PERSPECTIVE
NO MERCY

I didn't just read this journey; I experienced it.
Kevin, who lost a fierce battle against cancer just prior to publication

I needed this book. I'm going to go back and read it again.
Vic, a father of five and rock guitar player

A hauntingly beautiful story of Love's pursuit, restoring hope, and making us whole.
Heather, a mom of four, and volunteer church leader

This book must be an urgent matter in the heavenly realm.
Reny, a friend, Head Prayer Tribeswoman, and a CFO

A wonderful story.
Dianne, a mom to twins in heaven, and a Kindergarten Teacher

Really liked the explanation of how to get up after you fall down on snowshoes.
Will, a Director of Publication

Invited me to take a refreshed look at my life's main issues.
Lamar, a CEO, highly-decorated veteran, entrepreneur, and author

At times I feel you have been allowed supernatural privilege to view the film that plays in my soul, and at other times I am almost embarrassed, as I feel I have been privileged to view yours!
Amy, a mom, Paralegal, and poet

Great images. Really enjoyable.
Wade, a father of three, and Marketing Director for a technology company

Thank you for your interpretation of the story—His story and my story too—the greater reality that waits for me each day.
Karla, a mom to three under the age of seven

The book is rich.
Steve, an Editor

This book dispels the myth of pristine armor. It's the best portrayal of spiritual warfare I've ever encountered.
Marshall, a grandfather, and retired landscape designer

Writing is great. Very readable.
    Randy, a father of twins, and a Vice President of Residential Services

What a powerful story. I never want to put it down.
                Lindsay, a mom, artist, and an Executive Assistant

All I can say is, Wow!! Did not disappoint! I now understand the Bible better, and I feel closer to the Father, Son, and Holy Spirit because I now understand what the nuns in Catholic Sunday School couldn't explain.
            Cal, a father of two Marines, and owner of a bar and grill

NO MERCY

PRESTON GILLHAM

Bonefish

PUBLICATION™

PUBLICATION™

No Mercy is based on the historical record, but the work as a whole is a work of fiction with elements of allegory. This is not a literal work and should not be treated as such. The dialogue and characterization reflect the author's interpretation. *No Mercy* is a sweeping survey of life, love, and spirituality. It is not intended to be definitive, nor is it intended to be a parsing of theology.

Published and printed in the United States of America by
Bonefish Publication
2020 Wilshire Blvd.
Fort Worth, TX 76110

For information regarding special discounts for bulk purchases beyond those provided at www.PrestonGillham.com, please contact Bonefish Publication at, info@BonefishPublication.com

For further information about *No Mercy*, other works by the author, his blog, or to contact the author about speaking engagements or his consulting practice, please visit:

www.PrestonGillham.com

Library of Congress Control Number: 2010903590

ISBN: 978-0-9845103-0-6

10 9 8 7 6 5 4 3 2 1

To the
Prayer Tribe

For additional works
by Preston Gillham, visit

www.PrestonGillham.com

CONTENTS

Preface to the Reader. 11

No Mercy. 17

Acknowledgements 334

Additional Resources. 335

About the Author 336

About the Book. 336

PREFACE TO THE READER

Henry "Hank" Henderson's story is hard, even harsh in places. Momentous concepts like significance, trust, mercy, and forgiveness cannot be grasped unless their application is understood inside a meaningful framework. The temptation is strong to avoid harsh reality, but how can the anticipated dawn be celebrated if the dark night of the soul is not conceded and embraced?

The world is not a good place, nor is it safe. Hard things happen. People behave badly. There is fallout and life is not sanitary.

When I began this work, I had no aspiration to write a nice book. Rather, I determined to write an honest book in an unconventional style hoping it would embolden us all to consider profound failure, love's pursuit, heart's desire, and divine solution.

I know there will be critics of my book—strong and volatile—who will pronounce it heretical, shameful, and debauched for a variety of reasons. As I consider this, I pause—but only momentarily. I have looked into my heart and written honestly, passionately, and with conviction.

Reader, I trust you. You are an intelligent and thoughtful soul not willing to blindly swallow hook, line, and sinker what you read. Given this, I intend to take you outside your convention, but not without reason. I will push you to think about familiar concepts with allegory and metaphor. I believe in you and I believe in your ability to process judiciously what I put before you. If I did not, I would not have taken pen in hand. As with all things, eat the meat and throw out the bones.

Take your time. Read thoughtfully. Be skeptical of anyone who says they read *No Mercy* in a couple of hours on the plane. If you are a praying person, talk with God about what you read; there is a fair bit in these lines attributed to him.

Finally, thank you for joining me on this adventure. At the conclusion we will not be the same people who started the journey together.

Preston Gillham

Fort Worth, Texas
May 2009

"Look into thy heart and write."

–Sir Philip Sydney

NO
MERCY

BY

PRESTON GILLHAM

CHAPTER 1

July, SW Montana, USA

Hank and Vassar Henderson turned into Malden Creek Campground and Trailhead. As promised, the outfitter for Llamas to Go was waiting for them. Hank nosed their rental car into a vacant space next to the outfitter's stock trailer and shut off the engine. He and his older brother were on the cusp of their dream trip.

Rather than carrying their provisions on their own backs, they had rented three llamas to do the honors. Over the ensuing week, the brothers and their beasts of burden would follow Malden Creek to its headwaters high in the Absaroka Mountains. They were confident that within a few miles they would gain access to prime trout water—Brooks, Browns if they were lucky, Rainbows, and maybe Cutthroats—that few possessed the tenacity to reach and fish.

If all went as planned, they should get some fishing in before sunset of their first day. By the end of day two they anticipated seeing no trace of another human en route to their ultimate goal: a series of three alpine lakes nestled against the tree line.

They anticipated fishing their way up, spending two or three days at the lakes, then fish their way back focusing on favorite pockets of water they had discovered. One week later, at 3:00 PM, they would meet the outfitter, return the llamas, and start their reentry into the world of mobile phones, inboxes, and airports back home in Texas.

Vassar hatched the idea of an animal-assisted fishing trip eighteen months earlier. After considering its viability, he mentioned the idea to Hank as they sat on his patio beside the fire pit. Hank pledged to Google for outfitters the next day. The general location needed no discussion. Fishing in the Absaroka was a long-shared dream.

Within an hour of searching, Hank decided against the temperamental burro and stubborn mule, concluding the temperate llama was best suited for them. Llamas were easily picketed at night, ate indigenous grasses, got enough water from dew to stay hydrated—not that this would be an issue since it was a fishing trip—were surefooted, reliable, and gentle. Those qualities implied less llama time and more fishing time.

He discovered that llamas spit when unhappy, but mostly at each other over disagreements at feeding time, and rarely at people unless they felt mistreated. They kicked, but not unless provoked, and the probability of severe injury was remote given their size—250-400 pounds—and their soft, calloused feet. Since they had no upper front teeth, should they bite, their bite was not painful. This was a real plus for Hank. He had once been bitten by a horse. It was painful enough that he had never trusted horses again. Several of the articles Hank reviewed spoke of "llama kisses." This was intriguing, but as he discovered, a llama's kisses are not associated with affection but curiosity. Nearly every source described llamas as having a similar disposition to that of cats: you don't own them, they own you. Hank didn't know anything about cats, but Vassar did. So, the decision was made: llamas.

Over the next month, Vassar and Hank perfected their plans and made their reservations with Llamas to Go. The trip came together in short order. Waiting for the trip had been interminable.

But now they were out of the car, introducing themselves to the outfitter, and eyeing real llamas for the first time. The inquisitive, always-alert animals craned their long necks like periscopes to assess the brothers. Hank noted that they had wonderful eyes with long lashes and a split, upper lip, each side of which they worked independently. *The better to kiss you with,* he thought, *or spit at you, I suppose.*

While Vassar and Hank were giddy, the outfitter was matter-of-fact and not very personable. He offered a minimal introduction to trekking with and caring for llamas. His overview didn't cover spitting or kissing, but focused on how much weight to put in the animal's packs, how to ensure they were balanced, and how to make certain they were picketed at night. He made a passing comment about them eating natural vegetation, handed each brother a bag of llama treats, and then turned to the obligatory legal proceedings describing their responsibility should an animal be lost, injured, or heaven forbid, die.

After burdening them with onerous responsibility, the outfitter produced a form he said stated everything he had just declared, and pointed to a line where Hank was supposed to sign. As he was pointing, the outfitter casually mentioned that if one of the animals happened to hurt them or their stuff—or in any form or fashion compromised their trip or personal safety—Llamas to Go was not responsible. The inequity of the contract was clear, but Hank scrawled Henry H. Henderson above the designated line and confirmed the day's date in the designated space.

With his paperwork folded twice-over and stashed in the breast pocket of his western-style shirt, the outfitter untied the llamas from the stock trailer, handed the leads to Vassar, and headed to the cab of his truck. His farewell was a reminder that he would meet them in a week, same place, 3:00 PM. The transaction happened so quickly that neither Vassar nor Hank had time to formulate their questions before the outfitter was pulling out of the Malden Creek parking lot.

Men and beasts stared at each other, the llamas chewing their cuds, each brother hoping they were happy and not conjuring up fearsome spit wads. Much to his relief, as Vassar moved toward the rental car, the llamas followed. Hank fished in his jeans pocket for the keys and unlocked the trunk. Vassar handed the llamas' leads to Hank one at a time and confirmed that his younger brother had indeed secured each to the hinges of the trunk lid. Truth be known, Hank had tied each animal to the car with enough knots to moor a battleship through a typhoon.

Hank and Vassar looked at each other. They laughed and high-fived. Their adventure was underway.

With the precision of surgical nurses, they began sorting their gear and placing it in the llamas' packs. Heavier items went in first and closest to the animal's body; sharp objects were positioned facing the outside of each pack; lighter stuff went toward the top. The lash points on the pack flaps were reserved for sleeping pads, the tent, and the tubes holding their fly rods. Two of the llamas were about the same size; the third was smaller. The larger animals were packed with fifty pounds of gear while the smaller llama carried thirty-five.

Vassar and Hank each carried a day-pack with snacks, water, rain gear, a first aid/emergency pouch, and extra clothes. Experienced outdoorsmen, they knew they needed to be prepared to spend the night in the open…and potentially without the rest of their gear. What would the animals do if it thundered, or if there was a bolt of lightning? What if they saw a mountain lion, or a bear, or even something as harmless as a deer? Would they bolt and run? Kick? Buck? These were but a few of the questions that occurred to them about three minutes after the outfitter drove away.

Vassar noted as he returned from the campground restroom that the cinch straps under the llamas' bellies were slack now that their packs had weight in them. With some trepidation, the brothers tightened the cinches, the straps across their chests, and under their tails—and any other cord, webbing, or tie just for good measure. Neither would have been surprised if they had received a swift kick, but the tightening occurred without incident and both breathed easier. So far, so good, even though they had not yet left the back of the car.

Vassar untied the smaller llama and coaxed it around behind one of the larger animals. He snapped its lead to the other llama's saddle and then posed while Hank clicked a couple of pictures. Their digital posterity secured, Hank stuck the camera in his pocket, once again produced the keys from his jeans, and clicked the remote to lock the vehicle. For good measure, he pushed the "Lock" button again. The car's horn beeped twice and the lights flashed. Vassar jumped, but the animals did little more than twitch their ears a few times.

"Better put your keys away," Vassar said dryly.

Hank slipped the keys into a zip-lock bag, and stuck them into the bottom of a side pocket on his day pack. Hank lifted and shouldered his pack, hunched his shoulders, adjusted his waist belt before relaxing, and then tightened his shoulder straps. Last, he clipped his sternum strap and tugged on the tag end to pull his shoulder straps away from his arms and thus prevent his hands from tingling.

Vassar and Hank started their GPS units simultaneously in order to compare notes later. It was a silly thing, but it was part of their routine. As Hank was watching his GPS acquire signals from the navigational satellites orbiting Earth, a warm nose tilted his hat and nuzzled his sideburn. He turned and looked up at the wonderful eyes looking at him from six inches above his head and considered the hairy lips that had just planted their first kiss on his cheek. Vassar shook his head, amused. He and Hank had spent more time discussing this unique characteristic of llamas than any other part of their trip. Now, they were experiencing it.

Hank straightened his hat, glanced at his GPS, and coiled the llama's lead in his left hand. "I'm ready."

The brothers had trekked and camped and fished all over God's creation, but this was a new experience. They walked across the parking lot to the trail head, stopped to register in the loose-leaf binder hanging by a small chain from a wooden box placed there by the Forest Service, and then took their first steps up the Malden Creek Trail.

Neither Vassar nor Hank was interested in a sprint, but both were in reasonable shape for flatlanders and averaged a pace of two and half miles per hour. Not that they covered that distance. They stopped to look at Malden Creek and talk about fish. They stopped to catch their breath in the thin air while pretending to study Malden Creek for fish. They stopped to catch a flying insect to see what the hatch was and determine what the trout were feeding on. And they stopped periodically to rest—whether they needed to or not—for the llamas' sake. Apart from flicking their ears more than normal in response to Hank waving his hat to catch an insect, the llamas were contented trail companions.

Forty-five minutes into their hike, the trail was markedly less traveled. By the five-mile point, it was a spare, single-track jigging and jogging through the firs and alders alongside the creek. There were a few tempting fishing holes, but they had agreed to make the first-night's camp nine miles up the trail. If they made good time, found a reasonable site for their tent, and had wood gathered for the evening, they would fish, but not until then. So they kept moving.

The llamas were easily led, seemed unfazed by the weight they carried, were sure-footed, and their easy demeanor lent peacefulness that both Vassar and Hank relished as they decompressed from their demanding city lives.

Four o'clock in the afternoon, 9.6 miles up the trail, Vassar spotted a beautiful meadow at the edge of an Aspen grove and suggested they make camp. Hank was ready. They had achieved their goal. They suspected that within the next couple of hours a hatch of insects would occur, and if they were ready, they might open their fishing trip with dry-flies to rising trout.

They tied the llamas to the fallen trunk of an Aspen and began unloading each animal. Before Vassar and Hank undid the llamas' packs and saddles, they studied how the packs were placed on the saddles, and then how the saddles were secured to the animals. What was no doubt simple for the outfitter, looked like a graduate-level geometry problem to them.

Picking up one of the screw pickets and the picket line the outfitter had given to them, Hank trudged across the meadow studying the picket as he went. It was not unlike the giant corkscrew stake he had used years ago to tie one of their wandering dogs to. The dog had chewed through the line in short order and escaped. Hank wondered what would prevent the llamas from doing the same thing. Kneeling, Hank screwed the picket into the ground about half way before it resisted. He searched until he found a piece of wood to use as a lever. Slipping the wood through the triangle-shaped top, he finished screwing the stake into the ground. He secured the picket rope to the screw with a round turn followed by a bowline and a half hitch, stood up, and began uncoiling the line until he was certain it wouldn't tangle, then tossed the remainder across the meadow and returned to the screw picket.

Walking alongside the picket line, he stepped off twenty feet, knelt down, and tied a fixed loop in the line with a figure-eight knot. He stepped off another twenty feet and tied another loop, and then another twenty feet and a loop. Meanwhile, Vassar had screwed another picket into the ground and was ready to secure the line to it as soon as Hank tied his final knot. Vassar pulled the line taut—not tight—tied it off, and coiled the remainder of the rope beside the screw.

Working deliberately, the brothers unsaddled each llama, studying their harnesses and noting which saddle went with which animal. Vassar led the smaller llama to the center of the picket line and hooked its ten-foot lead to the fixed loop that Hank had tied. The two larger llamas were picketed on either side of the smaller one. Before turning to the duties of setting up camp, the brothers fluffed up the compressed hair on the llamas' backs where their saddles had been and gave each a Granola bar treat.

It didn't take long to pitch their tent; they had used the same style and brand of tent for years. It was an A-frame with a vestibule advertised as large enough for four people—provided the four people were five-year olds. It was a comfortable fit for the two of them and their gear. Four-season tents were popular, but the brothers had weathered a nineteen-inch snowfall once in their three-season tent. It performed admirably, was lighter, had more head room, and was a quarter of the price.

Vassar crawled into the tent and Hank handed him their sleeping bags, pads, and duffels of extra clothes before crawling in himself. They opened the valves on their sleeping pads, and accompanied by the sucking sound of the pads airing themselves up, the brothers pulled their sleeping bags from their stuff sacks, fluffed them up, and laid them out on top of the unrolling pads. Each had a camp pillow that also inflated when the valve was opened.

After zipping the tent door closed, the brothers went into the woods to gather fire wood. By 5:05 the fire was laid, ready to be lit later in the evening. They had also presumed upon the llamas to carry two, light weight, pack-chairs. These they set beside the rock fire ring.

As was their tradition, Vassar and Hank planned to eat steak the first night. Tonight, not only would they have steak, but they would have a hobo potato—diced potatoes, chopped onions, sliced carrots, bits of bacon, and a mushroom sauce. Later, when the coals in the fire had accumulated and were glowing red, they would lay out a double layer of aluminum foil, place the potatoes, onions, carrots, and bacon bits on it, drizzle the mushroom sauce over the assemblage, close the foil over it all, and place the package in the coals. If their timing was right—and it always was—they would serve hobo potato and medium rare steak simultaneously.

But the evening was young and dinner still a couple of hours away. The roiling and wriggling of Malden Creek as it tumbled toward the sea compelled them to turn their attention toward her and go in search of the deeper holes where wary trout lay in wait. Engulfed in the magic of late-afternoon, their compulsion became irresistible.

Vassar and Hank began assembling their fly rods. Each had chosen a two-weight rod for the creek, but had brought a heavier rod for the lakes. After greasing each ferrule of his rod with oil from his hair and putting it together, Hank dropped his hat on the ground, and placed the butt of his rod in his hat to keep the reel out of the dirt. He stripped line from the reel and threaded it through the snake guides. Running the leader through his fingers, he felt for abrasions on the tippet as he straightened it out. It was a habit. He had put on a new leader before leaving the house, as had Vassar. Anticipation. It was all part of the trip, part of the bond that Vassar and Hank enjoyed as they prepared for these adventures together.

"What are you tying on?" Hank asked.

Vassar held out his hand with a small, brown fly in his palm. Hank decided to tie on a similar pattern but with a bead head in order to fish deeper. If a hatch occurred and the fish started rising, he would adjust his selection.

Vassar and Hank had considered fishing wet, but decided to bring their lightweight, breathable waders at the last minute. If the weather turned unseasonably cool, or if they had more rain than normal, waders would enable them to keep fishing. As it turned out, Malden Creek was wider, deeper, and faster than they had expected. Bringing the waders was a good decision.

Vassar proposed trading the surprise of what Malden Creek held upriver for the certainty of the good fishing holes they had observed as they hiked. "I'll fish upstream," he said, "and let you start here—with the pocket water we've already scouted."

This small deference beside the creek was typical of Vassar. "Okay. Meet back here about 7:00 you think?"

Vassar agreed, put on his fishing vest and hat, turned his rod with the tip facing backward so it stood less chance of being caught in the brush, and headed upstream. Hank walked downstream about five minutes, just far enough to escape all the commotion they had created setting up camp, and edged up to the first hole of water.

He knelt behind a tangle of shrubs and studied the pool, watching for a rising fish. Nothing. He slipped away from the creek in an arching path that brought him close to the bottom of the pocket of water. Easing into casting position, he stripped thirty feet of line off of his reel, false casted three times to load his rod with the weight of the fly line, and delivered his fly to the side of the pool. He let the current take the sinking fly on a dead drift and collected the slack as it came back toward his position.

Hank gathered his line, false casted again, and placed the fly three feet farther to the left from his first cast. The fly drifted along the edge of a foam line on the water created by a boulder. He held his rod tip down; the line ran under his right index finger and through his left hand. There it was: the tug that fishermen yearn for. Hank lifted his rod tip while pulling slightly with his left hand. The hook was set and the fight on. His two-weight bent as he played the fish. A broad grin creased Hank's face.

He guided the hooked fish away from the roots and rocks along the bank, keeping it in the deeper water. As the fish tired, he pulled it closer to his net. It wasn't a trophy, but a wild trout of any size is a thrill. Hank suspected Malden harbored some big fish, but this eight-incher was a nice start. He removed the fly from the corner of the fish's mouth with a pair of forceps, supported it under its belly, and put it back in the water moving it forward and backward to revive it from its fight. The Brook trout recovered, and with three flips of its tail, darted into the depths of the pool.

CHAPTER 2

Upper Malden Creek Falls

Vassar hiked up Malden Creek like a man on a mission. Fifteen minutes up the trail there was a waterfall.

He heard the falls before he saw them. They were not majestic, but they were noteworthy for Malden Creek. As Vassar worked his way alongside the stream, he spied his route. He stopped to consider what lay before him, lifted his cowboy hat, and wiped the sweat from his forehead. It was hot by any standard, but especially so for the Montana mountains. After catching his breath, he reset his hat and moved to the edge of the waterfall, propped his fly rod against a tree, and visually scouted his path.

Vassar crab-walked past a protruding rock, placing his wading boots carefully so as not to slip and plunge into the pool below. Separating the ferns living in the mist, he crawled through and stood up. With the outcropping that formed the falls at his back and water tumbling from above his head, Vassar sidestepped behind the waterfall. A tangle of roots, brush, and ferns growing from a steep embankment awaited him on the other side of the passage. He grasped a root and began to climb, ducking under branches, and brushing away spider webs.

His shirt was damp with sweat, spray from the falls, and the mist that collected on the plants. The dampness was welcome relief from the heat, but as he climbed farther, cold air penetrated his thin shirt. He climbed farther, and as he did, it grew colder and colder. A few more yards and he was crawling through patchy snow, then more snow, and then the ground was covered.

The farther Vassar went into the world on the other side of the falls, the more radical the seasonal change was. *It's a nice change from the heat,* he thought, as he stopped to look around. *And, it's just like I remember it. That's good.*

Vassar used a thick vine to pull himself upright. He straightened his cowboy hat, rolled his sleeves down, and raised the collar of his shirt against his neck. *It will be good to see Father and Magician,* he thought, as he buttoned his top button.

Vassar's Father was the High King. Magician was the Kingdom's sorcerer and a powerful man. The three of them had discussed Hank at length earlier, but he knew nothing of it.

Over the years, Hank insulated himself from Vassar and his Father with emotional distance, personal privacy, and the convenient self-protection afforded him as a competent, successful, and very busy professional. Deep down, Hank believed Vassar was his Father's favorite, not because he saw his Father favor Vassar; he didn't. He just felt like Vassar was the favorite—and that he was the least favorite, worth less to his Father than Vassar. Because of this, Hank believed Vassar couldn't really identify with him—that he wouldn't really care about his issues and concerns. So, even though Hank and Vassar spent time together and had shared interests, Hank didn't engage Vassar personally. He didn't ask about Vassar's life, and offered precious little insight into his own. He knew how Vassar fished, what he did for a living, and who some of his friends were, but he would be hard-pressed to articulate his brother's dreams, struggles, joys, or aspirations.

Magician was a mystery. Hank rarely conversed with him, knew only bits and pieces of hearsay about what he did—and honestly, didn't care. Magician struck him as sort of weird. No. As outright strange.

But his Father was another matter. Hank didn't trust him, couldn't identify with him, didn't like him, and had intentionally sought independence from him as soon as he could. Hank was cynical toward him and his supposed love. Even though his Father's reputation was remarkable and his standing in the community was larger-than-life, Hank wasn't quick to acknowledge that they were related. His Father might be generous and gracious toward others, but such was not true for him—the least favored.

As far as Hank was concerned, his Father was a hard man with high expectations—impossible expectations, really. Hank felt he performed well. Better than most people, anyway. And he too held himself to ruthlessly high standards that he met with enough proficiency to feel justified in defending himself, but it was no use. Hank believed his Father tolerated him most of the time, but when he made a mistake, there was hell to pay—with himself and his demanding Father.

Hank felt abandoned in general, but especially now in the dark days he was weathering. Recent downturns in his business and personal life were weighing on him. He'd hoped—one more time—his Father would help him out, had even tried to contact him, but had heard nothing back. It frustrated Hank enormously, not so much that his Father was unresponsive—that was typical—but that he had once again allowed himself to hope that his Father would care…maybe just enough to provide some slack in life's tension.

Hank berated himself for hoping and turned inward toward his personal reservoirs of ingenuity and resourcefulness to self-maintain. All he could do now was hope his fishing trip would energize him for the rebuilding effort that awaited him back in Texas.

Such was the situation facing the King, Vassar, and Magician when they met to discuss Hank.

His Father wasn't worried about the stressors in Hank's life. They were remedied easily enough. He was far more concerned that Hank had a skewed view of his heart toward him.

To the King, the unsavory circumstances surrounding Hank were nothing more than the usual fallout of living in the midst of life's challenges. But the recent downturns in his son's life had thrown him off balance and created a different posture than normal. The king saw this as an opportunity to engage Hank, to demonstrate his true heart to him, and to draw his younger son in closer to himself and the family.

He intended to bring his considerable resources to bear on the window of opportunity afforded him by Hank's circumstances.

Undoing the misconceptions Hank harbored called for extraordinary intervention—removing him from his time dimension, compressing history, exposing him directly to the spiritual world, and bringing Hank face-to-face with the giants fighting for control of his soul.

The King was ready, waiting at Erymos. Magician was standing by. As expected, the forces opposing the King were on alert and their agents deployed. The stakes—Hank's wellbeing—were high for all concerned. Like any good leader, Vassar had come to see for himself what awaited his brother.

A breeze passed around him and Vassar felt a quick flush as goose bumps popped up on his body. He crept farther into the snowy woods. Paused. Heard voices.

Taking a slow deep breath, he stalked in the direction of the voices. The snow muffled his footsteps.

Stopping in the shadows, Vassar watched the platoon of mounted soldiers. They were deployed in a defensive perimeter, securing the nondescript clearing between them and the woods where Vassar hid. The officers clustered together inside the perimeter, chatting. Their helmets gleamed in the winter sun and their breastplates bore the crest of the High King.

Vassar listened and watched. He observed each mannerism, watched every exchange; he waited until an officer spoke to one of the soldiers to see if their discipline matched that of the High King's army. He studied the posture of the soldiers and the demeanor of the officers. They were in enemy territory. These woods—Gnarled Wood—were the domain of Zophos and his Dark Army. If these soldiers were imposters, they would not feel the darkness around them, would not be on high alert. They might present a convincing front, but Vassar knew the truth of their identity would be revealed in the nuance of their conduct. Soldiers in the High King's army would sit straighter. Their hands would not rest on the pommels of their saddles but on the pommels of their swords. They would be alert, as though preyed upon.

Satisfied, Vassar stepped to the edge of the woods. The horses sensed him before anyone saw him, but that drew the attention of the soldiers. Vassar raised his right hand and his power flooded the heart of each man in the platoon. They knew they were in the presence of the Prince, the oldest son of the High King, heir to the Kingdom and its throne.

The officers dismounted and knelt before Vassar with their heads bowed. Vassar strode forward, stretched his arms wide, and thanked them for their allegiance. He then ordered them to attention. The officers stood shoulder-to-shoulder, straight as arrows, with their right hands doubled into fists and placed over their hearts and the crest of the High King.

"Captain?"

"Yes, sir. Captain Alexander, sir."

"At ease. Your report."

Vassar listened as the officer detailed the High King's orders to bring his personal platoon to this place, set up a perimeter, and secure the area. He was to receive his two sons, coming from another time and place, and escort them to Erymos, the King's enclave about two hundred miles from the castle and its prominent Round Tower.

"Very well. And what of Zophos and the Dark Army?" Vassar inquired.

"Your Highness, Zophos has made incursions against the castle, the Round Tower, and those loyal to the High King. Thus far his attacks have not been out of the ordinary."

"And the condition of the troops guarding the Round Tower?"

"They report no difficulty repulsing Zophos' initiatives, sir."

His report interrupted by Vassar's question, Captain Alexander waited while the Prince thought. "Go ahead, Captain." Vassar could tell there was more on the officer's mind.

"With all due respect, sir. Your presence—and your brother's—will not escape the notice of Zophos. We can keep you under cover just so long before your presence is discovered. Even as we speak, the danger is escalating."

Vassar nodded and walked back and forth a few steps in front of the officers standing at his attention. Before issuing his final orders, Vassar asked the Captain if there was anything further.

"Yes, sir. There is one thing: your clothes. What are you dressed to do?"

Vassar chuckled, not just because of the Captain's question, but in anticipation of the myriad questions his very disoriented brother would pepper them with when they returned. "Captain, I'll tell you, but you won't understand."

Captain Alexander nodded.

"These are waders—twenty-first century clothing for fishing. The boots are soled with a rubber compound and titanium studs. Fishing in the world I have just left is a sport, not a matter of survival. My shirt is made of a synthetic material that will neither be discovered nor used in clothing for two hundred-fifty years. Underneath my waders I am wearing thermal tights—leggings—made by Patagonia, a clothing company named after a land you do not yet know exists and that faces an ocean you have not yet discovered. The hat is a mix of function and style, function for a job not defined in your world, and a style rooted in a territory called the American West that is just now being explored by Caucasians."

The Captain's widening eyes betrayed his stoic attention.

"Captain, I realize you're confused, but you asked. All that concerns you is this: I'm going back into the woods. In a few moments, I'll return with my brother. He'll be more confused than you are. He goes by, Hank, and he'll be dressed similar to me. Where we are camped, it is summer. While I'm away, assemble the appropriate clothing and equipment. I see you have horses for us. Once we've changed clothes, we must leave at once for Erymos. Oh, and by the way: My brother will ask a lot of questions. I haven't told him about this part of the trip. Your patience will be appreciated."

"Sir," the Captain straightened, "I understand." After a brief pause, the Captain corrected himself. "Actually, I do not understand, sir. But I don't suppose I need to. Your Highness, my men and I are at your service and will await the arrival of you and your brother. Safe travels."

"Captain, see to your men, and be alert. Zophos prowls like a lion looking for someone to devour. And you are correct: Our presence will not go unnoticed for long. Dismissed."

Vassar disappeared like an apparition into the woods.

He retraced his steps, stopping to listen, to hear if there was a breath out of place in the woods, stopping to sense if he was alone. Satisfied, he dropped to all fours, crawled into the thicket from which he had emerged earlier, felt the warm air return, and descended to the waterfall. He inched along behind the cascading water, crabbed around the protruding rock, eased down the slick face of moss-covered stone, and retrieved his rod. He noted a large Brown holding to the side of the pool beneath the falls and was tempted, but started his hike back to camp instead.

Hank caught and released three more fish. He looked at his watch, then decided to go back to camp early, get the fire started, check on the llamas, and finish getting the campsite in order before it got dark. They were small chores, but he wanted to finish them before Vassar got back—simple acts of kindness for his brother.

He reeled in his line, looped it around the foot of his reel, hooked his fly on the fourth snake guide, tightened the slack, and began the seven-minute walk back to camp. His heart was full. He was in the mountains, fishing for wild trout, hiking with llamas, and hanging out with Vassar.

Hank set his rod against a tree, took off his fishing vest and hung it on a stob, then turned his attention to starting the campfire. He selected a few pieces of dryer lint from a zip lock bag. Before leaving home, he had massaged Vaseline into the lint to make it both combustible and waterproof. He placed the pieces of lint under the tender of small branches laid earlier in the afternoon, flicked open his lighter, snapped the starter until a blue flame appeared, and held it to the lint.

Hank coaxed his fire into life, adding progressively larger twigs, and then branches, until the fire's warmth filled the campsite. It would take at least an hour to build up enough coals to properly roast their supper.

Hank scrounged through the llama packs until he located the treasured bottle of red wine—another Henderson-brothers' tradition—and carried it to the edge of Malden Creek. He created a cradle of large river rocks in six inches of water and placed the bottle there. By the time Vassar returned, the bottle should be chilled to perfection by the tumbling waters of melted snow.

Hank stood up. He took several deep breaths, holding each, trying to feel the mountain air permeate every pour of his soul before exhaling. He watched a Steller's Jay land in the tree above him. It hopped from branch to branch eyeing the camp for an opportunistic meal. Hank followed a piece of bark as it bobbed on the current toward the Gulf of Mexico. He turned and looked at the llamas. They were lying down chewing their cuds—content, or so it seemed. *They were a good idea. Peaceful too,* he thought.

Hank went to the packs, grabbed the three bells supplied by the outfitter, and tied them to the picket line. Should the llamas be disturbed in the night, the bells would jingle a wake-up call. Since trouble would most likely be a bear or a mountain lion, Hank hoped the bells would scare the intruder away before he had to investigate. Of course, he hoped not to hear any jangling bells at all.

Hank added wood to the fire, glanced at the bottle of wine to be certain it was still corralled, grabbed his water bottle, and sat down in a camp chair to wait for Vassar. While the fishing trip in Montana was a dream come true, given the recent demands of his life in Texas, it was also a welcome relief.

He was the Co-Founder and CEO of a marketing firm with its tentacles in media, publishing, and the nonprofit sector. Four months ago, his CFO resigned to start his own company—a competitive business. Ten weeks later, Hank discovered the man had stolen confidential customer information and was using it in his start-up venture.

He confronted the former employee. It broke the man and doomed his aspirations. Besides being unpleasant, it was the end of their friendship.

He used me to get what he wanted. What was he thinking? Hank had asked himself this question a hundred times in the last six weeks. He asked again now, but shook his head, no closer to an answer. What he did understand was that his CFO traded their relationship for a few names. *And they were poor contacts at that*, he reflected.

Part of Hank's job was writing—articles, blogs, books. All of these contributed to the handsome branding of his company. His last book had gone out of print in April after a short life on the shelf. The publisher hadn't marketed the book well. In fact, they didn't market the book at all. The publishing house was embroiled in a merger, he discovered, and apparently got distracted. *Hard to sell books when readers don't know you have a book to read*, he thought. *Clearly, my book wasn't as significant to them as it is to me.*

Hank had gambled by using a publisher, and knew in retrospect he should have self-published. But they offered him a nice advance, and the agent was encouraging. "They're a good company and will market your book aggressively," he had courted. "They have a stellar reputation, with strong relationships across the market spectrum…."

The letter from the publisher was cold. It was a form letter, and a pitiful one. The title of his book was hand written in a blank space at the top of the single page and signed at the bottom by someone he didn't know. The Marketing Director didn't return his call, or the call after that, or the one after that either. His agent sounded a sympathetic note but seemed more interested in acquiring his next manuscript. "I'm sorry, Hank," he'd said. "I really expected them to do a good job with your book. By the way, you working on anything new?"

Sure, I'll call you right away with my next book, Hank thought. *Heck. I write a book every month or two. Nothin' to it. And you did such an exceptional job with my last manuscript. Right. Don't hold your breath, pal. All that wining and dining and sweet talk to get my manuscript. I believed them—the editor, the publisher, marketing, all of them. They wasted me and my book. Used me. Nope, not again. Fool me once, shame on you. Fool me twice, shame on me.* Hank knew this was part of the business, but it was a callous and bitter disappointment.

The publisher offered to let him purchase the remaining copies of his book at fifteen percent over their cost, which he did. Thirty-two hundred books arrived a month before his fishing trip. He stacked them down the middle of his garage floor. When he was done stacking, the boxes were six-feet high and his back ached. Every box screamed that he was expendable. Insignificant. He had to walk around the boxes for days when he packed for his trip. The more he walked around the stack, the more he doubted his importance.

The proverbial straw that broke the camel's back soon followed. Partly because he was an author, but mostly because of his professional stature, Hank hosted a weekly radio program—live, during morning drive time, on a large station in Los Angeles—and served as one of the station's go-to experts on current events. It was a fabulous gig.

Live radio is not easy to master, but Hank had gotten the hang of it. His program delivered meaningful content and received good response. But five weeks after he'd been forced to destroy his former CFO and friend, three weeks after the shipment of his out-of-print books arrived, and one week before leaving with Vassar for Montana the Program Manager called to say his program was being replaced immediately by a local movie reviewer. Hank took pride in the belief that he was doing important work, but apparently not important enough to keep from being replaced by inane commentary on Hollywood drivel.

"It's what our listeners want," the Program Manager said.

While generally resilient to the jabs in life, these punches were a crossing right, an upper cut, and a knockout. Hank's confidence was shaken personally and professionally. He felt disrespected, unimportant, and insignificant.

He had prayed throughout his difficult year, more than he normally prayed, and for the last several weeks he had prayed fervently. But as usual, his prayers hadn't done any good. He tried hard to please God—pray more, read more, live better—but clearly, doing his best didn't garner any more value with God than it had with the Program Manager, the Publisher, or his former CFO. It seemed to Hank that God was anxious for him to be good, but when it came time for God to reciprocate and help him out, He was a no show.

More often than not, when God did turn up it was to point out where he could have improved—or tried harder, or prayed longer, or been kinder, or more humble, or more whatever. The list was long with God. No matter how hard he tried, it wasn't good enough for God. Never had been.

Hank didn't like God. He didn't trust Him either, but he kept these beliefs to himself. They were unacceptable views to have of God, especially around all the nice people at church. He'd learned a long time ago that Sunday morning was not a place for honest confession or genuine conversation. It was acceptable to have a health need or a family issue. Those could be mentioned for prayer and support. But it was not permissible to distrust and dislike God.

Hank never feared he would quit believing in God, but he desperately feared what he believed about God. *Hardly a Christian attitude,* he thought, chiding himself for his ungracious sensibility. *But you'd think he would've helped out some way, especially now.* His distrust rose above the gentle chiding. *I prayed, did my best.*

Like he'd done umpteen times, Hank took inventory of his efforts to get on God's good side, but he couldn't come up with any reason for God's indifference besides the obvious: *I'm not significant enough to matter.* As he had done for years, Hank distanced himself from God, preferring to keep to himself, try hard, and through his own effort to build a self-justifying case against this unreasonable God who liked to call Himself, Father.

Hank tried to be upbeat—and he was a good actor; he had everyone fooled—but he was despondent. He hadn't talked to anyone about his disappointments, wasn't sleeping well, and was drinking more than normal. He thought about mentioning it to Vassar, but decided against it. This was a fishing trip, not a therapy session. Besides, Hank guarded what he told Vassar, especially when it came to spiritual things. He never felt like Vassar could relate. It seemed to him that Vassar had a charmed life, whereas his was anything but. Just as he had done a thousand times before, Hank knew he could figure things out.

To begin with, he was determined to rebuild some emotional capital for the uphill slog he faced when he returned home in a week. *Yep. Montana is a good place for me to be,* Hank thought, as he forced himself to emerge from thinking about his funk and turn to the present.

He picked up a limb as big around as his wrist, placed the end of it on a rock, and stepped on it to break it into manageable lengths. He repeated the process until the stick was transformed into firewood and fed the fire again. He considered the coals and anticipated dinner.

Hank lifted the bottle of wine from Malden's chilling caresses, and eyed the wrinkling label. He opened the small blade on his knife and cut the foil wrap guarding the cork. He closed the blade, flipped his knife over, and opened the corkscrew. Sitting down in his camp chair, he held the bottle between his knees, inserted the corkscrew, and extracted the synthetic cork. He sniffed the contents of the bottle, cocked his eyebrow, and wrinkled his nose.

He poured a few ounces of wine into his camp cup. He swirled the wine for a few seconds to let it open and tasted it, letting it sit in his mouth a moment before swallowing, and then inhaling to measure the wine's finish. He drank the remainder from his cup and tasted a second time. Hank smiled and set the bottle aside. *Once this has opened, it'll be perfect.*

As a precaution because they were in bear country, Vassar had strung the small duffle containing dinner from a tree branch ten feet off of the ground. The steaks, potatoes, and accoutrements were wrapped—and wrapped again. A drug-sniffing dog couldn't have found their dinner. As Hank untied the cord and lowered the duffle to the ground, he wondered what the llamas' reaction would be to a bear. He suspected it would be a non event, but didn't want to test his hunch. *But a mountain lion would be a different matter,* he surmised. *I wonder if spitting is really the worst they can do?*

Hank wound up the accessory line Vassar had used to suspend the duffle and walked the thirty yards back to camp. He was just opening the duffle as Vassar approached.

"Do any good?" Vassar asked.

"Yeah, three or four. A nice Brookie."

"Really? How big?"

"Eight or so. Fought hard. How about you?"

"Not much. Saw a nice Brown, but was getting short on time," Vassar reported.

"Heck. You should've cast to him. Not like we have any place to be."

"I knew you'd have the wine open. Figured I'd better get back and see to my interests," Vassar joked, as he leaned his rod against a tree.

Hank resumed his efforts to untie the knot around the top of the duffle.

"Hey, before you undo that, let me show you what I found up the creek."

Hank looked at Vassar, his eyes asking if their camp would be alright.

"Everything's okay. Won't take but a few minutes," Vassar assured.

"Alright. But if something other than me eats my steak and potato, I'm not gonna be a happy camper."

"Me either, but you're not gonna believe what I found," Vassar promoted, as they left camp.

Vassar retraced his steps ducking and dodging the streamside vegetation. Hank followed six or seven feet behind.

"Sounds like a falls," Hank observed.

"Just wait until you see," Vassar replied.

Ten minutes after leaving camp, Vassar and Hank stood together looking at the waterfall. "C'mon." Vassar retraced his earlier route up to the edge of the waterfall. He glanced down at the pool and smiled back at his brother. "Watch your step."

Hank followed Vassar's footsteps and handholds up the waterfall, around the rock protrusion, and through the ferns until they were both standing in the recess of the rock with the cascade of Malden Creek tumbling past them an arm's length from their faces. Vassar looked into Hank's elated eyes, turned, and began sidestepping behind the waterfall. He didn't stop at the other side, but started climbing the embankment. Hank let Vassar ascend several feet before reaching up and grasping the exposed roots of a Fir. He looked down, kicked his wading boot into a secure footing, lifted himself up, and followed Vassar's lead.

Where the embankment fell away from near vertical, Vassar stopped and put his index finger in front of his lips. Hank crawled up beside him. "What'd you see?" he whispered, scanning the forest ahead.

Hank realized Vassar wasn't looking ahead, but rather was studying him. The brothers stared into each other's eyes—Hank questioning, Vassar assessing. "Hank, we've entered another realm."

"I'll say," Hank whispered back. "Lot cooler. Wetter. Wouldn't think the other side of the creek would be so different."

"That's not what I mean."

Hank looked at Vassar.

"I mean this is a different world. It's a different time."

Hank's eyes narrowed. "What are you talking about?"

"Hank, do you trust me?"

"Yeah. Why? What's the matter?"

"You have to trust me."

"I trust you, Vassar." He paused, looking at his brother. Uneasiness nagged in the vicinity of his sternum. "C'mon. Let's get outta here." Hank started to slide back down the embankment, but Vassar grabbed his arm.

"You know the things you were pondering beside the fire—your book going out of print, your CFO, the radio program being cancelled?"

"How'd...how'd you know that?"

"Look. I've brought you here. Planned every step."

"What are you...? We planned this trip together."

"I don't mean Montana. I mean here. Your confidence is low, and understandably so. But more than anything, you're doubting your significance."

Hank hadn't condensed his world into one word—one conviction, one fundamental necessity his soul needed—but significance, or the lack thereof, did capture how he felt. He didn't know how Vassar knew what he was thinking or how he'd seen through his all-is-well façade, but it didn't surprise him. Vassar was a smart guy—and he was right.

"Yes, it's been a hard year, and the last few weeks have been awful. Now let's go."

"God has heard your prayers."

"Vassar, you're freaking me out. Of course he heard. God hears everything. Knows everything. That's how come he gets to be God. But that doesn't mean he cares. If he was gonna help me he would've done it a long time ago. Now come on. I'm ready to get back. I didn't come to Montana to think about all that crap. I came to get over it."

"I know you did. God's heard your prayers, and this place—all that's around us—is his answer. He asked me to bring you here."

"Bring me where? Malden Creek? That waterfall? This muddy hill? We came to Montana to fish, not meet with God!" Hank's voice rose with irritation.

"Shh."

Hank looked around again. "Why do you keep telling me to be quiet? I don't see anything," Hank hissed.

"Just listen a minute. You're doubting yourself. You're doubting others. Your confidence is really low. Am I right?"

Hank didn't answer. He didn't need to.

"You've prayed, but gotten nothing—no answers, no help. But you're mistaken. God has heard. He's waiting for us now, at a place not far from here. Erymos, it's called. We're gonna have dinner together this evening."

"What in the? Have dinner with God. You're out of your...."

Vassar raised his hand for Hank to let him finish. "In your prayers you've asked God to speak to you, to help you. Well, when we passed behind the waterfall, we entered the spiritual world. You'll see soon enough, and God is anxious to talk with you about your disappointments."

Hank huffed out his nostrils. Vassar didn't acknowledge.

"But we've gotta be careful. This is a dangerous place. You've read about spiritual warfare?"

"Of course," he said.

"You're fixing to experience it, but there's nothing to be afraid of."

"Vassar, this is crazy."

"I know. That's why I asked if you trusted me."

"Yeah, yeah. Whatever." Hank's skepticism came out as irritation.

"Well? Do you, or don't you?" Vassar hissed.

Hank could smell his brother's breath in the humid cold. "Okay. I trust you." Hank looked at Vassar. "But, I'm going to reserve the right to change my mind. Because…did I mention this is insane?"

"Yes, you did."

"Okay, okay. Let's get on with it. I'm getting cold."

Vassar smiled and said, "Follow me. We're gonna have the most incredible adventure.

CHAPTER 3

Just beyond the Waterfall

"I'm glad you're with me," Vassar said to Hank, as he started crawling up through the mud and the snow and the progressing cold. "We'll take our time getting through these woods. Have to be quiet, so pay attention. Not far ahead Father's troops are waiting for us."

"Father? Troops? What are you...? Is this some sort of joke?"

"Nope. It's not a joke, Hank. I wouldn't do that to you."

"But how do you know all this?"

"I spoke with the Captain while you were fishing," Vassar said, as he eased ahead.

Hank stared out into the woods, mouth agape. Shook his head. Looked upward at his brother, and followed Vassar, crawling until he could stand up.

They moved through the dusting of snow toward the clearing where the High King's troops stood guard waiting for them. Vassar stopped before the soldiers noticed them and watched. After he was satisfied it was safe, he motioned to Hank, and they stepped through the remaining cover into the clearing.

The guards snapped to attention and the man who Hank assumed was the Captain knelt on one knee before Vassar and Hank, saluting them with his drawn sword. "Your Highnesses."

"Captain Alexander, as you were. May I present my brother, Henry Henderson?"

"Your Highness, the pleasure is mine. My men and I are at your service."

Hank was speechless, his mind racing to assemble the setting unfolding before him—to grasp the title the Captain used to address him.

"Captain, put your men at ease and pass the word," Vassar instructed. "From now until we reach Erymos, let's assume we're being watched. No more salutes. We'd be easy targets. Address me as Vassar and my brother as Hank."

"Sir." Captain Alexander acknowledged, turned, and motioned to another member of the guard, who walked over to collect two bundles, then brought them to Hank and Vassar. "We are ready to ride as soon as you are changed."

A couple of blankets were spread on the ground just inside the woods for Vassar and Hank to stand on. Hank wanted to laugh, but three puffs of air were all that escaped through his bewilderment. He turned twice around. Gawking. Each time, Captain Alexander nodded when Hank caught his eye.

Vassar grinned, said, "Come on, Hank. We've got to get moving." They stripped—their clothes, watches, rings, Hank's reading glasses—everything came off. Hank emulated Vassar in donning the strange attire. As they shed their clothes a soldier collected their twenty-first century belongings, folded them, wrapped them in an oiled tarpaulin, bound them, and then hid them close by. Hank took special notice. He'd paid $350 for his waders.

While Hank tracked where his waders and boots went, he lost track of nearly every other piece of the world as he knew it. He stopped and started, shell shocked by the time bomb Vassar exploded in his world. Vassar encouraged and coaxed. Hank started, then stopped. "Come on, Hank. You're doing fine. Need some help?"

Hank thought about asking Vassar a question, or two, or three, or four hundred. Instead, he just shook his head.

"Hank, I know this is all hard to accept. In time, it will make sense to you. Okay?"

Hank nodded. He had fallen behind Vassar getting dressed. His brain was working overtime to assimilate the situation but it wasn't processing fast enough. The switch from summer to winter was a shock, but the clothes, the soldiers, the time dimension, the royal title…. He stopped again and stared at Vassar. Turned to look into the clearing at the soldiers. "What? I'm, I mean, I don't. When did?"

"Just trust me, brother. Trust me."

"Trust isn't my strong suit."

"I know it isn't. That's okay. Give me all you've got though. Will you do that?"

Hank was mute again. He nodded. A soldier was crawling around on the blanket assembling his wardrobe in sequential order. Hank looked at the soldier, then the clothes, then Vassar, then the clearing, and then began the visual rounds again.

"Here you go," Vassar said, handing Hank the next piece of clothing to put on. Then another. "You're doing fine. Thanks for believing me."

Hank managed, "Sure—but I don't—I don't know what to believe."

As they emerged from changing, the Captain handed each a dagger. Hank pulled the eighteen-inch-long weapon, examined its blood groove, looked at Vassar, blinked, and then sheathed the weapon. He handed it to the soldier closest to him, intending for him to take it away, but the soldier strapped it around Hank's waist until it hung over his right hip. The dagger afflicted Hank with fear, not comfort. It was far too short for defense, heaven forbid, and much too long for a camp knife. He shut it out of his mind. It was the least of his worries.

A soldier walked up holding the reins to his horse. Hank stared blankly until it dawned on him, *He wants me to get on that horse.* "Is that? Do you? I mean, I'm not much of. It's a horse."

The soldier clicked his heels, bowed slightly, and said, "Yes sir. Indeed. When you are ready, sir."

Hank put his left foot in the stirrup, grabbed the pommel, and swung his right leg over the animal's back. As a soldier adjusted Hank's stirrups, Captain Alexander rode up beside him, "All set?"

"Huh?"

"Are you ready to ride?"

"Ride?" Hank was trying desperately to keep pace with all that was transpiring. "Yeah. Okay. But I haven't ridden a horse since I was in summer school at Colorado State."

"Colorado State? Where's that?"

"Fort Collins." Hank's mind was clearing as he felt the horse moving under him and smelled its musky odor.

"Fort Collins? Is that English?"

"No. American."

The Captain thought, then regrouped: "Whose flag flies over its walls?"

"No. It's not that kind of fort," Hank said. "Well, I guess it was at one time, but not now. It's a town, in northern Colorado, not far from the Wyoming border, with a university known for its Forestry program, and…." Now it was Captain Alexander's turn to be confused.

The Captain didn't have the slightest notion of what he was talking about. No clue about Colorado. No recognition of Wyoming. Didn't know what Forestry was. *America hasn't even been discovered as far as this guy's concerned,* Hank realized. "Never mind, Captain. Been a long day. Like I said, I haven't ridden in a while."

Gnarled Wood

The column of fourteen rode two abreast, Vassar in position five, Hank in eight. Captain Alexander kept them moving. Clearly, he didn't want to be caught in Gnarled Wood in the dark, and he didn't want to deliver the King's sons late for dinner.

They had ridden in and out of timber most of the trip. As they rode through a dense stand, the Captain signaled halt. The soldiers fell back and moved up beside Vassar and Hank while Captain Alexander and another officer rode ahead.

Twenty minutes later, they returned. "The High King is expecting us. He's ordered troops to escort us to Erymos. He spun his horse around and ordered the column forward with a hand motion.

The woods thinned allowing the squad and their two charges to see into a long meadow against a backdrop of more mountainous terrain. Fifty yards ahead were a hundred cavalry. Captain Alexander studied the situation, looked for movement along the edges of the meadow, monitored each change in the troops before them, and watched his horse's ears and eyes, trusting the animal's superior senses. He glanced at the officer who had ridden out with him earlier, his look asking for confirmation that he too deemed them safe. Only then did he motion his men into the open.

The uniformed troops closed rank around the more non-descript, elite guard escorting the princes. The company rode for the mountains and Erymos.

Their shadows were long when they approached the guarded entrance to a slot canyon. Captain Alexander joined the officer in charge of the company. They were briefed by the guards for several minutes. As they returned, the uniformed troops were ordered to form a perimeter in front of the slot. Captain Alexander sent four scouts from his squad through the slot while the remainder waited with Vassar and Hank.

Ten minutes later, the scouts returned, reported, and the contingent rode into the slot. The scouts led the way, followed by Captain Alexander, the brothers, and his troops. Two abreast was all the narrowness would permit.

The slot wasn't long, about an eighth of a mile. It opened into a steeply-walled, expansive canyon. At the far end stood a massive stone and timber structure.

Looks like the lodge at Yosemite, Hank thought. But unlike the park hotel that stands before a cliff, Erymos continued into the rock face.

Captain Alexander motioned for Vassar and Hank to join him. "Your Father has always enjoyed extraordinary entrances." He ordered his men to set up a perimeter in front of the building. Then he, Vassar, and Hank rode forward under a *porte cochere*, dismounted, and handed the reins for their horses to attendants.

While they were untying their few belongings from their saddles, the door behind them banged open and the High King bounded out with his arms open wide. Vassar, who was closest to the door, was grabbed in a bear hug. Father and son slapped each other on the back. The King pushed Vassar back, holding him by the shoulders to look at him, and pulled him close again. After another round of back pats, the King kissed Vassar on the head, released him, and turned to a wary Hank.

The King knew his younger son struggled with their relationship. He didn't want to make him uncomfortable with a gregarious greeting, but neither did he want Hank to conclude he was less favored than Vassar because he greeted him differently.

Hank did not rush to greet his Father, but neither did he resist his embrace. Once he had his son in his arms, the King held him, whispered in his ear how glad he was to see him, and then he kissed him on the head as he had done Vassar.

"Come in. It's cold out here." The King motioned them toward the door. "I've arranged a dinner this evening—a special dinner, in your honor—to show my appreciation for you and the pride I have that you're my sons." The King smiled. "John here will show you around and take you to your rooms," the King said, pointing to an aide.

Captain Alexander watched Hank closely. He knew the man was confused. Had seen it many times in the confusion of battle. He recognized the shock in Hank's eyes, the blank stare indicative of a mind that has more than it can manage. He witnessed Hank's glance at John when the King mentioned him, figured the King's words had registered somewhere inside Hank's head, but never expected what transpired. Hank turned and looked back at him—not at his brother, not at the King—but at him, a known leader of men. Captain Alexander reassured the uncertain Prince with a slight nod and quick pursing of his lips. It was the reassurance Hank needed, and the Captain knew it. Hank reached out and touched the horse standing close by, felt its warmth, and then woodenly turned to follow John.

Turning back to the attentive Captain Alexander, the King said, "Captain, thank you. Well done."

Captain Alexander bowed, "The honor was mine, Your Majesty."

Erymos

John guided Vassar and Hank up a sweeping staircase, across a balcony that looked down into the foyer where they had entered, and down a hall to their suite. Two Valets waited beside their door. John opened the door, handed a key to each brother, and entered. He toured them through their accommodations explaining that their armoires contained clothing suited to their status and the evening.

"Your Valets will lay your clothing out and assist you as necessary."

Hank stole a glance at Vassar. He'd heard the Prince of Wales had a Valet, but to have one himself?

"Do you need anything?" John asked.

Neither brother said anything.

"If anything comes to mind, let your Valet or me know."

"Thank you," Vassar said.

"One final thing," John said with his back to the door. "On the table in your sitting room you will find a gift from the King. He asked that you open them together."

John bowed slightly as he exited.

Hank didn't know what to do with a Valet, but figured the man knew his job. *I'll just follow his lead,* he thought.

Since passing behind the waterfall, about the only thing remotely familiar to Hank was riding a horse, and he could already feel the serious soreness of being a non rider settling into his hips. Hank disappeared into the washroom, not only to clean up, but for a break from the baffling new time dimension, Erymos, the King who he instinctively knew was his Father, and now of all things, a Valet.

Hank closed the bathroom door.

He stood motionless staring at the handle, but not really seeing it. Hank emerged from his trance. He eyed the bathroom's appointments, attempting to gain his bearings, and then engage some meaningful action. What to do with the wash basin and pitcher of water was apparent. What to do with his used wash water was not. Had it not been for his reading of history and chamber pots, waiting to go to the bathroom would have been an exercise in endurance.

Hank stayed in the bathroom as long as he felt he could without alarming his Valet, but his time away did little to help him recover his wits.

Hank was reasonably certain now that he was not living in a dream, but exactly where he was, he couldn't decide. He had indeed passed into a new dimension. Of this, he was convinced, because it was so cold. But convinced or not, he continued to struggle mightily to cope.

He splashed water onto his face and closed his eyes in the towel as he dried his face. He rubbed the towel around his neck and ears, took some deep breaths, and decided to eliminate all the stimuli he could postpone thinking about until later.

First on his postponement list was the Valet. Hank tossed aside his adult modesty and returned to his locker room days in school athletics when the guys all undressed and showered and dressed together. Thinking of his Valet as "just one of the guys," he opened the bathroom door and bravely began the process of undressing and dressing as if he knew what he was doing. Hank was appreciative that the Valet, for his part, was patient. He didn't laugh once—at least he didn't laugh out loud once.

After successfully dressing in his royal attire adorned with the King's crest, Hank's Valet handed him the elegant gift box. Vassar was waiting in the common area, his back to the room, staring out the window. Hank sat down beside him and they unwrapped their gifts. Each contained an exquisite, wooden box. They unfastened the latches and lifted the lids. Inside were custom-made daggers, each unique, but both bearing the King's crest on the pommel.

Hank was undone. "Vassar, whatever in the world am I supposed to do with this? I don't know how to use a sword, dagger thing. This whole royalty-Prince-King-knights-Your Highness-Valet-horses-and-soldiers deal...," he sat shaking his head. "I don't know."

Vassar sat quietly.

Hank looked sideways at Vassar, "And what's with you, anyway? All this worshipfulness Prince charade? You're going along with it! Who do you think you are?"

Vassar still sat quietly.

"To make matters worse, you've lassoed me into this melodramatic farce. Who do all these people think I am? Do I look like Sir Lancelot?" Hank paused for affect.

Vassar said nothing.

"Tell you what: If you introduce me to Guinevere, I'll buy into this traveling show." Hank put his face in his hands, then forced his hair through his fingers until he reached the back of his neck. He rubbed at the stiffness.

Vassar remained still.

Hank looked at his brother. "Well? You just going to sit there with your teeth in your mouth, or you going to give me an answer?"

Vassar acknowledged. "I understand your confusion. Father's going out of his way to make it a great evening, to let us know he's proud of us, and especially you. Like I told you just after we passed behind the waterfall, Father knows you need some encouragement. He knows you're struggling to feel significant. I believe the dagger is his attempt to remind you of who you are. And in answer to your question, no. You don't look like Lancelot. His hair was longer. You look like my brother."

Hank was not amused. "Can't we just go back to where we came from? You know, go fishing, like we planned? Let's go back to Malden Creek. I want to get in my sleeping bag and curl up. I feel like I've got a hangover and I haven't even been drinking. Speaking of which, I sure could use a drink."

"There will be wine at dinner."

"I wasn't thinking of wine," Hank snapped.

"I know. It'll have to do though. And no, we can't skip this. Father has prepared all this just for us. For you, really. You'll have a great time once you get in the swing of the evening. Just relax."

"And what about you, Vassar? You never answered me. Who do you think you are?"

Vassar smiled at his frustrated sibling. "We've got lots of time to discuss that later. Right now, it's nearly dinner time. Come on, trust me."

Hank was too overwhelmed to argue, let alone be belligerent. He looked out the window even though he couldn't see through the darkness. He thought, *A PR-banquet stunt,* and shook his head with disgust. He focused on his strange clothing. *And a costume party. Who thought this up?* His marketing mind wondered. *Don't I go to enough of these stupid events at home? I don't want to press the flesh with a room full of pretenders.* His thoughts ricocheted off the walls of his agitated mind. Hank shook his head again, incredulous, as if doing so would clear the cobwebs. *And the King. Of all people. Father, as Vassar refers to him. The one who cares—but not enough to return my calls.* Hank could almost taste the bitterness of his resentment. He was a hair-trigger away from bolting into the night to escape. *He's one of the last people I want to spend the evening with. How the heck did I get into this mess?* Hank paused to see if an answer surfaced. *I don't know. But I suspect, like the rest of my life, he's going to have it his way regardless. I should've guessed. Tonight, it's at the expense of my fishing trip. Yep. Plain to see why he's glad to see me. I'm sure I'm important to him. What an honor this will be for me, to help him feel better about the crappy job he's done being my Father.* The sarcasm was acid inside Hank, producing the familiar, burning resentment that scalded his soul. *Nothing like being used. Must be how a whore feels the morning after. 'Least she gets paid.*

A few minutes later, the valets entered carrying custom belts designed for the scabbards. Following Vassar's lead, Hank stood and let his Valet assist him.

"It's time for dinner, Your Highness," Vassar's Valet said.

"You ready?" he said to Hank.

"No. But I'm ready as I'll ever be I guess. After you, your Superiority."

Vassar felt the sting of Hank's doubt. Had felt it all before. He bowed ceremoniously, turned on his heel, and said, "Fall in, Lancelot."

Hank appreciated Vassar's effort to ease the tension, laughed, and followed Vassar into the hallway.

Up one floor, at the opposite end of Erymos, she stood naked before her wardrobe considering her options: *Black? I love black. The power, elegance. Hmm? Not tonight though. Too dark. And others will wear black—to compensate. I don't need black.*

She continued sorting, holding first one outfit and then another against her body, looking into the mirror. *Silver? This isn't a wedding.*

There was a knock at her door. She looked through the peep hole at the messenger, put on her robe, opened the door, and retreated back inside with the envelope. She broke the seal and read:

Princes Vassar and Henry are here. You will sit next to Henry—Hank, the King calls him. Valet says he is uncomfortable, quiet. Greeting the King was telling—like the King was hugging a post. Work your magic.

Don't be late,

Jester

She carried the note and a candle across the room, opened her window, and let the smoke from the burning paper escape into the cold night. She thought about Prince Henry as she closed the window and smiled.

Returning to her armoire, she spied her purple sheath. She examined the dress. Placing her hand inside the bodice, she spread her fingers and held the material up to the light. Her eyebrows rose slightly. Slipping the luxurious gown over her head, she slithered into its custom form, pulled it down over her hips—wriggled—tipped her head back and freed her hair from under the straps.

Turning again to the mirror, she edged a step closer. Running her hands over her hips and adjusting the gown under her breasts, her decision was made. With a deft touch, she reached behind her back and fastened the three buttons responsible for keeping her more-or-less contained. Focusing her green eyes upon her image a final time, she tossed her black curls with her fingers. *If a woman's glory is her hair, then I am glorious.*

Stepping to her dressing table, she inventoried the essentials in her handbag. Then, dabbing her middle finger with a vial of perfume, she slid it and its essence into her cleavage and then behind her ear lobes.

She was late to dinner, but fashionably so. What could Jester do? She was powerful and knew it.

Vassar got no farther than the drink table before being stopped to talk. Hank continued on to the first fireplace, hoping to be inconspicuous—not likely when you are a guest of honor. It wasn't a large crowd—thirty or so—though it was hard to tell with all the wait staff.

Hank didn't stay inconspicuous for long. He shook hands, smiled, kissed ladies on the cheek, and listened graciously to small talk. He behaved as he thought would be expected of him.

A handsome man with close-cropped, graying hair and a square jaw waited for a break in the discussion before interrupting. "Prince Henry, pardon the interruption. My name is Jester."

"Why does everyone keep calling me that?" Then Hank caught himself, but his irritation was evident. Jester looked quizzically at the Prince. Hank regrouped, "I'm sorry I was curt."

"No problem, sir," Jester said, with a slight bow of deference. "I addressed you as Prince because that's who you are, but I'll be happy to address you as you prefer."

"Fine. Just call me, Hank."

"Well, sir. With all due respect, I can't call you that, your Highness."

Hank winced at yet another royal title. "Why not? Hank's fine. It's what everybody calls me." He thought for a moment. "Except here. Nobody calls me that here."

"Sir?"

Hank could see Jester needed some middle ground. Even though the alternative was still awkward to his informal mind, he offered, "Okay. Call me, Mr. Henderson."

"But sir, you can't expect me to address you as a common guest." Jester swept his hand and arm in a broad sweep across the room of humanity gathered for the banquet. "That would be disrespectful and dishonoring. Sir, it would give the wrong impression. It would send the wrong message."

Hank wanted to curse at the obstreperous man, but managed to keep it to himself. He conceded. "We're not making much headway here. Just call me whatever suits you."

"Very well, Prince Henry. As you wish."

Hank flinched, but acknowledged with a tolerant nod and closed eyes. "You're welcome. Now, let me apologize. I reacted ungraciously, and must confess, I don't remember what you said your name is."

"That is not a problem, sir. Don't give it a second thought. My name is Jester." Again, Jester bowed a polite bow.

"Jester. Now that's a funny name," said Hank.

Jester didn't laugh.

"Sorry. It was meant as a joke. Not a very good one, I can see. Or polite. I'm still a little off kilter. I'm not from around here."

"No apology is necessary, Prince Henry. Now, if you'll come with me, I'll show you to your seat."

Hank excused himself to the people still waiting to speak with him. He thought about apologizing to them as well since they had witnessed his awkward exchange with the *maitre d'*, but decided against it and followed Jester toward the front of the dining room. He was relieved to be free of the chit chat, but was anxious about what the King had planned.

Hank looked around the room. The King's effort was noteworthy; the room was spectacularly prepared and appointed. But his thoughts quickly turned toward the same recitation he'd gone over countless times, *I wish he would just answer my prayers. Why can't he just do as I asked?* Hank wondered as he walked, but there was no insight. And as was his habit, he reverted to self-justifying introspection. *I tried hard, prayed, believed harder. I even tried to trust that he'd come through.*

The distrust he felt percolated through his stress. *The King doesn't get it,* he thought, as he followed Jester. The doubt turned into the familiar anger-on-a-theme. *Protecting my data, my company. Giving me a publicity break. Selling the books in my garage. There's a novel idea. Any of these would have been helpful.*

As usual, his rant spurred his descent into the caverns of his deep-seated resentment. *No. No break for me. Instead of helping me, he's throwing a party for himself and his friends. Gives me a big knife. What am I going to do with almost-a-sword? If I ever get home, maybe I can use it in the yard instead of that cheap machete I bought.*

With his PR smile stuck on his face, Prince Henry looked pleasant as he followed Jester. But his mind was in another century, grieving over his bruised significance, and profoundly doubting the one he wished would do something to help him. Hank ruthlessly drew himself up short. *Wish in one hand, spit in the other. See which one gets full first.* The muscles in his jaw tensed as he clinched his teeth.

Hank thought he was following the *maitre d'*, a graceful and genteel man in comport. In reality, Jester was one of the most powerful agents in the Dark Army, possessing the spiritual power of suggestion. Already, he was working to turn the bewildered Prince to Zophos' advantage by suggesting that the High King was self-serving, out of touch, and insensitive to his true needs. Although they sounded like his own thoughts, the suggestions Hank considered as he followed Jester to his seat at the table were Jester's. But his suggestions were so convincing, and his impersonation of Hank's thoughts, emotions, and behavior were so sophisticated, and correlated so well with his circumstances that Hank blindly adopted Jester's suggestions as valid—and, as though they were his own—one after another.

Hank glanced around the dining room. The ceiling was vaulted, fifty-feet high, he guessed, with exposed rafters. One side of the rectangular room was predominantly windows. Heavy draperies framed their view of the lawns and vistas of Erymos. Opposite this were three fireplaces, each six-feet long, each with mantles of granite supported on native stones half again as tall as a man. At one end of the dining room were doors leading to the staging area for the wait staff. At the other end, the face of the cliff against which Erymos was constructed. A narrow opening in the rock sliced the face from the ground halfway up. Guards stood on either side of the fissure. Except for the windowed wall and the rock face, tapestries and life-size portraits adorned the walls. The table was a long oval that would easily seat tonight's guests, and there was not a bad seat.

The head of the table was at the end closest to the rock face. The King was standing there, behind his chair, waiting for his guests to find their places. Vassar was to his right. Beside Vassar, Magician, the sorcerer. Jester led Hank to the chair on the King's left, wished him well for the evening, and nodded to the King as he backed away to return to his oversight of the evening. The seat to Hank's left was unoccupied.

The guests assembled around the table. The ladies were seated while the men remained standing. The room grew quiet as all eyes turned to the King. As he opened his mouth to speak his welcome, she swept into the room, ravishing in her elegant, purple gown. Every eye turned from the King. Jester, who was standing against the wall by the entrance, offered her his arm and escorted her toward the head of the table. The women watched with envy. Their husbands watched as though looking at a fine piece of art.

As she and Jester got closer, Hank eased the chair out in front of him, offering her the seat next to the King—the seat intended for him. He helped her be seated, nodded to Jester, and stepped behind the chair to her left where he waited for the King to resume his welcome.

Attention turned slowly from the beautiful late-comer back to the King. Resuming, he welcomed his guests, thanked them for coming to Erymos for this important occasion, and expressed his hope they would enjoy dinner. With that, he offered a toast to Vassar and Hank followed by a toast to friendship and the evening. As his guests sipped their wine, the King sat down between Vassar and the beautiful woman to his left, and nodded to the expectant *maitre d'* that service should begin.

Dinner was a pork loin stuffed with berries, caramelized nuts, and diced apples and pears. It was the most succulent piece of meat Hank ever recalled tasting. There was a medley of greenhouse-grown squash beside sliced, red potatoes seasoned to perfection with garlic and accented by sautéed onion.

Forgetting the time and place in the swirl of his dark thoughts and her perfume, Hank turned, and lifted his glass, "This is fine wine. What do you think, a Zin?" He could tell right away she was confused and remembered: *Zinfandel probably hasn't been invented yet.* "Never mind. Great wine."

"Yes it is," she said, smiling with amusement. "Hello, Prince Henry. I am Significance."

Hank stared at her, disbelieving, confused, doubtful he had heard correctly. Catching himself staring, he said, "I beg your pardon. I thought for a moment you said your name was Significance." Hank laughed nervously, embarrassed.

"I did," she said, touching her chest lightly with the fingers of her right hand. "I'm Significance."

"No you're not." Hank realized his rudeness and immediately wished he could take back his blurt of words. "I'm sorry. I apologize. I never should have said that. It's just that. I mean. Well, I've never. You can't be."

Significance leaned toward him and touched his arm. "Yes, Prince Henry. I am indeed, Significance. In the flesh and seated next to you. Oh my, you're blushing."

"Yeah. I imagine I am. I'm sorry. I wasn't expecting. I mean, gosh. You're, umm." Hank stopped. He took a deep breath and started over. "What I mean is, it's nice to meet you. Please forgive me. It's been a really long day. I go by Hank."

"Alright," she said, laughing. "Hank it is."

"You look lovely," he said.

"Thank you. You're kind to notice."

Hank blushed again, and thought, *How could I not notice? The whole room noticed.*

"And thank you for giving me your chair," she said. "It's an honor to sit by the King."

Hank smiled and turned his eyes away for a moment. Significance realized Jester's briefing was correct: *He really doesn't like his Father. That's why he gave me his seat—so he wouldn't have to talk to him. He is vulnerable.* And she went to work.

"So what do you do? Jester explained a little of your story—where, or more accurately, when you come from. I understand."

"You do? Enlighten me, then. I've never been so confused in all my life."

"It's alright. Let's just stick together. I'll help you understand what it's like here if you'll tell me all about there." Significance turned toward Hank and leaned in, her ear and hair and scent ever-so-close.

Hank reciprocated, their shoulders touched, and he began explaining how his marketing company worked. He told her about his successes, described campaigns on behalf of his larger clients, took her vicariously into the world of nonprofit shenanigans, and told her how he guided well-meaning nonprofits back to their missions of service and mercy. He told of endorsements and relational networks—and she hung on every word, asked astute questions, laughed appropriately, and affirmed his business acumen.

"Gosh, Significance. I've been talking nonstop ever since you sat down. You must be bored stiff with the sound of my voice."

"Hardly. I'm fascinated. Hank, you are an incredible man, a truly unique individual. I'm certain you must be highly recognized for your talents and skills."

Hank laughed deferentially. "Well, that's a discussion for another day. Enough about me. Tell me about you."

"Okay, but only if you promise to tell me more about you. You've told me about your work. But I want to hear what people are saying about you. No doubt this is why the King is hosting a banquet in your honor." She watched to see if he flinched at the mention of the King's presumed motive. Getting what she wanted, she continued, leaning over toward him. "So, do you promise? Promise to tell me more of the good stuff, the things about you?"

"Yeah, I promise. But it's your turn now."

"Well, I'm the daughter of a man who was a successful entrepreneur. Daddy had his finger in all sorts of different industries. He would start something, staff it, guide it to success, place it in the hands of a capable manager, and turn his attention to his next dream. Mom was an enthusiastic supporter and encouraged me to be all I could be."

"Did you work with your Dad?" Hank asked.

"Yes. I joined him after I completed the university. He lobbied for me to be admitted. I was the first woman graduate."

"Let me guess," Hank interrupted. "You graduated with honors."

Significance blushed and nodded.

"Your turn to be embarrassed," Hank sparred. "Go on. You joined your Dad after you graduated."

"That's right. He recognized that my ideas were astute and placed me in increasingly responsible positions. Jester told me what my title would be in your time dimension, but I've forgotten what he called it. It was all initials. Something 'financial,' I think."

"Chief Financial Officer?" Hank suggested. "CFO?"

"That's it," she said. "CFO. Is that an important job where you come from?"

"Very important," Hank said. "It's powerful and influential too. Same here?"

Significance blushed. "You've embarrassed me again. But, yes. It is the foremost position, second only to my Daddy. In all honesty though, I have a great team around me."

"I know you must," Hank said. "Tell me more."

"Like what?"

"What accomplishments are you most proud of?"

"That's not fair. I asked you first."

"I know, but you haven't talked as long as I did. Tell me, and then I'll answer your question."

Significance leaned against Hank's shoulder and lowered her voice so Hank had to lean close to hear. "I don't like to talk about it, but I brought health care to our employees, increased their productivity by letting them share in the company profits, and helped the communities where our companies are located by encouraging our staff to volunteer with community service."

"Great day! That's fabulous, Significance," Hank said. "Those are wildly innovative programs."

"Thanks for thinking so—and for saying it," she said.

Hank asked just above a whisper, "Has your father recognized your contribution?"

She leaned her leg against his and touched his arm at the elbow. "Has he ever. He has promoted, recognized, affirmed, given gifts…. Oh, my. What else? I don't know. I lose track. He has been so supportive."

"You sound like you really enjoy working with your Dad."

"Oh, I do, I do. Not everyone gets to work with someone they like. And not only that, I trust him beyond words. I know I'm important to him."

As nice dinners do, this one progressed slowly—as much event as dining. The King attempted to engage Hank in conversation a few times, but their exchanges proved brief, thanks to Significance. When the King tried to speak with Hank, Significance leaned forward—as though engaged. Conversation was awkward, especially for the King whose every move was observed in the room. To lean in front of Significance for long would be impolite—and inappropriate, given the cut of her dress.

In sharp contrast, the King's conversation with Vassar and Magician was robust. They shared ideas, reminisced, regaled each other with stories—some true, some embellished—and laughed. As the evening progressed, the King was certain Vassar knew how important he was to him.

But to his left, buffered by Significance, Hank was thankful for the distance. Jester strategically seated best friends to Hank's left, and as planned, they had little interest in small talk with Hank when they had a golden opportunity to enjoy being together. Hank barely noticed. He was smitten with Significance.

"Hank, that's a handsome dagger you're carrying."

"Thanks. It's a gift—from the King."

"Really? It's striking."

"Yeah. Gave it to me tonight. Gave one to Vassar too."

Hank slipped the weapon from its sheath, leaned into Significance, and showed her the gift holding it below the table in their laps. He could smell her perfume and feel her warmth as she leaned against his arm and touched his leg with hers.

"Vassar says the King gave it to me because I'm important." Hank's doubt was evident. He tried to rationalize. "Don't get me wrong," he said, where only she could hear, "the King and I just haven't ever gotten along like he and Vassar do. I received a gift because Vassar got a gift."

Hank put the dagger back in its sheath. Significance looked at Hank, her green eyes moist with empathy. Under the privacy afforded by the table, she slipped her hand onto Hank's. He felt the electricity, saw the admiration in her glance, and relished both. He felt important, recognized. Significant. And he sat a little straighter in his chair.

"Pardon me, please." A steward reached between Hank and Significance to refill his wine glass. Magician, who had been observing Hank and watching Significance's enticement from across the table, plotted to distract Hank from her. When he noticed the steward making his way around the table with the wine, he seized his opportunity. As soon as the steward stepped back to continue his service, Magician leaned between Hank and Significance, putting his arm on the back of Hank's chair.

"I'm sorry I didn't get a chance to greet you before dinner," he said.

"Magician. Nice to see you. How have you been?" Hank scooted his chair back from the table and stood, extending his hand.

"Oh, fine. Doing well thanks. You're looking good. Doing alright?"

"Yeah. I'm okay."

"Your Father has been telling your brother and me about you," Magician said.

"Oh? Good things I hope?"

"Oh certainly, certainly. The King thinks the world of you. A very proud father."

Hank deflected Magician's comments with a turn of his head, "Magician, let me introduce you to Significance."

"Significance," Magician said, with a slight tip of his chin. "We meet again."

"Yes. Our paths keep crossing," she acknowledged.

"So you already know each other," Hank observed.

"Our work overlaps from time to time," said Magician.

Irritated by Magician's shrewdness, and having no desire to address the King, Significance excused herself to refresh. Magician took her seat and motioned for Hank to sit down as he continued asking questions, talking about miscellany, and giving Hank other things to think about than Significance.

Jester saw her get up. They rendezvoused in an alcove off the main hall. "Got out foxed by the old master, didn't you?"

Significance curled her lip and hissed quietly through her teeth.

"How's it going?" Jester asked.

She assured him that Hank was skeptical of the King's intent, that he was interpreting his presence at the dinner as a polite inclusion, and that the real guest of honor was Vassar. "He told me about his job and revealed that the last year has been rough. A lot of disappointments and professional setbacks. His confidence is low and he feels unimportant."

"Good, good," Jester affirmed. "You're just what he needs."

Significance smiled and winked, "If I can get him alone, I'll also be what he wants."

"Come into my parlor, said the spider to the fly."

Significance grinned and walked back toward the dining room. She stopped in front of a mirror in the hallway, reapplied her lipstick, and pinched her cheeks.

Magician had turned the small talk with Hank to an affirmation of the King's opinion of him. "Your Father's proud of you, Hank. He wants to show you off. Let you know you're important."

Hank was paying attention to Magician, but then Significance returned and borrowed Magician's earlier move, slipping in between him and Hank when they stood politely upon her return to the table. Magician assisted Significance with her chair and patted Hank on the back before returning to his side of the table.

"You okay?" Hank asked her.

"Oh, yes. I ran into one of my girlfriends and started chatting. You men step out, don't say a word to anyone, and are back in a flash. But you know how we girls are."

Hank didn't say anything. Significance could tell he was immersed in thought. *No doubt Magician's influence*, she thought. She slipped her arm through his and pulled it close. Hank's attention was hers again. "You are clearly a dedicated and insightful man. What do you do to relax?"

With her questions she wooed him. With her caresses she drew him. With her attention she captured him. Each time she spoke his name, her affections tightened her grip on his senses. Hank's soul was thirsty for recognition. She provided it. He wanted more time with her, and she seemed to want the same with him. He relished the feeling of importance she brought to him, and felt the stimulation of being with her.

Their conversation wove in and out of various subjects. Discussion was easy and each other's company reassuring. She leaned into him and he relied upon her.

The dinner service had been removed by the wait staff, the table cloth cleaned of crumbs, and the drinks refilled. Dessert would come later.

The King stood, tapped his glass with a piece of silver, and raised his hand. "As you know, this is a special evening. My sons are here." The King introduced both, had them stand, and joined the room in applauding before continuing his speech.

"Vassar, my beloved oldest, and first in line to the throne is a true joy to me. Faithful. Creative beyond compare. Unselfish. Bright…." The King delivered a glowing tribute. He recognized Vassar's accomplishments, contributions, and affirmed his character as an honorable man.

When the King concluded, Vassar stood to the applause in order to make his acceptance comments. He was gracious, thankful, and recognized his debt to his Father's love. He thanked the guests for their attendance, thanked his Father for the blessing of being his son, and took his seat to another round of applause as the King stood once again.

Turning to Vassar, the King said, "Son, I've asked several of my friends to say a few words." He nodded to the first to take the floor as he sat down. Their comments were humbling in their recognition of Vassar and his position in the Kingdom. Each speaker concluded his remarks with a hearty toast.

While Vassar was being honored, Hank's resentful nervousness escalated. He had no interest in appearing gracious through what he felt was certain to be a disingenuous speech by his obligated Father—to do for him what he had done for Vassar, not out of desire, but because he felt obliged to his guests to not make them uncomfortable.

He sipped nervously at his wine and fiddled with his utensils.

"You're like a cat on a hot roof," Significance said into his ear.

"Yeah. I really don't like this. Just not right."

She reached, touched his arm, and gave it a gentle squeeze.

"I gotta get outta here," Hank whispered to Significance, as the table talk continued to venerate Vassar.

"The closest exit is through the opening in the rock," she advised.

"Where's it go?"

"I'll take you," she said, gripping his hand for reassurance.

A man and his wife at the other end of the table were making a joint presentation regarding Vassar's influence in their family. The guests around the table were captivated by their story.

Hank made his move. He ducked his head to avoid his Father's eyes and followed Significance as she walked quickly toward the rock face. Jester motioned to the guards on either side of the opening. In less than ten seconds Hank had slipped away from his Father's recognition dinner, escaped the unending recitation of his brother's accolades, and was following the allure of Significance into the darkening slit.

CHAPTER 4

Gnarled Wood, Zophos' Field Headquarters

Deep in Gnarled Wood on an island surrounded by swamps, miles from Erymos and hidden by dense vegetation, Zophos sat in his field headquarters brooding, immersed in strategy. After years of persistence, he was positioned to overthrow the King and gain the throne.

Zophos was not always dark, nor was Gnarled Wood always his haunt. His power, resourcefulness, and wealth originated with the High King. He served on the King's cabinet—one of three members—each carrying great responsibility and power.

But he became intoxicated with his beauty, intelligence, and position. He turned his power to his own advantage in an attempted *coup d'état* of the King. A third of the Army of Light's multiplied legions and accompanying compliment sided with Zophos. He knew then—as he knows still—that his rebellion was a desperate gamble. Defeat could not be an option. In fact, he had no contingency for losing. He had to win—at any cost.

The King proclaimed he would show Zophos and his breakaway army no mercy, pledging that the pit of the earth and the horrors of his vengeance would be Zophos' only consolation in defeat. As expected, Zophos retaliated with inflammatory rhetoric: "Since no mercy would be shown, no mercy would be granted," he went on record as saying. The gauntlet was thrown down and the universe plunged into war. Pitched battles raged with appalling casualties.

Zophos was a quick study. He honed his battlefield maneuvers, converted his Dark Army into a formidable force, and developed the fearsome tactic of transforming into a monstrous, red dragon.

But the war turned against Zophos. The King and the Army of Light surrounded him and his Dark Army and took them prisoner. In what some still consider an act of poor judgment, rather than bathe the worlds with the blood of the insurrectionists, the High King threw Zophos and his followers into Gnarled Wood. He planned to leave them there for a time period that suited him before rounding them up and throwing them into the lonely hell of his ultimate rejection. The King's rationale for delaying was that he needed time to prepare a place suitable for the likes of Zophos. Believing he still had a chance, Zophos regrouped and staged for another attempt at a *coup* with a fresh strategy.

Gnarled Wood was home to all of humankind, most of whom lived in or around the castle. The King did not rule like a traditional king. Most kingdoms function on political power and class systems, but not the Kingdom of Light. It functioned on love, at least that is what the King intended. His belief was that if he loved the people, the people would love him. In turn, they would enjoy a mutually satisfying and beneficial relationship and his reign would be legitimized.

In order to not delude himself with the false positive of a successful reign, especially given his intimidating power, the King gave the gift of an unfettered will—absolute freedom of choice—to every person in the Kingdom. No exceptions. The King was absolutely committed to love and absolutely opposed to manipulating anyone's freedom of choice. If people decided to love him, he wanted to know for certain they did so without coercion or intimidation. The King adhered to his conviction so strongly that he allowed dissent, outright rebellion, and even tolerated people who rejected his love and set themselves up under their own self-rule. Even insurrection, like Zophos', was tolerated.

Many of the King's senior advisors counseled him to create a legal standard and administer the Kingdom by that law. "Call it love, if you want, or doing what's best," they counseled him.

After a time, he agreed, and codified a simple legal code. But with humanity's use, it burgeoned into a laborious and onerous legal system.

The King was so committed to reigning based upon his deep love that he ultimately turned the impossible-to-keep legal system into an incentive to love and be loved. After all, the legal standard was a stark, weighty contrast to his glowing, rapturous love.

Lost in these reflective thoughts covering his history of conflict with the High King, Zophos was startled by his aide's knock. "Sir. I apologize."

"What is it?"

"The general staff has assembled for the briefing."

Zophos nodded, and turned to stare out again into the swamp surrounding his headquarters.

He, and many others, thought the King was insane with his love. They believed the Kingdom should be run with a firm grasp, and if necessary, an iron fist. But the King's power was formidable, his Kingdom pervasive, and his determination to love absolute. So, the King loved the people with undying hope the people would love him in return. Some did, some didn't, but the option remained for everyone.

This, Zophos thought. *This irrational love for everyone and everything. I can exploit this. He's left himself no room to maneuver.*

It was clear to Zophos that the King would not compromise his love. It was who he was. And he would not compromise people's freedom of choice. Love was bogus if unaccompanied by the absolute freedom to accept it or reject it.

The King has to know he'll have nothing but heartache from this policy of love, Zophos mused. *Says it's about relationship. Hmm. Whatever. Doesn't do him any good. He's gambling everything on love. Well, not me. If he wants to gamble on people, more power to him. Makes my job that much easier. People! Little fools.* "They're a means to an end," he muttered.

Desperate to escape the King's promised punishment and overthrow him, Zophos had conceived a master plan. *As long as I'm relegated to Gnarled Wood alongside humanity, why not turn the King's affinity for people against him? I'll make my stand here.*

This idea had simmered in his mind for some time, and as his thoughts blended together, his strategy had taken shape. Once satisfied with his genius, he had summoned the general staff.

Zophos stood up from his contemplation, belched, and swallowed. Tasted the bitter bile of his heart burn. *Okay*, he thought, assembling his summary to the forefront of his brilliant mind. *I need to review. Tell them what I'm going to tell them. Tell them. And then tell them again. No mistakes. No room for error. We must be overwhelming. No harm in that. I've got everything to gain and nothing to lose. The last time he and I met, I wasn't prepared. Landed me here*, he knew. *But Gnarled Wood is a good place to make our stand*, he reassured himself again. Zophos felt the familiar intensity, the plague of dissatisfaction. He burped again. Squinted at the taste and spit the brownish-yellow discharge onto the floor across the room. He wiped his teeth with his tongue, straightened his jacket, and made his way to the briefing room.

The command staff knew better than to sit down before Zophos arrived, and they knew better than to complain that he had kept them waiting. The correct time for the meeting wasn't the time stated in their order to appear at headquarters—it was when Zophos arrived.

The door opened. An aide stepped through, snapped to attention, and held the door until Zophos was through. The officers stiffened—in deference, self-defense, and dread.

"Sit down," he ordered.

He prowled back and forth across the front of the room. In his desperation to have what he wanted—the King's throne—he skipped his planned statement describing the rationale behind the meeting and launched straight into a recitation of the King's weakness. "Although the King's love is powerful and mankind's free will is untouchable, humanity is profoundly afflicted with weak discipline and frail frames."

There were quick glances around the briefing table. The staff scrambling to catch up to the rationale for Zophos' diatribe.

"They are vulnerable to peer pressure and influence. They are irrational in their pursuit of happiness. They are short-sighted, given to quarrels, slow to adopt change—even beneficial change—and are prone to disease and death. They are amazingly stubborn about maintaining their independence, even though it consistently does them a disservice. Oddly enough, the brighter ones in the bunch are more prone to this irrationality." Zophos paused to ponder this. "It's counterintuitive. The smartest are apt to be the greatest fools."

Zophos spun toward the briefing table. He commanded, "Pay attention to the poor, the destitute, the infirmed, the dumb—the simple ones among humanity. They are the savvier among the King's subjects. They're not easily led, can't be fooled for long. The smart ones—the smart ones are too smart for their own good."

Each general at the table nodded and frowned, as if fully capturing Zophos' rant, and to indicate full engagement.

Zophos turned away, his back to the table, his face toward a map of Gnarled Wood. He stepped up to the map and smoothed it with both palms, studied it, lost in his own world of thoughts.

Turning slowly, pensively, back toward the assembly at his table, Zophos resumed. "While the King sees in these peon people a great deal to love, I see in them a vulnerability to exploit. And that's what I intend to do. That's why I summoned you." Zophos smiled a condescending, wicked grin. "If these people are the key to the King's legitimacy as a ruler, then they are the key to his ouster. They are his soft underbelly, his vulnerability. If I create a deception that confuses their inferior reasoning, empowers their independence, and promises them peace they will side with me. In time, this will lead to a successful *coup*."

Zophos did not pause for feedback or questions. He expected those at the table to understand what he wanted. If they failed, or misunderstood, he'd replace them. Right now, he was more interested in voicing his bitter rage at the King's previous victory that had banished them all to Gnarled Wood. *Had a few things gone differently*, Zophos reflected, *I wouldn't be here. I'd be sitting in the King's chair.* He coughed, and spit.

Returning to the briefing table from the foray into the dark chambers of his mind, Zophos talked about *noblesse oblige*—doing what was best for the Kingdom and its people. But he quickly revealed his real objective was what it had always been: the throne. There was nothing altruistic about what Zophos wanted.

Fully immersed in his harangue bearing little resemblance to a briefing, Zophos regaled the room with his true intent. "And once the throne is seized, I will banish the King to the hell he stupidly believes he's created for me and I will coronate myself, sovereign." Zophos gloated in the thought.

He strode forward to the briefing table, leaned down upon it, and stared at each officer. He sat down, lowered his voice, and fixed his gaze. "If that means destroying Gnarled Wood, so be it. If it means destroying the castle, so be it. I don't care if it is the primary population center within Gnarled Wood. If it means destroying the Round Tower, so be it." The look in his eyes was frightening.

"But sir." The interruption came from the officer in the fourth chair, left side of the table. "The Round Tower is architecturally remarkable. If it were preserved, you could establish it as the seat of your kingdom."

"Idiot!" Zophos hissed. "I don't want my throne there—in people's hearts, as the King says. The Tower is only the seat of the King when he's with his people, and I'm not interested in his people. I want the King's seat of power in the universe."

The officer was obviously shaken. "I understand, sir. And, I agree," he quavered.

"I don't give a rat's ass if you agree or not. You'll do what I want. You all will," he screamed. "I haven't come this far to be defeated by your incompetence."

Every person at the table pressed against the back of their chair. To the person, they wished they could be anywhere other than in the room with Zophos' desperate hatred.

"I cannot afford defeat given the gravity of the King's preparations for punishment if you fail." It was perhaps the most honest statement thus far in the briefing. Beyond all of Zophos' railing, the specter of defeat was horrific. Far more than helping Zophos obtain the King's throne, the officers at the table were fighting to avoid the King's pledge of hell for their insurrection in siding with Zophos' first rebellion.

"Give me an update on the status of Gnarled Wood," Zophos commanded.

An officer leaned forward and submitted a terse overview. "Zophos. As you intended, sir. The air throughout Gnarled Wood is filled with confusion, delusion, intimidation, and manipulation. All living creatures, whether plant or animal, breathe your deception and desperation into every pore of their being. Communication, health, rationality, and length of life are compromised as a result."

The next officer waited a tense moment to discern whether Zophos had a comment, then began. "Sir, your systematic engagement in coercion of mankind's free will to elicit renunciations of loyalty to the King is proving effective. In exchange for their defection from the King, people are adopting as legitimate your promise of personal independence and acting accordingly."

Zophos reentered the conversation. "The more widespread people's independence, the stronger my case that the King is no longer legitimate."

"Yes, sir," the officer concurred.

Zophos continued, "Of course, once the King is overthrown, I intend to quash my new subjects' independence and free will decisively. Once in power, I'll renege."

"Sir, with all due respect," the officer began, but Zophos held up his hand.

"Don't question me," Zophos scowled. "The people's politicians, pastors, and public figures renege on their promises and pledges all the time. Like me, they are accountable to power, not the people."

To the person, each officer at the table looked down at their hands when Zophos gave his explanation. Each knew it was true, but they were all uncomfortable with the unvarnished candor.

Moving to the next item on his agenda, Zophos said, "I have four current interests in particular that I want to focus upon: Prince Vassar, Prince Henry, the castle, and the Round Tower."

The officers adjusted their attention and posture. The change of subject was a small relief from their discomfort, but it was a relief.

"The Princes are key targets because they are the King's heirs. The castle is important to me because it is home to the King's lovely people. The Round Tower is strategic because it is the home and institution of the King, the haven of those loyal to him. As goes the Round Tower, so goes the castle, and the Kingdom. If the King has said this once," Zophos reviewed, "he's said it a thousand times. But even if he wasn't vocal with this opinion, the fact that he situated the Round Tower in the center of the castle on prime property is an obvious clue."

There were nods of agreement around the table.

Zophos continued, "As you know, I developed and executed a plan to compromise Prince Vassar some years ago. My plan is ongoing. While containing physical components, especially in the beginning, my continuing attack on Prince Vassar is primarily psychological. Hear me, and hear me good: I will never miss an opportunity to question Prince Vassar's qualifications to reign. I expect the same from you. Utilize circumstance, manipulation, and inference—whatever it takes—to portray Prince Vassar as a liar at best, a lunatic at worst, but certainly not the Lord Prince of the Kingdom. Use this tactic. It works. Most folks in the castle and around Gnarled Wood don't give Prince Vassar a second thought."

There were a few sideways glances around the table. The statistic sounded compelling, and Zophos used it frequently to legitimize his claim to the throne, but it was hard to measure. He was quick to point out that if Prince Vassar and the King are such venerable leaders, then what's with the rising corruption of mankind? They had all heard this many times before, but the lack of substance was more troubling to them than it seemed to be to Zophos.

"Prince Vassar's brother requires a different tactic. I devised and implemented a plan several years ago to undermine the King's reputation with Prince Henry."

Of course, every person at the table knew this. They'd all been part of the implementation. But, they humored Zophos' need to stroke his ego.

"Most people don't realize that the boundaries of Gnarled Wood extend from here, to the waterfall on Malden Creek, and beyond into the world Prince Henry calls home: Oklahoma, Texas, and his fish camp in Montana. My informants tracked Prince Henry to Malden Creek and informed me when the Prince arrived this side of the falls."

Standing up for effect, Zophos began his pacing again. "Some—the young and impetuous—advocated killing Prince Henry *en route* to Erymos. I don't want to risk making the Prince a martyr. I have enough of those on my hands already, thanks to the poor advice from one of you who should know better."

The Brigadier's eyes opened wide with the realization of Zophos' implication. He turned to look at Zophos just in time to see the club coming down. Zophos' bludgeon struck him just above his left temple. His head exploded, spilling its contents on the table and spattering those close with the fluids of the disfavored officer's brain. His body slumped, limp, and slid under the table before knocking the chair over backward. Zophos stepped out of the way of the tipping chair.

Zophos twirled the club like a baton. The veterans of these meetings knew better than to flinch, look, or gasp. All eyes were on Zophos as the dead man's body drained beneath their feet.

"Killing the King's followers rarely works in my favor," Zophos continued. "It's easy enough to silence their voices, but their spilt blood cries out a continual endorsement of the King's reign. And you," he spun around pointing, "have yet to devise a way to silence their blood."

Every person in the room was watching the club.

"As it is, Prince Henry is playing into my hand by coming to this part of Gnarled Wood." Zophos laughed. "What's even better is that Prince Vassar and the King planned Prince Henry's trip."

Zophos remained at the front of the room, and although he still had the club in his hands, he had stopped pacing.

"I orchestrated the cataclysmic downturn of events in Prince Henry's life shortly before the fishing trip with his brother," Zophos said. "I always work to my advantage." Zophos paused, looked around the table, to be certain that declaration registered in everyone at the table. "That's why I will be victorious. I won't make the mistake the High King made. Victory requires ruthless, relentless focus on the objective. I won't be deterred. I won't be distracted. I will get what I want."

The tension in the room was thick enough to cut.

"I planned to undermine Prince Henry's life on the other side of the waterfall." Zophos shrugged. "But, no matter. Whether he is here or there is irrelevant." Zophos retreated into his own thoughts for a few long moments. Breaking his silence, he said, "However, it's probably advantageous he is here. I can achieve my goals more quickly."

"He's certainly more stressed," offered a bold officer desperate to ease some of the tension.

As though perfectly at ease with participation, Zophos concurred with the officer, "Yes, he is. He's off balance, disillusioned, and needs more desperately than ever to believe he's significant."

Seizing on the small momentum created by the other officer, another said, "Sir, sending Significance was perfect."

"You're right," he agreed. "She is alluring. I don't understand why."

It was a classic psychological demonstration of projection by Zophos—ascribing to another your own attitudes, feelings, and issues. And in classic manifestation, Zophos was blind to his projection. He was clueless that the desperation driving his rebellion against the King was his drive to be significant.

Zophos continued, "Under increased duress, Prince Henry will discredit himself as Prince and denounce the King's claim to the throne. Based upon the latest reports, this appears probable and the risk seems minimal. Given my advance work to destabilize him, the Prince is fragile. He will turn to Significance in lieu of the King's promises and look to her for affirmation, satisfaction, and importance."

"That would be a *coup* indeed—a Prince," several officers said, almost simultaneously.

Zophos' mood darkened noticeably. "The Round Tower, on the other hand, is formidable: virtually impenetrable, highly important to the King, populated with his loyalists, and secured by his Army of Light troops. I have assigned one of my brightest and sharpest minds, Ennui, to craft a strategy to overthrow the Round Tower."

The officers around the table mirrored Zophos' demeanor.

"Pay attention. The King is a cunning adversary. I'll send further orders."

Zophos dropped his club on the floor, turned, and exited the room. He didn't acknowledge the guard at the door.

Zophos' chief aide turned to the officers standing around the table and said, "Dismissed."

Zophos returned to his office, pondering all that was before him. An assistant to his aide entered with a fresh cup of hot tea, placed a folder in front of him, and announced that Competence and Ennui had arrived and were waiting outside for their briefing.

Zophos stared at the aide. As soon as he saw the man wilt, he snarled and said, "Send them in." The aide bowed his head and turned to leave as Zophos blew his nose on the floor beside his desk.

Competence and Ennui entered Zophos' lair and stood waiting.

Zophos motioned them toward his conference table. "Sit down. Let's begin with Prince Henry. What do we know thus far?"

Competence reported that he had received a dispatch from Jester just before the meeting indicating that Hank and Significance had a splendid meal at Erymos, and prior to the King's recognition of him, had left together via the slit in the rock.

Zophos nodded. "And…?"

"…And our plan is unfolding flawlessly," Competence continued. "As soon as our meeting is over, I will return to the slit in the rock. Jester has our operatives in place. Your objective has been made clear. Contingencies have been rehearsed. I think we're prepared for anything."

"Think?" Zophos snapped.

"We're ready, Zophos," Competence corrected.

Zophos was silent.

Competence squirmed in his seat, enduring Zophos' silent glare. He had seen others give reports, had witnessed Zophos' penchant for taking dramatic action—as if on a whim—to buttress his control. He'd watched Zophos slit people's throats from behind, leaving them gurgling and bleeding to death at the table. His mission was singular. His rule ruthless. His demeanor, merciless.

"Don't screw this up. I want the Prince broken. Humiliate him. Only then will he disgrace the King. Don't kill him. Let him suffer. The more he suffers, the more good he is to me."

Competence affirmed his understanding.

"Get out of here. Ennui, you stay."

As Competence left for the slit in the rock, Zophos' aide entered the office and announced that Nephilim had arrived and was waiting.

"Send him in," Zophos commanded.

Nephilim was a giant, a half-breed sired by a fallen angel and his human consort. He was larger, stronger, faster, and smarter. His corrupt spirituality and humanity made him a perfect choice for Chief of Military Operations.

No introductions were necessary. Nephilim and Ennui knew each other and knew why they were meeting with Zophos. "The castle's a formidable target," Nephilim sat down and began without fanfare, "but our assault will be overwhelming. They'll be demoralized. Victory will follow."

"Give me a plan, not hot air," Zophos hissed.

"Zophos, your archers have been equipped with ignitable arrows. Not only are they lethal, they also create doubt."

"So people doubt," he said indifferently. "I want more than that," he screamed.

"Under waves of fire from the archers, the catapult troops will move forward until they are within range. Of course, we have our normal artillery battalions, but for this battle, we've constructed new catapults that are larger. They can…"

"…how much larger?" Zophos wanted to know.

"Sixty-six percent."

"Go on."

"They can unleash a much heavier assault. In our tests, their projectiles created massive damage."

"Tell me more about how you'll demoralize the castle."

"The new catapults are capable of delivering sealed caldrons of flammable acid. The containers break on contact. By itself, the acid is lethal, but when paired with flaming arrows…." Nephilim's eyes glowed. "We tested the delivery system and the projectiles on an army of slaves. Most died, but it took awhile. Some were incapacitated. Their suffering was remarkable."

"Go on."

"We've also assembled a mobile force capable of flight. It will be the first time we've used this tactic, certainly the first time the castle will have seen anything like it. To be attacked on the ground and in the air will be overwhelming, and with our numbers and speed, their demoralization will rise with each assault wave."

"Anything more?" Zophos asked.

"We have the giant moles penned in caves we quarried out of granite cliffs. It's a real challenge to keep a mole caged. And fed. They eat so much it's a full-time job feeding them."

Zophos slapped his hand on the table, his signal that he didn't want to hear about maintenance; he wanted to hear about action.

"They will be turned loose behind the catapult line, sir. As they tunnel toward the castle, we can use their entry holes as supply depots. Once they are through, your troops will be supplied as they advance to the castle."

"Very well," Zophos stated, sounding bored.

"Ennui, you're responsible for penetrating the Round Tower."

"We have already begun," she said. Her precise speech—with nary a contraction—seemed incongruent to her lassitude. "After considerable analysis—by experts in all fields—our conclusion is that the Round Tower is not conquerable from without. The High King has seen to its defense and supply himself. While a frontal assault is part of the plan, as Nephilim described, our primary strategy occurs from within. My agents have already inserted themselves into the Round Tower, its culture, and its routine."

"Spies. Already inside. Well, well."

"That is correct, Zophos. My people are promoting a message of peace, purity of thought, and tolerance. Apathy toward anything outside the Tower is growing. It is our aim to see it become rampant."

"I like it," Zophos said, "but what about the battle for the castle? Won't they be alerted?"

"The true impenetrability of the Tower will be proven once the attack by Nephilim begins in earnest. We anticipate a slight rally inside the Keep—you know, for the cause and the King—and there will be a few heroic efforts. There always are. But as the battle progresses, the people in the Round Tower will realize they are safe. Their passion for the plight of the castle will wane as the risk becomes evident. They will withdraw into the insular safety of the Round Tower, lapse farther into apathy, and the rationalization they were suffering before the battle. In time, they will collapse under their own weight."

"Hmm," Zophos gloated. "When that occurs, the Round Tower will be a magnificent monument to the failed dream of the High King."

"And you can take your place on the throne," Nephilim summarized.

They relished a moment to consider such a victory.

"Very well," Zophos approved, bringing them back to the pending agenda. "I'll conduct the overall battle and will take responsibility for the psychological warfare."

"What do you have in mind?" Nephilim asked.

"I'm going to appear again as the Red Dragon."

Nephilim and Ennui leaned forward.

"It's not enough that our numbers are overwhelming. We must be ruthless. Defeat is not an option," he said, slapping the table with the flat of his hand. "I'll use our own casualties to create mental anguish."

"I like it," Nephilim said.

"We'll trample them—wounded, dying, and dead alike. An army ruthless enough to grind its own fallen under foot will send a clear message!"

"With your permission, I will inform your troops, sir." Nephilim gushed.

"I would be pleased for you to inform them." Zophos rose from his chair and leaned across the table into Nephilim's face. His breath was stale. "Tell their sorry souls that they better keep moving, better keep advancing. Always. At any cost." Zophos pounded his fists. "Tell them if they slow down, fall down, kneel down, or get down—for whatever reason—I'll run over them and their remains will squish up through my toes! Tell them, Nephilim. Tell them how it's going be."

Sweeping his hand over the expansive map of the castle, Zophos calmed. "This brute force—the attack, the catapults, the fire, the aerial bombardment—is a diversion."

"Sir?" Nephilim said.

"The primary objective is the Round Tower. Ennui's right. It's got to happen from within. Manipulation, deception, human capital working as spies to destabilize—whatever it takes. Ennui, don't disappointment me." Zophos' eyes glowed.

Ennui sat poker-faced, confident in her ability to achieve the desired result.

"This will take time," Zophos continued. "For now, I'll turn my attention to Prince Henry. What a genius that boy is." His tone was derisive. "Worried about work, his contacts, his stupid waders—and his ridiculous book. Doesn't trust his Father. Tell you what, if my boy walked out of a party I'd thrown, I'd skin him alive. On the spot, I'd take him out. But not the King. He's merciful. Loving. He's weak! No guts, no gumption."

Ennui and Nephilim leaned back in their seats as though to distance themselves from Zophos' hate. "Prince thinks he's smart. Thinks Jester's a *maitre d'* and that the King's dinner is a costume party." Zophos laughed. "Right about now the Prince is trying to get Significance and her purple dress into a dark corner. Meanwhile, the King and his guests are foregoing their toasts. Must be embarrassing for the High King."

Standing, Zophos said, with frightening intensity, "I'll conquer the High King. Prince Henry will turn away from him. He'll choose Significance instead of him. I'll win. Before long, the King's throne will be mine, not because of our superior force, but because the King's own people—starting with his boy, Prince Henry—declare their independence." Zophos stared at the two officers, his intimidation reinforcing the singular standard of victory.

"Dismissed."

CHAPTER 5

Slit in the Rock

As soon as Significance and Hank entered the slit in the rock, the guards stepped in front of the opening, just as Jester had instructed. Grasping his hand, Significance led him away from the King's dinner and deeper into the crevasse. Hank was blinded by the sudden transition from light to darkness. Significance giggled, squeezed his hand harder, and increased her pace. While he felt slight regret for abandoning his Father, and wondered casually what he would have said about him, Hank was enthralled with the anticipation of being led into the dark by an anxious, beautiful woman.

Hank could see the glow of a soft light ahead. Significance stopped, turned to Hank, pulled him close, and kissed him, half on his mouth, half on his cheek. "In here," she said, opening a heavy door leading down another hall. Hank closed the door behind them and followed her down the shoulder-width hallway. Significance waited in front of another door. Hank stopped close. She leaned back against him and reached between her breasts to collect the master key Jester had given to her.

They stepped into a cozy room. A fire crackled in the fireplace, its light dancing across the ceiling like an aurora. The floor was covered with elaborately woven wool rugs and the thick hides of bears and elk. Over-stuffed pillows made from silk and satin were piled in front of the fire. A bottle of wine awaited opening in between two glasses.

Significance closed the door behind them, locked it, and put her arms around Hank from behind. "I'm so glad you wanted to leave the dinner. I was tired of hearing the King go on and on about Vassar with you sitting there."

Hank put his hands on top of hers.

"Why don't you open the wine?" she said with a squeeze.

Hank worked to open the bottle with the old-style corkscrew. A fleeting thought of the wine he left open at their camp passed through his mind, which reminded him of Vassar. He glanced over his shoulder. Significance was settling into the pillows. He turned his attention to getting the cork out of the bottle.

Setting the bottle and glasses down on a low table, Hank sat down and leaned back beside Significance. She snuggled against him and put her nose against his neck. He put his arm around her and she pressed her breasts against his side and chest as she reached across his stomach. Hank ignored the decanting wine, turned more toward Significance, scooted lower, and kissed her.

Nestled in the furs, and the satin, and the silk, the fire's heat reflecting off the bank of pillows behind them, Hank and Significance cuddled. She wooed him with coy advances and retreats, allowing him closer and granting his hands more freedom. He nuzzled her ear and neck. She ran her hand over his hip. He caressed the small of her back, and tantalized her cleavage with his breath. She arched her back and he whispered how happy he was to be with her as he molded himself to her body.

They lay back kissing, touching.

"You know what?" she cooed.

"Hmm," Hank grunted, breathing heavily.

"I know of another place."

"This place is fabulous," he countered.

"It's even better."

"Better than fabulous?"

"Come, I'll show you," Significance said, wriggling out from under his arms and half-weight.

She adjusted her dress and re-buttoned it, slipped into her slippers, and sashayed across the room to what Hank had assumed was a closet.

She opened the door. "I'll wait in here," she cooed, tossing her hair with her fingers. "Ooo. Watch your step."

Hank tugged his other boot on, stood, and fastened his belt. There was a twinge of guilt as he adjusted the dagger on his waist, but it was momentary. Chasing after her, Hank opened the door and stepped through. The door closed behind him and it was dark. He reached back, feeling for the doorknob, thinking he would open the door, see where he should go, and give his eyes time to adjust to the dimmer light. He felt, and felt. He felt all around the jam. There was no knob, and the door was latched.

"Significance?"

"Significance?" He liked games, but this one had a weird feel.

"Significance?"

Hank's eyes adjusted to the ambient light, but it was faint. He moved forward, faster than he could see, anticipating Significance. He could smell her perfume on his clothes, remembered the sensation of her fingers, and felt again her voluptuous curves. He moved quicker, holding a hand up to protect his face.

But he forgot to watch his step. He tumbled down a short set of stairs and smacked his head smartly as he landed on his back. He took inventory, berated himself for not being more careful, and stood up— too quickly, became disoriented in his dizziness, and fell again, down an incline, and over the edge.

He plummeted, a twisted corkscrew of arms and legs. Bumping, tumbling, scraping—like being slammed upon a coral head by an angry wave—Hank landed in a heap on a pile of scree. His breath was gone; in its place, the writhing, gasping panic of desperate lungs.

And then it was quiet, save for his groans and gasps.

The Castle

Zophos, transfigured as the Red Dragon, stalked the perimeter of the castle in between waves of attackers who poured out of Gnarled Wood in hordes. He roared. He looked for the fallen and devoured them with intentional gore, dismembering them before chewing them up and spitting out their remains.

According to plan, Zophos' army loaded their catapults with a sticky-sweet, gummy liquid of spoiled fruit and fermented leaves. "Now!" the Dragon bellowed. The mess hurtled over the walls erupting in splatters. Again, and again.

The more those sullied by the morass of putrid refuse tried to wipe it off, the more it smeared. It permeated their clothes, clumped on their weapons, and was slick under foot.

The Dragon fumed as he signaled the next volley. He breathed fire. There was a stench like burned hair. His affect began to disarm even his own forces, but with keen timing, taking note of the critical moment when all eyes were on him, he belched one great eruption of horrific energy. "Turn them loose!" the Dragon roared.

Hundreds of crates placed across the plain surrounding the castle were broken open releasing thousands upon thousands of monkey-like creatures with four arms, giant faces, and powerful wings. They were famished, starved on purpose for this moment. They ran and flew straight for the rancid odor—and the castle—in their lust for nourishment. Swarming over the walls, they landed, shrieking and screaming and desperate to eat.

The soldiers inside the castle looked to their commanders for orders. But in that critical moment, when a commander must not flinch and a leader must lead, they hesitated, and fear seized a foothold in the King's army.

The hungry creatures bit, picked, plucked, and scratched at anything and anyone afflicted with the Dragon's sticky potion. Their jaws and fangs exacted terrible wounds, just as Zophos intended. Eyes, ears, fingers, noses—any soft tissue was fair game for the ravaged beasts.

As their appetites were sated, the ape-like animals' natural curiosity proved a plague as well. They grabbed anything shiny. Caches of weapons were knocked over by the swarming primates. Defensive measures stacked and ready to be used against the opposition were tipped, spilt, and scattered. Terrified animals swarmed in panic as the mayhem mushroomed like a wind-whipped wildfire. Confusion escalated exponentially. The beasts were too quick to be caught. Their screeching was deafening. Orders could not be communicated. Signals were lost. Runners couldn't get through.

The distraction proved a terrible turn of events inside the castle. Mistakes were made. Men fell, wounded by their own comrades who cut them, hacked them, or shot them while defending themselves. Discipline was in disarray. Each man did what seemed right in his own eyes. Confidence drained from the castle. Fear rose. The castle's coordination disintegrated.

The beasts provided the diversion Zophos desired. His hoards poured forward with little opposition, set up their positions, and began a withering assault against the gate. Zophos presided over the castle's imminent demise still embodied as the Great Dragon. He could smell victory. It oozed from the castle like a cloud of terror.

The Pit beyond Slit in the Rock

Right after Hank and Significance left the King's dinner, Jester stepped into the kitchen and slipped out a side door. He hustled through a little-used corridor, down a sweeping staircase, and into a large chamber where his team was assembled. "Significance and Prince

Henry left the banquet about five minutes ago," he reported. "Dis, get going." Jester nodded at Disappointment who turned and left.

Jester unbuttoned and stripped out of his *maitre d'* attire. Pity handed him his black pants, helped him into his shirt, and placed a chair behind him to sit on while he changed his boots. As he tucked his shirt in and fastened his belt, she helped him with his cloak while rehearsing the timing of her coordination with Dis' attack.

Competence and Envy unrolled a floor plan of the pit and spread it across a table. Once Jester was dressed and Pity finished her review, the four of them bent over the map. Competence pointed and reminded them of key intersections and confirmed rendezvous points. "Any questions," he asked.

Envy held a mirror while Jester blacked his face, darkening high spots and light spots and lightening dark places like his cheeks and under his eyes. As he worked on his rouse, he explained that they must maintain cover until his signal.

Jester explained that he would take advantage of the Prince's predicament by imitating his voice and suggesting thoughts to him as though he was thinking them himself. With any luck, the disillusioned and confused Prince would voice and appropriate Jester's suggestions thinking they were his own. If all went well, he would hear himself say things so powerful that their mere sound would sear a distorted conviction into his psyche, warp his thinking, wound his emotions, and further undermine his already doubtful opinion about his Father, the King.

Pity, Envy, Competence, and Jester checked each other again to be certain of their cloaked appearance. They eased out of the room into the pit and moved into position.

Prince Henry's scrapes, cuts, and sprains left him light-headed and nauseous. He heaved, and threw up on his chest. Gagged. Choked. Sat up. Vomited again between his legs, and fell back. He rolled to one side, heaved, spit, and then dry heaved.

He fell back and turned his face to the dirt and rock under him, tried to choke back his frustration. What little confidence and optimism he had brought through the falls to this side of Malden Creek was expended. His hope—his life—crumpled under his own weight.

He wanted a different life, wanted a different outcome, wanted Significance, and wanted to be recognized as an important person. He had been torpedoed and now he was sinking fast in this world Vassar had talked him into exploring. The rocks under him chilled his bones. Hank put his hands on either side of his face and cried. The volume of pain and sudden anger erupting deep within surprised him, and rather than expunging the poison from his soul, it scalded all the more with his acknowledgment.

As his senses could absorb more than his pitiable position, he realized he wasn't alone. His body stiffening from abuse and the cold rock under him, Hank labored to roll over and sit up. His royal robes were soiled and he sat in his vomit. His face was caked with mud from the pit's dirt and his tears. His Father's gift hung cockeyed from his belt. He blinked, wiped his eyes with his scuffed knuckles, and stared into the shadows cast by the dim light.

Dark eyes in ashen sockets watched him, surrounded him. Faces contemplated him as he considered them. Figures materialized in the inkiness and instinctively Hank recognized them. Dream state or alternate reality? He had given up trying to explain his physical circumstance, and how it was he knew these apparitions, and in some strange way, also this place.

Disappointment came toward him carrying shards of Hank's broken dreams.

Hank heard footsteps behind him and turned. Discouragement eased up behind him and removed his cloak. His body was bulky and he carried hemp ropes—hemp to cut, and burn, and splinter. His hands were calluses, his wrists wrapped with gauntlets of studded leather. Rope burns disgraced his forearms like cheap tattoos.

Depression emerged from his asylum in the depths, dragging chained manacles. His bloated figure and slow shuffle belied his persistence.

To his right, Despair inched in close and squatted. She was frail, smelled, and had a wheezing inhale and exhale. Hank felt his heart sink. He'd been hanging on, been hopeful his fishing trip would help his outlook, and that with a little time away he could come up with some creative ways to regain his confidence.

Significance had been in his arms. She was almost his, but now she was gone—just like his book, his media presence, and his corporate data, not to mention Vassar and any hope of pleasing his Father. In a whirlpool of the real and surreal, Hank's soul descended to the depths in which he sat. *Vassar got me into this mess*, he thought.

Disappointment removed his cloak and let it drop. It was his signal to execute the plan he had laid out before Zophos—the plan to break the Prince, to disillusion him, to convince him he was unimportant, insignificant, and to drag him farther into the depths.

With a flourish, a fifth apparition, Demoralization, whisked in from the darkness and set upon Hank in a disorienting dance and with merciless cracks from whips she wielded proficiently with either hand. Her lashing stung and distracted Hank just long enough for the others—Disappointment, Discouragement, Depression, Despair—to violate him with impunity.

They had their torturous way with Hank. He cowered in a ball, unable to escape, unable to defend himself. Chained in Depression's manacles, Disappointment cut him with his broken dreams. Taunting him, he sliced gaping wounds in his heart and poked at his eyes with his nails. Hank bled and he cried and he grieved his losses.

Discouragement tied ropes around Hank's skin and pulled them tight, burning him, chaffing him, and splintering the hemp barbs into him. He lashed his lines to the hopeless mooring of Hank's precipitous fall and held him captive, the victim of his own undoing.

Despair squatted on her haunches. Her wheezing and posture were a mirror of what Hank felt and who he had become. Her odor reeked of his plight and choked any hope of relief.

With flicks from the tip of her whip, Demoralization raised welts she then whipped until his skin erupted in a laceration. Cheeks, ears, groin. No tender place escaped the touch of her bitter, biting lash.

"Stop! Please! I'm begging. Have mercy. Please!"

Demoralization walked away, as if finished with her torment. But watching for Dis' cue from the corner of her eye, just as Hank's shoulders slumped, Demoralization turned and scourged him with a cutting strike to his neck that convulsed him.

Despair seized upon Hank's repeated failure to find relief. "There's no mercy for you, Prince." Wheezing. Gurgling. "You aren't worth mercy. Don't deserve it. Look at you. Mercy would be a waste on the likes of you. You insignificant prick. Think the King loves you, huh? If he loved you, you wouldn't be here. He doesn't care about you—but you're important to us."

Disappointment leaned over him. "Mercy, did you say? You want mercy?

"Yes. Please. Please stop," Hank whispered. "I'll do whatever you want."

"Tch. Tch," he clicked. "I'll give you mercy, Prince."

Disappointment handed Despair a shard of glass. She pulled open his robe and cut Hank's shirt away. She drew the outline of the letter "D" in his sweaty chest hair with her finger and backed away. "Let me see," Disappointment mused, as he sorted through his assortment of pieces. "Ah, here's a good one. Perfect!" With a shard of his broken dreams, Disappointment cut along Despair's tracing, carving the letter

"D" deep into his chest, almost to his heart. "There," Disappointment said, backing away, admiring his work.

"Nice," affirmed Depression.

"I'll say," said Despair. "He'll never be free of that."

Hank's writhing rendered Dis' hand unsteady. The "D" was jagged, its irregular form befitting the affliction it commemorated. Hank gaped at them with wild eyes flashing the terror of his torture and the confusion of his merciless plunge into the pit.

"Mercy! You want mercy, Prince? There it is," mocked Dis. "The mercy of the pit."

"We wouldn't want you to forget your dreams," Discouragement said, ripping his ropes from Hank's body.

"No. I should say not," Disappointment said with sarcasm. "That wouldn't be merciful."

"'D.' 'D' for "dreams," Despair observed wheezing. She pulled Hank's shirt back over his bleeding wound and patted his chest. A bloody "D" soaked through. Hank's field of vision narrowed, darkened to a tunnel, and closed.

The Castle

The assault by Zophos and General Nephilim gained ground against the eastern fortification. With implacable determination, the dark horde worked their way forward, exacting Zophos' plan on their enemy.

Archers bombarded the castle with sorties of flaming arrows. As if the distraction of the flying, climbing, monkey-like beasts and the myriad forces bearing down upon the castle were not enough, all available hands were diverted from defense of the citadel to fight the spreading fire of ignited acid.

Belief that life within the castle was impregnable faded. There was no safe place. No relief, and little hope.

But Zealot, an Army of Light commander, stayed focused and led well. "Vigor," he yelled to his lieutenant. "Regroup around those men holding their ground."

Vigor spun around to locate the soldiers Zealot referenced.

"There," Zealot pointed. "Rally those in retreat to stand with you."

Vigor was off in a flash, issuing orders as he moved to reinforce the small band of men defending against a breach. The confidence in his commands summoned the waning courage in many of those fleeing so that they hesitated in their retreat, and in their moment of hesitation, Vigor exhorted them. "Grab those weapons. Move in support here," he indicated, pointing, standing on a heap of rubble.

The men conquered their panic and responded as trained to Vigor's clear orders. The honor they regained being back in the fight was palpable—and it spread to others who needed their courage bolstered.

"Good. Good," Vigor yelled. "Focus now! Focus! Steady!" he screamed above the roar.

Twenty meters away, Zealot was also retrieving men splintered from their units and whose hearts were in disarray. "Form a firing line across here," he waved. "You men," he called to a disparate group of stragglers, "Gather the quivers from those fallen archers," he pointed. "Smooth the fletching. Attention to your training. Resupply this firing line," he ordered, in support of the men he'd just assembled. "Look sharp. Look sharp. I know I can count on you."

Motioning to Vigor, Zealot signaled for him to send four men. When they arrived, Zealot selected five of the men around him, and instructed them. "Three-by-three, rebuild the weapon caches around these positions. Put dirt on the sword handles and spear shafts. Rub them down so the troops can grip them. Pass the word to do the same with all the weapons. Look out for one another. We'll make our stand here. Be courageous!" And with a wave of his hand, they were off to carry out their orders.

Vigor noticed fifteen men about to be overrun. Grabbing a man close to him to serve as a courier, he said, "Run. Tell those men to fall back to a defensive line along there," he motioned with his arm. "Go!"

The men fell back as ordered. Vigor met them. "Nicely done. You four, provide covering fire with your bows. The rest of you, assemble what you can to make torches. The fire will protect us from the distraction of the monkeys. You're our flank. Hold until further notice."

In spite of the confusion and terror around them; in spite of the stickiness, smoke, and stench, every man fought gallantly under the steady leadership of Zealot and Vigor. In tandem, these leaders reassembled a formidable fighting force and staunched the enemy's progress against their sector.

On and on they came—in waves and by droves. Zophos ordered his troops forward without thought for their lives or remorse for the atrocity of his war. The swarming mass carried loads of rock and dirt, piled it against the fortress, and laid siege. What little retaliation they suffered from above by the afflicted castle was no deterrent. Zophos' army buried their fallen and wounded, dead-or-alive, under the growing heaps of detritus. With each wave of porters, the ramp increased. It was inevitable: Zophos and his troops would enter the castle sooner rather than later.

The eastern side of the castle was under full attack from land and air and under the earth. Great birds with enormous wings and talons dropped rocks and acid. The catapults continued launching. Nephilim ordered the giant moles loosed and they began tunneling toward the stronghold.

To add to the confusion, Zophos sent a secondary battalion to pummel the castle gate with a battering ram that seemed to be the weight of the world. For all the casualties suffered by the Dark Army, there was an endless string of reinforcements, each as adept and horrific as the fallen one he replaced.

Under withering cover-fire from Zophos' archers, his army leaned ladders against the castle wall. They climbed almost unimpeded and breached the castle's forces.

As the castle's defenders were neutralized, Zophos' porters constructed a great heap of refuse and efficiently built a siege ramp over which the Dark Army flooded. In short order, what was intended to be a diversion filled the castle with enemy legions.

The Red Dragon, Zophos, twitched his tail like a giant cat stalking a mouse.

The Pit beyond Slit in the Rock

Hank opened his eyes to a haze, closed them, tried to gather his thoughts, and opened them again. One worked better than the other—his world half blurry. He drifted back into unconsciousness.

He didn't know how long he had been out, but when he awoke again he remembered. It took time for his brain to work through the backlog of reports. What occurred was clear to him before the consequence registered. Freed from the literal bonds of his tormentors, but bound by their emotional fetters and affliction, Hank sat up. His clothes were stiff with vomit and blood. Hank rolled onto his hands and knees and began the painful, tedious task of standing up.

He reached to the wall to steady himself, and to his surprise, found a hand. He pulled himself up and held on until he was stable. In the half-light of the pit, Hank eyed his surroundings. He stumbled a few steps in each direction. The walls were immovable and impenetrable, but they were comprised of faces—hundreds, as far as he could see—a few entire bodies, some shoulders and legs and other parts, but mostly faces. Every eye watched him. Some of the faces were familiar, some angelic, some demonic. They watched him, stared at him, waiting to see what he would do.

For a long time Hank looked back at his audience. He was on a dais of his own making and those in attendance were waiting expectantly. He felt it, could see it in their eyes, and sense it in their demeanor. He had nothing to give, no speech, no statement, no explanation, no esteem—nothing.

All of his life Hank had met expectations, juggled his talents to keep people happy and impressed, and used his intelligence to prove he was significant. Until now he had been like a cat, always landing on his feet—but not any more. He overreached, and like a house of cards, felt himself imploding. Impossible expectations, professional derailment, and his feared insignificance collided and formed a perfect storm that left him in emotional bankruptcy. He had nothing to offer, nothing to hide, no resource to draw upon, and no position from which to speak. No amount of posturing could rationalize where he was and how he got there.

Hank unbuckled the belt holding his dagger and dropped it on the ground. He stripped off his stinking royal robe, wadded it up, and tossed it into a corner. Last, he took off his blood-stained undergarment and flung it into the dark night of his soul's torment. Branded with the horrific "D" on his chest as if it were a crest, Prince Henry lifted his hands to his head, wove his fingers into his hair, and wandered aimless, naked, spent, and crying throughout the endless pit of expectation into which he had scuttled his life.

He stumbled and crawled through the twilight-darkness, bruised, bleeding, and brutalized from Disappointment's merciless assault. His vision impaired with tears and sweat and swelling and doubt, Hank stepped in a hole. His ankle buckled. He smashed his nose and eyebrow when he fell. Rivulets of blood drained into his eye and mouth. Spitting and cursing he screamed for help in his horrid place.

Silence.

Jester and his accomplices waited, concealed. Their opportunity was imminent.

Hank broke. His frustration, hostility, and bitterness—compressed under the load of expectation he felt around him from the myriad faces—spewed like hot gas from a fissure. "Damn it! Where are you when I need you? Father? King?" Hank repeated the lines Jester fed to his psyche in his distress.

Silence.

Jester disguised another suggestion, and Hank voiced the thought, impugning the King. "You talk big. Say I'm important. Well? Well? Here I am. Where are you?"

Just like back home, in the real world, Hank thought, as his life there and his predicament in the pit coalesced.

The resentment Hank felt—the anger at his Father, so carefully protected, edited, and cloistered away from sight or visitation in a variety of nice ways—boiled out in an ungracious torrent and spread to Vassar as well. "If you won't help, maybe you could send Vassar, your favorite son." *Like that's going to happen,* he thought. *Probably still toasting one another's good fortune.*

He felt sorry for himself. "If only Vassar hadn't brought me here," he moaned, never recognizing Jester's voice disguised as his own. "I've tried playing along. Trusted. Believed. Worked hard. I've tried to say a good word now and then about the King. He's impossible. I studied our family history. Tried to get close to Vassar. If I hadn't invited him to go fishing—tried to find some common ground for us—I wouldn't be here. I've tolerated the King's friends—like Magician. All that empty talk about, 'If I can do anything for you—anything at all—just speak the word.' Where the hell are you now, Magician?"

Hank continued wandering down the corridors of the pit, talking to himself: "They're all talking small talk and celebrating the heir to the throne. But when they're done, the King will probably send Magician— after the fact—to set me straight. Got to protect his precious reputation, after all. He'll launch into everything I've done wrong, and how I can improve, and how I can keep this from happening next time, and how he expected better of me. Hell. Like I don't know already: 'Be wise. Learn from your mistakes. Trust the King. Your Father believes in you.' Blah, blah, blah. Right, Magician," he anticipated saying.

"Say the rest of it, coward. Say what my Father really thinks. He's disappointed, thinks I ought to try harder and be more like Vassar; wishes I'd quit fouling up and making him look bad. Why doesn't he just come out and say it? 'When will you ever learn, Hank? You stupid incompetent.'"

Stupid: Hank's pet name for himself—and with his Father as well, he believed. For all of his talents, accomplishments, and successes— walls and walls filled with recognitions—his core belief about himself boiled down to this despicable moniker.

When it came to others, Hank was almost infinitely patient, understanding, and tolerant, but when it came to himself, he was ruthless—in keeping with what he felt the King expected of him, and what he expected of himself. In his private world, Hank never heard or used his given name affectionately. When he heard God speak his name, his tone was equally stern; his degree of expectation demanded no less. When he screwed up, "Stupid," echoed through the hollow caverns of his soul until absorbed by his heart. By all appearances, Hank looked like the pristine Malden Creek teaming with life, but inside he felt like a dead river, silted-in with polluted waste.

Hank stumbled along, stubbing his toes until they bled—skinning his hands and breaking his nails when he fell and clawed at the floor of the pit to arrest his fall. He dumped years of harbored venom into the stagnant air. Like an addict who falls off the sobriety wagon and binges on his drug of choice, the poison gushed out of Hank in an increasing torrent. *As long as I've said enough to incur the King's wrath, why not say how I really feel? He's going to torment me anyway,* he thought. Then snarled, "I'd like to think this was the end, that you won't bother me here. Nothing I did in life was good enough to please you. Maybe I'll be free of your critique now—once and for all."

Hank wandered farther before reconsidering. "I doubt it. You've never missed an opportunity to rub my nose in my failure before. Why would you start now?"

Hank screamed into the darkness, "Come down here, King. Tell me all about how you love me, think the world of me, see potential in me. Foist your noble ideals on me while you hold me down and rub my face in the shit of my life. Until I give up. See it your way. All the while grinning and telling me about your love. I know better. Even when I yield, it won't be good enough for you. Will it? Hold my face in the steaming pile until I pledge to try harder and do better and be more like Vassar. 'Sorry' isn't good enough for you, is it? Never has been.

"Others think you're fair. I don't see it. King!? King!? You're duplicitous. Your reputation may be sterling, but you've tarnished mine to make your own. Push me down, elevate yourself. 'Tell them what I did for you,' you say. 'Tell them how much better off you are now than you were,' you push.

"You don't give a flying shit about me.

"I didn't stay at your party, so here I am: condemned to a pit. Getting even, aren't you? Because you can. You don't get your way, so just as I have a chance with Significance, you throw a tantrum. All eyes weren't on you, so you interrupted, didn't you?" Hank threw his question for the King into the void.

Son of the High King! Blessed, he tells me, Hank rehearsed in his mind. "Gives me a stupid knife." Hank shook his fist in the night. "If this is your blessing, if this is your care, no thanks. I've had enough of your love. You show up late—after the fact—once I'm afflicted, to correct me. Tell me how great you are and how sorry I am—'building my character,' you call it. 'Loving me,' you say. 'If only you'd listen'—I can hear it all now. All your inane cover-ups. I may be stupid, but I'm not a fool. I don't need your love.

"When was the last time you noticed I'd done something right? Huh? I can't hear you. Father? Speak louder. King? Why don't you come down here and talk with me, man-to-man?

"You know I'm right, don't you?"

Hank listened. Hollered, "I'm not incompetent. I'm important." Waited.

I'm significant, he thought. *I've got to be.* "I'm significant. Whether you think I am or not. You hear me?"

Waited.

"King! Magician! I'm waiting. Vassar! Where's that brotherly love you're so big on?" Hank was hoarse from yelling.

"Damn you. Damn you all!"

He bellowed the finale prompted by Jester and collapsed, spent from his emotional purge, alarmed at his string of expletives, empty from his aborted entitlement as a child of the High King. The pollution had erupted out of his soul like an abscess. Disappointment, discouragement, despair, depression, demoralization: The bondage swept through him, doing inside him what his tormentors had done to his body. Anger, distrust, bitter jealousy, and envy: The ugliness seeped through him like stain.

Hank pulled his knees to his chest. It was ominously quiet, like the low pressure before a tornado. He dared curse the King, Vassar, Magician; even his own heritage. He had fallen professionally, fallen in reputation, and was fallen from his family's grace. *Stupid.*

Jester pushed thoughts-of-choice to Hank's self-addiction. "This cursed darkness is my home now. I thought it was a nightmare, wished it was only a dream, but this pit is my future. I've disgraced the King and ruined my standing in the Kingdom."

Pity eased in closer to Hank, goaded from the shadows by her prudent boss, Jester. She smelled incontinent. Her body was waif-like, her skin sallow, and her hair oily. She picked at the dried blood on

Hank's wounds with her dirty fingernails, fidgeted with the tangles in his hair, and leaned against his back.

Pity hung on Hank's aching shoulders repeating Jester's disparagement. Pick, pick, pick. Prince Henry slumped lower under the weight of Pity and Jester's endless condemnation. He choked in the cloud of her stagnant breath.

The Castle

Zophos' slaves and troops ferried supplies from Gnarled Wood over the besieged wall and into the castle under the watchful command of Nephilim. The embankment was a veritable thoroughfare flowing with reinforcements as Zophos' army occupied the courtyards, nooks, and crannies of the citadel. Troops assembled in glutted lines surrounding the castle, each waiting his turn to march through the gates, scale the ladders, or walk up the earthen embankment.

The noise of battle, the stench of charred wood and flesh, and the cries of desperation mushroomed like a giant canopy over the castle and Gnarled Wood. The steady advance of the dark forces indicated the decisive turn in the battle.

Having assembled a hundred men under each of their commands, Zealot and Vigor flanked each other's troops and staged a strategic retreat toward the Round Tower. The troops' discipline and determination to follow Zealot's and Vigor's leadership proved costly to their enemy. The soldiers with the torches guarded their rear and dispelled the monkeys who wanted nothing to do with fire.

Other pockets, warriors loyal to the High King fought shoulder-to-shoulder and back-to-back, but it was a losing cause. They were gallant and confident in their belief that the High King was worthy of their life's sacrifice, but they were crushed and trampled by the advancing army. While they believed the High King would be victorious, and were faithful to the end, they would not live to see the deliverance they believed in.

CHAPTER 6

The Pit

H ank sank lower under Pity's weight and the burden of his losses. While she picked at the bloody mats of hair surrounding the wounds to his chest and neck, Hank looked into the ever-present faces observing him, illuminated by the diffused light. "All you care about is what I'm gonna do," he said. "You're like everybody else in my life. You're voyeurs. Like gawkers at a wreck on the highway. Just looking for blood. You've offered no help, no cover, no consolation. No nothing. All you do is stare. Haven't you ever seen a naked man before?"

Their expressions were unchanged.

Hank put his head down against the floor of the pit. He ached—inside and out. He thought about his pain, the sum of it focused behind his sternum like oppressive heartburn, only duller and deeper. He'd never felt his heart before, but now it was unmistakable.

With Hank's head down and facing away, Jester caught Pity's attention and motioned for her to be more aggressive. "No mercy," he mouthed. He couldn't risk a mistake. He held up the flat of his hand, twisted his wrist, and made a quick fist.

Pity took off her robe, laid down naked against Hank, and covered them with her garment. She pressed against him. With her apparent kindness, touch, and warmth Pity turned Hank's attention from the rudimentary awareness of his heart to her. With her affections she wooed him, drew him, and consoled him. Hank felt the desperation of his condition and turned to her to assuage his loss of Significance. He held onto her for recognition, embraced her for affirmation, and lay with her under her cloak. He clung to her as if she had his best interest at heart. Just as he had done with Significance, Hank did what seemed best to him in order to regain control, find a semblance of confidence, and tend to his immediate wants. Hank buried his face in her oily hair, stroked at her sticky skin, grasped her buttocks, and gave himself up to her.

Pity heard footsteps and looked over her shoulder at Jester. He motioned for her to join him in the shadows. Hank was exhausted and sleeping hard, but Pity was still careful not to wake him as she got up. She wrapped her robe around herself and retreated to Jester's concealed position.

Hank awakened cold and stiff. As his swelling and inflammation increased, and scabs began forming, his pain intensified. It didn't take long for him to recall his circumstance, to remember Pity, and to understand she had gone, leaving him naked and in need. He also noticed his pit was lighter.

He pushed against the ground, rolled over, and stared up into the eyes of the High King, Vassar, and Magician. The King's countenance glowed, accounting for the light. The three people he had cursed, berated, taunted, and deserted in hopes of finding Significance, were now looking at him. Hank pressed himself onto all fours, and finally into the bent-over stance of an old man. Teeth clinched, he straightened by degrees, his scabbing chest granted him an upright position only after painful negotiation.

Naked, dirty, stained, and stale, his chest crested with the despicable "D", Hank lifted his head, straightened his shoulders, and set his jaw. "I've been looking for you."

Silence.

"I stepped out with Significance—to get some fresh air. I was bored, and so was she."

Silence.

"We had a good time. You were busy—with Vassar—probably didn't notice I was gone. We figured I deserved better."

There was no reply.

"Significance values my opinion—listens to my ideas. You never asked, never noticed, and didn't pay attention."

The King, Vassar, and Magician listened.

"I gather from your silence that you disapprove. Have you stopped to consider my viewpoint? My reasons?"

Nothing.

"I didn't think so. You're indifferent—intolerant of my efforts. You don't even notice when I do something right."

No response.

"I called for help—*cried* for help—but you didn't come. Magician, you said, 'If I can do anything, call me.' Well, I called. I hollered. Hell! I even screamed. But did you come like you said you would? Would I still be here if you'd been faithful?"

Magician did not defend himself.

"It's your way or no way, isn't it?" Hank said to the King. "Blind loyalty. You expect me to fall in, march lock-step, and parrot what everyone else says about you. You expect me to be like Vassar. So you can feel better about yourself. Feel important. Believe you are somebody. Well I need that too. I need to be significant. Need to feel important. But no. You can't let that happen. I get a bit of momentum going—with no help from you—and you get in my way. Cause me to stumble and fall. Then, when it gets tough, and I need help, you're nowhere to be found."

Not a nod or a blink.

"Did you note my disappointment? In my despair, did you comfort me? Did you encourage me in my discouragement? No! You abandoned me in life and in this dark place until you finished your meal, had dessert, and savored your brandy. But now—now that it's convenient— you show up late, really late."

None of the three made a move.

"No doubt you're here to point out all the ways I screwed up. That's what you're best at: hindsight. What an astute gift," Hank mocked. "Look! Have I not paid sufficiently? Are you satisfied? Or do you want to rub my nose in it some more—like you always do? Want to build a little more character in me, King? Show you care by demanding I see things your way?"

No reaction.

"Why are you here? What do you want?"

It was very quiet. Hank looked around. The wall of countenances watched. His thoughts swirled like a dark eddy, *I've done it now. Father will abandon me forever. I deserve to be executed and my remains thrown in some corner of hell to rot.*

Hank thought of Significance, could feel her form in his memory, had no clue of Jester's complicity in his self-defense. *I wish she was here,* he thought. *I want her. She would validate my reputation. If only she was here. I would be equal to Vassar.*

His thoughts turned in a whirlwind to Pity: *If only the King could understand; show some mercy.*

And then his thoughts swung back to his entitlement, *I still want to know where he was—where Magician was. Where were they when I really needed them?*

"Hank?" The King spoke his name in the darkness of degradation. His tone was not condescending or demanding, wasn't condemning, but it was determined.

"Hank?"

Hank turned from the empty promises of the pit toward the face of the High King. He could see through his eyes, like windows, into his Father's soul. There was a flicker of understanding, a moment of awareness: *I slighted him. Wounded him. I humiliated him lusting for Significance. But still, he's here.*

The High King waited.

Hank retraced the last hours. *He abandoned the important matters of the Kingdom to search for me. He missed me. He knows my name. He laid aside his reputation and position to search for me in this hell hole even though I disregarded him.*

Lurking in the shadows watching Hank, Jester sent an urgent dispatch to Zophos by Competence. "Report that the King's been wounded by Prince Henry. They're both in the depths of the pit. The Prince has compromised himself with Pity and cursed the King. Please advise."

Gnarled Wood outside the Castle

Zophos, the Red Dragon, had scorched the beleaguered castle with the fire of his jealousy. He hated the High King and all associated with the Kingdom of Light. He despised the castle and its inhabitants, but they were advantageous in the long run.

As he had done at the birth of Prince Vassar, he swept stars from the sky with his tail and hurled them at the citadel. He fed upon the fallen, even his own. With his great claws he lacerated the earth to its bowels so that those around him fell screaming into its depths. With these three—the fire from his mouth, the slinging destruction of his tail, and his great claws to rend the earth to the depths of its darkness—the Dragon wielded his fearsome intimidation against hope.

Traveling upon the airwaves, Competence arrived seconds after he was dispatched from the pit. Zophos received the brief from Jester with a gloat. "So, the High King's son has denied him?"

"He has. Heard him myself," Competence confirmed.

"Our strategy is working better than I hoped," Zophos mused. "We can't be too cautious. The Prince is compromised, but he's not conquered. It's essential that he declare self-rule repeatedly—until it is so habitual he doesn't even think—until he sabotages the King's right to the throne, and until all those watching him are convinced that loyalty to the King is a losing proposition. Then—then the King will be compromised, set-up for my *coup*."

"I understand," Competence stated. "Ingenious, sir."

"Tell Jester, Prince Henry's not defeated. Do not underestimate the force of his will or the triumvirate of the High King, Magician, and Prince Vassar."

"Yes, sir."

"Once his denial of the King is secured, the Prince must be wrecked. Got that?"

Competence acknowledged.

"Ruin him on the rocks of remorse. Don't flinch! Not for a moment!"

"Yes, sir," Competence snapped.

"Dismissed."

In seconds, just as he had gone, Competence returned on the airwaves at the speed of light, down into the pit, and relayed Zophos' commands to Jester.

Jester acknowledged. "And the battle for the castle?"

"Our forces control the air and the bowels of the earth under the castle, but the Round Tower remains impenetrable. However, they were staging to attack the Round Tower as I left. The Army of Light is failing."

"This time Zophos will win," Jester said.

"Any progress here?" Competence inquired.

"Yeah. Nothing works in our favor like entitlement," Jester said. "The Prince has it. Feels he's owed, that because of all he's done and who he is, that he's due."

"Feels warm to him now," Envy observed. "Look at him, standing there naked in front of the High King, shoulders thrown back, chin high. Couldn't be going any better."

"Check out that 'D' on his chest," Competence noted. "Disappointment does good work."

"Uh, huh. Before long the entitlement will become arrogance and will be like a seeping cold in his bones. It's my little surprise," Jester snarled.

"How much longer do you think?" Envy asked.

"A few minutes—time for arrogance to permeate him. That self-important lust to be noteworthy apart from the High King affords us the leverage necessary to accomplish Zophos' wishes."

Competence, Envy, and Jester continued to observe Hank.

"There he goes, just like you said. Entitlement breeds arrogance," Competence said.

"Arrogance becomes resentment," Jester stated. "Resentment turns into bitterness. Bitterness becomes rage. Before he knows it, he'll be consumed, eaten up with rage at the King."

"And with himself," added Competence. "He will be so hostile it will boil out of him like lava."

"Once the Prince diagnoses his infection, bitterness will be coursing like a cancer through every cell in his soul," Envy said.

"Okay. We're getting close. No mistakes, you two," Jester said. "Do this right and we will get him. Come on."

Jester led, edging through the shadows closer to where Hank stood making his defense. Competence and Envy eased along behind him. The walls of faces watched, expecting.

Competence stood a head taller than anyone else. He was handsome, powerful, efficient, and decorated like a general for his achievements. He watched Prince Henry's every move as he postured in front of the King, Magician, and Prince Vassar. Even though puffed up with self-importance, clearly Hank's bravado and self-assertion were no match for the King's gracious patience.

Prince Henry and the King stood eye-to-eye. Jester knew the High King's winnowing gaze would sort out the Prince's true heart from his attitude of entitlement and arrogant posturing if he waited any longer. Action was imperative.

"Now!" hissed Jester to Competence. "Get him now!"

Competence stepped up behind Prince Henry, drew two knives, and with deft skill plunged one into his right hip and the other into the small of his back. The Prince screamed in agony and collapsed. Gasping for breath, spasms escalated up his spine and down his leg. He writhed, tormented and twisted, in his awfulness.

The Pit

Hank's wounds were not mortal, but they were heinous. Competence's dagger to his hip entered at an oblique angle, cutting cartilage, severing tendons, and lacerating the large muscles that enabled his hip to work.

He was crippled.

The knife to his lower back sliced through discs and nerves, and before Competence was finished, he bent his blade and broke the point off inside Hank's spine. It would serve as a constant and jagged reminder of his attack.

The stabbing pain in his back robbed him of comfort or consolation.

Competence retreated to Jester's position. "He won't sleep much, Jester."

"No. I suspect not."

"Fatigue is a powerful tool," Competence counseled. "In a few days the Prince will be open to any opinion you wish to offer."

"True enough," Jester concurred.

"Thing is, the King, Magician, and Prince Vassar were right there— the whole time. I didn't think I'd get close, let alone carry out my plan. Caught them off guard. Totally."

Jester was quiet—watching, thinking. "Something's not right," he whispered.

"Yeah, look. He's wounded and they aren't even helping him."

This was too easy, Jester thought. *Something's up.*

"They've played right into your hands, Jester," Competence said.

"They really *can't* be trusted," added Envy, as he observed their indifference.

"That's interesting," Competence concurred. "The Prince will agree."

"Maybe. Just maybe," said Jester. "But we mustn't underestimate those three."

The Castle

Skirmishes could still be heard, but for the most part, the King's Army of Light had retreated into the Round Tower. Their dead littered the battlefield. Hundreds were captured, relocated deep into Gnarled Wood, to await their fate as prisoners of war.

Zophos' commanders set up their headquarters. Across the castle area flags were raised to distinguish levels of command. Officers assembled their ranks and guided soldiers separated during the confusion of battle back to their units. Lines of communication were established, fresh orders were communicated, and the battlefield was prepared for the next phase of attack. Zophos ordered his troops fed with the dead and wounded from both armies.

Reinforcements for the Dark Army poured into the castle. A steady stream of reports was fielded at Zophos' headquarters. His staff analyzed each and collated them for Zophos' briefings. Maps and diagrams of the castle, the area of Gnarled Wood surrounding the castle, and the Round Tower lined the walls of Zophos' situation room adjacent to his field office. These were updated continuously by his staff, none of whom were permitted a break from duty.

Unlike most camps, the fires among Zophos' army never died. Their fatigue fueled a hostile, maniacal fervor. All through the Dark Army men gnashed their teeth anxious to find relief from their labor. But under orders from the top, the army was a constant hive of energy. Apart from the company headquarters, there were no tents since there was no rest.

The Pit

Crumpled on the rocky floor of his dreary place, Hank grieved his wounds. He knew his health was broken—sensed these injuries would haunt his dying day—knew his prowess to woo others to himself with strength, appearance, and ability was gone, knew he was compromised. He felt his body splinting his wounds with scar tissue. He gasped for each breath as pain's vise prevented his lungs all but the sparsest measure of air. He bit his lip until it bled in a futile attempt to bear the pain. Beads of sweat leaked from his skin.

Jester slipped from his place in the shadows. As usual, he deceived with impersonation. "If only I hadn't left the King's dinner, I wouldn't be in this pit, wouldn't be hurt. If only I could have stayed with Significance. I'd be wrapped in her arms and legs. Stupid move. Stupid. Stupid. I'm no use to anyone now. Cripple! I've wandered so far into this pit I'll never find my way back."

Prince Henry repeated Jester's suggestions, taking his counsel and making it his own without a second thought. He was too focused on his pain and the immediacy of his predicament. Thus he left unprotected his vulnerability—distrust—and Jester jabbed at it like a fighter jabs at his opponent's cut.

"The King could've prevented this, could've done something," Jester suggested to Hank. "He was right there. He just didn't want to. He had to see it coming. Had to. Vassar too. Had to see I was going to be attacked, but he didn't protect me—none of them did. And Magician? All talk. Incompetent coward. Might as well not even exist."

Jester fueled the resentment building in the Prince as though fueling a fire. One stick of doubt at a time, he coaxed the flame higher and hotter.

"Father says I'm important to him. Says he loves me. He doesn't give a shit about me!"

Jester's work was ruthless. Seizing upon the Prince's vulnerability, he exploited Hank's wounds. Hank believed Jester's thoughts were his own, never recognizing Jester's voice. Never realizing the first-person pronouns were not his own. Jester's fire grew to a firestorm of distrust in Hank, disheartening him, and escalating his doubt.

The shadows in the pit were gray, but the darkness Hank felt was inky. "I'm abandoned," Jester suggested. Hank concurred. Conceded. Acid tears of resentment poured out of his eyes already abused from his fall.

Though observed by hundreds of eyes in his dungeon, none offered comfort. "I'm lonely," Jester offered, and the tears scalded Hank's cheeks.

Jester called to Competence, "Bring me something to shield this wretched soul from the rock beneath him. He's suffering."

Grabbing what he could find, Competence brought a woven mat for Hank to lie on. Putting it beside the Prince, Competence helped Hank roll onto the thin pad. It was scratchy, but it afforded him some mercy from the hard cold. Never mind that Competence had just wounded him. In Hank's habitual, self-reliant desperation, he turned to him for assistance rather than look elsewhere.

For hours, like those that crawl by during the night watch, Hank lay on his grass mat on the rocky bottom of the pit. In the half-light he could see the walls of faces watching. In the quiet he could hear them breathing. From his mat, no matter how he examined his situation, it seemed hopeless.

"Hank?" He closed his eyes and listened. Concentrated.

"Hank?"

He opened his eyes. To his surprise, Vassar and Magician were there.

Magician got down on his hands and knees and put his face close to Hank's. "I will give you treasures you never dreamed of possessing in this dark realm. I have hoarded wealth and unspeakable riches buried in this pit. I will give all this to you. If you will allow me, I will shelter you with my power and nurture your soul back to health with my own life."

Hank listened. But he was wary. He felt a slight compulsion—a desire—to trust, but felt desire and doubt tangle and clog in his throat like a hairball.

Magician knew Hank was paying attention. He realized that while his words were easy enough to understand, they carried a message that was challenging for Hank to comprehend. He paused for him to digest, then continued: "But make no mistake: I will not accommodate your affairs and I will not facilitate your independence. It's not in your best interest. I'm merciful, and I will be merciful to you, but I will show no mercy for your self-reliance, self-rule, selfish pursuits, or self-sufficiency. *Capiche?*"

"I understand," Hank whispered to Magician, who remained not more than eight inches from his face.

"One more thing"—Magician's breath was hot on Hank's chapped face—"I expect you to adopt the same attitude I have toward these illicit lusts you've chased—searching to belong, seeking worth, and trying to prove your ability. Give them no quarter. I don't."

Magician's face was so close Hank felt his eyes crossing. He knew deep within that Magician was telling him like it was. Quite literally, he was in between a rock and a hard place.

Hank agreed.

Vassar stepped onto Hank's mat, bent over his broken form, and reached down to his brother. For a moment Hank hesitated, torn emotionally between the brother he felt abandoned him and the brother with whom he'd fished the great rivers, but with a mere fraction of belief he granted Vassar the benefit of his doubt and grasped his forearms. Untaxed, Vassar lifted Hank to his feet.

The knife point twisted against Hank's nerves. Fire shot down his leg into his foot. He attempted to straighten his leg, but the adhesions and scarring tore with frightful fury. "Oh, God!" Hank screamed, as Vassar and Magician supported him.

His pain and predicament provoked the doubt planted by Jester. "Why are you hurting me?" he spat, questioning Vassar's intent and integrity. Engulfed in pain, with nothing left but his pitiful mat, Hank forgot his agreement with Magician made seconds earlier and focused instead on his immediate affliction. "Why don't you heal me?" Entitlement spiked like malarial fever.

CHAPTER 7

Hank's Mat

Vassar never left his brother's mat, and for his part, Magician didn't either. As time passed, their constant presence registered inside Hank, and he suspected they had been present with him the whole time, even as he fled the King's dinner with Significance. He'd heard Vassar speak from time-to-time about how he valued loyalty, but this was different; he wasn't talking—he was demonstrating faithfulness. Magician was too. It made no sense. He was glad they were there, but wouldn't blame them if they left. He knew he wasn't good company and knew there were better places they could be.

Vassar and Magician's faithfulness wasn't the only odd thing Hank noticed about his disgraced dungeon: there was always light, but no apparent source—no candles, no lamps, no fires—just diffused light from somewhere. When he awoke, there was light. If he needed to see better for some reason, the light increased.

He had gone spelunking once with his friend, Scott—back in his other life—in Georgia. They each carried two, extra flashlights, just in case, because the cave was totally dark. Once, on vacation, he'd toured Carlsbad Caverns. Part of the tour involved turning the lights out inside the massive cave. It was dark—totally. He slept in Ed's basement once. Like a cave, it was black as pitch. But not here. Not this cave. In his pit, there was always light.

Hank also thought about the faces surrounding him: *Don't these folks have anything better to do? I know why I'm here, but…*"what's with these people?" Hank said aloud to Vassar. "They're always looking at me."

"I've noticed. Like they're waiting, expecting you to do something important."

"Folks," Hank said, turning to the faces, "let me tell you: This mat's no bully pulpit. I've got nothing to say. I lost everything I thought I had on my way here. I don't have anything for you. No position, no authority, no influence. I lost my dagger—threw it away, actually. Ruined my robe." Hank paused to ponder. "Heck. I don't even have any clothes."

As time passed, Hank talked more openly with Vassar and Magician. They talked about everything. Big ideas. Small talk. Hypothetical. The more they talked and the more time they spent together, the more Hank realized his viewpoint was changing. Intensity does that. Vassar and Magician were not pushy. They waited for Hank to engage them and then responded.

But he felt something that was hard to identify. These conversations were like an internal massage working out the soreness in his soul and promoting healing deep inside. He was still crippled from Competence's attack. He still hurt and still didn't sleep much, but new desires were surfacing. He attempted to describe these to Vassar, who listened, but offered nothing more than, "Those originate in your heart."

"Maybe, but I don't know," Hank said. "Could be my stomach, or ribs. Maybe something else. I don't know. Whatever it is, I can feel it."

Vassar didn't care much what Hank called his heart. What was important to Vassar was that his brother recognized input from another source deep inside of him, and he did.

For one thing, Hank felt his caginess—his doubt—relaxing a bit. While it still flared, he felt like he could trust Vassar and Magician a little, but only a little. He remained guarded, but was glad for some relief from the oppression of his distrust. The more Vassar and Magician talked about life, him, them, and the King the more Hank felt he understood.

But Hank had distrusted his Father too long and had too much evidence to support his doubts. Just because Vassar and Magician were convincing with their positive view of the King, the torment of the pit, added to the losses Hank felt in his real life, exacerbated his wariness.

He had heard his Father had supernatural power to heal; had heard the same was true of Vassar and Magician, but it hadn't happened for him. In the darkness and persevering pain, Hank lost track of time. He wondered if his Father would heal him; wondered if it would hurt when he removed the broken blade, or if it would be painful when he stripped the scar tissue out of his muscles. It hurt like fire when he stretched, or turned the wrong direction, and tore the adhesions loose. *Will it be like that, only worse?* he wondered.

Hank spoke to Vassar and Magician about healing. They confirmed that the King could, and did not deny they possessed the same ability. Hank asked them to send a message to the King requesting healing, but he couldn't verify whether they did it or not. He asked the same consideration from his brother and Magician. They said they understood his request, but they didn't do anything. He waited for a miracle, believed one could occur, but when it didn't his hope waned and left him vulnerable to Jester's bias.

Hank decided he had either done too much wrong to be entitled to healing or that the King was withholding healing to let the pain toughen his character. Hank landed where he had landed most of his life, thanks in no small part to Jester's ongoing counsel, that his continual suffering was probably a mix of both reasons—but mainly the latter.

The King's a demanding, hard man, he thought. *Besides, I'm not as important as Vassar. Father likes him.*

In Hank's mind and emotions, he had fallen too far from the King's graces to be worthy of mercy, and given his prior experience, the King seemed prone to coerce character development in him whether he wanted it or not. Hank concurred with Jester that it was an abuse of his power. *But what can I do?*

Jester offered from the darkness, "That's just the way the King loves me," and Hank repeated his opinion as his own.

Hank felt his Father was justified in withholding his mercy. But as time passed, Jester wondered how long the King could justify withholding his healing. He seemed petty. Hank agreed with Jester, and the more he mulled this over, the more this point of view permeated his thoughts. The implication was evident to Hank: If this is the way his Father loved him, then he wanted to stay as far from his Father's love as possible.

In contrast to Jester's opinion and his painful predicament, there was Vassar's repeated reassurance that Hank could trust Magician and him. The discussion was often heated. When Hank asked Vassar about the lack of relief, the failure of the King to rescue him, and his dismal circumstances Vassar always sounded the same note: Father is trustworthy. He told Hank stories of others being healed, delivered from dungeons, and saved from terrible onslaught. Hank admitted the stories were entertaining, but what he really wanted was a story of his own to tell. Vassar always said he understood and then would add, "Trust me, Hank. I'll take care of you."

At first Hank was courteous. He didn't want to offend Vassar or Magician, especially in front of all the expectant faces constantly observing. Later he tried to trust—like Vassar encouraged him to—but then he doubted under the burden of persistent pain. As more time passed, he resented. After resentment accumulated and reached critical mass, he exploded. "Damn it! I don't want your hollow promises, Vassar. You're all talk, just like the King. When it comes down to it, you don't deliver either. I'm hurting like hell and getting worse. You could help, but you don't. What don't you understand? I want to be rid of this pain."

Hank didn't erupt with a cursing fit only once or twice. It was more frequent—enough that he concluded he could no longer accept their forgiveness. When his frustration with pain's antagonism boiled over, his vehemence spewed out. More often than not, the King was his target, but Vassar caught a fair bit too. He felt remorse after he vented the cauldron of his resentment, but no sooner would he blow and relieve a bit of his pent-up anger, than it would begin building again like a pressure cooker.

In the pit, the passage of time fell into two categories for Hank: an episode or an eternity. With no sunrise or sunset, no watch and no calendar, his world revolved around fitful, irregular sleep patterns. He knew his life was passing before him, but didn't know how much.

Pain persisted, never flinched, and never wavered. Pain was honest and demanded to be taken at face value. Pain tolerated no delusion of grandeur and insisted Hank grip the reality of his condition moment-by-moment. Pain would not be denied.

Pain was like being screamed at every waking moment. Initially it was disarming, but in time Hank developed some proficiency in thinking through the pain, focusing in spite of it, and living with its relentlessness. It was a slow process. Hank might not have recognized his progression had Vassar not pointed out his brother's mental tenacity. The more Vassar recognized Hank's development and pointed it out to him, the more Hank realized his development. He was overcoming with the consistent help of Vassar and Magician. Time, intensity, focus, and persistent coaching from Vassar and Magician were transforming agents.

In spite of its ferocity, Hank began to view pain, not as an enemy or an antagonist, but as a demanding mentor. Instead of spending the majority of his day focused on illusions—like being healed, being out of the pit, being with Significance, being recognized, being important—Hank began spending more time considering the views Vassar and Magician shared with him. They told stories from the past, offered observations about Hank's situation, and presented new ideas about the King. All while pain screamed and discomfort tortured his attention span.

While not what Hank would have choreographed, the time he and Vassar spent on the mat was forging a closer bond between them—even closer than fishing. In addition, he was growing to appreciate Magician. He had not had the opportunity—rather, had not taken the opportunity—to spend much time around him. Now, all he had was time.

His former life was remote, lost in hours, and days, and weeks—maybe years. Hank didn't know. Time was impossible to gauge. Prior to the pit his days were jammed with emails, text messages, phone calls, deadlines, payables, receivables, friends, family—on and on it went: the dog had to be walked; he had to work out; the oil needed to be changed in the car; he had to stop by for the laundry; needed to go to the grocery, *ad infinitum*. Not anymore. Two things vied for his attention now: pain and his mat.

One of the more curious things to Hank was his changing attitude toward his mat. The woven, grass rectangle was home. He felt secure on his mat. It was a known quantity in a mysterious, dark world filled with expectations he couldn't meet. As much as he disliked his grass mat, Hank realized that his confinement to its insignificance afforded him an unprecedented opportunity to focus on what Vassar and Magician were saying. At times he even felt a sense of authority standing on his own place. Granted, it was a place with tortured memories, but it was his place and he knew it well.

This security didn't last long. It felt like no sooner did he accept his mat than he sensed dissatisfaction with it. This would have added to his frustration had he not been adopting more and more of Vassar and Magician's counsel about his heart. Hank sensed the desire for more than his mat offered. That was a good thing according to Vassar.

Vassar called Magician over to the mat and said to Hank, "Tell us more about your desire."

"I don't want as much as I used to, but I desire…" …and he would get tangled up distinguishing between wanting and desiring. The first seemed shallow and selfish—like mind-candy with an emotional high and corresponding low. The second was deeper…and something else…maybe more intense, more important, more profound…more something. Whatever it was, desire had a permanence that his wants did not.

"I've wanted all sorts of things—importance, notice, appreciation, value. In a word, I've wanted significance. Wanted desperately, lusted I guess."

"I'm following you," Vassar encouraged. "Go on."

"Those wants are still there. If I think about them, they surface, and if I think about them long they grab hold of me. But what you call desire is stronger—deeper in me. It's like it's coming from my belly or my chest. I'm not sure where it's coming from, I just know it's not coming out of my head. I think these desires are coming from my heart."

"And your heart is a deeper, more important place, than your head?" Magician probed.

"Yeah. I think so," Hank mused. "Am I making any sense?"

"Little brother, you're making lots of sense. Your realization is profound. Wouldn't you say, Magician?"

"Definitely. Most men go their entire lives never recognizing their heart's desire. But now you know, and knowledge is power."

"I agree," said Vassar. "Now that you know about your heart, the power to access it and live from its desire can fuel your spirit and soul."

"But you need to nurture it," Magician chimed in.

"And that's what we're doing together—on the mat—right?" Hank asked.

Vassar and Magician agreed.

Hank thought about all this. "You know, thinking back to the King's recognition dinner…. Can I be honest with you?"

"Of course," Vassar said.

"I wanted Significance so bad. The longing drove me. I still think about her, want her, want her acceptance. I want to feel the importance of having her." Hank paused to think. "But, as badly as I want Significance, there's something different; there's a desire—and that's new—a desire to be loved."

The three were quiet. Then Magician asked, "Loved by whom?"

Hank's eyebrows raised, then turned down into a frown of confusion. "It's weird. It's like I have a desire to be loved by the King—by Father—like you are, Vassar. But that's crazy. Why would I want to be loved by him?"

"You don't trust him any farther than you can throw him, do you?" said Magician.

Hank turned away. "No. I don't. That's what's strange about this desire."

"You know," Vassar began, "Father doesn't play favorites. I know you feel otherwise, but he doesn't. I'm his first-born. You're his second-born. Our birth order is different, but we're both his sons, and he loves us. I am loved absolutely. Everything in Father loves me. You're loved too, Hank. Absolutely. Father loves you with all he's got."

Magician could tell another voice would be helpful. "Hank, let me tell you how I see things. Everything about your brother has its genesis in the King—his life, his value, his identity, his ability, even his significance is wrapped up in your Father. Your identity is the same—whether you agree or not. Hank, you're significant for the same reason Vassar's significant: You're the son of the High King."

Hank looked from Magician to Vassar.

"Let me tell you something," Magician said. "Your Father sent me to be with you. His instructions were simple: 'Go to my son. Do not leave him. Guard his heart. Help him see the truth about himself, about me, and about our relationship.'"

"He said that? He sent you?"

"Your Father did not set you up to fail, Hank. He didn't cause your pain. You made some poor decisions."

"You can say that again," Hank concurred.

"Your Father hasn't given up on you. He's working hard to turn your predicament to your advantage—the pit, the mat, your wounds, your mistakes—all of it. Had it not been for all this, you wouldn't have discovered your heart, and you wouldn't be reconsidering your relationship with your Father."

Vassar said, "When you invited me to go fishing, I knew it was the chance of a lifetime for you—for us, really. You've been bogged down with work and life, your independence and distrust—and your doubt—for so long. You needed a fresh lens, a different view."

"So you arranged the passage behind the waterfall into this world?"

"That's right. I discussed it with Father and Magician. Father felt if we could get you out of the routine, you'd stand a fighting chance of getting ahead of your doubts. He felt if you had the opportunity to face your fears, you might realize how much he loves you."

"I see," Hank said, fighting through the battlements of distrust to listen to Vassar.

"Brother, it worked. You're free—free to do as you desire," Vassar said.

By the look on Hank's face, he was thinking hard about Vassar's comments.

"Hank, what do you desire?" Magician asked.

"I want out of here." Hank looked around at the walls of expectant faces. "I want my health back. I want to be freed from this relentless torment in my body."

It was an accurate response—for want. Magician said, "You misunderstood my question."

"No. I didn't, Magician," Hank said. "I understood your question."

"So, what do you desire, Hank?"

"Magician, I know the right answer." Hank waited. "But I'm so tired of right answers that are shallow and dishonest."

"Good for you. So give me an honest answer," Magician said. "You told me what you want. Tell me what you desire."

"I think Father loves me. He has to love me, as I think about it. But that doesn't mean he likes me or wants me around."

"Hank, Father's committed to you," Vassar contributed. "Committed to your thoughts, your projects, your concerns, your pressures. You name it. He desires to be integrally involved. There's nothing more important to him than being with you."

"Then where is he, Vassar?" Hank's hostility at the King flared in concert with Jester's tailored perspective and his own distrust.

"Look around. You're consumed with your mat, your pain, your future, your needs, your wants—all that stuff Jester says is important."

"Yeah, well. Seems like about all I've got." It was Jester's retort, but Hank voiced it as his own. "What's your point?"

"How is it you can see down here? Whose light illuminates this darkness? Who was it that came to you and called your name out in your darkest hour?" Vassar paused. This was a new idea—that the King was the light source. He allowed time for this to sink into Hank.

"If Father had abandoned you, you wouldn't have heard his voice in the darkness, would you? He didn't forsake you. You fled from him! You chased after Significance—through the slit in the rock. You ran down the corridors of your own ingenuity, groping for Significance, listening to Jester—like he's being honest with you. Father promised to take care of every need you have, tried to approach you, to bless you, to welcome you. But you ran from him. Don't you get it, Hank? He ran after you into this pit—even to the darkness of your fornication. Right now, he honors your wish for distance by keeping his. But he's still close."

"He might be close to you, Vassar. He's not close to me."

"You can see can't you?"

CHAPTER 8

The Castle

With the Army of Light in retreat toward the Round Tower, Zophos ordered his front-line troops to pull back for resupply. Fresh troops would take their place.

Confident in his military strength, Zophos made it appear as though his army was retreating as they pulled back. To the confused and demoralized Army of Light, it appeared the Dark Army was in full withdrawal. With all the smoke and diversion, and anxious to retake lost ground, the Army of Light surged in careless, over-confident pursuit.

Fresh troops met them in the smoky ruse. Whole battalions were annihilated. Their blood poured copiously onto the already-saturated ground. The dazed survivors retreated toward the Round Tower wading knee-deep in the blood of their comrades. The wounded drowned in it.

Wagons full of fresh equipment, food, and clothing were moved forward behind the fresh troops. Rather than taking time to sharpen their weapons, Zophos' army tossed their dull blades in piles as they withdrew, moved on to designated supply depots, and replaced them with sharpened weapons. Slave labor sharpened the dulled weapons and restocked the supply depots in preparation for the next troop rotation.

The battlefield was cleared of obstructions. Ruined machinery, felled trees, empty containers—the collateral of the assault—was piled in berms rising twenty-five feet high, covered over with pieces of homes and the dirt of fertile fields, and packed down for defensive insurance. Zophos did not intend to be driven from the castle, but he would not be caught unprepared.

Zophos' supply chain moved unimpeded into the castle.

Hank's Mat

Hank was getting stiff and hurting from sitting.

Magician noticed him squirming. "The wounds inflicted by Competence were desperate measures ordered against you by Zophos. He wants you destroyed, wants your soul wrecked on the rocks of regret."

"Zophos! Why would I matter to him?"

"Because you matter to the King," Magician replied.

"The plot thickens," Hank said. "Zophos wants my soul wrecked with regret?"

"Yes."

"Well, I don't want that. I'm not clear about much, but I'm certain of that."

"Good. Neither does the King," Magician said, seizing Hank's initiative. Magician moved closer to Hank. "You're weak, Hank. Your Father will be your strength. You're disabled, but he will be your ability." Magician moved back, stood up, and said, "Jester says you are abandoned. I say you are loved by your Father beyond your wildest imagination."

Hank felt the pressure behind his sternum that he had tried to describe to Vassar and Magician earlier, the tugging-longing-aching they said was his heart's desire.

Vassar said, "Your wound is an unintended gift from Zophos. What he means for your destruction, Father means to use for your benefit— your transformation."

"Transformation into what?"

"Into a warrior of light," Magician said emphatically.

Hank blinked at Magician in disbelief. "A warrior? Of light?"

"That's correct."

Hank laughed. "Look. I sweat when I try to stand up. I can't fight. I'm a cripple."

"This war is different," Magician said. "It's a battle over trust. The naïve believe battle is ordered and rational. The warrior knows it's primal and ugly. Confusing. The fight to trust the King isn't a sanctioned match. It's a brawl."

In an awkward way, Hank was relieved by Magician's explanation. He knew his doubt wasn't an acceptable problem. He knew it wasn't a difficulty he could talk about with the folks back home, especially at church, the place everyone said he was supposed to turn for comfort, support, and guidance. Failing to trust the High King was treason. Fearing the reaction of others and the stigma of his distrust, Hank hid it and grappled with his doubt all by himself.

As if seeing into his private chamber, Magician said, "The battle to trust plunged you into a lonely struggle waged in isolation."

"How'd you know?"

"The shame of not trusting seems too great to confess, so you hide it to spare yourself the disrespect and dishonor from others. It's an insidious problem—like an abscess you don't lance for fear of the mess. The shame festers when you hide behind smiles and well-constructed façades called success."

"I guess that's why it's so important to get my professional legs back under me."

"Probably so," Vassar said. "The isolation's brutal. I was never so happy as when you invited me to come fishing with you. I hoped you might let me behind the façade."

"Well, you're my brother."

"Yeah, I am. And I'm advocating for Father in your life."

"Father, huh?" Hank mused.

"Yep."

"Man, oh man, Vassar. I don't know. You and the King get along better than he and I do. Always have. I wish it was different, but I haven't trusted him for years."

"I know. It comes down to this, Hank: You'll never learn to trust him until your confidence in him is put to the supreme test."

"It's been a test lately. That's for sure."

"This is what happened to you in the pit," Magician said. "Jester capitalized on your recent disappointments and assaulted you with half-truths about your Father. You believed him and your distrust grew."

"Are you saying it doesn't have to be that way?"

"Uh, huh. This is one reason Vassar and I are here. If you want, we'll help you learn to trust."

"How will you do that?"

Vassar said, "I'll start with a promise. Over time, it will look like I've broken my word. Jester, and circumstances—and your pain—will all appear to support the accusation that I lied to you. But in time, you'll see. I will not break my promise."

"So we're back to your definition of trust."

"That's right. You won't learn to trust me until your confidence in me is tested."

Hank looked at the faces staring at him. "Alright. What's your promise, Vassar?"

"Hank, I will not in any way fail you nor give you up nor leave you without support. I will not, I will not, I will not—I cannot—in any degree leave you helpless, nor alone, nor let you down, nor relax my hold on you. You're my brother, my family."

Hank studied his brother. "You know, you didn't leave yourself much room to mess up, Vassar."

"No, I didn't, did I?"

"Look, Vassar. You don't need to do this. It's not worth it."

"You mean, *you're* not worth it," Vassar corrected.

Hank shrugged, acknowledging.

"I know I don't need to promise you anything, Hank. Know I don't owe you anything. I *want* to be with you though. It's my choice. And you *are* worth it."

"Well, I don't know," Hank demurred.

"Besides, I promised Father," Vassar said.

"You know, brother. For somebody as smart as you are, you sure did hem yourself in with me."

Vassar laughed. "Yeah, yeah. I know. But I went into it with my eyes wide open."

Hank looked back to Magician, "Well, back to this warrior of light business. You used the word transformation."

"That's right," Magician said. "The King wants to transform you into a warrior of light."

"Yeah, that's what I thought you said. I gather this transformation is going to occur in the battle you mentioned?"

Magician nodded.

"And since we've been talking about trust, I'm assuming my confidence in the King is going to be tested."

Magician nodded again.

"Well, that shouldn't be too hard. Don't have much confidence to begin with."

Vassar said, "It's not just confidence in Father. It's confidence in me too, and in Magician."

"I see," Hank said.

"Hank, I've not left you since you laid down on this mat. Neither has Magician."

"That's true," Hank acknowledged.

"And let me point out again, you've never been without light, not from the moment you left dinner with Significance."

Hank thought back. His thoughts stopped in the small room with the fire place and pillows. He thought of Significance. Remembered her touch and the feel of her.

"Even making out with Significance in that cozy, little room there was light," Vassar added.

"How'd you know what I was thinking?"

Vassar just smiled.

"So, what's your point about the light?" Hank followed up after collecting his thoughts.

"Just that you recognize you've not ever been in total darkness."

Hank thought carefully. "Okay. So?"

"So, Father has never been far from you, even though you tried to escape and leave him."

Hank looked around. He could see the faces and details surrounding him. "You're right. It's been dusky, but never dark, never dark like it should've been."

"That's Father," Vassar said.

Hank looked at his surroundings. Studied the faces. Knew their expectations. Felt their stares. There were no shadows. He hadn't noticed that before, but it was true. He pondered the meaning of that, but shook his head to clear the implications. *The light's everywhere*, he thought.

"What are you thinking?" Vassar asked.

Hank thought some before replying. "I'd like to know more about the light." Hank paused. "And for what it's worth, I believe your promise, Vassar."

The Path Out

To hedge against defeat, Jester sent two platoons from the Dark Army Special Corp to sabotage the path out of the Pit. Riding on the airwaves at the speed of light, his platoons deployed at the head of the path and hiked a short distance before beginning their work.

Jester's orders were that the Princes and their party should be discouraged from proceeding, not killed. "Turn them around," he had said. "Zophos wants the Princes to wander in the pit, especially Prince Henry. Kill the others."

Under the watchful eye of their commander, the troops rigged a variety of deterrents. They created a log pendulum that when released would swing out, hit a man, and kill him instantly. They placed animal traps—bear and wolf—in the footpath and concealed them. They dug a pit extending from edge-to-edge of the trail, ten-feet long, and eight-feet deep. They cut the shafts of twenty-seven spears off three feet below the head and buried the butt-ends a foot into the ground in the bottom of the pit. The pit was too long to jump and the ceiling was too low to allow a man to vault over. There wasn't room to go around and it was lethal for anyone who fell into it. They disguised the pit with a fake floor.

For each trap, the officer in charge positioned Special Forces, reiterating that the death traps were for anyone other than the Princes. "Do whatever you want to the Princes, just don't kill 'em. Zophos' orders," he repeated to each group.

Just beyond the final trap—the pit of spears—a full platoon of Zophos' best were positioned. While it was unthinkable that anyone could navigate through the traps, it was better to be certain than face the ire of Zophos. Before the officer in charge left to report back to Jester, he issued his final order to the Lieutenant of the platoon, in spite of Zophos' command. "If anyone, including the Princes, makes it past our traps and reaches your position, kill them."

Hank's Mat

Hank nudged Vassar with his elbow. Three figures were lurking in the shadows, hooded, and wearing packs. After assessing their situation, the three moved closer to Hank's mat, and stopped again.

Hank felt like he was being stalked. They took another step toward his mat. Hank called out, "Who are you and what do you want?"

They stopped at the challenge in Hank's voice. "We are knights, loyal to the High King, and the Kingdom of Light. The King has sent us to join you."

"And your names?" Hank asked.

"This is Faith," the third character said, pointing and stepping forward to take the lead. "He's Hope, and I'm Love."

"I know these men," Vassar said.

"Me too," Magician confirmed.

"What do we do?" Hank asked.

"That's your call," Vassar said.

"My call?" That was an interesting responsibility Hank had not expected to carry. He stared ahead. It was amusing to him that everyone was patient while he tried to think. *You know, it's crazy. I'm used to making big decisions all day long, but I don't know what to do,* he thought. *It's like I'm just learning how to make decisions.* "Okay. Well, I think I need all the help I can get."

"Even if the help is sent from your Father?" Magician asked.

The incongruity between his distrust and anxiousness for assistance didn't escape Hank's notice. *Probably why I'm having difficulty making a decision,* he thought, before answering. Hank looked at the three men, then Magician. "Yeah, I think so."

It was a small step of trust. Vassar and Magician smiled.

"Welcome to my mat," Hank said, spreading his arms open with an inviting flourish.

The men approached Hank's mat, set their packs down, and took off their cloaks. They each had on breastplates bearing the King's crest. Faith was diminutive. He had a steel stare and squinted eyes. His nose was crooked, clearly broken in some altercation. Hank suspected right away that there was much more to this man than met the eye. Hope appeared the embodiment of determination: He didn't walk; he strode.

His jaw was square, his gaze penetrating. He was the tallest. Love was a squat, powerful man, with legs like tree trunks and powerful arms. He was handsome and bore the look of a man who could do whatever it took to convince you of his opinion. He was the leader.

After they greeted Vassar and Magician and were introduced to Hank, they opened their packs and laid the contents in front of Hank's mat. There were three breastplates, one of which was new, a set of clothes, a pair of boots, three helmets, three shields, and three swords.

"What's all this?" Hank asked.

"You can't be a warrior if you're not equipped," Magician said.

Hank looked at Magician and Vassar, then at Faith, Hope, and Love; the contrast between them and him couldn't have been starker. Jester noticed and seized the opportunity to whisper an accusation from the darkness that Hank voiced under his breath, "I'll never be a warrior."

Vassar countered, "Hank, trust me."

"Let's not kid ourselves, Vassar. I can't even stand up straight."

Hank thought of Faith's crooked nose and how he must have gotten it—a thought given to him by Magician, although he didn't realize Magician had this ability and didn't recognize the thought as coming from him. Hank had a lot to learn about the battle for his mind.

Jester countered Magician's thought and Hank repeated his notion like a well-trained Myna. "I've dishonored the King. Heck, I don't call him Father, even though he is. I'm disloyal." Sweeping his eyes across the faces of the five, Hank said, "Look at you guys. I'm not knight material."

Love said, "Hank, the King believes in you."

Faith added, "But you must abandon your ways for his ways and your history for his future. You must decide to walk in his light. Give your heart to him, trust him, believe that he has your best in mind."

Hank replied, "There was a time when you all were probably right, but now? I'm not so sure."

Faith said, "You've misjudged your Father. He's not proud, as you imply. If he were, then he would've rejected you outright a long time ago."

Love entered the conversation, "The King's not like other rulers. When it comes to you, he has no consideration for his reputation."

"How do you know that?" Hank asked.

"We've talked about it—at length. He determined to come here—to this degraded place—because of his love for you. He wanted to be close to you. I watched him prepare. He changed everything, risked everything, and gave up everything in order to be with you."

Magician spoke again, "They're telling you the truth. Your Father's not proud, but he's realistic. He won't accommodate your independence. In fact, if you accept his invitation to knighthood and decide to live in his light, he'll do everything within his power to wean you from dependence upon yourself."

"And he doesn't mean a little bit," Love added. "Your Father loves you too much to abandon you to yourself."

Not understanding that these five warriors had been sent by his Father to guide him, train him, care for him, and teach him to walk in the light, Hank still assumed his transformation was his responsibility. Based upon that false assumption, Jester suggested and Hank voiced, "I can see okay in the dark. Besides, I don't know anything about living in the light."

Vassar stepped in front of his brother. "Hank, give me all you have. Right now. Everything. Trust me."

Hank laughed. "Vassar, I don't have anything. In case you haven't noticed, I'm naked."

"Believe me. I noticed. We all noticed," Vassar said, amid laughs. "But you have plenty of things to give me: hopes, dreams, wants—your lust for Significance. What about your disappointments? Your despair? Don't forget your affair with Pity. Give me your talents, your competence, your wounds, your losses—including the ones at work back home—your fear, your reputation. And what about your mat? You have that to give."

Hank hesitated, but once he started handing things to Vassar, he gathered momentum. At first he placed things deliberately in Vassar's hand, but soon he was collecting stuff as Vassar mentioned it and flinging it at his brother, not in anger, but with abandon. Vassar didn't mind. He was glad to see Hank trust him. Magician, Faith, Hope, and Love gathered Hank's jettisoned goods and put them at Vassar's feet.

"There. That's it. I don't have anything left—except this "D" on my chest. Can't get rid of that," Hank said, breathless from his flurry of activity. "And my mat. That stays. I have to have somewhere to live."

Patience, Vassar, he counseled himself, seeing Hank's provision for his shame. *Patience. In time he will understand.*

Vassar said pointing, "Love, Hope. If you all will look behind that outcropping of rock over there you will find all the provisions necessary for my brother to have a bath."

Faith, Hope, and Love built a fire and heated water for a wash tub. The warm water felt sublime to Hank as he submerged in it. He scrubbed, washing off the grime he'd collected in the pit. Magician washed his back, tending to the tender scars there. Faith added hot water to the tub. After he'd soaked a while, Hope placed a towel on the mat beside the tub for Hank to stand on. Love draped a thick, white towel over his shoulders. Hank eased the towel back and forth across his back. The friction felt good to his healing skin.

Once he was dried off and the tub set aside, Vassar pointed to the clothing laid out in front of Hank's mat and Magician handed the items to him. First there was underwear, fresh and white. Next a shirt, then some pants; each fit well. Faith set a squared-off log on end for Hank to use as a seat while he pulled his boots on. They fit perfectly, which amazed him; finding shoes that fit had always been a problem. He stood up and finished buttoning the sleeves of his shirt. Just like at home, sleeves were always buttoned last, usually while driving to work.

Vassar pointed and Magician handed him a robe. Hank pulled this on over his head until he noticed the crest. "I can't wear this," Hank said, as he started removing it. "It has the King's crest on it. I'm not worthy."

Vassar raised his voice, "Hey! Don't give me that. If you're hoping to wear a royal robe when you're deserving of it, you can forget it! You wear this robe because it's who you are. Father said so. Okay?"

"Okay," Hank said, after a deep breath.

"Good," Vassar said. "And quit listening to Jester, will you? You follow his input like it was the holy grail."

"Yeah, you're right. Sorry about that. Gee, I'm a slow learner."

"Don't worry about it," Vassar reassured. "Now fasten this belt around your waist."

Hank did as Vassar instructed. Almost at once he felt the stiffness of spasms spreading across his sacrum and spiraling around his thigh. He grimaced. Beads of sweat formed on his forehead. He tried to straightened up, but couldn't. He undid the belt and held it by the buckle like a dead snake. "This makes my back and hip hurt worse."

"I know," said Vassar. "But this has nothing to do with helping your physical pain and everything to do with helping you overcome the distraction pain brings. This is about focusing in your heart and soul on what's true—regardless of how you feel."

Pointing to the belt, Vassar said, "Now put that thing on. Cinch it up tight."

While Hank tightened his belt and adjusted his robe, Vassar motioned for Magician to help him with Hank's new breastplate. As he and Magician fastened the buckles holding the front of the breastplate to the back, Vassar said, "Your breastplate's like mine. Has the family crest on it. It's the same crest that's on your robe." Hank was raising one shoulder, then the next. He'd never worn a breastplate before. "This covers your vital organs, especially your heart, and that's important. It's where desire comes from. You know that."

"Yeah, I think so," Hank said. "But I forget sometimes."

"We'll help you remember. Your heart's like a spring of life. It must be guarded."

In his no-nonsense way, Hope said, "Nobody wears that crest unless his heart's straight with the High King."

Hank caught a whiff of Pity's condemnation from somewhere in the darkness, and fielded Jester's jaded opinion. "Look Vassar, I appreciate your confidence. But I live with me. My heart's not right. It's divided. Part of me desires to see myself like the King sees me, but another part of me wants to chase Significance into bed for a romp every chance I get. Getting all dressed up like this was a bad idea. Help me get out of this stuff."

Love stepped in front of Hank. With his left hand he held Hank's chin; with his right, he held his cheek bone. He pinched Hank's cheek onto his teeth for leverage, pried his mouth open, and looked inside. "Open up, lemme see in there." Hank squirmed, but Love's grip was firm. Vassar smiled at Love's tactic. "How are your teeth? Okay?" He let go of Hank's face.

"Of course. My teeth are fine," Hank said, rubbing his cheeks. "What's that got to do with anything?"

Love chested-up to Hank. "You bit hard on Jester's bait. I wanted to be sure your teeth were alright." Hank tried to move his face away from Love's. He was so close he was blurry. "If your heart's divided how come we bonded like we did? Do you think I'd tolerate the company of a treacherous heart? Do you think the High King would be here, lighting your way, if your heart was rotten?"

Hank needed to hear what Love was saying, and he knew it. He could hear Jester protesting, but Love was formidable. "Your heart's not divided any more than mine is. That's just Jester's sales pitch. Sounds right. Feels like it. But it's hogwash!"

Love turned away from Hank and said to Magician, "Since when did Jester become the paragon of truth?"

"Last time I checked, he wasn't."

"Agreed. He's deceitful."

"And manipulative," Magician added.

Not to be left out, Hope added, "Hank, the condition of your heart's dictated by who you are, not what you do. You have a heart for the High King because you're his son. You can chase whatever delusion or illusion Jester brings across your path. Heck, you can live like Zophos himself. But the condition of your heart's determined by the fact that you're your Father's son. Besides, a divided heart's a broken heart. Your heart's not broken. Matter of fact, it's been working overtime—to make its desires known. Love's trying to help you see that."

"Here's the deal," Magician said. "You can lust for Significance, want her, want her affection—she's beautiful, no question about that—but your heart's desire is to be important to the King."

"Want versus desire," Hank said, to let Magician know he was tracking.

"Right. Ignoring your true desire has created the conflict you're feeling. You can live like hell itself, Hank. Won't change your status in the Kingdom, but it's a bad plan. It'll wound your heart and your Father's heart, not to mention the consequences of bad decisions."

"I know that's right," Hank agreed.

Vassar grasped Hank by his shoulders and turned him back around. "Magician, let's finish getting this breastplate on him. We're gonna be in a fine mess if the enemy shows up and our stuff's scattered all over."

Regaining some humor, Hank added, "Yeah, Magician. Looks like we're having a yard sale."

Magician handed Hank's shield and helmet to Vassar. "I don't mean to rub it in," said Vassar, "but your mental game's been lacking. Jester plays on your mind at will." Vassar helped Hank put on the helmet. "You're the King's son. Jester may strike at your head, but you're protected. Got it?"

"Got it," Hank parroted. While Hank and Vassar adjusted the helmet's straps, Magician attached a sword to Hank's belt.

"Step back. Let me look at you," Vassar said.

Hank stepped backward into the light illuminating his mat—the King's light. The armor glowed with a golden sheen. His heart jumped in his chest. "Here! Hold this." Hank handed his shield to Vassar. "Hold it so I can see myself." Vassar held the shield like a mirror. "Wow! Check it out, Vassar! Look at me. I'm ready for battle, just like you. I've always wanted to be like you, and just look at me!"

"Only one thing left. Magician, please." Magician handed Vassar a bundle of cloth. Much to Hank's amazement, Vassar unwrapped Hank's dagger, the one the King had given to him, the one he had discarded in the pit, the one signifying his identity as a son.

Hank drew his dagger from its sheath and looked down the gleaming blade. The butt felt good in his hand. The balance was perfect. Unlike earlier, when he'd shown the weapon to Significance during dinner, the blade felt natural, like an extension of his arm.

He slid the dagger back into its sheath, fastened it to his belt, opposite his sword, and straightened up. With newfound freedom, he spread his arms in the shape of a cross as if to absorb the moment and the King's light into the pores of his being.

CHAPTER 9

Hank's Mat

"Hank, you're standing taller," Vassar observed.

"Thanks," Hank said, straightening his shoulders.

"I'm proud of you. You're behaving like my little brother again—for the first time in a long time."

"Well, you have a knack for seeing things in me I don't see."

"It's true," Vassar said. "There's a fire in your eye that hasn't been there in a long time."

"Yeah, well, maybe." Jester could see where Vassar was headed with this conversation and went on the offensive with Hank, taking advantage of the pity he felt.

"Hey! Don't discount what I'm saying. I've poured my heart and soul into you. When you discount yourself, you discount me. The time will come when you feel more of what I see in you."

"I guess I already do, to some extent," Hank conceded.

"I think you do," Vassar said. "In your heart you see yourself differently than you used to."

"That's true."

"See, you're progressing, in spite of what Jester says."

"Yeah, I've been starting to think about how he works and about his perspective."

"I know. Hank, there are those who stand up straight because they believe in themselves. They beat on their chests and draw attention to their accomplishments. You've been tempted this way, when you think about it. Thought it would get you what you wanted in life and with Significance."

"When I contemplate Jester's thoughts, and I'm really paying attention," Hank said, "they seem shallow, like they're connected to an old version of me."

"Great way to put it, Hank. They are tied to the old. Father's offering you a new way and equipping you to live in that new territory. For one thing, he's surrounded you with us so you won't be alone."

Hank stretched from side to side. He was intrigued with Vassar's ideas, but pain was screaming for his attention.

"Hurting?"

"Yeah, I am. Tightening up. This belt makes it worse."

"I understand," Vassar said. "One of the greatest gifts any man can have is an impediment."

"What do you mean?"

"You lacked heart, passion—awareness of your deep desires. Your wounds stripped away all the extraneous so you could see these important aspects of yourself. Before you landed in the pit, you had no vision. Everything you had going for you masked your ability to see beyond yourself. Now you have that chance—to see and to live."

"I think I'm following you."

"The man who hasn't suffered a wound is intolerant of the wounds in others. The man who hasn't faced death will never seize life around the shoulder. The man who's not aware of his heart's desire will not summon the courage to abandon his transient and tangible wants—that stuff Jester talks about. He'll believe making love to Significance—and other illicit lovers—makes him a man. Such is not the case. I believe you know that in your heart—thanks to your wounds, thanks to the pit."

"Yeah, I suppose so," said Hank. "My mat hasn't left me much to worry over."

"No. Don't believe it has," Vassar agreed.

This moment, compounded with the moment before that, and the moment before that—all the moments Vassar had spent next to Hank on his mat—was forging a deep bond.

"Can I tell you something?" Hank said to Vassar.

"Sure."

"I have a confession."

"What's that?"

"Well." Hank hesitated. "I'm scared."

"About what?"

"About how I feel about my mat. As weird as it is, I'm comfortable here. I feel secure on my mat. It's like an accountability factor for me."

"You're afraid that if you leave your mat you'll lose track of your heart's desires," Vassar reflected. "That you'll regress and revert to your old life."

"Yeah, I think so. I don't like it, but I know it. I can function here. The pain's a distraction, but it keeps my priorities in focus. That's for sure."

"I think I hear a 'but' coming," Vassar interjected.

"But there's something else, something in me that wants to leave this place, to leave my mat."

"And go where?"

"Well, that's what's so strange. It's like I want to go walk in the light of the King, and I don't even like the King. I'm just scared, Vassar. Just scared, I guess."

"Is leaving the mat what scares you most?"

Hank thought for a minute, and said, "I don't know. Maybe what I'm most scared of is what the High King will say when we see each other in his light."

"This mat's been good for you, hasn't it?"

"I think it has, Vassar."

"Hank, fear's the false belief that you can go somewhere or do something that's beyond the presence and capability of the High King. Fear's the belief that what you do is greater than the High King. Fear's the belief that you can find yourself alone, abandoned by Father."

"Hadn't thought of it like that before."

"There's no place you can go that's so far away that Father won't travel with you. There's nothing you can do that will cause Father to abandon you. There's nothing that can separate you from Father. Nothing! You're his son—we're his sons. He won't ever disown us or leave us destitute or abandon us."

"So what do I do with my fear, Vassar?"

"You reject it. Disown it," Vassar declared. "It's based on Jester's lie that Father isn't close."

Skulking in the shadows, Jester was worried. He had to do something, had to change the momentum. There would be hell to pay with Zophos if the mission to compromise Prince Henry failed.

On cue, the broken tip of Competence's dagger twisted in Hank's back. He winced and turned unnaturally. The scar tissue from the wound in his hip tore. Burning, stabbing pain screamed through his body. Hank gasped. His legs tingled. He slumped to the right as strong spasms wrenched him over, contorting his posture. Hank dropped his shield and turned his attention from Vassar to his pain.

Seizing the opportunity, Jester's Special Forces lunged from the shadows in a vicious, slashing attack. They were upon Hank before he could collect his thoughts, let alone draw his sword. He hunkered down, grasped his dropped shield, and held it over himself. The noise was horrendous! Metal on metal. Yelling. Screaming. Cursing. The confusion was disorienting. Hank rallied, more with anger than resolve, and struck back.

But in his panic, Hank didn't breathe and tired quickly. He lowered his shield—ever-so-slightly—but just enough to allow the glancing blow of a chain mace to clip the top of his helmet.

His world became a blurry haze. Hank felt himself kicking and swinging his fist, but his head sounded like a belfry. He slipped and fell. A kick landed in his groin. Nausea rose up inside him. Hank writhed in pain on his mat, sucking to regain his breath and control the heaves convulsing his abdomen. He was dressed like a warrior, prepared for battle, but wallowed indignantly on the ground.

As quickly as they had come, the terrorists retreated to the shadows. Vassar and Magician bent down to aid Hank while Faith, Hope, and Love guarded them. Hank was shaken and scared, but he could hear Jester's assessment: *I'm not a warrior and never will be. I failed.*

Hank struggled to his knees. With great effort, but as ceremoniously as possible, he drew his sword from its scabbard and his dagger from its sheath and dropped them at the feet of Magician and Vassar. "I'm not a warrior. Never even drew my sword, just wallowed on my mat, kicking like a girl. It's no use. I wanted it to be different, but it's not."

Vassar picked up the pristine dagger. "Here, put this away. You handled yourself admirably. Battle isn't graceful. It's ugly. A confusing, desperate struggle for survival. Those who've never fought to survive don't understand. They don't get the desperation. Those who have engaged in the madness of warfare, who have witnessed the humiliation and naked failure of their vaunted courage—and lived to tell about it—can't describe it to those who just talk about it or live it vicariously."

Hope stepped closer to check on Hank. "You fought well, Hank. Did what you had to do."

"But look at my breastplate. It's scraped and dented. I vomited on it."

Taking a scarlet sash from his waist, Vassar wiped his brother's breakfast from his breastplate.

"I never drew my sword." His lament reeked with condemnation. "And my head hurts like hell!"

"That's because your helmet has a dent in it shaped like a mace," observed Magician.

Hank removed his helmet and stared at the sizable dimple. "Great! Now what?"

"Let me have that." Magician took Hank's helmet and tossed it to Love who pounded the dent out of it with the butt of his sword.

"Here you go. Good as new!"

Hank cursed. Vassar and the others seemed nonplussed. He felt humiliated.

Love said, "Hank, Jester's deceiving you. He's playing upon the uninformed image you have about what battle is supposed to look like versus what it is in reality. Battle's not glorious, but there's glory in fighting beside those you're loyal to. There's honor in fighting for what you believe in and hold precious. What's important here is that we trusted each other and fought together. That you fought lying on the ground is neither here nor there."

Vassar sat down beside his brother. "Hank, let me tell you a story.

"Years ago the High King commissioned me for an incursion into enemy territory. It was a daring mission. I hand-picked a group of twelve men, knighted them, and soon we were fighting the enemy in pitched battles on multiple fronts. We fought well, but we were a ragtag bunch. They weren't seasoned. Hadn't been trained. They didn't know about Magician and his strength. That was a big deal. As you're learning, his sorcery is powerful, but he wasn't part of our squad."

Hank nodded at Magician to acknowledge Vassar's affirmation of him.

"One of my twelve guys, Avarice, perhaps the most trusted in that he cared for the group's finances, was caught off guard. He got isolated from the others and was lured by an enemy faction into a treasonous plot to overthrow the Kingdom. Their plan included kidnapping me and holding me for ransom. Once they extorted the ransom from the King, they planned to kill me, and overthrow the King while he had no heir."

The beginning of Vassar's story sounded vaguely familiar, but Hank had not heard it recounted this way before. And certainly not in this context.

"I knew something was not right and talked with Father about it," Vassar continued. "Based on the intelligence we had, he and I concurred.

We knew these people were being driven to action by Zophos, but we also knew Zophos' greatest weakness."

"Which is?"

"Lust. Unbridled lust for power. We decided to exploit that propensity to overplay his hand."

"How?" asked Hank.

"In his lust to gain power, we knew he would show his true colors—show that he was all about power and corruption and deceit. People would see that he had no intention of being noble, and certainly not of being gracious and benevolent, like the King. If we were right, then instead of overthrowing the King, he would solidify the King's rule and reputation by his greed, the Kingdom would be strengthened, and its people resolved against Zophos. If you'll think about it, he's trying to do the same thing with you that he tried with me—blackmail, extortion, ransom, deception—even murder. He doesn't have any new angles."

"So what happened?"

"What followed was the most desperate fight I've ever been in. The enemy began staging the battlefield for an all-or-nothing attack during a celebration dinner my knights and I were enjoying. I could tell Avarice was preoccupied during dinner. I'm a patient man, but I was ready to get on with it. So I said, 'Avarice, I believe you have another obligation this evening.' He just looked at me, feigning innocence. I said, 'Go on. Do what you need to do.'"

"What did he do?"

"He excused himself. Didn't offer any explanation. None of the others suspected a thing. It was common for Avarice to come and go, and to do so in secret sometimes because of the amount of money he carried. There wasn't any point in confronting him in front of the others; his failure would weigh heavy enough on him later. Besides, his betrayal was necessary to advance the Kingdom and to ratify the covenant between the High King and me.

"When the attack occurred, I was with the other knights in a garden. It was late. While I'd been to this garden many times, this time was different—the darkness was full of unnatural sounds. I was scared, brother. Like you earlier, I felt like there was a strong possibility I could find myself separated from Father and separated from my buddies. There's no loneliness quite like that. Warriors are trained to fight together, just as we did a few moments ago. But I was by myself that night."

"Where were the other knights? I thought they went with you to the garden."

"My friends were asleep. Avarice had assembled quite an army—over 600 crack troops, plus a local militia. Probably close to 700, all totaled. And that was just what Avarice brought with him. Just in case we decided to try to fight our way out of the trap, Zophos brought thirteen legions of his own."

"Thirteen legions?" Hank exclaimed. "How many is that?"

"A legion's typically 5,500 to 6,000 men. So, what's that?"

"Oh, somewhere between seventy and eighty thousand. What's a few thousand here and there when you're up against eleven men?" Hank said, doing the math and capturing the irony in Vassar's story.

"Yeah, right. We were surrounded, and I mean surrounded. Avarice and his guys were around us in the garden, but Zophos' Dark Army encompassed us."

"Encompassed?" Hank asked.

"All around us, as well as above and below us—backing up Avarice's army. The fight was over before it started. I haven't ever felt more hopeless or alone than I did that evening." Vassar was quiet as he remembered.

Hank was next to his brother on sacred ground recalling an important anniversary of the heart. He honored Vassar's reflection, anxious for him to continue, but reverenced his pace in telling his story.

Vassar glanced at Hank and continued. "Avarice singled me out by kissing me with the affection of a friend. I was betrayed with a kiss. Betrayed by a trusted colleague and a breach of honor. As Avarice backed away, I heard blood-money rattle in his pocket."

"He was bought off?" Hank asked.

"Yep. And it was chump change."

"Avarice betrayed you for a pittance?"

"That's right, brother. It messed with my head. I believed I was worth more than that. Thought I was more significant. But in the end, I was sold for the same price as a dead slave and Avarice had the proof in his pocket."

"A dead slave?"

"By law, if you did something to kill my slave, you had to reimburse me, but not to replace my slave. You only had to reimburse me for the inconvenience of disposing of my dead slave."

"So this wasn't the depreciated value of the slave," Hank interrupted. "This was a disposal fee for the body."

"Right. That was the price Avarice negotiated for me."

Hank shook his head in disbelief; didn't know what to say. He glanced at Magician who raised his eyebrows confirming the sad truth. Hank turned back to Vassar.

"I know what it feels like to be insignificant, but not like that, Vassar."

"I know."

"I mean, it's one thing to have a book go out of print or have a program cancelled for a movie review—you know, all that stuff that was going on when we headed to Montana. But to be sold out cheap…. Wow."

"I was hauled away by this throng," Vassar continued, "and dragged before a variety of people, all loyal to Zophos, all scared to death of me, and threatened by me. I'd been around them every day for years. They could've taken me anytime they wanted. Anyway, they took me inside the castle and loosed their goons on me."

"No!" Hank was defensive for his brother.

"They jumped on me *en masse*, a half dozen or more at a time beating me, spitting on me, kicking me. It was an attack similar to the one you just endured. Not pretty. So believe me, I know how you feel."

"But you were alone. I wasn't."

"I hunkered down. Blood coursed down my face. You know how cuts are to your face and head?"

"Yeah. Bleed like nobody's business." Hank touched the scar on his eyebrow.

"There were so many cuts, especially on my face. I was blinded by the blood. Couldn't see, couldn't anticipate the next blow. They held me down and whipped me. Peeled the skin off my bones. I threw up, too. Nearly passed out. Wanted to pass out, but didn't. I got dizzy from being hit in the head, and I suppose as well from the loss of blood. I saw blood, swallowed blood, spit blood, and when I fell down I wallowed in my own bloody sticky vomit. They spit on me, peed on me."

As Vassar talked about his suffering, Magician, Faith, Hope, and Love straightened in rapt attention honoring the sacrifice of history's greatest hero and the epic battle of the universe.

"The more they beat me, the more furious they became. They picked me up and dragged me out onto a porch overlooking the castle courtyard. They rounded everyone up and forced them to come over and watch. There were a lot of people. They stripped me naked in front of women and children. They made fun of me. Hit me in the crotch until I vomited again—in front of everyone—but it was the dry heaves by then. I tried to get up. Got to all fours. They poked me from behind. I doubled up in a ball. Tried to protect myself, but couldn't. I don't know if they lost interest or wore out. All I know is I just lay there. Couldn't do anything else. I was covered in my own blood, vomit, and mucous. I was naked, wanted to get up, but couldn't. I was beat."

"Vassar, I don't know what to say."

"You know, Hank, I didn't look much like a warrior that day. Those who watched the beating will never forget it. Those who weren't there will never comprehend its atrocity. But you understand something of it, and in that way, we're privileged to share in each other's suffering."

Hank was uncomfortable with the idea that his battle was anything similar to Vassar's, but felt honored that Vassar included him. "How long did they hold you captive?"

"They tortured and abused me for three days."

"Three days! That's an eternity."

"If you only knew. Eventually, Zophos got in on the action. Words can't describe." Vassar waited to see if a description would surface, but none did. "I'll tell you, I came close to giving up, especially when I looked and saw Father sitting on his throne, high above, in all his glory. General Michael was standing beside him, respectfully, but I could see he was anxious—really fidgety. That was a bad sign. The Army of Light was formed in rank across the heavens ready to charge the Praetorium at the nod of the King. Their white horses pawed the ground and the dust of heaven rose under their hooves into an ominous storm cloud filled with electricity. The earth shook under them, like an earthquake. They waited and watched for Father's signal. General Michael waited and watched Father. I watched as well."

"And?" Hank whispered.

"Father never signaled. Never said a word and didn't lift a finger. I descended into deep darkness, brother. A hell-of-a pit. I was tempted to give up on Father. Tempted to quit trusting him. It was immensely hard, but I didn't give in."

They sat in quiet thinking.

"You obviously escaped," Hank said. "How'd you do it?"

"I didn't! Father came and got me."

"Father did?!" Hank couldn't believe the turn this tale was taking. "The High King rescued you—after he abandoned you?"

"The Mighty Warrior himself delivered me. Could've sent someone else—Michael, the army, any number of qualified folks—but determined to do it himself. Risked the Kingdom to come rescue me.

Avarice thought I was a chump, but Father believed I was a champion. You've never heard a battle cry like he let fly when he raided Zophos' stronghold and freed me!"

"Holy mackerel! This is incredible!"

"I was a mess. I had the filth and grime of hell itself matted into my pores. I was so vile I was cursed. And, I was afraid. It sure did seem like Father had abandoned me. Plus, when I started seeing this plan unfold—from the meeting in the garden on—I wondered if Father knew what he was doing. When I was in the pit of hell I wondered aloud if he cared. Wondered where he'd gone. I had no idea if he would tolerate questions like that from me."

"One thing about it, we ask the same questions," Hank observed.

"That we do."

"This isn't the end of the story," Hank said.

"Father came into pitch blackness, found me, resurrected me from certain annihilation, and elevated me back into prominence in the Kingdom."

"That's phenomenal." Hank sat shaking his head. Magician, Faith, Hope, and Love leaned closer, anticipating what was coming next.

"Vassar, why didn't the King stop them? Why didn't he send Michael and rescue you—when he had the chance—before all your pain and doubt?"

"Because he knew then that you and I needed to have this conversation today. Hank, he allowed it for your sake, so that through my experience you could discover trust in your heart."

"You agreed to go through all that—in cahoots with the King—for my benefit?" Hank said bewildered.

"Yes. Here's the deal: It was that conflict that distinguished me as a great warrior and set me apart. I wouldn't wish what I went through on my worst enemy, but I wouldn't trade the experience for anything. Had I not gone through that torment, I wouldn't be able to identify with what you're enduring right now, would I?"

"Well, I suppose not," Hank conceded. He couldn't argue with Vassar's logic, but it was difficult to wrap his mind around.

"You can't think your way through this, Hank," Faith said, sticking his crooked nose into the conversation. "You have to believe it in your heart. Right, guys?" Faith said, tapping his chest and looking for input from Hope and Love.

"That's right," they confirmed.

"He's telling you like it is, Hank," Magician said, making the opinion unanimous.

"I can tell you this," Vassar said, "we're warriors, you and I. Warriors of light. And what's more, we're in this fight together, all of us—you, Magician, Faith, Hope, Love, and me. We are not alone."

Hank looked at the knights surrounding his mat. Their breastplates glowed in the light.

CHAPTER 10

The Round Tower

Located in the central part of the castle, the Round Tower—also known as, the Keep—was designed, and built by the High King. It was a striking fortress built upon a massive rock dome surrounded by cliffs and a profoundly steep ditch. From its place of prominence, the Round Tower rose into the sky, its top obscured by smoke billowing up from fires burning throughout the castle's courtyard.

The Keep was constructed of granite blocks hewn to fit together. From a distance, its surface appeared dark grey, almost black. But when examined in good light, it was red, grey, pink-rose, and black. From its tiniest pebble to each giant block, the Round Tower fit together perfectly. Once constructed, its surface was polished with fine-grade quartz sand containing fifteen percent emery, the hardest stone known to man next to the diamond, and the most efficient means of polishing the Round Tower to its sheen.

A broad road bent toward the Keep as it approached from the castle. The road narrowed and constricted to an even narrower bridge that partially crossed the grassy moat toward the Tower. Unless the drawbridge of the Keep was down, the bridge across the moat ended in mid air. If the drawbridge was down, it completed the bridge and permitted approach to the first in a series of four portcullises. Each portcullis was a massive iron grating capable of being raised to permit entry or lowered to block passage.

Traffic entered the Keep through the first portcullis and stopped while it was lowered behind them and its corresponding door closed. There they waited—between doors one and two—as though entombed, until the second door opened and its portcullis raised.

Each chamber created by the portcullises had arrow loops in the walls for archers and murder holes in the roof from which stones and missiles could be launched or dumped onto helpless captives below.

Between portcullis three and four, a ninety-degree turn was required before entry was gained into the Round Tower. Given the turn, no enemy could gain either mass or momentum, nor seize the advantage of a straight run at the portcullis and doors with a battering device. And should a forced entry be attempted, the trapped attackers would meet certain death in any of the three murder-chambers.

Inside, the Round Tower had multiple floors, each supported by the domed roof of the ceiling below. Provisions of food were warehoused in catacombs in the event the Round Tower had to be defended for an extended period. The Keep was constructed around a pure spring, so fresh water was abundant. Inhabitants of the Round Tower could live a lifetime of comfort without ever having to venture outside its safety. It was a magnificent and impenetrable fortress.

Gazing from the upper floors of the Round Tower, it was clear the castle had sustained heavy damage and that its people were suffering under the cruel hand of Zophos. Seeking relief, many were collaborating with the Dark Army against the Army of Light.

The Army of Light had held defensive perimeters around the Round Tower while workers further supplied its already burgeoning warehouses. Even though they had sustained substantial losses, the King's soldiers were focused and gallant in their planned retreat and held their ground until the impregnable fortress was abundantly supplied. From the Round Tower they could seal themselves off from the castle, the Dragon, and the unpleasantness of Gnarled Wood. They could heal and sustain a war of attrition against the Dark Army. To attack the Round Tower would be suicide for the enemy.

Nevertheless, the wrath of the Great Red Dragon was atrocious. In his lust for controlling power he sent wave after wave of attackers against the Round Tower. Soon its walls were scorched and the moat ran red with the blood of Zophos' fallen. Even for battle-savvy veterans, the incessant sound of suffering was torture. Sleep—what there was of it— was fitful. Stress from the constant noise escalated to a fevered pitch.

In the beginning, for the warriors inside the Round Tower, life was one of resolute determination. Discipline was unswerving. No mercy was shown to schedule deviations, personal care, mental discipline, or military preparedness. No mercy was shown the enemy. While it seemed less than noble to mow them down from the safety of the Keep, they were faithful to carry out the standing command from the High King: "Fight fiercely. Take no prisoners. Utterly destroy them!"

Zophos conscripted many men from the castle to support the Dark Army and his assault. The desperation of the battle deteriorated the souls of mankind and drove them to live for themselves and crave nothing beyond personal gain. Each man lived every moment wanting but never receiving to his satisfaction. They lusted but never had. They banded together out of fear, Zophos' compulsion, and the expediency of self-preservation.

The culture of the Keep was greatly affected by the war with Zophos. In their disdain for what transpired, it didn't take long for them to institute standards inside the Tower to distinguish themselves from those outside the Round Tower.

After undergoing trauma and threat, it is not uncommon to pull back to a life of fundamentals. This is what the Army of Light and members of the Tower did. They read the same books, listened to the same music, used the same phrases in their speeches, sent their children to the same schools, enjoyed the same activities, and wore the same clothes. They held each other and their families to strict standards and combined their efforts to eliminate any perceived threats to their beliefs. As time passed though, the fundamental disciplines became the singular focus, usurping the original intent of the Round Tower: a sacred place for the High King and his followers.

There were a few who either demonstrated an inability to meet the expectations of the Round Tower or who questioned its standards. The Army of Light was merciless to anyone who failed to meet expectation, let alone who expressed an idea commonly associated with Zophos or the Dark Army. Accountability groups adhering to rigid curricula were recommended for these weaker members and poor performers. But while the theory of the accountability groups was vaunted, their practical reality was unrealistic. As a result, those who failed to find accountability and overcome their failure to meet expectations either lied about their repeated shortcomings, posed as though successful, or were found out, rejected, and cast out into the castle.

As the days and weeks turned into months, the Keep settled into a standardized, disciplined, and predictable routine. After a time, without perceived incursion by the enemy into the Round Tower, the Army of Light declared victory over the Dark Army. They attributed their success to the standards instituted inside the Round Tower. As a result, they codified their standards and expressed them as expected behavior for everyone living in the Tower. Poor behavior made a person immediately suspect.

Given the fundamental and sacred nature of the disciplinary standards, the diversity of culture and the creative abilities of people was limited to the classical, standard, predictable, and acceptable definitions set by the Round Tower's leadership. Anything drifting outside these parameters was deemed countercultural.

The most adept at living by the Tower's standards were solicited by the leadership to develop training programs and literature about how they achieved their success. These proficient performers gained notoriety, popularity, recognition, and wealth.

In short order, the people in the Round Tower built redundant systems to ensure their safety from the outside. Inside, they enhanced their ability to live independent of any exterior influence. For most, there was no need to leave the confines or culture of the Round Tower or to question its systems.

The lack of a broader vision, creative expression, and an outlet for imagination began to take its toll. Predictability was the norm. Souls designed to take flight with creativity suffered under the inertia of the Keep's narrow expectations. Hearts withered for lack of opportunity to scale the heights of challenge. Initiative sagged. Change was resented. Motivation was lacking. Children rebelled at the expectations placed upon them. Ingenuity was left wanting. Art was patterned, music formulaic. Stories ended alike—"And everyone lived happily ever after."

Expectations were met. Discipline was maintained. The routine was preserved.

But the peoples' eyes grew dull.

Hank's Mat

Following Zophos' propensity to lash out with maniacal desperation and overplay his hand, Jester regularly requisitioned troops from the Dark Army. Zophos generally concurred without question. No sooner would the soldiers arrive, than Jester would send them against the six warriors of light. The attacks were vicious and random, sometimes frontal, at other times oblique, and frequently by stealth in the night. Jester intended to overwhelm Prince Henry's growing confidence and demoralize his escalating trust, but Hank and his counterparts were adept at overcoming the attacks.

Often just the discussions they were having about the King and the Kingdom kept the enemy at bay. Hank noticed this and thought, *How is it that the mention of the King's name causes my enemies to turn and run but being his son doesn't mean that much to me?*

He didn't know it, but the King whom he tried to ignore, closely monitored Hank's preparedness, activity, and progress. Each enemy attack was permitted only within stringent standards that worked to Hank's ultimate benefit and the eventual resolution of the problems in their relationship. The King communicated telepathically with Magician, and together they coordinated the formative development in Hank's life.

After many skirmishes, the awkwardness of his armor was all but erased and Hank began to feel secure in his training as a knight and warrior of the light. He sparred with the other knights, exercised, practiced, and was getting more adept at compensating for the impediment of his wounds from Competence. Each day began with stretching and strengthening that afforded Hank time to focus for the day. At first the routine was a burden, but in time he realized it was a gift. Never before had he entered his day mentally tuned, but now he did—pain insisted upon it.

Hank had the appearance of confidence before he passed behind the waterfall into Gnarled Wood, but his confidence was self-confidence, rooted in how he felt about his accomplishments, recognition, and abilities. This rendered his confidence tenuous, dependent upon circumstance, as evidenced by the personal crisis that consumed him when his professional props were compromised. But during his time in the pit and on his mat, his self-confidence had disintegrated. Now his confidence was in Vassar, Magician, the other knights, and to his amusement, to some extent he felt confident in the High King whom he had doubted all his days.

It was ironic: For years Hank proclaimed his confidence in the High King and the Kingdom's ideals. But as he had learned in the pit, trusting the High King was in reality his most profound weakness. In a strange twist, no sooner had he realized this than his confidence in the King began to increase.

Jester noted that the effectiveness of his attacks on Hank was waning. *No sense doing again today what stopped working yesterday,* Jester thought, and he returned with a vengeance to his psychological warfare, knowing full well Hank's trust in the High King was speculative: trust was forged, not decided upon during a discussion.

So. After all his years of distrust, the Prince believes he knows what it is to trust. We'll see about that, Jester decided. He knew fresh confidence often belied over-confidence—and that could be exploited.

He'd had a suspicion Hank might progress with the help of Magician and the rest, so he held Envy in reserve for just such a time as this.

Envy stepped into an ante chamber with Jester, closed the door, and stripped out of his black clothing into clothing with the appearance of light. While he changed, Pity dyed his hair blond. Jester handed him blue lenses for his eyes. Once the disguise was complete, Envy stood still while Pity and Jester examined him for imperfection.

"Listen for my counsel and do exactly as I say," Jester instructed.

"Will do." Envy managed his irritation at Jester's micro-control as he left the chamber disguised with fabricated light.

Instead of the subtle illumination Hank was accustomed to, the light in the pit increased dramatically to a harsh glare as Envy approached. Hank squinted and his eyes watered.

Envy marched as trained—confidently, brazenly—to Hank's mat. The knights allowed him to approach, and as anticipated Hank mistook the fabricated light for the light of the King and assumed Envy was his emissary. This, along with the decrease in outright attacks, left Hank vulnerable to Envy's deceptive message.

On days when the pain in Hank's back and hips shrieked in crescendo, Envy rounded up the ugly, destitute, and debauched and paraded them past Hank's mat. None of these lost and degraded souls walked with a limp. None suffered. They walked, and bent, and laughed without a trace of physical pain.

"Look at that guy!" Envy said, as a sorry soul passed Hank's mat. Envy was parroting Jester, as ordered. "He has no interest in the High King and no regard for the Kingdom. He's a lost cause. If only I could walk like that—without aggravation, without a limp—like he does." Envy's thoughts resonated with Hank's entitlement to be pain free.

"Why can't the King heal my affliction?" Envy tempted. "That's a reasonable expectation. After all, I'm his son. Just think what I could do if I didn't hurt. I could really tighten my belt like Vassar and Magician do. I could be a real warrior."

Envy's reasoning was rational, reasonable, expedient, and was cloaked in apparent light. As Hank considered freedom from pain and the resultant fame of being a great warrior, he envisioned parades and honors—and perhaps finding and reuniting with Significance.

Envy paraded a reprobate and his girlfriend in front of Hank's mat, then offered his editorial, "There goes a guy who's ruined his life! He abuses himself with drugs, poisons his health with a slut, and has no more social grace than to grope her in public! But look. He's not crippled. He's consumed by darkness, but he doesn't limp. Yet here I am, sitting on a cheap mat, polluting myself with the fantasy that it's advantageous to be a child of the King. If the King loves me and has the power to remove my pain, why doesn't he do it?"

While Envy hammered Hank with enticements capitalizing upon his lack of trust, Magician talked with Hank about his reluctance to trust the High King. The milieu of thoughts from Envy, Jester, Magician—and Hank's own thinking—created a discordant cacophony.

"'Why' is an important question, Hank." Magician didn't say a great deal—and when he did it was in a lower, quieter tone—but when he spoke, Hank knew to pay attention. Magician was a wise man and Hank had developed a good deal of respect for him. "But just because you ask 'why,' doesn't mean you're going to get an answer. And when you do get an answer, it may not be satisfactory in your estimation."

"I realize the King doesn't owe me an explanation, or even an answer. Who am I to question him? In fact, I admire his patience—or tolerance. Whatever it is. If the roles were reversed, I wouldn't put up with my questions," Hank confided.

"But when pain intensifies—when it gets in the way of my ability to do what I want to do—no matter how resolved I am not to demand an answer, 'Why?!' howls through my teeth like an express in the night."

"And with fiery agitation," Magician added.

"You can say that again. Fact is Magician, I'm not proud of it, but I have screamed and cursed at the High King, 'Why, damn it?! Why? What do you want from me?! What's the point?! You want me to hurt like hell?! Is that it?! Tell me! You have something to say?! Say it! I'm listening!'"

Hank and Magician sat in silence before Hank said, "It's very quiet after one of my outbursts. I wonder what the King's thinking."

"How do you feel after venting?" Magician asked.

Hank thought, then said, "I feel condemned, I guess. Distant. Shamed. But condemned is probably the best description. And destined to keep on hurting."

"Why?"

"Partially because the King's not going to do anything for me and partially because I've made him mad. He's going to get even."

"You see him as capricious?"

"Capricious? That's a different word, but yeah. I suppose that's it—in a word. Capricious. Petty works too."

"As you've said, Hank, pain's a distraction."

"Yeah, can't concentrate. It's like being screamed at all the time."

"Pain's a raving fury," Magician said.

It was affirming to Hank to hear Magician acknowledge the formidable foe he faced.

"If a man isn't careful," Magician said, "he can miss the whole point of life contending with pain. He can be deceived and believe if he conquers it, he'll be content. It's a compelling idea, and when it's constant—like yours—it's relentless."

"It's proving to be exactly that," Hank confirmed.

"You know," Magician continued, "pain played a similar role in Vassar's life. Pain could have torn him apart, but instead it gave him the gift of steadfast endurance. I've seen Vassar sweat blood to maintain his focus."

"You're kidding!"

"Nope. Not one bit."

"That's incredible! Makes me admire him all the more."

"Know what you mean," Magician said.

"You used the word 'relentless' to describe pain," Hank said.

"Uh, huh."

"Most nights there's a period—right after I lie down—when I don't hurt. On a good night, the relief is about twenty seconds. Other nights, maybe five or ten. Bad nights…well…."

"On a bad night there isn't any relief, is there?"

Hank shook his head.

"It's merciless," Magician said.

"Yep. It is," Hank concurred. "Magician, I'm tired. If you don't mind, I think I'll take a nap."

"No problem. Thanks for talking with me. I'll let you know if anything stirs."

Hank closed his eyes.

Some folks place great stock in dreams, write them down, and tell their friends about them after they awaken. Hank believed in dreams—

and visions, for that matter—but not readily; they were too irrational. He was a skeptic. But that some had visions portending the future, or saw revelations invisible to the rational mind, was within the realm of possible Hank believed; it was just not probable or routine.

It was a good thing Hank had room for this belief, even though it was marginal, because after he went to sleep a vision unfolded. He saw himself...

...standing on his grass mat in the dark circumference of spectators. Hank watched as a parade passed his woven viewing platform. Leading the parade was a troupe of dancers carrying banners before the throng of admiring faces. The dancers twirled and leapt with their flowing banners. The participants sang and clapped in rhythm. It was such an enchanting, mesmerizing display that Hank was caught up in the emotion of it all, clapping and tapping in time with the singers and dancers.

As Hank's dream progressed, he realized the parade was in his honor. The songs were about him. The dances were dedicated to him. And the banners were tributes to him.

There were banners portraying the battles he had fought in the pit. Banners with pictures of the books he had written back in Texas. There were banners with his titles: Chief Executive Officer. President. Founder. Author. Host. His resume was being acted out in dance and song. It was compelling and creative and totally cool. Hank felt pride rising up in him. The more of the parade that past, the more grand the recounting of his accomplishments and the more glorious the recognition he felt—at last.

Hank was caught up in the moment, anticipating the next accolade, and relishing the acknowledgement he was receiving. As if approaching the climax, the grandest banner of them all—taller, more elaborate, larger—came into view. It had his image on it, dressed as a warrior... and with his foot on the neck of the Great Red Dragon whose tail curled around and framed the cloth.

He was a hero! Exalted. When those in the parade saw that Hank understood the message on their banner, they cheered frenetically and danced more furiously. Hank raised both arms in a "V" and basked in their affirmation.

As the banner got closer, he saw her. Carrying this tribute to him was Significance, and was she stunning: legs a mile long, her figure a feast for the eyes. Her gown was sheer, her skin flawless, and she gyrated in a hypnotic dance with her black hair flowing. She smiled at him, celebrated him, recognized him. The honor was his—the parade his. It was all about him, his accomplishments, his titles, his place, his significance. She offered herself to him.

That's when Hank realized something was amiss. While the parade accurately portrayed his life before passing behind the waterfall, he'd learned in the pit that life is about far more than him and what he wants. Life is about desire—heart's desire—desire to connect with Vassar, and Magician, and the others—and maybe one day, to connect with his Father. But there were no banners recognizing any of them. Hank looked down the parade route. There was no banner honoring the High King in whose light they marched and in whose light he lived. No banner recognizing Vassar who'd protected him, stood by him, and pledged his faithfulness to him. Nothing for Magician. Nothing for anyone—except himself.

The eyes of Hank's heart were opened.

He understood what Envy was trying to get him to believe: that he was entitled, and that if the King didn't do what he wanted, then the King was whimsical, petty, capricious, and unworthy of his loyalty. For the first time, Hank truly realized that Jester was fueling his distrust of the King. Jester impugned the King's reputation because he didn't do what Hank wanted him to do—as if the King were obliged to do what Hank wanted versus what he knew was best. Based upon Jester's perspective, Hank was King. But Hank saw that even this was a ruse.

Jester wasn't promoting him over the King. He was advancing himself and his agenda, and he was in cahoots with the King's enemy, Zophos.

As the pieces of his life's puzzle fit together in rapid revelation, Hank saw that by accepting Envy's conjecture, Jester's counsel, and Pity's comfort he was commissioning and hosting this parade in his own honor.

The parade throbbed in front of him. Significance danced for him. Hank said to himself, *I have life backward. It's not about me. It's about the King. It's not about what I want; it's about what I desire—and I desire to know my Father and celebrate his Kingdom. I want this parade, but I don't desire this parade.*

Hank thought back on lessons he'd learned from Faith, Hope, Love, Magician, and Vassar. *A warrior lays his life down so another can live. If called upon to do so, a warrior must be prepared to die on behalf of the King. Honor in life is not having your own parade.*

Hank looked out from his thoughts. Significance's beautiful body glistened. Her sheer dress clung to her, revealed her. *Honor is faithful to the end,* Hank rehearsed, *faithful to the High King. Faithfulness is being put to the test and not flinching.*

The picture came into focus for Hank. Not out of duty, but from deep within his heart-of-hearts, his conviction shifted from his wants to his heart's desire and the High King's viewpoint. Passionate desire—greater than his own life—boiled up from his heart. The look in his eyes changed from dull to fiery. The set to his chin tilted down. The muscles in his cheeks clinched into knots. His spine straightened and his breastplate rose as his lungs filled.

In a fluid motion honed by his training and battles, Hank reached into the parade, grabbed the giggling Significance, and pulled her to himself.

"Hey, big guy! I've missed you," she said saucily, flinging her head back, inviting.

He turned Significance around and wrapped his left arm over her shoulder and across her chest. He held her in a vice-like grip.

"Ow! Not so hard! You're hurting me. Let go!"

Recognizing in an instant that Hank had tipped in favor of the High King, Jester ran out from the shadows screaming his warning to Significance. Morphing back into her natural state, Significance turned into an elegantly colored constrictor. She wrapped her body around Hank and squeezed. With each breath he took, she tightened. Twisting her head, she struck Hank's neck and held him with her fangs. Her determination to dominate him, to suffocate his life, and to take him into herself was unchanged but her method was more apparent.

The hours of mentoring by the knights paid off. Reaching to his side, Hank yanked out his dagger, plunged it into the snake's side, and drew the blade toward its neck. Significance's coils loosened. Hank seized the serpent behind the head and pinched its jaws to pry its fangs out of his neck. As its life gurgled away, he dropped the twitching reptile at his feet and picked up the banner Significance had carried declaring his honor. Sensing Envy's approach from behind, he broke the banner's staff over his knee and spun deftly with the jagged end in his hand. Just as Envy reached for him, Hank stabbed him through the heart. Hank braced his legs, gripped harder, and rammed the pole again. He pushed with all his strength. His bloody hands slipped. He wiped them on his pants and shoved again until the banner itself plugged Envy's mortal chest wound.

Hank raised his clenched fist into the air and screamed into the darkness rife with expectant faces, "My allegiance is to the High King of Glory. I serve him and him alone! Here I stand, so help me God!"

Hank sat bolt-upright. "What happened, Magician? Where are they?"

"You tell me," Magician said. "What'd you see?"

Hank stared into the darkness, collecting his thoughts. *What did just happen?* he pondered. *It was so real! Must have been something I ate…or how much did I drink last…?*

"Hank, don't over analyze," Magician said. "Just because you think rationally doesn't mean the High King does. Your Father's a man of many resources and great ingenuity. He'll do whatever he deems in his best interest and to your greatest benefit. Take what he gives you at face value. Trust him, even if it doesn't make sense right now," Magician said.

Hank stared at Magician, thought, and reached for his dagger. The handle was sticky.

Hank's Mat

Hank knew he couldn't stay on his mat. Didn't want to anymore. He wanted to follow his heart's desire to know the King, but every time he considered leaving—doing what Faith called, "running for the light,"—his desire got tangled up in his impediment. *How can I—a cripple—run in the light? And what am I going to do with my mat?*

Magician sat down beside Hank. "I couldn't help but hear you debating," he said. "May I offer some thoughts?"

"Oh, by all means. I'm not getting very far on my own."

Magician took a deep breath, "I have authority from your Father to share my sorcery and power with you."

"Wait, wait. I don't understand," Hank said.

"But I just started," Magician protested.

"Yes, I know, but you already lost me."

"Here's the deal," Magician began again. "I will walk through you, run through you, fight through you, and if necessary, I'll die through you."

"Why?"

"Because your Father asked me to. In the process, I'll access your heart more deeply than you ever dreamed possible. I will extract the desires of your heart, place them before you, and you will realize their fulfillment before your very eyes."

There was a confident resonance in Magician's words.

"So the question is not whether or not you can keep up. Not whether you can fight like the others. These are inconsequential. You'll do fine," Magician reassured. "The decision you face is whether or not you're going to run for the light—just like Faith challenged you. It's that simple." Magician chuckled, then said, "It's simple, but it will affect the rest of your life. Well, take your time thinking about it. Listen to your heart, and don't forget my offer."

Magician pointed to Vassar, Faith, Hope, and Love. "While you're thinking, I'm going to slip over there and be sure those four aren't telling taller tales than they really were."

The Round Tower

While his enemy had consolidated into the Round Tower, Zophos' Dark Army was dispersed and distracted with the demands of occupation. It was part of success he had not accounted for, and as a result, the overhead demand created frustration among his staff and exacerbated the inefficiency of his top-down management, especially given his focus on the Round Tower.

Zophos' plan was counterintuitive and costly, but he believed it would achieve his ultimate objective. He continued ordering Nephilim to throw the Dark Army against the Round Tower in a series of major assaults. Each attack was more heinous, terrifying, darker, and more horrific than the previous. Zophos' logic was simple: the more atrocious his attacks, the more quickly those inside the Round Tower would recognize they were safe, relax, and then let down their defenses.

The people inside the Round Tower accepted Ennui as balanced, the picture of stability and confidence. This opinion was galvanized when they saw her calm composure during Nephilim's driving assaults against the Tower. She was unfazed, slept well, ate calmly, dressed nicely, and moved placidly through the hallways of the Keep making small talk. Her demeanor inside the Tower, midst the chaos outside, elevated her to a place of admiration.

Day by day, the emotional atmosphere inside the Tower calmed as the people turned their attention inward, paying less attention to the war outside. They invested their energies on their creature comforts, socializing with friends, and personal advancement. Fueled by Ennui and her staff, a healthy suspicion mushroomed toward anyone propagating awareness of the war or advocating intervention and relief for the castle.

Zophos' and Ennui's plan appeared to be unfolding perfectly.

"So how's your nephew doing?" Zealot asked, as he and Vigor sat at a corner table in one of the Tower's restaurants.

"Better," Vigor said, as he watched how Zealot gripped his glass. *Index and middle fingers only. Others away from the tumbler. Left hand.* "You know, he must have contracted something from one of his little buddies. Was sick as a dog for a week, maybe a little longer."

Zealot moved the glass to his right hand and put his palm flat on the table, the stem of the glass between his middle and ring fingers. He waited until he was certain Vigor noticed. "Well, I'm glad to hear it. Poor guy. No fun being sick like that." Zealot turned the glass clockwise.

Vigor counted the rotations: *One. Two. Three.* They continued chatting. "No, it's not. His sister had a stomach ache last week. Was pretty miserable too."

Zealot took a sip of his drink, set his glass on the table, and turned it one turn counter clockwise. Stopped. Made a few irrelevant gestures. He tapped the table softly three times with his knuckles.

Vigor looked into Zealot's eyes, blinked, and thought, *Store room behind the auditorium. He will arrive 7:45. That means I'm to arrive 8:15.*

Vigor walked casually, but with purpose, through the labyrinthine hallways of the Round Tower's seventh floor. He often walked these passages. Thinking. Contemplating. It was a quiet area. The regulars were accustomed to his frequency, nodded when they passed him, but didn't engage him in discussion. They liked the quiet of the seventh floor too.

He stopped, pretending to examine a months-old bulletin posted on the wall outside the auditorium. He glanced right and left. Listened. Quickly, but carefully, he opened the auditorium door, slipped inside, and closed the door after him. He waited to let his eyes adjust, then moved through the foyer, into the auditorium, and sat down—as was his custom—second row from the back, two seats in.

He waited, measuring time by reciting to himself the early lines of Chaucer's tale, *The House of Fame*, about a poet who falls asleep in a glass temple adorned with images of famous people. Their deeds are written on the walls, and the poet's guide through the temple is an eagle. Vigor enjoyed Chaucer's contemplation of fame, fortune, reputation, and his subtle cynicism as to the tale's veracity. *Not unlike the Round Tower,* he thought, standing up after several minutes and a number of lines.

Vigor quietly moved down the aisle. His senses tuned raw for any sound, smell, or movement. He ran his hand along the leading edge of the stage and moved stage left, eased up the stairs, and behind the curtain. He stopped again. It was darker still. He knew the path like he knew the back of his hand. *But what if someone has been here? Has moved something? Is waiting to intercept me midst the antiquated sets?* There was nothing new about Vigor's worries. They plagued him without fail each time he came to the auditorium—or any one of their other secret meeting places.

As satisfied as he could be, given the risks and circumstance, he crept through the staging. He sensed the wall before he could touch it. Knew it had to be close. Hand out, he touched the wall like Braille. He followed along the wall, turned behind it, took five steps, and felt for the handle.

He tapped the brass handle lightly—two quick, then a third—with his fingernail. He touched the dagger hidden under his cloak. He caught his breath as the door pulled away from its jam. Waited for a count. Two. Three. Gripped the knife's handle harder. His triceps tightened.

"Hello, friend," Zealot whispered.

Vigor stepped into the store room as Zealot closed the door behind him.

"Any difficulty?" Zealot asked.

"No. Pretty routine. How about you?"

"Same for me, although there is a new face on the seventh floor, at least new to me. A woman. Had a little different look in her eye than everyone else. I think it's just that she's new though," Zealot reassured.

Vigor didn't show it, but even though Zealot downplayed his encounter, the woman bothered him, and he could tell she bothered Zealot as well.

"It's probably nothing—this woman." Zealot voiced Vigor's thought. "But we should probably let this meeting place lie fallow for a while."

"Agreed. We have other options," Vigor said.

Zealot was quiet for a moment. Vigor could sense his discomfort, and it spread. "Tell you what. Just to be on the safe side, let's postpone our talk this evening until the fourth," Zealot said. "We'll rendezvous out in the castle at the Plowman. Have some dinner. We can talk there. It's loud enough, no one can overhear."

"Good. I agree," Vigor said. "I've got some important information for you on the Dark Army's training and troop movement."

Zealot nodded. The two men hugged, and according to their plan, Zealot waited until Vigor had time to leave the auditorium before he made his exit.

Zealot stopped at the side door behind the stage. There was no way to know if anyone was on the other side. He pulled a flask of whiskey from his pocket. Took a swig and sloshed it around in his mouth. It burned mightily. He let some of the amber trickle out of his mouth, down his chin, and onto the front of his shirt. He repeated his ritual. Swallowed.

He grasped the door handle and swung it open clumsily. Waiting a dramatic moment, he stepped into the hall, acting unsteady on his feet— mimicking a closet drunk to anyone who might be in the hallway.

The commotion startled her. Letizia's heart jumped to her throat and she whirled around.

Zealot played his part, trying unsuccessfully to find his pocket for the flask. "Begging your pardon, ma'am. I was jest tryin' my time. I mean, takin' my time—some time, that ish—to myself."

Letizia stared at Zealot for a long moment. Enough to take inventory of him. He was certain of that. Inventory of what, he couldn't be certain. She glared a hard glare, and turned away.

CHAPTER 11

Hank's Mat

Hank stood on the edge of his mat staring into the chasm, scanning the faces in the dark sphere. *My mat's my stage, the place where I'm featured.*

He paused, recognizing that his thoughts had the familiar sound of Jester's voice. *My mat's the same stage as in my dream. Heck! It's the same stage as my life, just the second act—or the four-hundredth.* "Damn you, Jester," Hank growled.

No. I won't take my mat with me, he determined. *If I'm gonna make a run for the light, I'm going without my mat.* Hank glanced over where Vassar and the others were talking. *None of them have mats. None of them make provision for themselves. They don't seem concerned for their lives, not like I am anyway.* Turning back toward the dark sphere created by the King's gracious ray of light, Hank vowed, *Neither will I. If I'm going to adopt their opinion of me as a warrior in the Army of Light, I'll embrace their view completely or not at all. Whatever accommodation the High King makes for them, I'll accept as mine too.*

I'm not interested in playing the same old part in the theater of life. I'm tired of the expectations, tired of trying to be significant, and tired of trying to get the audience to recognize me.

It dawned on him that his distrust in the High King had nothing to do with the King's character, as Jester suggested at every turn. Rather, his doubt was rooted in the role reversal he had adopted in the darkness of his own drama. Hank shook his head in wonder at the simplicity of his revelation. As he modified his view and installed the King as the lead on life's stage, the incongruities and distrust he had wrestled with for years dissipated.

I perform a supporting role—not the featured part, not the one I've crafted in consultation with Jester, rooted in my own independence and ingenuity. Don't want to perform that role any longer. I want to follow my heart's desire. Hank could feel a climax in his heart, as though there was a symphony building inside him. He felt anticipation, a dawning in his soul that he would not—must not—ignore.

"I won't stay on this mat and I won't take it with me. I will seize my heart's desire!" he stated into the darkness.

Hank had been so deep in thought he hadn't noticed the silence behind him. Vassar, Magician, Faith, Hope, and Love were standing in a shallow semi-circle looking at him—a solitary figure—occupying a cheaply-woven mat, in a dark and forbidding dungeon, filled with enemies, and expectations. Each of the knights had his sword in front of him—point down, pommel up—with his hands resting on either side of the guard.

Hank faced their silent stares. At first he was surprised, but ascertained that this moment was not only significant to him, but to them as well. His decision was made. His mat was too small to contain his heart. Just as Magician had promised, he had realized treasures in the darkness that were not available any other place, but the time to move was now. The chance of a lifetime awaited him and it was embodied in those standing before him.

Hank reached across his breastplate, grasped his sword with a hand now accustomed to its feel, and drew it hissing from its scabbard, flashing a glint of blue steel in the King's light. He raised it in a salute to the knights before him.

"Vassar. You've never once failed to stand beside me, even in my selfishness. You've taught me from your heart. You've transferred your skills to me. You've been the embodiment of Father, often at your own expense and reputation, and often as the brunt of my anger. I recognize what you've done and I'm grateful. If I had something of value to give you, I would."

Vassar acknowledged Hank with tears gleaming in his eyes.

"But all I have to give you are my dreams, brother. I dream of walking with you in the light of the King. I dream of defending you with all I possess. I dream of hearing you say—one of these days—that your life was richer because I stood beside you, just as mine is richer because you've stood beside me. Because of you, I understand that there's no greater love than laying my life down for a friend so he can live. This is what you've done for me. I dream of doing the same for you. I give you my dreams, Vassar. All I hope is that we pursue them together."

Vassar nodded.

"Magician, I don't want to betray your confidence, but you whispered to me that you would run through me, fight through me, live through me, and if called upon to do so, would die through me. If your offer still stands, then I accept. I have nothing to offer except my will, but with all I possess, I choose to reject my independence and adopt your strength, your way, and your viewpoint."

Magician winked.

"Hope. I'm weak and vulnerable, crippled, wracked by pain. I'm all dressed up like a warrior, but my confidence is low. I realize I have a growing heart for the Kingdom and the High King, but I'm easily distracted by these infirmities. It's with profound relief that you've joined this band of brothers." Hank placed his hand on his chest, covering his heart, and the emblem of the Kingdom. "Would you be here, close to my heart, and upon your honor would you protect me from delusion?"

Hope doubled his right hand into a fist and placed it over his heart as he nodded his head.

"Love. I must admit, you're not what I expected."

Love smiled. It wasn't the first time he'd heard that confession.

"I've heard about you all my life from many who claimed to know you. I knew I needed you, but much to my disappointment, following the lead of others—not the least of whom has been Jester—I looked for you in all the wrong places. And, I'm guilty of pointing others to apparitions and fantasies and telling them they were you. I apologize. I've given myself to an array of poor facsimiles: Significance, Recognition, Pity, Importance, Competence, and others. I've called my unfaithfulness by your name, and in so doing, I've used your name in vain. I apologize for that as well. Love, I lack focus. I lack discipline. My heart desires to be faithful, but I'm vulnerable to distraction. I ask that you guard my vision, protect my focus, and provide a safe harbor for me and my heart?"

The muscles in Love's forearms rippled as he gripped the blade guard of his sword. He bowed his head for a few dramatic seconds, and then just as Hope had done, Love doubled his right hand into a tight fist and held it against his heart as a vow of his allegiance.

"Faith. I doubted you," Hank began. "I'm sorry. I misjudged you—because of your size."

Faith's mouth slanted into an angled grin.

"But you know, I figured there was more to you than met the eye. Your crooked nose gave you away, and as silly as it may sound, I decided to trust you because of your nose. I figured you got it broken fighting, fighting for something important to you. After watching you, I've concluded that my hunch was correct. You've fought for me, believed in me, and given me everything your heart has to give. I like what you're made of. I desire to believe like you believe, but I have a long way to go. Would you help my unbelief?"

Faith stepped forward. He turned and looked at the others, stood as straight and tall as he could, throwing his shoulders back and his chest out, he struck a pose befitting his attitude, and then turned to face Hank. He took a deep bow, held it, and then twirled his sword before placing his fist over his heart and moving back into rank.

"Well. There you have it," Magician goaded.

Hank knelt on his mat. Vassar, Faith, Hope, Love, and Magician lifted their swords and brought them to rest on Hank's shoulders. Somewhere in a dark corner, Jester guffawed. Hank gave no consideration to his implication. The five knights withdrew, sheathed their swords, and Magician helped Hank to his feet.

In honor of his courageous stand, the others allowed Hank the privilege of determining their next move. Looking at his fellow warriors, Hank said, "I've heard voices in the dark while I've been awake in the night, unable to sleep. They say there's fighting on the eastern revetment of the castle. They say Zophos, disguised as a huge, red dragon has breached the wall and is laying siege to the Round Tower. I hear the Army of Light staged a defense, but retreated into the Keep, and is hard pressed to do any good against the enemy. I think it's a good day to distinguish ourselves on behalf of the High King."

"Indeed it is," said Faith.

"I agree," Magician said. "What do you think we should do, Hank?"

Hank looked down at the edge of his mat. He turned and looked at Magician. Then he shouted, "Let's make a run for the light," and stepped from his mat.

In the Pit, Running in the Light

They followed Hank's lead away from the mat and were engulfed in the brilliance of the light. Hank blinked and his eyes watered. He was accustomed to the shadows. This radiance was splendid and he exulted in his decision. He felt immediate relief that blossomed into what he assumed was freedom. Freedom from the onerous darkness. Freedom from the expectations surrounding him. Freedom to relax. His heart throbbed. He relished the moment, ran a bit farther, and relished that moment. He looked around. He was surrounded by dazzling light. He threw his arms open in the illumination of the High King.

His eyes grew more accustomed to the magnificence. Squinting, blinking, Hank looked around as his new surroundings became more defined. The light reflected off the warriors' faces, armor, and weapons. It revealed what was true in Hank and of his fellow knights. The light was so magnificent it was difficult to distinguish between the source of light and those who reflected it.

Hank looked back into the dark chasm. It was now a charcoal-colored abyss. It was as though he had stepped from a dark cellar into stunning sunlight, allowed his eyes time to adjust to the sunlight, and then turned to look back into the cellar. He was blind to the detail of the darkness even though not yet out of the pit. He couldn't see whether the faces were watching. He was free to walk in the light without expectation or judgment.

"What do you see?" Magician asked.

"Not much. Not much of anything," Hank said. "But I remember."

"You know, if you stand here and look long enough—with your back to the light—your eyes will adjust and you'll regain your ability to see in the shadows. But you can't have it both ways, Hank. You either live in the darkness or walk in the light. You can't live in a gray twilight that knows neither the defeat of your way nor the victory of the High King's. You can't accommodate Jester's view and your Father's. They're incompatible."

"I understand," Hank said.

"You gave it a heck-of-a try, but you'll never comprehend the light by studying the darkness. Only light overcomes darkness."

It took a moment for Hank to realize Magician was testing him: Did he really want him to live through him? Magician was waiting to follow Hank's lead.

Hank turned to look at the warrior with the uncanny sorcery and propensity for always being close at hand. "Magician, I have lived a lifetime in dark places. I'm proficient at coping with murkiness and living off the remnants I'm able to scrounge from the deeps. I've even rationalized living in the darkness as a noble calling, and no doubt, there are treasures in my heart that only could have been mined from the caverns of my soul's darkness. But it's a new day! I was curious to look back, and I'm glad I did, but I choose to live in the light."

Hank turned into the light and took a few steps, stopped, turned back, "And yes, Magician, I do want you to live through me."

Gnarled Wood

Not wanting to face Zophos himself, Jester sent his report to Zophos via a messenger. Zophos didn't believe the messenger's report—that everything was under control—anymore than the messenger did. If everything was under control, the Prince would still be naked, filthy, and on his mat. That he was clothed in the armor of the Kingdom and walking in the light was a clear failure.

Zophos grunted at Jester's messenger and then summoned his aide. The aide knew the look on Zophos' face, stepped back out, and returned with the guards. As they stepped into his office, Zophos sat at his desk and scribbled a note:

Jester—

I'm disappointed.

Z—

Zophos folded the note, inserted it into an envelope, let wax from the candle on his desk drip over the flap, and then mashed his signet ring into the cooling wax to complete the seal. He flipped the envelope over and wrote "Jester" on the front.

Zophos sat back in his chair and looked at the messenger. He looked at his aide and the four guards and nodded toward the messenger. "You may need a little help," Zophos said. The aide stepped outside and returned with two more guards.

Zophos picked up a short blade off his desk that he used to open correspondence. While the guards held the messenger, Zophos sharpened the blade on a whetstone. The messenger began to protest, "I'm just a messenger." He tried to reason with Zophos. He pleaded and begged. Zophos didn't acknowledge.

After taking his time with the blade, Zophos rose from his chair, and came around his desk. The messenger struggled, but it was a futile effort. The guards held his arms and legs, and seeing that Zophos was eyeing the man's face, they grasped his head. They pried open his mouth. Zophos glanced at the guard on his left who used his sleeve to grab the messenger's tongue. When it was stretched out, Zophos cut the messenger's tongue out. He wiped his blade on the messenger's shirt and told his aide, "Wrap that up."

Zophos' aide took the messenger's tongue and the sealed note for Jester and put them into the messenger's bag. "Get this man something soft to eat," the aide said.

"And he better not choke," Zophos added with a snarl. "Get him back to Jester, and make sure he personally delivers my message."

The messenger was bent over in front of Zophos' desk bleeding and drooling, making guttural sounds as he cried and gasped.

"Get him outta here, and clean that up before it gets sticky."

In the Pit, Walking in the Light

Each day Hank dressed in the light. He took special care polishing the crest of the Kingdom on his breastplate and spent hours touching up the edges of his sword and dagger.

The six spent hours discussing tactics and strategy. They understood that they would have to work as one in the coming days. And while they relished the relative peace of this place in the light, the darkness of the pit was a turn of the head away. Hank was always amazed at the gray abyss that stared back.

It was amusing to Hank that Jester remained tenacious, even in the light. One couldn't fault him on determination. He worked every angle, and while Hank found it easier to discern Jester's counsel in the light, he suspected this would not be the case for long. Jester was too shrewd to not modify his tactics to keep his prey off balance.

The Castle

The blitz on the castle had gone better than Zophos thought possible. The castle, its courtyard, the surrounding area, and out through Gnarled Wood were now his domain.

Thousands of captives were marched into Gnarled Wood where they became hideous creatures, tormented by the goons who guarded them as well as by their own regret, which filled their days and haunted their nights. They lashed out at each other, took selfish advantage of everyone and every opportunity, and were consumed by personal survival. They were like drowning ants whose mound is flooded by spring rains. Scrambling over each other to get to the surface, they showed no regard for the fatal price they exacted upon others.

In their torment, they lived bitter lives, shirking any semblance of personal responsibility onto the one individual they blamed for their predicament: the High King. Most of their projections began, "If only the King…." They reasoned that if the High King would give them what they wanted—tranquility, stability, ample provision, health, friendship, success—then they would be happy. But since their circumstances indicated otherwise, they questioned the King's love and power with bitter, hard hearts.

While thousands were carried away into Gnarled Wood, thousands of others were left as shields and accomplices to Zophos who wanted one thing: to occupy the High King's seat. He lied, deceived, accused, confused, and manipulated in order to get what he wanted.

The Round Tower

Zophos adjusted his tactics. *What better strategy than to create the appearance that tranquility has returned, that a new day of peace has arrived? I will portray myself as the embodiment of their hope—a benevolent and caring conqueror. Guardian of peace.*

The King also promoted peace, but it was peace within—an intangible. Zophos envisioned peace in the neighborhood.

Zophos created an illusion of tranquility replete with the possibility of abundance almost within arm's reach. All around the Round Tower he positioned enclaves of his subjects living in rebuilt prosperity as though he was providing the very things the High King would not—or could not: peace, happiness, fulfillment, financial security, meaningful work, a better life, family, recognition, and so forth. There were dozens of programs. Whatever they wanted, he provided. Their children thrived. They were active socially. Their businesses were in the right place, at the right time, and flourished. Welfare was evident.

The delusion of peace—peace within the castle and its courtyard—was the new order-of-the-day. Crime was down and the streets were safe once again. Zophos hosted outdoor parties with copious amounts of food, live music, and activities for the children. He established business networks to stimulate the economy, trade, and reciprocity. He aggressively reconstructed the infrastructure destroyed by his war. Optimism bloomed throughout the castle.

Zophos used his supernatural power, ruthless intolerance for patience, and superb supporting staff to hurry the pace of time. More quickly than normal, a public opinion formed both inside and outside the Round Tower that the war was over.

The vocal and visible heroes in the castle battle were systematically neutralized, but not so quickly as to raise suspicion. Some were tripped up by Zophos' staff. They had affairs, entered unethical business agreements, and seized power at the expense of their honor. Others were neutralized by silence and shame, believing with no small amount of assistance from Zophos' staff, that their conduct in the war was ignoble. And, there were a number of influential voices silenced by a contract on their life. As the number of those who had fought the enemy diminished, the stories of those who had fought were forgotten or recast as fables.

Soon, it became reasonable and desirable to deny the war occurred. The idea took hold, and with Zophos' and Ennui's nurturance became the *en vogue* opinion. Prosperity proclaimed a new day whose dawn was apparent. Naysayers—skeptics and radicals—found themselves progressively hard pressed to counter growing, public opinion. After all, seeing is believing.

Inside the Round Tower the lust for peace was so great, and the denial of pervasive threat so strong, that it birthed a denial that Zophos and his Dark Army lurked outside. Under the direction of Ennui, many came to question Zophos' existence.

Some asserted Zophos was a metaphor; nothing more than an idea. This was the perspective Ennui pushed the hardest; it was the most advantageous to Zophos and her agenda. After all, if Zophos was a metaphorical idea, that would make his counter-part, the High King, metaphorical as well.

While many adopted this metaphorical concept and then didn't give it—or its principles—any further thought or credence, some needed something to believe in. Since it was politically incorrect to believe in one power—nobody wanted to be a radical—they believed in a host of ideas, concepts, philosophies, practices, superstitions, and powers. This was fine by Ennui. The more diverse beliefs that proliferated, the greater the majority of folks became who believed in nothing beyond living in the moment. When pressed, by conscience or conversation, it seemed best to embrace the notion of a higher power. But for most, their higher power didn't have enough power, authority, or recourse to govern life and action. So, they did what worked best for them.

Ennui was adept at discerning which statements, actions, beliefs, people, and practices were important to the goals she and Zophos established and which she could ignore. Tranquility. Harmony. Separation from the castle. The people in the Round Tower prided themselves in the conviction of their belief, but in actuality, apart from preferred affinity groups and routine, there was little to distinguish their beliefs from those of the people in the castle. When it came right down to it, the majority of humanity inside the Tower and outside it lived independently, for their own good, and by whatever standard seemed best to them. They gave no thought to Zophos, acknowledged the King only socially, and showed little deference to either.

"Let tomorrow take care of itself. Today let's eat, drink, and be merry," they said. "Live in the moment," and inside and outside the Round Tower, this is what transpired.

Zophos' reconstruction continued to flourish. Ennui's concerted efforts to move the Tower's attitude toward indifference continued unchecked. Peace and prosperity seemed to abound.

Balance-in-life and balance-of-power became key ingredients to peace, harmony, living together—to nearly everything—especially the visible assessment of stability and security. At a visceral level, balance was the key indicator used to ameliorate the conflict between the amorphous concepts of good and evil.

If Zophos is akin to the idea of evil, then the notion of the High King is akin to the idea of good, went the reasoning, especially when talking to younger people. Those who mused about such things were hired to teach on the subject. They lectured and wrote books and did research. They formed a collective and diagramed their ideas with what they called the yin-yang. The younger set loved it. It felt edgy and new and meaningful. They invested long hours, late into the night, discussing "what if," and "if, then." It was like double-entry bookkeeping for philosophers.

As their collective grew and enjoyed recognized status, they formed into an association, lobbied Ennui with their finds and preferences, and soon their diagram replaced most of the crests inside and outside the Round Tower. To the majority of people, the collective's initiative was neither here nor there.

Having achieved notoriety, the association next adopted the initiative of maintaining *feng shui* in their homes, offices, and clubs. For all the support they initially enjoyed from Ennui, she was repeatedly unavailable when pressed to meet on the *feng shui* project. It was as though she didn't care. But the association numbers were strong enough that they could proceed on their own initiative. And their influence grew. Those most committed to balance were considered *avant-garde*, admired, and were emulated.

To be considered tolerant was a highly-sought compliment, so much so that irrationality grew rampant as people compromised their sensibilities to rationalize their tolerance. Intolerance, it was believed, upset the balance of society—the overall *feng shui*—making it the major enemy of peace. As long as things seemed peaceful—which Zophos was ensuring to be the case—then the status quo was protected. Never mind if heart and history declared otherwise.

It was soon *en vogue* to renounce violence and repudiate with elaborate denials—even bordering on preposterous—any suggestion that war remained a reality. "Look for yourself," was the simplest and strongest argument floated over dinner tables and in coffee shops. All around the Round Tower life appeared tranquil and routine. Skirmishes were to be expected, and they did occur, but they were quickly quelled.

The history of the war was not denied outright. Neither was it taught or recounted. But the idea that it was still being waged was not lent much credence. War heroes were memorialized and then their stories neglected and their sacrifice discounted. That some would win and some would lose, the rationalization went, was part of competition and suitable for games, but was intolerable and soundly denied as part of life's routine.

Consequently, essentials to the health of the human psyche—passion, aspiration, courage, creativity, leadership, self-sacrifice, vision, heroism, tenacity, all of which are forged in the fires of conflict—starved like cur dogs in the alleys of men's souls.

A few people asserted that the tranquil scene around the Round Tower was in reality a deception. These few paid attention to their heart. For them, there was no escaping that the world was infected with insurrection. But it required courage to march against public opinion. It necessitated resolve to listen with the heart. To grow quiet and contemplative, to listen for the heart's desire, and then pursue its compulsion was a challenging quest not many recognized, few discussed, and fewer still pursued, especially when under duress by the culture inside and outside the Round Tower.

Zophos observed that those occupying the Round Tower took great pride in maintaining a polished appearance and noted that this could work to his advantage. So driven toward the perfection of their image were the inhabitants of the Round Tower, that they rejected and/or refused entry to those who returned from battle to tell of the ugliness of their fight. They smelled of smoke and death, which upset the peace. Their armor was stained with the dregs of survival, a clear challenge to the paragon of tolerance and the motto of, "live and let live." These warriors spoke of fear and confusion in battle. They reported of engaging in whatever tactic was necessary to be victorious. Their eyes and hearts were fierce. Their hands and swords were blemished with other's blood. Their stories were unsettling—some heroic, but not all.

These fighters were labeled intolerant and their tales resented because they burdened others to think about unpleasant things. They were considered suspect because they tarnished the polished appearance inside the Tower. This news brought a sinister smile to Zophos' face.

Gnarled Wood

No one would ever guess Ennui commanded a crack company of agents trained in special-forces warfare. She had large, dark eyes—almost black—set midst long lashes that gave her a lazy, inviting look. Her skin was a cocoa-olive color and devoid of flaw. Her black hair cascaded in long rivulets and she always wore it down. She coiffed herself perfectly, never hurried, rarely raised her voice, avoided contractions when she spoke, and eschewed complex sentences in order to mask her strategic and brilliant intellect.

Ennui was a role model held in high esteem within the Round Tower because of her unflappable tolerance, dispassion, and balance. She was trusted to provide wise guidance to the inhabitants of the Keep because she knew about life on the outside. Those inside the Tower believed she could guide the development of their values and opinions. They placed her on boards and committees and other places of prominence. They modeled their thoughts after hers: "Let's make another study, shall we?" "Don't worry about that. Let me think about it." "Let's table that until our next meeting." "Let's not do anything we'll regret tomorrow." "Since we don't have a consensus, maybe it's best if we wait." "Please. Calm down." "There's no need to be angry." "Let's all be nice." "It's better to say 'perhaps,' or 'maybe,' or 'we'll see' than to say, 'no.'" "We don't want to hurt anyone's feelings." "If we work harder, then we can all get what we want." "Be happy."

Ennui's attitude pervaded the atmosphere of the Round Tower. Her anger only flared if the peace was broken, the balance upset, or intolerance demonstrated. Whatever and whoever was the cause, Ennui's action was decisive, efficient, and expedient.

Ennui and her assistant, Letizia Pintaro, passed through the last portcullis and onto the narrow bridge connecting the Round Tower to the castle road. They traveled deliberately, speaking to people along the way. This was her routine, part of her strategy. Her consistency over time disarmed any alarm that her regular business took her into Gnarled Wood. As soon as they were past the castle grounds, they flipped their hoods up and covered their faces to conceal their identities. At the junction, they took the left fork, headed down the low road, and passed into the depths of Gnarled Wood.

The aide knocked and stepped into Zophos' office. "Ennui is here to see you, sir. As usual, right on schedule."

Zophos nodded, and motioned for the *aide-de-camp* to show Ennui into his office.

"What have you got?" Zophos demanded. Neither liked the other, but they shared respect.

"The inhabitants of the Round Tower are succumbing to apathy. Their will to endure, to focus, and to discipline their minds is rotting like a forgotten melon."

"And their opinion of the castle and the battle for their hearts?" Zophos asked.

"No clue, collectively. But still too soon to tell for certain. There are a few who do not subscribe to your deception of tranquility. But these are discounted by the majority."

"Good."

"Perhaps," Ennui said apathetically. "We are portraying those who remain unconvinced as troublesome, intolerant, not nice, and in some cases, dangerous to group wellbeing."

"Your thoughts on the timing of our next phase?"

Her answer was concise, "The time is right to launch."

Zophos leaned back in his chair and glared at Ennui. "Dismissed."

As she departed, he hollered after her, "Don't disappoint me."

As they had come, Ennui and her assistant returned. The guards in the first portcullis announced their entry, as did the guards in the subsequent chambers. Passage back into the Round Tower was routine.

Letizia returned to the office. Ennui deliberately meandered, greeting all she saw and appearing normal—just another day, another routine trip. As she encountered her agents within the enemy Keep, she greeted them, and shrugged her left shoulder. It was their sign to prepare for Zophos' next phase of attack.

The Castle area surrounding the Round Tower

Zophos issued a new set of orders covering diversionary squads, the Dark Army's appearance, delusionary tactics, his own role and appearance, and the objectives in his plan. Messengers delivered his orders at light speed via the airwaves.

Re. diversionary squads: Small bands of raiders shall be formed and attack periodically in order to recreate belief within the Round Tower that there is indeed a noble fight somewhere on behalf of the High King. These squads shall be comprised of poorly trained, weak troops. They are to attack only high-visibility targets in broad daylight. They are to do nothing that might cause the inhabitants of the Round Tower to think life in the castle or the Round Tower might be different than it appears, i.e. safe and tranquil. To ensure the diversionary squads do not reveal their fate ahead of time or during their slaughter for the cause, their tongues are to be cut out prior to the engagement. The squads shall be permitted to inflict an occasional casualty to build resentment through heartache and disturbance. Every effort shall then be made to blame the High King for not securing the peace.

Re. appearance: Nothing shall jeopardize the illusion of comfort created by Ennui. Facades of pleasure, beauty, peace, and self-realization are to be marketed and worn at all times by all troops and commanders stationed in Gnarled Wood within eyesight of the Round Tower. The High King has promised his followers tribulation, difficulty, misunderstanding, and self-denial. I, Zophos, will create an illusion of just the opposite.

Re. delusion: An illusion of light shall be created. Bluing will be buffed off of all armament, including but not limited to chains, tent stakes, tack, and kitchen utensils. Any metal worn, used, or carried by the Dark Army shall be scrubbed down to bare metal and polished to sheen. No tarnish will be tolerated. Fires shall blaze throughout the night. Shields, breastplates, etcetera shall be positioned to reflect light toward the Round Tower. During daylight hours troops are to stand at attention positioned to reflect sunlight from their armor toward the Tower. Black crests are to be removed. The Dark Army shall appear to be the Army of Light until further notice.

Zophos' orders went on to indicate that he would disguise himself as a cabinet-level minister in the Kingdom of Light. He would ride a white stallion, wield a sharp sword, and quote phrases attributed to the High King. Upon occasion, he would turn his sword on his own diversionary squads as they approach the Round Tower. These would die martyr's deaths while he appeared a defender of the Tower.

Deception is imperative! Under no circumstance will the illusion of light or its disguise be jeopardized.

Re. objectives: In time, driven by the immediate and shortsighted wish for the peace of heaven upon earth, the Round Tower will become irrelevant. The inhabitants of the Round Tower will simply open the gates of the Keep and amalgamate themselves into the placid scenes of light created in the castle. By the time its inhabitants realize the Dark Army is disguised with an illusion of light, it will be too late! Their hearts will be weak, their minds ill-prepared, and their souls ill-equipped to defend against the onslaught. Person-by-person, group-by-group, they will be led like sheep to slaughter in Gnarled Wood. As they face their destruction they will suffer under the misconception that it was the High King who failed them. In their disillusionment, suffering pitiable fates in Gnarled Wood, they will with their consequential denial of the King undermine the legitimacy of his reign.

Zophos' orders concluded by stating, "With the King's legitimacy in doubt by a preponderance of the Round Tower's subjects, I shall ascend the King's throne and assume power given the people's vote of no confidence in the High King."

After Zophos completed issuing his orders, he sat back and reflected as the next group of aides entered his headquarters. He joked to his assistants that his greatest concern was getting fat gorging on prisoners taken from the Round Tower. As he laughed, Zophos stripped off his outer garments and put on fresh, white clothing and polished armor. He would appear to be again what he once was, clothed in light.

Outside, a raging stallion waited. A white stallion.

CHAPTER 12

In the Light

During a rest stop on the path out of the pit, Vassar said to Hank, "I brought this for you to put around your waist." He held a scarlet sash for all to admire. "It's a reminder. As you know, I'm big on reminders. I think they do wonders for focus, and given all you've been through, and all that lies ahead, you need all the focus you can muster."

"Thanks, Vassar. I like it. What's it supposed to remind me about again?"

"That you're redeemed, ransomed by the High King."

"I thought that was what my breastplate signified."

"It does, but it's much more than that. You're also forgiven, chosen, honored, and valued as special by the High King. But specifically this sash is to assist you in waging war against Jester's accusations that you're condemned and that Father doesn't care about you. These are two weaknesses you must guard against."

"You can say that again," Hank agreed.

"What lies before us is not easy," Vassar continued. "It's a treacherous, difficult journey. We'll encounter many foes and suffer great heartache."

"That's encouraging," Hank deadpanned.

Vassar offered a slight smile, then continued, "All of this is in addition to the struggles you created for yourself."

"Significance…."

"…Significance, Pity, Competence."

"Yeah, and this pain." For a man who had denied responsibility, Hank's ownership of his actions and their consequence was real progress.

"So you need a reminder. This scarlet sash is visible, it's striking, and believe me, it was expensive!"

Magician stepped up behind Hank and helped him tie the sash around his waist.

"Remember that you were once lost, but now you're found. You were distant, but now you've been brought near. You were destitute, but now you're an heir. You were alone, but now you're comforted. You were desperate, but now you're confident. You were insecure, but now you're secure. You were weak, but now you're strong. You were worthless, but now you're invaluable. You were your own, but now you belong to the High King. You were cursed, but now you're blessed. You were insignificant, but now you're significant. As a matter of fact, you were dead and now you're alive. You're a reclaimed man with a noble heritage, a high calling, and a heart in tune with the desires of the High King and his Kingdom."

Faith stood up from their break and stretched; his signal that it was time to get moving. Vassar said, "Love, if you'll go before Hank, and Hope, if you'll come after him, I'll lead the way. Faith, you're with me. Magician…"

"…I'll bring up the rear," Magician anticipated.

"Good," Vassar said. "We've got a climb in front of us, but tonight we should camp outside the pit."

"I'm for that," Hank said, moving forward in the light.

They hadn't walked more than half an hour when they reached a fork in the trail. The trail to the left matched the one they had been on. The trail to the right narrowed, became obscure—marked only by cairns—and was noticeably difficult. Vassar waited for the others to form up, and turned right.

"Are you sure that's the right way?" Hank asked.

"Yes."

"But this other trail looks better."

"I know, it is, and it's the most direct path out of the pit."

"So why not go that way?" Hank inquired.

"I'm going to take us via the narrow way. It's tough going, and it will test us, but I've been this way before."

"Just for the heck of it?" Hank wanted to know.

"No. Zophos has sabotaged the wide path. You're ready for a fight, but you're not ready for a fight like the one that lies down that path. In time you will be, but not yet."

The climb out of the pit was arduous and steep. Hank's thighs burned. His unhappy hip complained to his back and his knees, but he kept forging ahead, willing his body to follow his heart's desire.

Hank followed Love's footsteps. He learned right away that picking his own climbing line resulted in a slip and a clattering cascade of scree. But Love's steps were solid and graceful.

Hank was thrilled that each time he paused and looked back from the light ahead into the pit behind all he could see was graduated gray-to-black. The faces watching him, expecting from him, were dim. But even though he was focusing on walking in the light, he could still smell and feel the stale, humid pit.

He was anxious to escape and became the morale of the little platoon urging them back to the trail after their respites. His heart's desire led the group.

Hank stopped. Sniffed. Tipped his face left and right. Felt it and smelled it again, for the first time since passing behind the waterfall from Montana: fresh, cold air. "Smell that, Hope? Feel it?" he said. "Come on, we're close," Hank encouraged, not waiting on Hope to reply.

The group emerged through a narrow fissure into an old-growth forest about mid afternoon; light snow was falling. While he had been walking in the light since his momentous decision to step off his mat, Hank was finally out of the pit, breathing fresh air.

Love, Hank, and Hope waited together while Vassar, Magician, and Faith scouted the area. Half an hour later, they were satisfied they were safe.

That evening the band of brothers sat around their fire and talked about the adventure they had shared in the pit. Hank was gratified, not just to be out of the pit, but that he was part of the celebration, a contributor to the story of the light, and was a redeemed man surrounded by warriors in the service of the High King.

Their story connected them, bonded them. They knew each other's strengths and calling. With these mighty warriors in his company, Hank's weakness and doubt were guarded from any illusion of independence or self-sufficiency. He was part of a unit, a team, and the story told around the fire promoted their tie and reinforced their loyalty to the King as warriors for the Kingdom of Light.

The dancing fire calmed to a waltz of embers. "All my life I've longed for the light, but didn't recognize it," Hank said. "I've ignored it and fled from it. Tried to compromise it. Now, here I am. Bathed in it. Surrounded by it. Camped with men who have lived in the light for years. But I still don't understand it."

"The light's the truth about your life," Love said. "It's how the King sees things, how he does things. His perspective can't ever be nullified."

"Not to be argumentative," Hank said, "but I ignored the light. I didn't live according to the truth."

"True enough," acknowledged Love, "but that doesn't change the fact of the light. You can cover your eyes and claim the sun isn't shining, but that doesn't change the fact that it shines, only that you are behaving irrationally. Denial may change your behavior, but it doesn't change the light."

Magician, who was sitting cross-legged next to Hank, reached inside his breastplate and pulled out a scarlet cravat made of the same material as Hank's sash. Like Hank's sash, Magician's cravat was reminiscent of redemption, but when Magician pulled this cravat from around his neck his sorcery was astounding.

Through Magician's power, Hank understood. "So the light is that I truly am the King's son, just like you, Vassar."

Vassar smiled, "Just like me, Hank."

"But even though I believed that my life was all about me, and rode that belief all the way to the pit, it didn't diminish the light?"

"Nope," said Magician. "Remember, the King came to the pit himself to rescue you."

"He did indeed," Hank concurred, touching his scarlet sash and recalling his redemption. "He came and got me, just like he did for you, huh Vassar?"

"Just like he did for me, Hank."

"I don't want to return to that dark place," Hank said. "I'm tired of doing things my way. My heart desires to be where the High King is, living in the light, headed toward wherever he's going, and hanging out with you guys."

Hope, who had been quiet, said, "If you'll think about it, your brother is the light personified, the embodiment of the King. While you were stuck on high center, sitting on your mat in the pit listening to Jester yak, Vassar was right beside you, telling you what your Father thinks of you, and showing you your Father's heart."

Faith poked the fire with a stick. Hope resumed his staring. Magician retied the scarlet cravat around his neck and stuffed it into his breastplate.

Hank glanced at Vassar through the fire and rearranged what he knew of his brother based on the things Hope said. He liked his brother, liked fishing with him, trekking the woods with him, and enjoyed going to the high school football games with him on Friday nights back home in Texas. He'd never thought about doing those things and walking in the light simultaneously.

He tested the character of Vassar that Hope introduced against the person he knew and liked. He was relieved to discover he was still the same old Vassar, just more likable.

Faith went to sleep with the poker in his hand. Everyone assumed that meant he planned to tend the fire through the night. Fatigue wooed each of them into the woolen warmth of their cloaks. The snow stopped and the woods held them and their conversation in confidence.

Hank awoke to the smell of breakfast. Performing these honors was none other than the High King.

When he recognized who was in camp, he scrambled to his feet. His clamoring startled the others awake, ready to defend themselves. When they saw the King, they gathered around him, each giving and receiving a hug.

Hank held back. He had not seen the King face-to-face since his degrading display of arrogance in the dungeon. The memory flashed across his mind: Naked, his disgusting "D" still an infected scab on his chest, the stench of Pity on his skin, ...*and I dared raise my chin to him,* Hank recalled. *I set my jaw. I was defiant. He was gracious. I was defensive. Audacious. He listened and cried, more for my suffering than the wounds I inflicted on him. He was vulnerable. I acted as though I was entitled—that he owed me.*

A great deal had changed since that awful encounter—for the good. Hank knew he was not the same man. *Had it not been for Competence's attack and this unsparing pain, I'd still be crawling like a chameleon on the floor of the pit.* It felt odd to be thankful for his affliction.

Pain had hardened him—overly—and his confidence became brittle. When the stuff of life bombarded him it shattered his bondage to self-reliance and set his captive heart free to build trust. Pain rescued his soul by unshackling him from the burden of expectation and giving him permission to carry the bare essentials. Pain had proven to be a demanding coach, but pain had also become an honest and reliable mentor.

Hank braced for what had to be coming. His failures were stacked like cordwood. *I'll do the only reasonable thing,* he decided. *I'll surrender my sword and give him back the dagger. Then I'll just leave. Do I go back to the pit? That's where I belong. It's what I deserve.* Hank's mind raced, examining his options. *Got to think. Come on, Hank. I've got to get this right, got to behave. Maybe I could slip away. Heck, who am I kidding? They'll see me. Maybe if I kneel—no, grovel—on my belly—then, he'll....*

Lost in his thoughts—failing to recognize they were more of Jester's condemnations—Hank jolted into the present. The High King was standing in front of him. Hank's knees felt weak, his stomach queasy. Unlike in the pit where he darted his eyes around the dungeon in defiance, he stared into the King's eyes.

The King's eyes reddened and brimmed with tears. He reached out and held Hank by his shoulders. He focused on first his left eye and then his right. "Son, I have all the words of all the languages in all the world at my disposal, but words escape me. I can't tell you how proud I am of you."

Hank's knees buckled. He fell face forward against his Father's chest and the High King wrapped his arms around him. Hank expected to fall, but the King held him.

In that magic moment, far from where he had once been, Hank sensed the bond between his heart and the heart of his Father. For the first time in a long time—if ever—Hank recognized his Father's love. The King's light cut like a torch through Hank's steely allegations of favoritism, hardness, indifference, ruthless expectations, provisional acceptance, and disapproval. It was as though the King invited Hank into the sanctuary of his heart for a look around. Expecting the condemnation Jester spoke about and that he knew he deserved, he found instead a place prepared for him in his Father's heart.

It was a long time before the High King spoke. He was relishing the moment. In fact, he held Hank so long that Faith and Hope tended to breakfast.

Pressing his face against the right side of Hank's neck, the High King reiterated to his younger son the famous words spoken publicly to Vassar. "Hank, you are my much-loved son. I couldn't be more pleased with you than I am today." Then, motioning to Vassar, the King put his arms around both of his sons, kissed them each on the forehead, and blessed them for the joy they brought to his heart.

Breakfast was like any breakfast eaten on a cold morning, outside, around a fire. Steam rose from the oats and shrouded their faces in fog. There was no conversation—oats are no good cold. They also enjoyed smoked fish and dried fruit and more coffee, except for Faith, who was enjoying tea prepared just the way he liked it. The King hadn't missed a beat. It would have been easier for the King to serve either coffee or tea, but he wanted each to know their value in his life. As breakfast tapered off, conversation resumed.

Then as quickly as he had appeared, the King was gone—and the dirty dishes with him—but his light remained; brighter than Hank remembered. They soon realized that not only did he leave them packages of leftovers for their morning journey, he filled their packs with ample provisions for the road ahead.

The Round Tower

"Army of Light Prevails," read the bold headline in the *Round Tower Tribune*. The article began, "Prevailing against formidable odds, the Army of Light was victorious and once again occupies the castle and Gnarled Wood." This seemed the case. In all directions—even at night—the light of the army could be seen.

"The Red Dragon's been defeated," the rumor mill declared. And it appeared true. No one had heard his roar, been scorched alive, or consumed lately. "What other explanation can there be? He must have been defeated. It's the only rational conclusion," the experts asserted during Round Tower forums.

There were others, like those promoting yin-yang and *feng shui*—fancying themselves brighter and more rational than the rest—who asserted that the Red Dragon was a figment of the imagination, nothing more than a delusion. Most tolerated this notion whether they agreed or not; no one wanted to be dogmatic or condescending. That wouldn't be nice. The important thing was that regardless of what one believed about the Dragon, peace was apparent, and on those infrequent occasions when conflict arose, it was dealt with right away.

Someone—no one knew who—had given an extraordinary Ambassador command of the castle. He was frequently seen—at all hours—and was ruthless toward troublemakers. "He's in firm control," was the Keep's consensus. "It can be observed from the Tower windows," they said.

Single-handedly he destroyed attackers. His power grew in the minds of those in the Round Tower by the day. Screaming insults at his foes while quoting the High King, he slayed the dark raiders without mercy, hacked them to pieces, and then trampled upon them with his white steed. Clearly, the dark forces could not stand before his indignant anger. Many in the Tower consoled themselves with these reports.

Some people in the Round Tower told personal stories of encountering marauding gangs only to see the Ambassador, mounted upon a raging animal and clothed in white and light, come to their defense. To be rescued was wonderful, but to be rescued by the Ambassador was extraordinary. These people enjoyed celebrated status in the Tower. Stories of the Ambassador's deliverance circulated and his reputation spread throughout the Round Tower.

Of course, this was all Ennui's doing as she and her agents promoted apathy—as peace—throughout the Tower. Her power grew, but no one noticed or seemed to care.

It was only a matter of time before word passed within the Round Tower that posting guards was not necessary except for ceremonial occasions and public relations events. No one knew the origin of this initiative, but it did make sense in light of the peace.

One of Ennui's agents with a remarkable reputation in the Round Tower suggested they should open the Tower gates now that peace prevailed. His rationale was clear—and cost-efficient—and was adopted by those considering themselves forward thinking. "The army has conquered the Dragon, our troops occupy the castle once again, and peace prevails," went their reasoning. "We are safe—anyone can look from the Tower and see that!" they said, usually with a tone of condescension. "We should open our gates to everyone," they contended magnanimously. "Accommodate. This is what the High King would do," the persons of influence and persuasion asserted with piety. "Peace must be nurtured with understanding," some counseled high-mindedly. "Now is the time! If not now, then when?" It was like a political rally building momentum. "We must work together to maintain peace, tolerate the ignoble, reach out to those less fortunate, and separate ourselves from the barbarism of conflict. We've known war. Let us embrace peace." The agents' speeches were flowery, pithy, and appealing.

But people from the other side of the argument, administrative types, played upon fear and counseled that caution should be exercised. "What if we open our gates and our provisions are compromised, or unwanted persons come in, or our routine is upset?" There were a hundred "what if's" that fueled fear and promoted their agenda of caution.

After much wrangling, the majority was persuaded based upon fear for their own safety that the Round Tower's entrance should remain closed and protected except on market days: Monday, Wednesday, Friday, Saturday, every second Tuesday, and on Sunday. After all, it had been Round Tower policy for as long as anyone could remember to keep the portcullises down.

Ennui could not have cared less about these debates and discussions. The wrangling among those in the Round Tower always found unity in a celebration of the general peace. Many of the debates within the Keep were tabled; no action taken, no conclusion drawn. "Why does it matter if we delay this decision?" was the question that brought a discussion to a shoulder-shrugging conclusion.

Ennui watched with pleasure as apathy secured a stronghold. "Let them call it whatever they want," she said to Letizia. "Peace, tolerance, apathy. I do not care, just so long as they are complacent. If they are clueless, it will not matter if the gates are open or closed. It is a moot point."

"Yes, ma'am," Letizia said.

Ennui's plan was working.

Few noticed the subtle clues that all was not as it appeared outside the Round Tower. But those few discussed their observations over coffee cups and after work. "Why are the troops in the castle always polishing their armor?" ran one line of curiosity.

"Must be something their commander requires. You know, a discipline thing."

"But our armor doesn't tarnish. Why does theirs?"

"Who knows? Might have something to do with being outdoors."

"Yeah. That's probably it," they all agreed.

This sort of postulating went on-and-on. None but "the radicals"— as they were termed—thought for a moment that all the polishing was to cover a ruse.

"Rumor has it that the Ambassador is quick to punish anyone with tarnished armor," someone noted. The Ambassador's actions reinforced the sense of security in the Keep.

The regal posture of the Ambassador on his white horse was pointed to as an encouraging sign that all was well. There were a few—but only a few—who questioned his mixture of blessing and cursing. He frequently quoted the High King, but his quotes were often taken out of context or mixed with his own opinions. While he claimed to speak for the King, it alarmed some that his messages rarely—if ever— acknowledged the honor due the High King.

Ennui and her agents pointed out these discrepancies inside the Round Tower and used them to build a tolerance for the modification of beliefs. It's easier to fix another's shortcoming than your own. "For the finger you point, there are three pointing back at you," they preached.

It was working. All but the most cynical elevated the Ambassador to an almost mythological status.

The inhabitants of the Round Tower demonstrated no notable concern that their membership statistics were inconsistent. Membership growth was reported but not analyzed. Ennui manipulated the numbers in a shell game of deception. In reality, much of the apparent growth within the Round Tower was attributable to inhabitants moving from one area to another within the Keep. It wasn't true growth.

Reports of people leaving the Keep were associated with conflicting beliefs. Most of those who left were inconsistent in their commitment to the Round Tower's standards. They did not get involved and saw no point to the initiations, promotions, or programs in the Keep. They were indifferent to the Tower's standard and lifestyle. When they left, there was a general feeling of good riddance, and they were not missed.

Other losses were rarely reported. While striving for peace, ongoing costs are to be expected, said those who gave this any consideration at all. Besides, few knew anyone personally who had been lost in battle. Most felt that hearing the information alone was sufficient to show they cared.

And so life went on inside the Tower. Ennui told them they were courageous and engaged in noble endeavors. She and her agents put glorious posters on the walls and the people projected themselves into the printed glory.

Peace was apparent, but it was neither lasting nor absolute. There was always conflict somewhere. More often than not, when the skirmish was examined, the inhabitants of the Round Tower found that it involved one of the radicals who believed all was not as it appeared outside the Keep. They believed that peace in the castle was an illusion and that the Round Tower had been lulled into apathy.

The leaders in the Round Tower insisted the occasional lack of tranquility was not as these radicals asserted. Accusations against Ennui were dismissed as impudent character assassination against an innocent public servant; nothing more than the ranting allegations of radical minds.

In their defense, the radicals pointed out inconsistencies between the High King's known point of view and that stated by the Ambassador. But the leadership had seen it all before and dismissed their arguments. People on the fringe become vigorous zealots in any field, even in service to the Kingdom and the High King. "Moderation in all things is a much safer tack," asserted the leaders in the Round Tower.

The Keep's leadership was committed to tolerance, unless people like these radicals behaved intolerantly by not tolerating others. Then, they meted out unflinching justice to preserve the peace for the good of all. Tolerance had enemies that could not be tolerated. Their preferred method of dealing with disruptors was to isolate them within the Round Tower. This way, they could exact retribution and still appear tolerant. But if given the opportunity—any opportunity—they were banished from the Tower altogether.

When one of these radical sorts suffered a wound in battle, or revealed a vulnerability, they were taken away and dispatched by the ceremonial guard, some of whom were Ennui's agents. Their remains were thrown into the castle yard for others to clean up. While it was unpleasant duty, it was necessary for the cause of peace, the preservation of the Tower's traditions, and to maintain the standard of tranquility.

Gnarled Wood

"The ingenuity of our plan is apparent, Zophos," said Ennui.

"*My* plan," Zophos corrected her. "Continue."

Ennui shrugged. "The Round Tower is disintegrating from the inside. If guards are posted at all, they are slow and fat."

Zophos shook his head in amazement, pondering, *What's the King thinking? No guards that matter? No offensive? Why doesn't he do something about this?* "Go on."

"You have no doubt noticed the ingress and egress of a number of people dressed in black. These are my agents. The Round Tower considers them advisors. Believe it or not, they pay my agents to do the work they do not want to do. They even send my agents out to fight on their behalf."

"And?" Zophos asked.

"I send them out. They rough each other up a bit, and return with tales of victory for the High King's forces."

Zophos laughed and shook his head. "I told you so."

Zophos and Ennui agreed the day was approaching when the Round Tower would be irrelevant. "This is already the case in parts of the Tower," Ennui said.

Zophos smirked at his good fortune. "Any sign that the Army of Light is preparing for battle?"

Ennui thought. "Not that I can tell. I suppose it is possible that I have missed something, but I do not see how. I have agents throughout the Round Tower."

"Are they being bought off?" Zophos asked.

"I doubt it. Every agent is redundant. They might buy off one or two, but not three or four—sometimes more—depending on the area they have infiltrated."

Ennui reported about the meetings inside the Round Tower— endless meetings, both in duration and number. "They have committees on committees," she said. "Each has a precious *raison d'être* with just enough power to intoxicate the members with their importance. A few do have important mandates, but most perpetuate pettiness in the name of either tolerance or some ideal they claim is important."

"But they're not important?" Zophos inquired.

"No. Not that I can tell. Every time I walk past some obese sentry guarding a meaningless passage I think, There is a picture of the Round Tower."

Zophos leaned back. "So, they're committed to peace. Tolerance is preeminent. And they pride themselves in their ideals, but their ideals are irrelevant."

"Pretty much," Ennui confirmed.

"Alright, then. Your conclusion."

"I suspect the Round Tower will collapse under its own weight—its politics and culture, its indifference, and its apathy. It will happen just like I told you it would."

CHAPTER 13

The Old-Growth Forest, dappled in Light

Their bellies full with the King's breakfast and their hearts replete with his blessing, Hank and the other knights assisted each other with their armor. Breastplates were buckled. Tunics tucked out of the way. Swords and scabbards and daggers fastened at their sides. Helmets and shields fitted for battle.

As a final act of preparation, Magician assisted Hank in tying the scarlet sash around his waist. Giving little thought to whether or not it was appropriate for a warrior to weep, Hank let his tears run down his face.

They kept a quick pace and vigilant eye. None doubted that the enemy was contemplating how to regain his advantage. Hank's decision to step from his mat into the King's light and take the offensive in his life, had no doubt scuttled the status quo. With each step Hank seized territory that was once the domain of darkness but now belonged to the Kingdom of Light.

The six knights assumed a two-three-one configuration determining this to be their best defensive configuration given the narrow way. Hope and Faith took the point, acting as the group's ears and eyes. Love brought up the rear, or drag. Vassar, Hank, and Magician trekked in the middle, close together. They were the power of the small team, and the core around which all would form in the event of an altercation.

The point of attack was not ideal in Jester's mind, but it was the only feasible location down wind. Given the rancid odor of his beasts, the band of knights were sure to smell the ambush before it was upon them. But with the stiff wind, Jester believed his plan had a chance.

Faith and Hope stopped and scanned ahead and above. Still watching behind them, Love backed forward to join Magician. No birds flew. None sat in the scrubby trees along the trail or above them. Their vision was blocked by house-size boulders and the twists in the trail. To make matters even worse, the wind was at their back.

Hank whispered to Magician, "Something's wrong. Fight through me. Live through me."

Faith took a half-step forward, heard a clawing in the scree to his left, and retreated just as the party was pounced upon by savage ogres. The beasts leaped from the boulders and shrubs with yelps and shrieks. They were like catamounts; nimble, muscular, lean, but covered with wiry hair like a hog's. Their faces sported powerful jaws and exaggerated canines. They swiped at the band of knights with slashing claws capable of slicing a man in two, certainly of severing an arm or leg.

Backed together and wielding their swords with disciplined abandon on multiple targets, the knights fought a gallant defense. Determination to survive and the careful training he had endured in the pit served Hank well. He fought with confident skill, and his sword was effective.

The ambush escalated, and it appeared the Princes were overrun, but attacking them was akin to attacking a bowling ball with Porcupine quills. Back-to-back, shoulder-to-shoulder, each guarding the other's vulnerability, the knights held their ground, fended off the initial attack, and dulled the momentum of the ambush. Then they took the offensive. With each thrust or hack the life of a beast exploded and spattered the knights from head-to-toe. Bodies piled at their feet, and still they came charging wildly toward the slaughter.

Even as his losses mounted, Jester sent more of his beasts to their deaths against the six. A moral victory was as precious to him as a triumph. The loss of a relative few from Zophos' legions was inconsequential if it positioned him for the larger battle yet to be prosecuted.

The ambush disintegrated as Jester's beasts were decimated. The survivors scattered. Hank and the others killed the wounded and straggling.

Smeared with the residue of the pitched battle, Hank looked at the fallen. He had exacted heavy losses upon his nemesis, Jester, and he had done so in spite of his pain. He fought alongside trusted warriors. He had depended on Magician, trusted him, and his trust had worked. But most important, he had fought alongside Vassar and now stood victorious.

Hank thrust his arms into the air! "Send us more of your beasts, Zophos," Hank yelled, his challenge echoing off the canyon walls.

Hank stepped from the perimeter of the fallen assailants and taunted the enemy again. He walked further into the surrounding shrubs and rocks searching for survivors, killing those he found. He hurried, compelled to not let any escape. The farther he went, the more aggressive he became. Stabbing a struggling beast wasn't enough. After felling it, he hacked until its head was severed—and in the process his sword was dulled from hitting the dirt and rocks. His confidence rose. He could feel his strength surging. As he went he proclaimed victory for the Kingdom of Light.

The Prince had taken Jester's bait. He emerged into a small clearing surrounded by rocks and shrubs, perfect hiding places for Jester's reserves.

The beasts leaped upon Hank. He fought with courage, whirling, and twisting to fend off the enemy attacking from all sides. He called for assistance, but had wandered too far from his band of brothers. He was isolated by his overconfidence, but was holding his own. He heard Jester's encouragement, "I can do this. I'm winning. Victory is mine."

Hank swung right, slicing a beast's head like a cantaloupe. He dodged a swipe that tore his sleeve, but then reacted against the off-balance beast, thrusting his sword into its chest. The blade punctured lungs and life, but wedged in its rib cage. Hank abandoned his stuck blade and drew his dagger.

Twirling to his left, he thrust his dagger through the open mouth of an attacking monster. He jerked his arm and dagger free, but in his whirling dervish of self-defense and misplaced confidence, Hank wrenched Competence's old wounds. The scar tissue in his hip tore. He fell in a searing tear of sinew and adhesions. The tip of Competence's dagger stabbed his nerves as though it was the first time. Hank collapsed like wheat after a sickle.

In a flash, he went from offense to defense. He rolled in the gore of the fallen, caked with the mud of their blood and his sweat. His strength failed and the battle turned against him. He was struck in the head from behind. Like a punch-drunk boxer who drops his guard, Hank took a crossing blow to his face that lacerated him from his right-eye socket to his ear. He struggled to straighten his helmet and clear his vision, but was hit again. He cursed at being left to fight and die alone. He felt the powerful, all-too-familiar wave of pity and distrust boil to the surface. It tasted metallically bitter, like blood.

Hank was hit again—hard. The blow spun him around and left him flat on his back. A beast pounced on him, knocking the breath out of him. He heard Jester scream his tempting accusation against the King, "Why have you abandoned me again after all I've done for you?" With this his final thought, Hank's world faded from dark to black.

Gnarled Wood

A cadre of aides rotated in and out of Zophos' office updating troop positions and battle lines on maps spread across his conference table and hung along the walls. His senior staff fielded, screened, and organized the myriad messages that arrived around the clock. Zophos wanted an update at the top of each hour, but if something noteworthy transpired, he wanted to be interrupted. If he was masquerading as the Ambassador, a messenger was to be sent on the airwaves.

Zophos had learned to ignore the hive of activity in front of his desk. Inactivity was a greater distraction. For an army that never rested—by edict—a dearth of reporting meant either no news or bad news. During a campaign of the magnitude surrounding the Round Tower, no buzz in headquarters portended bad things.

Clicking his heels in front of Zophos' desk, the aide bowed slightly, "Sir," and handed the abbreviated message to his commander. Zophos looked first at the signature and then began from the top:

Ambushed Princes.
Prince Henry isolated. Abandoned. Down.
Holding position,
Jester

Zophos screamed a string of expletives while penning a terse appendage to Jester's note:

Jester—

No one holds their position in my army. Seize the momentum. Show no mercy.
I won't.

Z—

Zophos signed his distinguishing "Z", sealed the note, and handed it to the waiting aide, "Deliver this to Jester at once."

Zophos stood and flung off his dark cape. "Get my stallion!" he scathed.

The Narrow Place

Cold caromed off the walls of his mind. He ignored it. There it was again. The icy intrusion demanded his attention. And again. Hank tried to open his eyes, but although his brain commanded both to comply, just the left obeyed. His right eye was swollen and sealed shut with the congealing blood from his wound.

A fuzzy, lopsided picture appeared. Daylight was an affliction. He closed his eye. The cold came again. Through the fog, Hank made out the form of Magician hovering over him. More cold. Demanding. He blinked away enough of the haze to realize that Magician was swabbing his face with the scarlet cravat from around his neck.

"Am I alive or dead?"

"Oh, you're very much alive." Magician pressed harder.

Hank winced.

"See?"

"Uh, huh."

"You wouldn't be talking to me if you were dead, would you now?"

"Where am I?"

"You're in the light."

"How'd I get here?"

"You marched here, with the rest of us."

Hank's mind began to clear. "I thought I died."

"You would have," Magician said, continuing to clean Hank's cut.

The ordeal came back to him. "What happened?"

"Your brother happened. Near as I can tell, one of those animals was dragging you away by the neck. When I came up a moment later, you were lying in a heap with its severed head on your chest. Its mouth still around your neck. Vassar had his sword in one hand, dagger in the other. It was something to see. Never seen anybody do what he does, especially when he's angry."

Hank reached up and touched his face. "Wow. That hurts."

"Yep. Bet so," Magician said, as he continued. "Faith, Hope, and Love have secured the area. Vassar's off thinking, I believe. I carried you here. It's safer. Gotta get you cleaned up."

"I was doing so well. Beasts dead at my feet, piling higher. Next thing I know, I'm looking at you."

"You made two mistakes."

Silence.

"You listening to me?"

"Yeah. But I can't see very well."

"You don't need to see to listen."

"I know. I was just saying I can't see."

"You sure you can hear okay? You took quite a shot to the head."

"I'm listening," Hank mumbled.

"Tell me your Mother's maiden name and give me your date of birth."

"Magician, I'm listening! Tell me what happened."

"First, you got off by yourself. Warriors don't let themselves get isolated. Big mistake. Second, you got over confident. That's also a big mistake."

"Over confident? I didn't know you could do that," Hank said.

"Uh, huh. You were drinking the success of your early battles. Started feeling strong. Confident. An unguarded strength is a tremendous weakness, Hank. There's nothing more vulnerable than an isolated warrior or more dangerous than an unguarded strength."

"Say that again."

"I knew you were still fogged over in there. I've wasted all this breath trying to explain to you."

"Magician, I heard you. I just want to be certain I heard you right. I don't want to have to repeat this lesson."

"No. Doubt you do. You're wise, like your brother. I said, there's nothing more vulnerable than an isolated warrior or more dangerous than an unguarded strength."

"Got it. Thanks."

"Oh, sure. No problem."

"So, how's it look? Am I gonna be okay?"

Magician nodded and continued swabbing the laceration.

The cut looked worse than it was. The claw had just missed catching his eye socket, in which case it would have torn his head apart. But as it was, his face would bear a scar, but he would be none the worse for wear in a few days.

Hank closed his left eye. "Magician, I failed. My chest hurts."

"Maybe it's because that beast landed on you," Magician said.

"Maybe, but I think it hurts because I believed Jester again. That's the last thing I remember—his words. I cursed Father for abandoning me. Cursed you too, and Vassar, and all the while it was my mistake. Same old entitlement. Same self-reliance. You know the drill. Believing it's up to me, I keep making the same mistakes, Magician—in the dark, in the pit, in the light, in the fight. Doesn't matter. Hell! You'd think I could at least make a new mistake."

Magician grunted to acknowledge Hank's confession.

Hank didn't say anything more; just lay still while Magician tended to him. After a moment of silence, Magician rubbed the wound too hard. Hank reacted with a jerk. Magician pulled away—just far enough so Hank could focus on the scarlet cravat. The reminder of redemption in Magician's hand was stained with the blood of Hank's failure. Once again, he was reminded: *I am redeemed.*

Hank smiled, closed his left eye, and let the comfort from Magician's sorcery work its way into his heart. He thought of the High King, thought of the scarlet sash around his waist—given to him by Vassar—and in his heart he focused on the indelible place of prominence he occupied in his Father's heart.

Hank opened his eye. Ten eyes were looking down at him. "Brother! I swear! I can't find you. Come looking, and here you are with a wild beast hanging around your neck. You did some mighty fine damage to them."

"Yeah, but look at me."

Vassar didn't acknowledge Hank's pity. "Here you go. I made this for you." Vassar bent down and fastened a necklace around Hank's neck. It was made of claws from the beasts he had killed.

While Hank was thinking about this new adornment, Hope and Love put their arms under Hank and stood him up, stabilizing him while his dizziness cleared.

"Wow, guys! I'm in trouble," declared Hank. "I can't see." And about that time, the stiffness in his back and hips fired up spasms from lying on the ground. "My old wounds are heating up something terrible. I should just stay here for awhile. Go on without me. I'll catch up."

Hank started to sit down, but Love and Hope held him up. "Magician," said Vassar, "would you please take my brother's sash from around his waist and tie it around his face so he can see it better?"

Love took a more direct approach. "Look, Hank. It's not possible for us to go on without you. Even if you'd been chewed into a thousand pieces, we couldn't return to the High King without you. No one's left behind! Ever."

"And that includes you!" Hope added.

"So here's the deal," Love said. "I can carry you, or you can walk. Your call."

Knowing he could squander his suffering with pity, or seize the moment to his advantage, Hank made a decision—deep in his heart. "Well, now that you've explained it to me, I understand. Why didn't you say so earlier?"

With his good eye, Hank stared at Love, taunting him. Love raised an eyebrow—the closest he would come to flinching. Hank had rebounded, thanks to his friends. He slung his left arm over Love's shoulder and his right arm over Hope's. "Let's go!"

The Round Tower

"Radicals. They disturb the status quo," Ennui said to her assistant, Ms. Pintaro.

"Yes, ma'am," Letizia acknowledged.

"Hmm. Well, enough of this. Contact Captain Nekros. See to it yourself. Tell him Zealot is making our work in the Tower difficult. Tell him he is disturbing the peace. He has been holding covert meetings. Insurrection. Insertion."

Letizia waited to see if there was anything further from Ennui. When her boss turned her head to other matters, Letizia left for Captain Nekros' office.

Working under cover, Zealot had infiltrated and networked among Zophos' troops searching for inhabitants of the castle dissatisfied with the enemy's occupation. After building a relationship with them, Zealot would win their confidence, and then lead them into a conversion of loyalty from Zophos to the High King. Given their less-than-stellar past, these proselytes were not always welcomed in the Round Tower.

Most of those whom Zealot brought into the Keep were not versed in its culture. They were passionate, like children waking up to a summer day of possibility. The Tower was staid. They used the wrong lingo—some even said curse words—did not dress correctly, ate and drank in the wrong places, told inappropriate stories and jokes, and talked at the wrong time during meetings. They asked odd questions and wondered about inconsistencies long-term residents of the Keep knew to ignore. Converts created chaos in the routine.

While tolerance was a noble ideal, it did not go far beyond convenience. Since proselytes like those Zealot brought into the Tower disturbed the peace, they were shunned from the Round Tower's society. Many returned to the castle and their old way of life. Some stayed in the Keep, but suffered a long, torturous initiation period into the Tower's clubs and cliques. By the time they were accepted, most were burdened into submission under the Keep's onerous expectations. Once accepted, they looked the part—and acted peaceful and tolerant—but their hearts were broken by the demands of the Round Tower's fraternity. Zealot, and those like him, was regarded a troublemaker.

Zealot, and his old friend, Vigor, were returning to the Tower from dinner at the Plowman. They turned from the castle road onto the narrow bridge leading to the first portcullis and gate. Traffic was sparse and the gate was closed.

"That's odd," Zealot said to Vigor. "Don't remember the last time the gate was closed."

"Me either," Vigor concurred.

"Hello, the Keep!" Zealot called to the guards.

A guard's face appeared in a window high above the gate. "Identify yourselves."

"I'm Zealot, a resident of the Round Tower, and loyal to the High King."

"I'm Vigor, also a resident of the Round Tower, and loyal to the King."

The guard looked down on the two, ensuring they were alone, and raised the portcullis. The gate opened behind it. The guard made certain Zealot and Vigor were alone when they entered Chamber One.

Once inside, the gate closed and the portcullis lowered behind them. Zealot and Vigor repeated the exercise again, identifying themselves to a guard, who like the first, observed them through a hole to ensure they were alone.

Portcullis two and its gate raised and opened. As before, they closed in place behind them, locking Zealot and Vigor in Chamber Two.

"Security is tight today," Vigor observed.

"I was thinking the same thing," Zealot said.

The two men waited for the routine in Chamber Two to commence, but the guard did not appear to question them.

After waiting a few minutes, Zealot called, "Hello!"

Nothing.

He and Vigor chatted about their contacts in the castle and the meetings they'd had.

"Guard? Guard?" Vigor yelled. He whistled through his teeth. The shrill sound reverberated in the small chamber.

Above them, the covers over the murder holes were removed. "Who are you?" demanded a voice from the ceiling.

"I'm Zealot."

"I'm Vigor. We're returning home."

There was shuffling above them. The two friends didn't think much about it. The Round Tower had become a bureaucracy, and true to bureaucracies, the Keep was often inefficient. Their passage from Chamber Two into Chamber Three, and then into the Round Tower and home for dinner might be slow, but it would occur soon enough.

There was no verbal command, just a single nod from a hooded figure.

Bubbling-hot oil poured from the murder holes above splashing on Zealot and Vigor, scalding them. Their screams would not escape Chamber Two. They tore at their oil-soaked clothes trying to distance themselves from the burning. Skin peeled off with their clothes.

A second nod and salt rained down on their raw exposure. Trying to brush its burning crystals intensified their wounds. Zealot and Vigor couldn't escape Chamber Two and couldn't quench their torment.

Their screams turned to hoarse cries.

With the third nod, rocks as big as bread baskets dropped through the holes. Zealot and Vigor were stoned into silence—and death— eventually. Their torture and demise was concluded.

The man who had quietly directed these attacks gave each guard a few coins and instructed that Chamber Two should be cleaned after the midnight watch when no one would notice. "Spread the salt you sweep up on the road to kill the weeds," Captain Nekros instructed. Letizia

Pintaro nodded to the Captain, smiled slightly, and turned to go back to her office.

In the Light

Hank's armor and body bore the marks of battle. His face wasn't as handsome as it once was, and his back and hip plagued him, but he was proud of the scuffs on his shield, breastplate, and helmet. They were badges of honor. He had been in the battle, had met the enemy, and lived to tell about it. The abrasions also served notice: I am a veteran!

The knights descended for five days from the narrow place of rocks and scrub brush—from the cold, windy snow and elevation—into thickets of tangled undergrowth and low lands. For the better part of a day they weaved through the brush, but soon the undergrowth became twisted webs of briars and vines from floor to canopy. The crisp mountain air they had all enjoyed was traded for dense, humid air, stale with the musty decay of the swamp.

The briars were tough. Their thorns tore at the moist leather of their muddy boots, not to mention ripping their clothing and skin.

Hank unsheathed his sword and began whacking to blaze a path.

At a break, Hank sat down against a tree, worn out. His shoulders and neck ached. Sweat stained his shirt and pants. Love sat close by. "Whew! I thought killing beasts was hard. This is tough going."

"Yeah," said Love. "You've been hitting it pretty hard."

Hank noticed Love was enjoying the break, but he wasn't the sweaty, winded mess he was.

"You know," Love said, quietly enough that the others couldn't hear him, "you're so worn out from whacking vines that if the enemy shows up you'll be too tired to fight."

"You've got that right."

Love let the conversation lie fallow.

"I'm curious," Love said, after chewing a handful of nuts and drinking a swig of water: "What's the weed whacking doing to the edge on your sword?"

Hank picked up his sword. It was dull from hitting the dirt and streaked with sticky sap. The tip had some dings in it from hitting rocks.

"It doesn't look so good," Hank reported.

"Didn't figure it did. Noisy too. All that hacking and huffing."

Love took another drink. "You know, if you'll stop using your sword like a hatchet, you'll save yourself and your blade a lot of abuse."

"But these briars are tearing me up."

Love nodded, as he examined a tear in his pants and the cut underneath. "There's no denying they'll cut you. But briars are part of the woods, and these swamps and woods are on our journey in the light."

"Wonder why we couldn't go around?" Hank said.

"Don't know," Love said. "On rare occasions the High King guides us around challenges, but most of the time he leads us through them. Part of the adventure."

"Adventure," Hank said, as he thought about the implication. "Okay, but what about the cuts?"

"What about 'em?"

"They hurt!"

"Oh, that. Yeah, I know. Cuts are a distraction. That's all."

"I'd just as soon do without them," Hank said.

"Me too, but that's the distraction. The goal isn't to get through the briars with no cuts. The goal is to stay focused on the light while you're in the briars."

Love let that sink in, then added, "Same's true for your other pains too—your back and hip."

"Yeah, Competence did a number on me," Hank said, voicing the self-pity long-recommended by Jester.

"Your pain's a distraction," Love continued. "All of it—small niggles like the briars and big bites like your back. Focus on the hurt and you open yourself up to the counsel of Jester. Recognize that pain is a distraction and you're repositioned to listen to your heart's desire."

Hank sensed Love was right, but his hip was stiff from sitting. He straightened his leg. There were twinges in his back and the cuts on his legs burned as the skin around them stretched.

"So I'm supposed to just wade through the briars?"

"Certainly not! That'd be dumb. It'd be denial, denial of the circumstance and denial of your pain."

Love stood, reached down, and pulled Hank to his feet. "Walk with me." He led them out of the clearing where the others were resting to a nasty tangle of briars. "Now, do exactly as I do."

With precise care, Love stepped on the base of the briars in front of him, mashing them under his boot into the ground. Then he stepped high and pinned other briars under his foot. With each step, he paused to assess his situation, one to plan his next step, two to note any disturbance in the woods. Like a dancer, Love stepped through the woods, navigating with choreographed deliberation, moving briars away from his face, and easing them down behind him. Hank watched and followed, stepping where Love stepped, mimicking his every move.

Love stopped. Listened. Satisfied, he said, "What do you think?"

"I've got it," Hank said.

"Good. Let's go back. You lead, and as you do, think about the King."

Hank copied Love as he worked his way back through the briars. He thought about the King with each step.

"Take your time," Love encouraged. "Be aware of yourself and what's around you."

Hank considered the satisfaction inside his chest as he moved among the tangles. He noted that the birds stayed on their perches rather than flying as they had done during his previous commotion. He winced each time a briar rebounded and snagged him, but paused, collected his thoughts, and continued.

Once Hank caught his knee in a briar and couldn't get free. Love helped him get extricated, reassured him, and said, "That get you?"

"Yeah. It sure does burn."

"I know. Use that to your advantage."

Hank's brow furrowed.

"You can focus on the burning and be distracted, or you can note the burning and use it as a catalyst to set your mind and heart on the King and your next step."

"Ah. Got it," Hank said with new resolve.

As Love had shown, he stopped to plan his next step, to listen to the woods, to focus on the King, but also to listen to his heart. There was a song inside him. It was a resolute rhythm with a simple, repeating verse affirming that he was a blessed man. He listened—took in the moment with a deep breath, felt it waft through his soul, exhaled, and took his next step.

Several times Hank stopped, acknowledged the burning pain, then set his mind on the joy that he felt in his heart and the blessing given to him by his Father. On a couple of occasions he even spread his arms out, breathed deep, and soaked up the light of the moment, taking it into himself, and annexing it as new territory for his heart.

Vassar and Magician watched. "Looks like our trek's turned into a dance," Magician said.

"Umm," Vassar concurred. "Father knows what's he's doing."

CHAPTER 14

The Briar Swamp

Hank's skills in the swamp and briars improved. For three days he implemented Love's instruction, moving adroitly, light on his feet like a dancer, stepping through the impediments and irritants of the undergrowth. But the demands of the brush and briars, and the high-stepping required to navigate the swamp, sapped his strength.

Jester never slept and his temptations were unrelenting. Like pain, his persistence was powerful. A flood of water won't erode rock, but a constant drip will. Neither pain nor Jester missed a beat.

Even a casual observer could recognize when Hank was vulnerable: He grimaced when his back stabbed him; his arms and legs bled dribbles where the briars cut him; low groans rattled in his throat as he lifted his legs to step over a thorn.

What do I have to do to get the King to let up on me? Jester suggested to Hank's mind, as if the King was cutting Hank, or that the dagger point was his, or that the pain was his fault and his affliction. Distracted by pain's relentless goad, Hank fielded Jester's insistent doubts, owned them for himself, and replaced his heart's song with a pitiful dirge. To make matters worse, he couldn't sleep.

Jester never missed a cue. "If only I could sleep a little, I could make it. I could overcome these distractions. I just need a break," Jester offered.

"I wonder how much longer he's going to make me endure this?" Jester questioned.

Each of Jester's suggestions—temptations—played to Hank's independence, pity-filled entitlement, and latent distrust.

"I wonder if he's even noticed that I'm doing better, getting stronger, trying harder than ever before?" Jester suggested.

One night, after the others had gone to bed and the fire was dying, Hank sat alone on a log staring at the gibbous moon. He didn't hear Magician slip up behind him until he was stepping over the log to sit beside him.

"Can't sleep?"

"Nope. Not much."

"I've noticed," Magician said. "Sleep deprivation. It's an effective torture over the long haul."

Hank looked steady at the moon. He'd not used that word to describe his experience, but "tortured" seemed a fair assessment. He heard Jester's spin, *Why does Father torture me?*

As Hank thought about Jester's accusation, Magician said, "You know, Hank, I admire you."

"Admire me?!"

"Yeah, I do. You're a good man. I'm proud to be your friend, proud to march with you, trust you in a tight spot. I admire you."

"Don't mess with me, Magician! I'm not a good man. My days are spent stumbling, fumbling, and cursing. My nights are spent tossing, staring into the dark, and doubting."

"Oh, I know that," Magician said, "but that's not what I was referencing. That's the stuff Jester keeps ranting about. I'm talking about you. I admire you. I admire your heart. You have an amazing passion for the High King. I can see it in your eyes and in the way you carry yourself."

"Talking with you makes my head hurt," Hank said.

"Everybody says I have that effect on them, except for Faith; he's too hard-headed." Magician chuckled. "The deal is, you've agreed with Jester. He's been suggesting that you are what you do, or don't do. Know what I'm saying?"

"Yeah, I know what you're saying."

"Jester's a smart guy, but the stuff he's telling you is akin to what horses leave behind them on the trail. Think about that."

"I am," Hank said.

"And another thing, have you noticed that the pain gets worse when you adopt Jester's views?"

"Well, hadn't given it much thought," Hank said.

"You're who the King says you are. Whether you act like it or not is another matter altogether—a discussion for another day, but not now. You do remember what your Father said, don't you?"

"Which time?"

"He said it to your face in front of us, 'This is my son.' Am I right?"

"Yeah, that's right. That's what he said."

"Well, if you'll recall, you hadn't exactly been performing too well when he said that."

"But Magician, I'm failing. I'm foundering in these swamps. You all can't ignore that—I can't ignore that. It's a fact!"

"No, you can't, and I didn't say you should. What you do in these swampy woods is important—vitally important—but that's not as important as *how* you get through these swamps."

Hank considered what Magician was saying to him and then began to process it in his heart. *I'm back to the need to focus, like Love said. I've got to set my mind on what I know—the truth about the King, the truth about me, the truth about my circumstances. And I must take Magician at his word. He offered to live through me. I need to renew that determination with....*

"...Magician, I was just thinking (not realizing that his thoughts had been Magician's thoughts), I desire to take you at your word. Will you empower me—through your sorcery—to live life?"

"I have been!"

Magician could see by Hank's expression that he was confused again. *How could I be empowered and fail so miserably?*

"Look. Just because I extend the light of life to you doesn't mean there'll be no briars or that you won't bog down in the swamps."

"But I don't want to bog down."

"I know. Listen to me. There are many good men who have died in the briars and in the jaws of wild beasts and their bodies rot away in the swamp. As you would suspect, Jester contends that the High King failed to protect these warriors. But not so! He ushered them into the Kingdom through a different door than the one he's leading us toward."

"I see what you're saying. It's just so hard to stay focused."

"Yes. It is," Magician said.

They sat quietly before Magician said, "You've been listening to Jester. In fact, you've made the mistake of believing his thoughts are your own."

"Gee. How you come up with these insights, I don't know. But you're right."

"Well, I've been at it awhile. Hank, your heart doesn't condemn you, and the High King certainly doesn't. Condemnation is Jester's angle and his alone. You know you can't make any provision for Jester. Right?"

"Yeah, I know. But I haven't been doing too well remembering."

"And do you understand that as soon as you recognize Jester's counsel, you can't think about it or believe it's true? Can't give it any quarter?"

"Yeah, but I've been pondering on it a lot."

"I know. Live and learn," Magician reassured. "You must think fiercely! Make no provision for the trappings of your old way of living!"

"Get the eye of the tiger back," Hank summarized.

"The eye of the tiger," Magician confirmed.

"Thanks for talking to me, Magician. By the way, have you noticed that we're being watched?"

"Yeah. For the last couple of days."

The Round Tower

The Round Tower ran on routines. Like any other successful club or membership organization, members of the Keep formed into homogeneous groups. There were many groups, all in a hierarchy, that if diagramed would resemble a pyramid. Moving between groups was accepted practice so long as the status of the group entered approximately matched the status of the group departed. This shell game of membership was one of Ennui's brainstorms to prevent residents of the Round Tower from becoming alarmed that their numbers were shrinking. There was always the illusion of growth somewhere.

Groups that were "growing" were anxious to showcase their success. Over time, an elaborate system of programs developed that those groups enjoying less success could use to emulate the programs of the more successful groups. More and more emphasis was given to programs in search of recognition and distinction. Even though dedicated in name to the High King and the Kingdom, discussion of the High King was not part of the culture in many groups. Programs focused on the group and self-realization.

Ennui met with Zophos on a regular basis to tweak their strategy. Most of their meetings were short since there was not a great deal to talk about; the Round Tower was permeated with apathy. The single tenet always reinforced in their meetings was that anyone promoting change or advocating on behalf of the High King was to be dealt with. Immediately.

At night, the Round Tower's gates were usually closed in keeping with tradition. But during the day, security was lax. The portcullises were lifted and the gates open more often than not. People came and went as they wished. As intelligence was gained by Ennui's agents, Zophos and his commanders modified their illusion of light such that it became almost impossible to distinguish between the Army of Light and the Dark Army.

Given the Round Tower's growing apathy to the High King, his original vision for the Kingdom was relegated to myth. His concepts were talked about and quoted on occasion, but were not viewed as applicable to daily life. Rather than the arcane teaching of the King, the culture of the Round Tower was the guiding principle for most circumstances. Had these ideals been examined, it would have been apparent that the philosophies of the Round Tower were an amalgamation of what the High King was reputed to have said at some point in history and the philosophies bandied about in the castle by Zophos and his agents.

When speaking of success and leadership, the High King had taught that the first will be last and the last will be first; that if anyone wished to be a leader, he should adopt the attitude of a servant. Leaders in the Tower referenced this teaching and offered themselves as cases in point. However, in practice they behaved no different than the leadership of the castle. Even though they said one thing, by their lifestyle it was apparent the leadership of the Round Tower and the castle both believed the High King's teachings were antiquated, and if pressed, irrelevant.

Judging by their lifestyle and achievement, the leaders were correct and the High King was wrong; they were esteemed, powerful, and enjoyed status and financial security. At first blush, those who believed what the King said—that the last would be first—usually were simply last.

The majority of members in the Army of Light who lived within the Round Tower embraced the values of the castle, looking to social and professional success to provide the meaning and significance they wanted. Of course, no one talked about this lest they be perceived as slighting the High King.

Saying one thing, while doing another, didn't cause much alarm in the Round Tower. While Zophos instituted rules and regulations in the castle for dealing with conflicts, the same was not done in the Round Tower. If the rule of law in the castle was broken, punishment was meted out according to the law. The rule of law within the Round Tower was arbitrary and broken with impunity—just as long as the law-breaker had the power to enforce his action. Since the Round Tower had the reputation of being a nice place, those who exploited the law to their own advantage did so smiling, talking about the High King, and promoting their unlawful agenda as beneficial to the Kingdom. Radicals, like Zealot and Vigor had been, who pointed out inconsistencies between the High King's standard and the Keep's actual practice, were resented and suspect.

Gnarled Wood

Ennui's plan was unfolding just like she projected. The Round Tower was adopting the castle's values at the expense of the High King's standards and in spite of tragic, historical precedent. Ennui and her staff charted its eventual demise.

But in spite of his escalating success, with some frequency Zophos' madness to have the High King's throne drove him to over extend. He couldn't help himself. Just as radicals like Zealot and Vigor upset the equilibrium inside the Round Tower, Zophos' desperate compulsion upset the equilibrium as well, not only in the Tower, but in the castle. This was unacceptable, and in his rational moments, Zophos knew this better than anyone.

The mute diversionary squads and their skirmishes proved the perfect outlet for his seething, and given his genius for deception, worked to his advantage. The fire fights appeared to be legitimate incursions by enemies of the Round Tower and the castle. None of the skirmishes were large enough to threaten the Round Tower or create undue alarm in the castle, but they were frequent enough and bold enough to remind the Round Tower and the castle of conflict in the world.

Zophos' pattern was to send a diversionary squad into the castle. After they had upset a sector, he would attack them with ruthless efficiency, reestablish the equilibrium, and look like a hero and protector of the peace at the same time. In this way, humanity depended on him for tranquility.

Ennui encouraged the Round Tower to reach out to the castle-at-large as if collaborating with an ally to prevent attacks. This promoted the value of equilibrium and tolerance for all, and it further distracted the Tower from the King's priorities in exchange for the prospect of imminent peace.

Zophos and his marketers spun his skirmish indiscretions as just another unfortunate conflict of good against evil. They decried the evil, but celebrated the triumph of the restored peace at the decisive and determined hand of the Ambassador—whoever he was.

His approval rating soared. His desperation was written off to the amorphous "evil" in the world. As hoped, the Army of Light within the Round Tower reached out to the castle for reassurance and collaboration to "Achieve the Higher Good" as the new program was dubbed by the marketing department.

Soon, the spin was routine and convincing. News reports of the skirmishes always concluded with the reporter's trusted voice and unblinking eyes, "Once again today, good triumphs evil and peace is preserved."

To Zophos' surprise, the more the ideology of good was enabled, and the more he was categorized as an amorphous evil, the less the residents of the Round Tower believed him to be a real power. It was another stroke of genius. His power actually grew, and with it, his pride.

The Round Tower's complacency became more pervasive. Good was not a powerful enough concept to inspire men to take action. Evil was, but not the myth of evil. Ennui's sensibility proved remarkably shrewd.

But it made Zophos angry that people did not attribute to him the recognition he deserved. His aides tried to appease him while managing his lust. "Keep the end in mind," they said. "Soon. Very soon, the High King's throne will be yours."

Zophos' response grew in intensity and was always a variation of the same theme, "And then! Then there will be hell to pay by all those who discounted me."

The Briar Swamp

Hank was on point, leading as Love had guided. Each step he took was planned, thoughtful, and followed by attention to any detail around him that might indicate trouble. He had modeled himself after Love and gotten better at moving through the briars and thickets of the swampy woods.

He noticed a change in vegetation on the floor of the woods, glanced at the trees surrounding the anomaly: black spruce and tamarack. He sniffed. The peaty odor finalized his definition. He stepped away and conferred with Magician.

While Faith stood watch, Hank and Magician gathered three saplings apiece, each about twelve feet long, and approached the muskeg bog Hank had identified. Hank laid the first three saplings side-by-side on the surface of the muskeg; Magician handed him the others. They repeated their effort. In less than ten minutes they had constructed a rudimentary bridge spanning the muskeg. If Hank had missed the signs and stepped into the muskeg, he would have sunk to his arm pits in the ooze of decaying matter, moss, and sedge.

The party crossed the muskeg and never sunk deeper than an ankle. Willows awaited them along the shoreline of a gorgeous lake. They stopped, drank, rested, and refilled their canteens before resuming.

Two hours after crossing the muskeg and winding their way through the willows, the troupe began a steep climb. An hour later they came upon and followed an elk trail zigzagging up the mountainside. It was an irregular trail, but Hank trusted the animal's intuition more than his own eyesight and sensibility.

Three days later, the sky spit snow and sleet at them. It was a welcome relief from the treachery of the humidity and briars. Hank felt reborn, stopping to lift his face to the precipitation. For the first time in several days, he could see. Sometimes he turned a complete circle to take in the vista. The light of the High King seemed more tangible to him here than in the swamp, even though he knew it was only a feeling. The High King's promise, and the affirmation of his compatriots, was that his light was constant.

At times he ran in the light. Sometimes he walked. And there were plenty of times all he could do was shuffle. Progress and speed were not the point, Hank had determined. What was important was that he lived in the light rather than focusing on and walking in the darkness as he had done most of his life.

They stopped to refresh their plan. It was decided that Hope and Faith should recon ahead and report back. "No longer than an hour," Vassar reminded them as they departed.

Hank sat down next to his brother. "You know, I'm having the time of my life, Vassar."

"What do you mean?"

"I mean I'm thrilled we're headed for the castle and all—the Round Tower, and whatever else—but I don't feel like *I have to go* there or anywhere. It's more than enough to be here with you and the others just living, enjoying, and being on the journey. It's an adventure."

"It is," Vassar said. "I'm with you. Just think of the adventures we can recount!"

"We've had a few, haven't we?"

"You can say that again. And you know what?"

"What?"

"I think more await us," Vassar said.

Eight or ten chickadees flitted past in a panic. Hank and the others froze; their senses on high alert. There was rustling. Then quiet. Love touched the handle of his sword.

"Vassar?"

Vassar exhaled. "Here," he said.

Hope and Faith emerged from a few feet away, a testimony to their stealth; there were none better.

They reported two bits of news, both good: first, that the terrain got easier, and second that they met a representative of the King. There was relief to hear that the trail was less onerous, but that was overshadowed anticipating the details of the meeting.

Vassar quizzed Hope and Faith about the representative. "We can't be too careful," he said.

They agreed and were happy to have Vassar double check their belief about the emissary. Satisfied that he was sent by the King with a message for them, Vassar pursed his lips indicating that Hope and Faith could continue. They explained how they met the man and recounted each aspect of their brief conversation. He confirmed that they were indeed to proceed to the castle, acquaint themselves with the situation, and that their next instructions would come to them there.

Retracing their steps, Hope and Faith led the way. As reported, the trail flattened and the terrain opened up. The weather remained raw, but it didn't matter. They were all happy to be trekking instead of slogging. They walked in an irregular cluster to appear like ordinary travelers. The closer they came to the castle, the greater the chance they would encounter others—day laborers, farmers, herdsmen.

As they crested a rise, the castle and the prominence of the Round Tower appeared on the horizon. They stopped. Looked. Listened. Studied the territory between them and there. They made certain their cloaks covered their breastplates, fixed their minds upon their destination, and headed for the castle.

CHAPTER 15

The Castle

As expected, Vassar, Hank, and their companions encountered more and more people as they approached the castle. What they did not expect was the downcast and despondent demeanor of these folks. Their hair was dirty and long, hanging shroud-like over their faces. Their clothes were soiled and worn. Vassar greeted those they passed, but none responded. Few looked up. Most edged closer to their side of the road.

While they were still a long way from the castle, they smelled a pungent odor. At first it would arrive with a random breeze. Then it was persistent. It became overpowering, nauseating—a breath-robbing stench unlike anything Hank had ever smelled.

As they reached the top of a hill, there before them was the source of the fetid smell. A massive dump occupied several acres on either side of the road. Vassar was first to cover his nose and mouth. He used his scarlet scarf. The others followed his lead. Hank undid his scarlet sash.

The dump was mounded with the trash of Zophos' campaign against the castle: decaying animals, body parts, ruined equipment, and spoiled crops. The pile steamed and smoked and burst with occasional fires of spontaneous combustion.

People lived here—not by the dump, but in the dump. They had dug caves in the refuse and covered them with the carnage of Zophos' war to shield themselves from the elements. They crawled over the mound of waste searching for nourishment, subsisting in Zophos' realm as human rats.

Why don't they go to the Round Tower? Hank thought. *There must be plenty of room there. I bet the people in the Keep would welcome them.* He wanted to ask Magician, but none of them were saying anything to each other as they passed through Zophos' heaping refuse.

A putrid river demarcated the dump from a shanty town. Hank assumed the people who lived in this town were a step above the souls living on the rubbish heap. It wasn't a big step. *But it's a step*, Hank thought, as they crossed the river on a derelict footbridge.

A dilapidated sign stood askew in the mud at the end of the bridge: "La Faim." *Why would anyone name their town after hunger?* Hank thought. He glanced at Hope and noted a dark lament in his eyes.

Gangs of young men hung out beside the road—young tuffs backed up against a dead end. The hair on the back of Hank's neck stood up as they came to the first group. Unlike most of the people on the road, these guys stared at the band of brothers with seething caldrons of anger.

Three dead-enders stepped into the road. Behind them, a cadre assembled and blocked the way. As Hank and the rest approached, the gang formed a defiant funnel on either side of the road and then closed in behind them.

Magician stepped forward to negotiate on their behalf. He waited for the gang's leader to state his terms. Fueled by his peers and the bravado of his age, the young man looked around at his accomplices and stated the price of his bribe, an exorbitant amount. Magician agreed without debate and reached into his cloak for the sum.

It was too easy, too fast. The young thug became angry. He bucked up and increased his requirement by a third. The gang jeered Magician in support of their leader's moxie. Magician smiled and agreed.

His compliance ignited the gang leader's emotion. The tuff stepped toward Magician snarling and demanding an amount double the last stated. He leaned toward Magician and reached menacingly. Like a serpent's coil and strike, Magician seized the young man's wrist, turned him in a flash to a helpless disadvantage, and with his own dagger blade pressed against the side of his neck held him at death's door. In a simultaneous instant, the knights spun into a defensive hive, swords drawn, with looks daring anyone to advance a step.

Magician watched the gang members. He eased his grip on their leader and turned him to face him. Magician took his scarlet cravat and wiped the blood from the small cut on the young man's neck. He spoke reassurance to the dead-end youth while cleaning the accumulation of grime from his hairline, eyebrows, and cheeks. He smiled and said, "I'll send someone soon to you and your friends. There's a better way, a way of hope and confidence, a way that will prove once and for all that you are people of great value and significance."

Magician handed the young man's dagger back to him, then reached into his cloak, withdrew his money pouch, and paid the last amount demanded by the young man. Magician smiled again at the young man, touched his shoulder, and said again, "I'll send someone soon with a message of light to illuminate the way out of this dark place."

The gang was motionless. Magician replaced his money pouch inside his cloak, took a deep breath, and said, "Well guys, we should get going." The five around him relaxed their stance and resumed their journey. Several of the gang members followed.

Hank noticed as they walked on through La Faim that the few older men they saw were either ancient or passed out, their brains pickled in the local hooch. But there were no men that mattered, no men who could make a difference, no men to lead with courageous grace like Magician had done.

The road was rugged and rutted, not just because of the winter weather and freeze-thaw cycles, but because it was badly constructed. Drainage was poor. There weren't enough ditches and those that had been dug were ill-conceived. They carried not only waste water but solid waste—human waste, animal waste, and garbage. Where this slow moving muck was impeded, it backed up, and found a new route over the road, filling the ruts and forming unavoidable quagmires. Hank thought of the muskeg bog and wished for saplings to put over these swamps. There was nothing to do but slog through.

The road through La Faim was lined with sorry dwellings and a few store fronts catering to travelers. Their wares were cheap junk. A few peasants laid potatoes and onions on the ground for sale. They sat beside the sad displays with sadder stares. Whores displayed themselves saucily and offered the band of brothers group deals. They called out cheerfully, but their cheerful voices disguised their desperate plight.

La Faim improved to hovels the closer they got to the castle grounds, but the odor of the dump lingered. Fuel came from the combustibles scrounged out of the dump. The people living in the hovels bought wood from the folks living in the dump who were taxed by the folks living in between in the shanties of La Faim. It was a subsistence economy that left everyone smelling like Zophos' waste.

At the far edge of La Faim there was a row of better homes. Each was surrounded by a wall crowned with shards of glass or metal. These were the dwellings of the power brokers. The walls protected them from the angry, disdainful people they capitalized upon to work for them. Dogs stood at the gates barking. Guards sat around smoky, inefficient fires watching as the band continued along the road.

The road wound through an open area—uninhabited and untended—lying between the property belonging to the bosses of La Faim and the castle proper. Scavengers had carried away the ruins of the war and the earth was reclaiming Zophos' erosive offense against it with grass and vines. The knights breathed more easily here, but their respite was short-lived. Ten minutes after leaving La Faim, they entered the castle's outskirts and encountered the army's first outposts.

"This doesn't feel right," Magician said in a hush to Hank, as they entered the castle grounds.

"I agree. What do you think it is?"

"To begin with, these soldiers polishing their armor. The Army of Light doesn't polish their armor."

"You're right," Hank said. "It's issued by the King. What do you suppose…?"

"Why don't you ask?"

Hank and Magician walked up to a group of soldiers sitting in a circle, talking and polishing. "Good afternoon," Hank said.

"Afternoon," they said, more or less together.

"We've just arrived. Is there a pub in town you like?"

"You just lookin' for a drink or you wantin' supper too?" asked one of the men.

"Supper sounds good."

"Hoi Polloi's where I'd go."

"Me too," a couple more agreed.

"Is it far?" Hank inquired.

"Not far," offered another, who'd been quiet to this point. "Down that street a ways," he said, pointing with the handle of the axe he was polishing. "Once you get to the bend, bear left. It's about a block, on your right."

"Can't miss it," added the first man.

"Okay," said Hank. "Hoi Polloi it is. By the way, what are you guys doing?"

"What's it look like?" one retorted.

"You *are* new to town, ain't you?" said the man who'd given directions.

Hank shrugged, but didn't move.

"Not bein' military hisself, don't guess he'd have no way of knowin'," one said to the first man who had spoken.

"If our armor ain't polished—if it's got any tarnish—there's hell to pay."

"With the Ambassador," added the direction giver.

"Fact is, there's a guy next group over, or was a guy anyway," another soldier began, pointing with his head and continuing to polish. "Anyways, yesterday, he was discovered with a dull spot on the butt-end of his boot-knife. Most likely just hadn't finished cleanin' with a fresh cloth. Anybody could make that mistake, especially if it was gettin' on toward dark. But the Ambassador come by, inspectin' like he does, and pulled him up then and there, right in front of God and everybody."

"I ain't never before heard nothin' like that," the direction giver said.

"Me neither," he resumed. "Gave him a tongue lashin' to beat all dressin' downs. Turned the air blue. All about how he was tarnishin' the light, and his reputation—as Ambassador, that is—and how he was a sorry disgrace to the Kingdom."

"He get the usual?" asked one of the others.

"Yeah, on the spot. Ambassador done the work hisself, used the guy's own knife."

"His boot knife?" asked another, as he paused his polishing.

"Cut both his hands off, about three inches above his wrists. Told him if he was ever caught with a dirty weapon again, it'd be his head next. Then the Ambassador polished the butt of the knife on the guy's shirt."

"Damn," remarked another soldier.

"That's right. Then he dropped the knife on the ground beside him, right where he'd been bleedin'."

Hank was stunned, but hid it well. He stood for a moment looking into their fire, his mind racing at the cruelty, but honoring the silent ruminations of the group.

After what he felt an appropriate time, he exhaled hard and said, "Well, polish hard guys."

"That's what we're aimin' to do."

"Thanks for the tip on Hoi Polloi. Take it easy."

Hank and Magician reported the conversation to Vassar and the others. "This is a deception," said Magician. "These troops are not part of the Army of Light. They are the enemy in disguise, and no doubt this Ambassador they referenced is either Zophos or one of his higher ups. This wouldn't be the first time he's tried to appear as one who lives in the light. It's an effective deception, and he's excellent at fabricating light."

"We shouldn't talk about this right now," Hank suggested. "If Magician's correct, then we're surrounded by the Dark Army."

"We must keep our wits about us," Hope exhorted.

"I agree," said Vassar.

"Those guys recommended Hoi Polloi. It's just down that street," Hank said pointing.

"I'm ready!" said Love.

They had to ask for additional directions twice before finding the entrance to Hoi Polloi. It was on the street the soldier told Hank it was on, but the entrance was hidden down a narrow alley. The sign was a small, brass plaque indiscernible in the fading light. Faith figured out they were in the right place by feeling the recessed letters on the name plate until he discerned "Hoi" to his satisfaction.

They seated themselves at a round table in the corner next to the fireplace. Magician, Vassar, and Faith sat so they could watch the door. Judging by the four steps down and the lower-than-standard door height, the room was a cellar at its creation, but sometime eons ago was transformed into a pub. Stone columns supported the roof and low ceiling; exposed-beams added to the insular atmosphere.

"Hi, boys. What can I get you?" Hank imagined the waitress might have been beautiful once, but the wrinkles and hard edges in her face belied a hard life.

"What are you most proud of?" asked Love.

"Probably the special," she said, pointing to a sign on the wall above the bar.

When she returned with the wine, they each ordered a bowl of stew. Then they ordered an assortment of boar, stewed horse, and beef ribs with potatoes, onions, peppers, and bread. As she was heading to the kitchen, staff appeared with large napkins that they tied around each man's neck. Everyone took this in stride and continued talking except for Hank who thought this seemed reminiscent of putting a bib on a baby. He started to laugh. Faith asked what was funny. Hank started to explain, but after a couple of false starts decided it best to say, "Never mind. It's nothing," and change the subject. Before the staff left, they provided each man with a bowl of hot water in which to wash his hands. There were no towels. The first purpose of the bib was now apparent to Hank.

The soup came in bread bowls and kept them occupied right up to the serving of the main course. The waitress, followed by additional staff, marched single-file to the table carrying three platters of meat and vegetables. It smelled superb. Wine glasses were refilled and they were left to their meal. This was Hank's first meal sitting in a chair since the King's banquet.

They offered quiet thanks with their eyes open; Vassar did the honors. "Father, we are grateful for this meal. We recognize it's a clear sign of your provision and care. Guide our conversation, please."

Grasping their choice of meat with one hand, they cut it free with a knife—the only utensil—in the other hand. Conversation died. They ate and ate and ate their fill, and just about when they had decided they couldn't eat any more, the waitress came with a slab of pork ribs, "Compliments of the chef," she said, raking them into the middle of the table on top of the existing food. They continued their feast, but slower than at first.

The waitress returned and goaded them as lightweights, even though each had eaten a prodigious amount of food. Once she was satisfied they were happy—and full—she motioned for the table to be cleared while she discussed the options for a dessert. It was a slow night at Hoi Polloi. There was only one other customer—a single man. The waitress introduced each dessert with a detailed description. This was followed by a roving discussion around the table. She enjoyed the attention and they enjoyed thinking about something besides being in enemy territory.

They decided on one baked cinnamon apple cut into six pieces, a bottle of port, and six glasses. She feigned frustration—said she just didn't understand men.

The waitress poured the port and passed the glasses around. They asked her for recommendations about places to see, local news, and eventually her thoughts on the Round Tower.

She knew all the local gossip and shared her information without hesitation. Among her more fascinating revelations was the poor reputation of the Round Tower versus admiration for the Dark Army, even though she didn't call them that.

"So, are you a follower of the High King?" Hank asked.

"Of course. We're all followers of the High King, aren't we?" she replied. "Everyone's got their own way of following, I suppose. But heck, yeah. I mean, hey! I live here, don't I?"

"Well, yeah," Hank said. "But I didn't know where you live had anything to do with being a follower of the King. I thought you were a follower if you followed him."

"Whatever," she said with a shrug. "That's the kind of thing those folks in the Round Tower believe."

"Speaking of which," Vassar interjected, "Should we go there while we're in town?"

"Oh, I don't know," she said. "I probably wouldn't waste my time on it."

"Why's that?" Vassar asked.

"Well, it's a pain to get into for one thing. If they're guarding the gate it takes forever to listen to all their damn rules. It's boring beyond endurance. And their rituals are just plain strange! Apart from that, I suppose it's an okay place."

They laughed at her sarcasm.

"It's all just an act, near as I can tell."

"What do you mean?" Hope asked.

"Well, take the gates for example. One day they're wide open. Come and go as you please. The next day, they could be closed. Whole place locked up tight as a drum. There's no rhyme or reason to it. Just a bunch of petty bureaucrats. You know how people are if they have a little power. Goes to their head. Know what I mean?" she asked, not expecting an answer or allocating space for one. "So they use their uppity attitude to talk down to everyone and make themselves appear better than the rest of us."

"Doesn't make much sense, does it?" said Love.

"Gosh, no. It's like visiting a foreign country, not that I've ever been to one. But they talk all the time about being tolerant and open minded and stuff. But hey! You mess up inside the Round Tower and they'll throw your ass out right now! Seen it too many times."

"I thought the people in the Round Tower were followers of the High King," said Love.

"That's what they say. Can't get too excited about the High King myself though, at least not if he's like them. Now the Ambassador, he runs a tight ship. As long as you don't cross him, life's alright. But you get crossways with him…. My, my. But you know what? That's the military. It's the way they do things."

"And the King?" Love probed. "He a hard man like the Ambassador?"

"Beats me. Don't get me wrong. From what I hear, the High King has some good things to say. But you know how politicians are. Near as I can tell, looking at those folks in the Keep, can't see the King's done piddle squat."

"So what's the point?" Love asked.

"My point exactly," she said.

"Who lives inside the Round Tower?" asked Hank. "Is it just the Army of Light?"

"I'm not sure, but I don't think so. I guess most of them do, but some live in the castle too."

"You don't sound very certain," Hank said.

"Well, no. I'm not. But gosh a'mighty. Some folks say the Dark Army is part of the Army of Light, and others say the opposite. Hard to tell. I just hear 'em talking sometimes. Mostly bar talk, I figure. You'd think you could tell them apart, but you can't. Can't tell one from the other. They all strut around, acting important. Most of them that come in here are a pain in the you-know-what. Excuse me for sayin' it. You guys have been real nice though."

"Thanks," Vassar said. "No reason not to be kind, especially to someone who's looked after us like you have."

They all nodded their agreement with Vassar, and then he returned to the subject. "You were saying, you can't tell the difference in the two armies."

"I think the only difference is that the folks who live in the Keep have a better view, but the hassle of getting through all the red tape just to have a view? Not me. I'm happy just to make ends meet. We're all just muddling along anyhow. Work hard, live life, have a few friends, and enjoy the family you've got. Be honest. You know, that's about all a person can do these days."

"I understand," Hank said.

Three soldiers entered and sat down on the other side of the pub. Hank nodded their direction, "Those guys over there, polishing their armor?"

The waitress looked. "Yeah, Army of Light guys. They're regulars."

"They all polish like that when they come in?" Hank pressed.

"Yep. Well, every once and awhile there's one who doesn't polish like a fiend. But for the most part, they all polish like there's no tomorrow."

With a recommendation from the waitress, they found lodging for the night in a *pension* not far from the pub and settled into their rooms. After getting cleaned up and ready for bed, Vassar and Hank sat in the dark talking.

"That was sure a disheartening conversation," Hank said. "The Army of Light isn't distinguishable from the Dark Army? Hard to believe."

"Brother, prepare yourself. There's no more dangerous place in the castle than the Round Tower. I'm afraid many of our friends there have been listening to Jester."

"Jester. What a pariah. His voice is incessant in my head," Hank said.

"He's got an accomplice, Ennui. Pretty lady. Smart as a whip. Been operating inside the Tower for some time. She's established herself among the leadership."

"Really?"

"Yeah. In fact, she's gained enough power that she's influenced the whole culture of the Keep."

"How so?" Hank asked.

"With high-sounding ideas like tolerance, peace at any cost, openness, absence of absolute knowledge...."

"Ah. Yeah, what do they call that?" Hank quickly answered his own question: "Relativism. That's it."

"Uh, huh," Vassar said. "Result is, the Tower's indifferent. Apathetic. In fact, apathy's demoralized them. Their lack of passion for Father indicates they've succumbed to Ennui's subtleties by degrees. They've grown stale and insecure. Their hearts know better, but they don't recognize their heart's desires because they haven't guarded them, listened to them, or treasured their value."

"Whew. Been there," Hank said. "And I suppose they're every bit as desperate as I was in the pit?"

"Every bit, and very insightful, brother. Desperate people do desperate things. It's like they're drowning in their attempt to be independent of the King."

"Those are treacherous waters."

"They are, and you know as well as I do, a drowning person will drown their rescuer in an effort to keep their own nose above water."

"Uh, huh."

"I have a sneaking suspicion Father didn't send us by way of the castle just so we can have a nice dinner and sleep in a real bed. I think he wanted us to get a feel for how things are going."

"You think Father wants us to do something about the Round Tower?"

"Wouldn't surprise me," Vassar said.

"What do you think we should do?"

"Until we hear otherwise, we act like travelers, but think like infiltrators. We gather as much insight as we can about the castle, who its power brokers are, how the people live, and try to discern what this Ambassador's up to."

"Hmm," Hank mused. "And do the same for the Round Tower?"

"I suspect so, but we must be careful."

There was a knock on the door. Hank could sense Vassar's suspicion in the dark. They unsheathed their daggers. Vassar stood against the wall by the hinges of the door with his dagger ready. Hank unlatched the cover over the peep hole and looked into the face of the proprietor.

"Good evening, sir. I'm sorry to bother you so late."

"That's alright," Hank said.

"I have a message for you—an envelope," he said. "It arrived a moment ago. It's urgent."

"Are you alone?" Hank watched to see if the man cut his eyes away or told the truth.

"Yes, sir," the man said, looking to his right and left.

Hank closed the cover over the peep hole and unbolted the door. As he opened the door, Hank stepped to the side in case the door was rushed. The inn keeper was alone. He handed Hank a sealed envelope. "It was delivered by special courier. Said it mustn't wait until morning, otherwise I wouldn't have awakened you. Sorry."

"No problem. We were up. Thank you for bringing it to the room. Good night." Hank closed and bolted the door.

Vassar lit a candle. Hank tore the seal on the envelope and read the enclosed message:

Travel west—before dawn. I will meet you.

He handed the note to Vassar and said, "What do you think we should do?"

Vassar read, eyed the script that was familiar to him, and said, "I think we should depart before dawn. You?"

"I'll tell the others," Hank said, as he headed for the door to the hallway.

CHAPTER 16

Headed West

After a fitful night, Hank and the other knights wrapped themselves in their cloaks. It was cold as a wedge. They didn't sneak out of town, but neither did they take the main road. Working their way west from their *pension* they passed the Round Tower. The first portcullis was down and the gates open. A couple of guards chatted around a fire pit to the left of the entrance.

Hank felt an odd but familiar sense that it took him a moment to place. He slowed his step and dropped back alongside Magician. "This place feels like the pit."

"How so?" Magician asked.

"Dark."

Magician paused, then said, "Does, doesn't it?"

It felt good to be away from the shadowy castle and the foreboding Round Tower. Their trek to the west followed a river on their left that flowed faster as they gained elevation. The water tripped and splashed in a torrent like children running toward the sea. After an hour, there was no sign of human presence. The wind was sharp out of the north. Snow began mid morning. Hank relished the inclement weather as if it was a metaphor of his life. After flowing west to east, the river turned north.

Faith and Hope climbed to the top of a rise for a better look, and then returned. "The river runs from due north through a series of meadows," Hope said. "We know it has to bend back west at some point, but can't see where, and we could see a long way." Hope pointed to the promontory they had descended.

Hank considered Hope's report, looked at Vassar, and said, "The message said 'travel west.' North with the river isn't west. My gut tells me—bad as I hate to say it—that we should cross the river. What do you all think?"

The men considered the river's current and depth. "You know," said Vassar, "I've enjoyed this river all morning. It's beautiful, especially in the snow." He paused. "But it doesn't look all that inviting now."

"I'm with you," said Love. "Getting wet on a cold day isn't on my list of fun things to do."

"But I think Hank called it right," said Vassar.

"Me too," said Love.

"Me three," said Hope.

Faith nodded, and said, "We should cross."

Magician knew the drill—they all did—and was already stripping and tying his clothes and belongings in a bundle. Their teeth chattered. Within moments, they had their bundles of personal affects hung around their necks.

Magician stepped in first, Hope second.

By the time Vassar was knee deep, Magician was up to his waist. He bent his arm at the elbow and looked to Hope who linked arms with him and looked to Hank. They formed a human chain with locked arms, supported one another, and fought the numbing cold and current as they inched their way across.

Once ashore, they danced and jumped up and down and shivered, fumbling to untie their bundles, dry off, and get dressed. They exulted at the adventure they had just endured, kidded each other, and remarked that whoever it was that sent the note saying they should travel west, no doubt knew this river crossing was involved.

His pain was predictable in instances like this, so it didn't surprise Hank that as he sat on the ground trying to get his boots laced, the wounds inflicted by Competence flared up. The slicing and stabbing at his waist and hip were excruciating, taking his breath away, even more than the cold water had done. Hank grimaced.

Jester seized the opportunity. *I can't let them see me hurt,* Jester advised. His commentary played to the lingering burden of expectation Hank felt others had of him. *I can't give in to my handicap,* Jester recommended. Seizing a bit more turf, *If only the King would remove this, then I could make it.*

The pain intensified as spasms twisted him around the whipping post of his spine. Jester stepped closer and voiced Hank's latent resentment: *Not now, damn it. I've got a long way to go over slick ground. How will I make it? If only I weren't crippled. I'm just going to slow everyone down. Look where we're headed! The mountains will be treacherous in the snow.*

Fresh from the exhilaration of crossing the swollen stream, locked arm-in-arm with great warriors, Hank was being sucked down under the torrent of pain, resentment, and hopelessness. The endless cycle of victory and defeat was demoralizing. If Jester surprised him, he got whipped. If Jester approached him head-on, he got whipped. The whirlpool of gloom sucked him toward loneliness.

He waited in his isolation, acting busy, until their backs were turned. Then Hank began the awkward torture to stand up. He rolled onto his hands and knees like a wooden animal and stopped to catch his breath. Working one leg up to his chest, and bracing against his knee, he leveraged his infirmed body toward upright. He opened his mouth like a winded runner, but the spasms shackled his lungs in iron-clad ribs.

Putting on his Spartan face, Hank said, "Tell you what, I'll be drag on this leg." *Maybe the pain will subside,* he thought. *If I'm last in line, they won't notice I'm hurting.*

Vassar assumed the point, followed by Love, Hope, and Faith. As they started off, Magician looked into Hank's eyes, waiting for his invitation....

"Magician, I'm hurting like hell," Hank whispered. "That cold water did me in. Can't breathe, can't hardly move. I need you if I'm going to make it."

"I understand. Thanks for relying on me."

Magician massaged Hank's back, but not with a feel-good massage. He worked the tight spots, pressing them, loosening the tissue, then used his elbow to reset the trigger points. As cold as it was, Hank sweat with his labor against pain. As the spasms eased, Magician popped Hank's ribs back into place one at a time with his thumb. Half an hour later, Hank wasn't fighting to breathe and the pain had subsided to a manageable level.

Magician produced a flask from his pack. Pouring a cup full, he handed it to Hank. "Here. Drink this."

"What is it?"

"It looks like water—tastes a lot like water, come to think of it—but it's my strength and healing. Drink it down."

Hank drained it dry. "Thanks. I'm ready to go."

"Glad to help," Magician said, as he put the cup in his pack. "Before we get moving, tell me what you've decided to do with Jester's suggestions."

"Oh, that stuff?" Hank ducked and shook his head. "I told Jester to go to hell."

Magician laughed. "Good for you." Magician grabbed Hank's pack and helped him put it on. "Come on. We'll both pull drag."

The others were just around the corner, out of ear shot, but close enough to keep an eye on Magician and Hank while they worked things out.

The trail was steep. They all huffed and puffed in the thin air, but the burning in their chests was energizing. As Hank hiked, pain backed off a degree or two. Magician shared from his flask three or four more times and stayed close. Hank felt his courage bolstered.

Two squirrels chirped and scampered through the trees above Hank and Magician as they brought up the rear of the party. Hank stopped to watch. More than anything, he stopped to catch his breath.

They raced through the highest branches. Stopping. Jumping. Chirping. Chasing. Around and around. Through and through. Back to the heights.

How in the world do they do that? Hank thought, watching their antics. They leaped after one another. The follower caught the same branch as the leader, but the limb snapped.

Clinging to the broken branch, the squirrel plummeted. Twenty feet from the ground, he clipped the end of a lower branch. Rather than breaking his fall, it sent him cartwheeling to an awkward landing on the rock shelf a few feet from Hank.

One moment Hank was enthralled with high-altitude acrobatics and the next he was horrified by the acrobat's precipitous plunge. He bent over the little animal, already bleeding from his nose and mouth.

The squirrel eyed Hank's monstrous form poised over him. Summoning his will to survive, the squirrel moved, dragging back legs that no longer worked and a tail that no longer twitched. Overcome with compassion, Hank scooped his hands and forearms under the wounded animal in order to move him away from the precipice inches away. The squirrel expelled a fearful huff. Blood snorted from his nose onto Hank's hands. He tensed and his claws punctured Hank's forearms.

Hank knelt on both knees and laid the squirrel down on a bed of grass. He stared into the black eye of the squirrel who stared back in terror. *He thinks I'm a predator,* Hank thought. He whispered, "You don't understand. I'm not going to hurt you. I rescued you. I want to help. Look. You wounded me when I saved you. I'm bleeding, but its okay."

The squirrel did what he'd always done. Given his belief about mankind, he turned his black eyes from Hank and dragged himself away from his rescuer.

In an instant, Hank understood. The distrust he saw in the squirrel was like his distrust of the King. The compassion, mercy, and longing to care for the squirrel that he felt, he recognized in the High King for him. Looking into the black eye of the fear-stricken squirrel, Hank understood what the High King saw when he looked into his eyes. Hank caught a fresh vision of his Father's heart toward him.

Hank thought of his precipitous, cartwheeling fall after his antics chasing Significance. He relived clawing his way through the dark pit, dragging himself along the rock ledges of his disconsolation. He thought of clinging to Pity, groping at her for comfort in the depths. He felt again the fear that consumed him as Disappointment pummeled him—touched the careening distress in his soul as he fled from Discouragement's abuse.

In his reflection into the pit, Hank remembered that the High King had come to him in his predicament, had called to him in the darkness; that he had not left him unattended. The persistence he once resented and distrusted, he now recognized as the determined love of his Father. No matter his ungracious predicament, his Father's mercy and grace were constant.

Hank lay down on his side under the weight of his revelation. He pulled his knees and bleeding arms to his chest and wept into his blood-spattered hands. His tears were a mix of sorrow, repentance, and revelation of the light. His outlook that had been tipping more times than he could count since his fall into the pit tipped yet again. No longer was he inclined away from the High King. He leaned into his Father.

The simplest of creatures unraveled the complex tangle in Hank's heart and soul by giving his life. At the right moment, in his providential love, the High King gave up life to create life.

Standing in a circle around him, Hank's brother and friends guarded him while he worked his way through the maze of independence that had misled him. Love took off his own cloak and covered him. Hope improvised a pillow with his knapsack. Faith brought water. Using his scarlet cravat, Magician dried Hank's tears and washed his face. Vassar touched his brother's arms and healed his wounds. In the recess of his heart, his Father's light mentored him into the security of his true identity and position as his son whom he loved with all his heart.

Hank didn't know how long he had been curled up on the ground. It didn't matter. He had shaken loose from his fetters of distrust and his heart had emerged from its dark brooding into the light. His heart was free of another shackle and he knew it! He sucked gulps of mountain air. Like opening the windows in a stale room, the cold blew through his chest filling his heart with the grace and lovingkindness of his Father.

They were all curious about the mysterious note they had received, all except for Vassar and Magician; Vassar knew and Magician suspected, but they remained mum. They discussed who might have sent it, whether they were being led on a wild goose chase, or more ominous, were they being led into an ambush?

"Whoever sent the note," Faith said, "knows the territory better than we do."

"Agreed," said Hope. "We can't let our guard down."

They decided to hike another hour and begin looking for a suitable place to spend the night. Hank volunteered to take the point, with Magician second. Love would pull drag.

As the afternoon shadows got longer, Hank started watching for a good campsite. Finding a spot was proving to be a challenge. They were in dense, north-facing timber with lots of dead fall. Progress was slow and the temperature was dropping. He needed to find a clearing.

Hank started to duck under a branch, but stopped dead in his tracks. He turned to Magician, put his finger over his lips, and motioned for him to move forward beside him. Hank had noted that the wind had been fluky most of the afternoon. In addition to indicating a possible weather change, it required them to be more careful. "Do you smell that?" he whispered in Magician's ear.

Taking a whiff, turning his head and taking another, Magician whispered back, "A fire. We're not alone."

"Is it dead ahead?"

Magician sniffed again. They studied the wind's direction. "I think so. Coming from the west."

"Okay." Hank signaled back for the others to form up, then he led them forward.

Hank felt his body fill with adrenaline. *Whoever sent the note has to be by that fire. No one else is around. What's he want? How'd he know where to find us? How'd he know we would find him? Pay attention,* he reiterated to himself.

Silence is tedious work. As it got colder, the snow had gotten crusty. Hank chose every step, secured his balance, and reassessed. Darkness—an enemy when establishing a camp but an ally when sneaking—was creeping up as well. Magician followed Hank. Faith and Hope flanked Vassar. Love guarded against a surprise from behind.

The wind had steadied. That was a blessing. He continued following the smell of the smoke. What little noise they made was swept away with the hushed breeze.

Hank stopped and squatted, motioned for Magician to join him. "What's up?" Magician whispered.

"Want you with me."

Hank and Magician inched forward. They were close enough to hear the hiss and pop of the fire. Slinking forward—half crouching, half crawling—Hank and Magician took cover behind a log.

Hank snatched a quick, one-eyed look over the edge of the log. A solitary soul stood with his back to the fire.

Magician glanced. They watched, and though not spoken, shared the same questions and analysis: *Is he alone? Doubtful. Too many provisions. Must be several. Where are they? We saw no signs. Did we miss something?*

The man noticed something on the backside of the fire that displeased him. He walked around, picked up a stick, and squatted down to tend the flame. His face was illuminated. Hank looked at Magician. They looked again toward the fire. Hank scrambled up from his hiding place, "Father! Wow! I hoped it would be you."

Hank waved to the others to move up. Hank waited until last to approach the fire. Jester, who had followed closely, was consulting with him: *Careful. He may not be what he seems. He's shifty. And just because I feel different about him, I've still fouled up beyond imagination. Why would he be glad to see me?*

The High King greeted Faith, Hope, Love, and Magician. He hugged Vassar and Hank, kissed them both on the head, looked them over from head to toe to satisfy himself that they were alright, and then reminded them how blessed he was to have them as his sons.

"Well, then! I'm glad you're here," the High King said, turning from his greetings. "Dinner's ready!"

"I'll say it is," Love said, looking at the spread of food.

"I'm so hungry," Hope said.

"Me too," agreed the King. "And you guys are right on time."

Right on time? Hank thought. *How could he know? There's no way.* Hank pondered Jester's opinions. *The river crossing, my back spasms, my limp, the squirrel—me lying on the ground…. How'd he get all this stuff up here?* Laid before them was a feast—multiple courses, wines, breads, desserts. He looked for pack animals. None. *I don't get it.*

Magician noticed Hank's reticence and positioned himself close to him while they were serving their plates. "You and Jester having a nice conversation?" he whispered.

It was the impetus Hank needed to retake the advantage from Jester.

Vassar, Magician, Love, Faith, and Hope carried the conversation after dinner. The King and Hank sat next to each other enjoying the banter.

There is no substitute for the bond between friends sitting around a fire encircled by darkness, cold, and wilderness. The raw message spoke into Hank's heart: "These friends are all I have—they are all I need."

Hank thought, *The King—I mean, Father—is sitting next to me, because he chose to. He could be talking with the others, but instead, he's sharing my mood and moment. He could be with anyone, anywhere, but he's chosen to be with me.*

He paused. Then drew his conclusion, *That makes me significant.* There.

He had thought it, had said the "s" word inside the confines of his mind. The belief—I'm significant—was absorbed by his thirsty soul. He felt sated. *It's true!* Hank realized.

He retraced his mental steps and arrived at the same conclusion: *No one occupies the same space and time with Father as I do, and that makes me significant. Others are significant too, like Vassar and Magician, but they are significant for who they are with Father. I'm significant for who I am because Father has chosen to spend his time with me.*

Hank thought back to the "real" world—a distant, surreal memory—and his professional losses. He reflected on his quest for importance and recognition. He jumped in his memory to Erymos and the King's banquet. He envisioned the room, touched his doubt and distrust again, and felt the burn of jealousy for Vassar's favor with the King. He remembered how beautiful Significance was, smelled her perfume, and felt her against him. He touched her and could almost feel her breath against his neck. *I was desperate,* he recalled, *willing to do anything to have her affirmation, to be important. Desperate enough to give her my soul—so desperate that I missed the point—until tonight.*

I'm significant because my Father spends time with me, not because of Significance.

But the next thought brought Hank to a hard stop. *Is this significance enough for me?* Hank pondered this notion while he stared into the fire.

Is it enough for me that I am significant because Father spends time with me? Or, do I want—require—something more; someone more, besides Father?

Hank knew the expected answer. But he had been spouting the right answers all his life. They were expected of him by all those staring at him from the walls of the pit and the corridors of his real-world life. What he wanted to discern was his heart's conviction. *In my heart, I believe Father's enough; he's plenty, in fact—more than enough.* Hank considered the implications: *Of course! My significance is secured by him and in him and through him—and that's plenty good for me.*

Hank knew this was a great revelation. He had been searching for significance all his life. In his desperation, he had clung to its persona all the way to the depths of the pit. *I know this will be tested. Has to be. It's radical. The stakes are too high for Jester to let my realization become conviction. He'll fight me over this, probably more than ever before. But Vassar, Magician, and the others have taught me well—and they'll defend me against hell itself.*

Seizing upon the courage embedded in this confidence, Hank upped his heart's stake with conviction. *I know they will,* he reassured himself.

While it was still dark Hank awoke to his Father's hand on his shoulder and his finger on his lips. "Shhh. Get your things together and walk with Vassar and me. We'll let the others sleep," the King whispered.

While the High King stoked the fire and Vassar prepared breakfast, Hank limbered up his back and hips by stretching his knees up to his chest. On a good morning, it took twenty minutes to become functional. On a hard morning…. Today was one of those. After thirty minutes of tedium, he accepted that today's pain would have to be endured rather than managed. He limped over to the fire and knelt down to savor his coffee and breakfast. Sitting was not an option given the spasms. The porridge with dried fruit, a few nuts, and a sprinkle of brown sugar was the staple, but there was also a thick slice of cured meat for good measure. After seconds of the meat and two cups of coffee, Hank was sated and smiling.

"You about ready?" the King asked, amused.

Hank nodded and began the process of standing up, taking his knapsack up with him so he wouldn't have to bend over again to pick it up. He had learned certain efficiencies from the persistent mentoring of pain.

"Here," the King said, holding his pack out to Hank. "You carry my pack and let me carry yours today."

"Oh, that's okay, Father. I can get it."

"As you wish."

Hank struggled to shoulder his load. It was awkward and heavy for a man with a bum back and gimpy leg. While he got the pack on his back, the searing ache made it difficult for him to get his breath, but he didn't say anything. He wanted his Father and Vassar to be proud of his Spartan effort and determination.

They hiked north, following no trail that Hank could discern. It was snowing and getting deeper by the minute. Their hike slowed to a trudge. The King stopped after an hour, swung his pack off his shoulders, and set it on the ground against a rock.

They gnawed on jerky and ate more dried fruit with nuts. "Got to keep the internal fire stoked," the King advised between bites.

"Glad you brought these fur hats," Vassar said.

"Me too," Hank seconded. "Back home they say you lose most of your body heat from your head."

"Back home, they would be right," said the King. "And you'll lose most of your body heat through your head here as well." He chuckled.

Hank knew people kidded those they like. But he hadn't thought in terms of his Father liking him before. Hank reached up and touched his hat. *Is it possible that he likes me?* Hank wondered.

The King pointed to a dead-fall of logs and boughs propped haphazardly upon a cluster of rocks as big as cars. "Hank, if you'll go to the other side of that dead fall, you'll be able to crawl under it. You should find three pair of snowshoes and some staves; ought to be six."

Hank kicked away a drift of snow, crawled under the dead fall, and returned with the snowshoes; he had to go back for the staves. A healthy man would have been able to get all the equipment in one trip, but given his condition, Hank had to brace against his infirmity with one hand while grasping a load of equipment with the other.

Hank dusted the snow off of a log and sat down to examine the snowshoes. Vassar said they were made from white ash. As far as Hank was concerned, they could have been made out of redbud and he wouldn't have known the difference. The wood was bent into a teardrop shape. A woven mesh of leather strips held the bent wood in its shape and provided flotation in deep snow. Toward the front of each shoe there was a leather binding to secure the shoe to his boot. Their purpose and how they fit were self-evident, but Hank had a sneaking suspicion walking with them would take some time to perfect.

Struggling to reach his feet against the objection of his recalcitrant back, Hank laced the snowshoe bindings around his boots, tightened the heel strap, and sat back to catch his breath.

"Ready?" the King asked his sons, as he handed Hank a pair of walking sticks.

Hank grabbed the staves and his Father pulled him to his feet. "Thanks. I'm ready," Hank said. The King resumed his trek up the mountain using his staves for balance as he ducked under low branches and stepped over dead falls. Hank followed, but his progress was tedious. With each duck and step and slip his back grew angrier.

Attempting to navigate a narrow draw, Hank stepped on his trailing snowshoe, lost his balance, and fell headlong. Given the depth of the snow, his fall didn't hurt, but the snow was so deep he couldn't reach the ground. It was an odd predicament. He stabbed his arms again and again into the snow, searching for a purchase to push himself upright. But to no avail. He may as well have been pushing his arms into the ocean. He was stuck.

Noting that Hank was not visible, the King returned to where Hank was stranded. "Hank. Cross your poles in an "X" and place your hand at their intersection. They'll provide enough resistance for you to get back to your feet."

Hank did as his Father recommended. It was awkward, but it worked. He felt embarrassed by his lack of proficiency.

"Just like life in the real world, Hank."

"Huh?"

"Snowshoeing. It's like life. You can't live posing for everyone, hoping to convince them you have your act together, or trying to meet their expectations. It'll break you. You have to live with gusto! No matter what."

Hank wasn't certain he followed his Father's logic. His doubt must have shown because the King elaborated. "Hank, remember when you were a little boy back in Oklahoma watching cowboy shows on TV?"

"Yes."

"Who was your favorite?"

"Cheyenne Bodie," Hank said right away. It was an easy question.

"Why'd you like him better than, say, the Lone Ranger?"

Hank revisited his childhood, fighting imaginary bad guys. "Because when Mr. Bodie fought he always lost his hat."

The King laughed. "Right, and the Lone Ranger could jump off a speeding stagecoach, tackle a guy on a galloping horse, tumble down a hill…"

"…but he never lost his hat," Hank finished incredulously.

The King chuckled again with the reminiscence. "Do you remember your blue cowboy hat?"

"I do. I fought a lot of bad guys in that hat."

"Indeed you did."

"And it had the rodeo creases to prove they were tough fights."

"That's what I'm talking about, Hank. Some people expect you to be like the Lone Ranger: never lose your hat, shirttail never comes out, never get dirty, never get a bloody nose. But that's not life. You've lived under the weight of those expectations for a long time."

"Just like in the pit with all those faces watching me," Hank said.

"Just like in the pit," his Father agreed. "Those folks, with a lot of help from Jester, have insisted that I have the same expectations of you."

Hank didn't move, didn't blink. He'd been caught flat-footed—dropped his guard—and now the King held his most tender, profound doubt in his hand.

The King stared back, unblinking, unflinching. "Hank, you're with me—on an adventure. I'll lead and break trail. Even if you fall down and lose your hat, or bloody your nose, or fall into a pit—I'm not disappointed in you. You're my son. I'm just happy we're together. Trust me. I won't leave you. Nothing you can do will cause me to abandon you."

Hank looked down at himself. He looked like the abominable snowman after his ungracious wallow in the snow. His Father began dusting the snow off of Hank.

In the process of extracting himself from the ditch, Hank had shed his pack. The High King stepped into the ravine and retrieved Hank's pack while he was tightening his snowshoe bindings. Setting Hank's pack down alongside his own, the King said, "I won't take your pack from you. If you insist on carrying it, I'll honor your decision. But if you'll trade with me, I'll take your heavy load and give you my light load. What do you say? Trade with me?"

"Father, that's okay. I know I need to pack my own weight."

"Who said?"

Being cautious, Hank said, "You did."

"Me!?"

"Yes, sir. Think so."

"Not me. Doesn't even sound like me," his Father said.

"I'm sorry. I didn't mean to offend you."

"You didn't offend me," his Father said, with a dismissal of his hand. "But I'm curious. Who says you have to carry your own weight?"

With his first answer dismissed, Hank realized he didn't have a second one queued up. Hank thought for a moment or two. "Well, everybody I guess. I mean, to be responsible, I need to carry my own weight, take care of myself—and given my competencies, I expect I should help others too. I can do it. I just lost my focus."

"You can do it?"

Sensing he was getting backed into a corner, Hank thought before responding. "I think so. Isn't that what's expected?"

"Oh, sure. It's what's expected, but it's not what I expect," his Father said. "When you say, 'I can,' you're declaring your strength. When you say, 'do it,' you're proclaiming your capability. Son, you've tried being strong and capable. If memory serves me, that's how you landed in the pit."

"Well, that's true. Got me into the pit back in the real world too."

"Here's the deal, Hank. I'll be your strength—if you'll let me. And the capability you're relying on? That inflames the wounds Competence inflicted upon you."

"You sound like Magician," Hank said.

His Father just smiled.

"Father, I can't deny I'm a strong man. I can't deny my capability. Fact is, I have so many capabilities they confuse me."

"I'm not suggesting you deny your strength and capability."

Hank shook his head, confused.

"Tell you what. How about I offer you a new plan?"

"Sure," Hank conceded.

"I'll set the expectation. Deal?"

"Okay. It's a deal," Hank agreed.

"Before you take on any responsibility, consult with me. If the responsibility's something I believe you should carry, I'll recommend you take care of it. On the other hand, if I recommend you not take responsibility for whatever's in question, then you leave it where it lies. I'll deal with it. What do you say?"

"Hmm," Hank mused. "Okay. Sounds reasonable enough."

"Super! We're agreed then," his Father enthused.

Hank reached down to pick up his pack. His back stiffened and complained. Hank straightened up and thought about his options—considered the agreement he'd just made.

"Father, do you still want to change packs with me?"

"Sure. Offer still stands."

"Alright then. Let's trade for a while."

His Father's pack was much lighter. As he adjusted the straps, Hank felt ashamed that he had traded his heavy load for an easier weight. *I ought to be able to carry my own pack,* Hank heard in his mind. *If only I was stronger. What if Vassar notices? What will he think?* Hank felt embarrassed. He had let himself down. He expected better of himself; expected he could make a good showing.

"How's the pack fit?"

"Oh, it's fine." Hank was sheepish. "It's lighter," he said, while fiddling with his sternum strap.

"Son, the voice you hear in your head? That's not me—and it's not you. It's Jester. He's piling his expectations onto the expectations you already feel. He wants you to adopt his thoughts."

"How do you know?"

"I should…. I ought…. If only…. What if…? Thoughts like these, all of which come from Jester by the way, breed dissatisfaction. Believe them and your significance is now tied to your ability and strength."

"What do you think I should do?"

"I recommend you drop those expectations like a hot rock—all of them. They're not yours, so why haul them up the hill?"

"Hard to argue with that," Hank said.

"Yeah. Meant for it to be. Come on. Let's find Vassar."

Hank had followed in his Father's footsteps since leaving camp, but when they resumed, Hank walked beside his Father, enjoying what his Father noted, and pointing out his own observations. The morning turned from a difficult trudge into an adventure alongside his Father and brother. When he hiked behind his Father, his ache for significance was dulled, but when he walked with his Father—beside him—it was assuaged.

They saw the brush strokes of an owl's wings in the snow mapping her discovery of breakfast. They heard the occasional pop inside a tree as it warmed from a sub-zero night. They stood motionless, not breathing, and felt the yearning in their ears for any sound at all—then exhaled into the exhilaration of absolute silence and watched their breath rise like crystal stars that cooled and fell to earth.

Midday the High King proposed they stop and eat lunch. They were above the tree line so they took shelter behind a massive outcropping of boulders. The wind had drifted the snow on the lea side of the giant rocks and exposed bare ground. The High King, Vassar, and Hank sat down shoulder-to-shoulder to eat trail mix and jerky.

"So, where are we headed, Father?" Hank asked.

"Here."

Hank looked around, expecting he had missed something in the high desolation. "This is it? You brought us here?"

"Yes."

Hank eyed their surroundings again. He looked at his Father to discern if he was joking. His face yielded no hint. "Okay. I give up."

"I brought you to this place because it's raw and genuine. It's not a place to be trifled with. In fact, it's dangerous. Exposed. It will kill you."

Hank listened, but he didn't understand.

"Hank, I want you to take off your breastplate." Hank got to his knees and did as his Father requested.

"Now your shirt."

Hank hesitated.

"Take off your shirt."

Again Hank hesitated, not because of the cold, but because of the shame he felt for the "D" on his chest. The grotesque wound had never healed. The scar tissue ripped when he stretched his arms. It didn't matter if he was putting on his breastplate, stretching in the morning, or skipping a rock. Any tightening of the skin on his chest created a fresh wound. His chest hairs around the scar were ingrown and the puss-filled boils there grew more irritated as his shirt rubbed against them. He feigned modesty when his traveling companions and he bathed at the end of the day. While they cleaned up together, he walked up river—out of sight—to bathe and scrub the blood and puss stains from his shirt. It wasn't modesty that marched him upstream. It was shame.

"Son, I asked you to take your shirt off."

Hank began his obedience. He pulled his shirt over his head and dropped his soiled garment on his breastplate.

The High King eyed the nasty "D" while Hank hung his head. Not a day passed that he did not grieve the "D." Kneeling in the cold in front of his Father and Vassar, a morass of memories clogged his mind. He felt the sting, the bite, the burn, the agony—the broken dreams. Disappointment. Discouragement. Depression. Despair. Demoralization. They had tortured him then. They tortured him now.

The King reached to touch Hank's chest, but he withdrew. "Please, don't! It's infected."

Blowing snow chaffed at his tender skin. Tears trickled down his cheek, freezing where they dropped. His nose ran to expunge the cold and grief. He shivered as his soul's light dimmed.

And then there was warmth. Vassar had removed his breastplate and shirt and pulled Hank tight to himself. Hank felt Vassar's tears drip and run down his back. He felt Vassar trace the scars on his back and neck with the tip of his finger. His shivering stopped. He wrapped his arms around Vassar, wiped his mucous off his shoulder where it had dribbled, and thanked him for coming to him midst his shame.

Vassar gave Hank an extra squeeze, patted him three times, and backed away.

Hank rubbed at his eyes, wishing they would quit watering. Blinked. Wiped. His "D" was on Vassar's chest! The scars that marked his wrists were now on Vassar's. The gouges afflicted on him in the darkness were now on Vassar's back and side. Hank's heart was filled with light—remarkable light.

Vassar picked up his own shirt, clean and white, and tossed it to Hank. Then Vassar wriggled into Hank's stained shirt.

The hike home was easier; it was downhill. Hank's mind whirred through the day's events trying to assemble a rationale for what Vassar had done, but he didn't get very far. Vassar's overture was a simple hug, but his gracious exchange was so exorbitant it defied words. A few times Hank thought to say, "Thank you," but decided against it each time as too trite. Vassar had taken his grief, his sorrow, and his shame. "Thank you" didn't seem enough. Hank wracked his brain for something commensurate to do or say given the magnitude of Vassar's sacrifice. Nothing came to him.

Hank stayed close to Vassar all afternoon. It seemed enough. Together, they enjoyed the woods, followed a fox's trail, cawed at the ravens, and treasured their Father's antics as he led them on a circuitous route back to camp. Shared experience was the currency of their communication.

As the three got closer to camp, Vassar lagged behind the King to have a private word with Hank. Grasping him by the shoulders, Vassar said, "Hank, you can never repay what I did today up on the mountain. So, don't try. Anything you attempt will cheapen my sacrifice and indicate that you don't understand my gift."

"But Vassar, I need to do something for you," Hank pleaded.

"All I ask is that you be my brother. Walk with me, talk with me, listen to me. Cause me to laugh."

"Cause you to laugh?"

"Just be you," Vassar said. "Don't edit yourself. Don't try to make others like you. They won't, no matter how hard you try. Don't take on the burden of trying to meet their expectations. You can't. Live out of the light in your heart—the passion in your soul. You do this, you'll cause me to laugh with delight."

Hank grasped Vassar by the wrists, felt the scars there—his scars, by all rights—"You got it, Vassar. And for what it's worth, thank you."

CHAPTER 17

Camp at 10,550 feet

Magician, Faith, Hope, and Love had been busy. As Vassar and Hank walked into camp, supper was nearly ready. They cleaned up and joined the others for fish, greens complimented by berries and nuts, baked bread, and a complex red wine. Where that and the fresh fish came from, no one was confessing.

While the others were cleaning up the dishes, the King pulled Magician aside to help him gather wood. "It's imperative that Hank understand the conversation Vassar and I are going to have this evening about our covenant. Sit by him. Be certain he understands."

Not far away a wolf pack howled in seven-part harmony. The sky shed a fresh blanket of snow and erased the day's coming and going. Hope stoked a good fire fed with the hardwood gathered by the King and Magician. They refilled their glasses and found places that suited them around the flames. Magician claimed a spot next to Hank.

"Father, after a similar meal years ago, you and I made a covenant together," Vassar said.

"We sure did," the King reminisced. "We should remember our agreement again this evening."

The King prepared three pieces of bread, stacked them on top of each other, and wrapped them snug in a linen napkin. He handed the bundle to Vassar who unwrapped the cloth, removed the middle piece of bread, lifted it for all to see in the fire light, and broke it in half. Looking around the ring, he said, "This piece of bread represents my body, broken on your behalf, so that you can live a full and complete life."

Vassar placed one of the halves back in between the other two pieces of bread and wrapped them up again. He handed the remaining half to

Hank, told him to tear off a fragment, hold it, and pass the half around the circle. After each had a piece of bread, Vassar said, "Eat and remember."

He took the remainder of the torn bread, wrapped it separately, and laid it aside out of sight.

Magician leaned close to Hank. "Before you were born, Vassar and your Father entered into an agreement—a blood covenant: Vassar agreed to give his life in exchange for your life. It was the only way to keep the family together. The High King agreed—reluctantly. He piled all of your failings and flaws onto Vassar, taking from you all that was wrong with you, and making you into the transformed man you are today."

"I recall him telling me about this during a conversation in the pit. Of course, I had heard the story before, but hearing him tell it made my heart hurt, and it sure changed my view of Vassar."

"Right. I remember that discussion as well," Magician said.

"I still struggle with why Father did that to Vassar."

"Your Father didn't do that to Vassar. Vassar voluntarily agreed."

"But why?"

"He volunteered because you're his brother and that's what big brothers do," Magician said.

"Yeah, well. I should've suffered my own consequences."

"That would've been the right thing. But in addition to being just, the King's also merciful."

"I follow what you're saying, but I'm not sure I understand," Hank said.

"The King noted that you were hopeless, afflicted with fatal flaws. If justice was his only character trait, you would've been executed for your failings."

"I understand that part," Hank said. "Can't go to church for too long before that point is crystal clear. It's mercy I struggle with. I get forgiveness, at least conceptually. But it seems to me mercy is in between justice and forgiveness, and there's a major gap there. Did Father just overlook my failings and jump to forgiveness?"

"Hardly!"

"This is where Vassar comes into the picture. He took everything the King couldn't stand about you upon himself, carried it to Zophos' lair, and dumped it all. Every bit of it. The stench and filth overwhelmed Zophos."

"Oh, wow! That was pretty shrewd," Hank said.

"It was. So while Zophos was sorting through the dregs of your life—trying to regroup and reformulate—Vassar freed you from your curse and failure and brought you with him before the High King."

"You know. I've heard about that too. The intercession stuff. But why'd he do that?"

"To vouch for you, to confirm to the King that your debt was paid in full. In so doing, the King's justice was satisfied by his heart of mercy embodied in Vassar."

"Vassar is Father's heart personified." Hank's comment was as much an affirmation as a statement of fresh revelation.

"Yes. What he and Vassar did for you on the mountain is a reflection of what they did for your whole life."

Hank looked at Magician for a long moment before turning toward his brother.

Vassar had paused while Magician explained the ceremony. Lifting his cup of wine, Vassar said, "This wine is symbolic of the covenant between the King and me."

As Vassar handed the cup to Hank, he said, "Drink it. And always remember."

Hank took the cup from Vassar, then turned to Magician for assistance, sensing there was more to this action than he realized.

"Hank, a covenant is stronger than an agreement, or even a contract. Both of those can be changed, or even dismissed, but not a covenant."

"I didn't know that." Hank was beginning to understand.

"Remember, because of his mercy, Vassar gave his life on your behalf."

"And this is when Father came to rescue Vassar," said Hank.

"Right—and you too. The King rescued both of you from Zophos. It was a daring strategy, but it worked."

"I'll say it did! It worked great," Hank agreed. "Boy, this mercy thing is overwhelming."

"As it should be. Your Father's mercy toward you is fresh, just like each sunrise, which he created as a reminder of his lovingkindness. You'll spend the rest of your days soaking in it and benefiting from it, but you'll spend an eternity understanding it. Only your heart's capable of an adequate response to his mercy."

Hank had made tremendous strides in his ability to connect and live from his heart, but the switch from his head to his heart was still not automatic. Magician could tell Hank was performing the function of switching by sheer act of will and afforded him time to accomplish the feat.

"That's a lot to soak up, Magician."

"Yes, it is. And understand: A covenant like the King and Vassar have is unique in that it is between equals, is unchangeable, irrevocable, and exists in perpetuity."

Hank stared into the blood-red wine in the cup as he thought and remembered. "Since Vassar redeemed me from destruction by Zophos, I belong to him. He bought me—with his life."

"Keep going," encouraged Magician.

"He gave his life so I could live."

"You're doing fine," Magician reassured. "Go on."

"So since I belong to Vassar, when he and Father entered into covenant together, they got all of me—and I received all of them," he finished.

"Bingo. You've got it."

Hank looked at Vassar. "Is all this true?"

Vassar nodded at his brother.

"And is Magician correct about the terms of this covenant—unchangeable, irrevocable, in perpetuity—all that?"

"Yes," Vassar said.

"And the most important aspect of life—the thing you want more than anything—is for us to spend time together?"

"That's about it," Vassar said.

"And spending time together makes me significant."

"More than you'll ever know."

"And affirms your significance as well?" Hank asked, seeking confirmation.

"More than you'll ever know." Vassar said, "Time is life for you, little brother. When you spend time with Father and me, you give us your life, and there's no greater love and demonstration of friendship than for a man to invest his life in his friends."

Hank looked again into the cup and heard Vassar's words echo in the chamber of his heart: "Remember." By eating and drinking he was participating in the reality of his Father and brother's covenant. He was part of Vassar. Vassar was part of him.

Hank looked up—snapped back into the moment. It was as though he and Magician had retreated to their own hideaway to talk at length. In reality, only a few seconds had passed since he'd taken the cup from Vassar. Twelve eyes watched him. Lifting the cup, Hank said, "Here's to you Vassar, my brother, and to you Father, the High King of Glory. You gambled on me, sought me while rebellious, redeemed me though worthless, resurrected me, and loved me with no regard for your future. I honor you. Thank you. I vow with this drink to never drink red without remembering." Hank touched his lips to the cup—paused, looked first to his Father and then to Vassar—drank, and swallowed.

The Round Tower

Except for a few renegades and employees of the Keep, the Army of Light had hung their uniforms in their cedar closets—right next to their formal attire. Their swords were on shelves underneath seasonal clothing.

As one wandered through the Round Tower, it was not clear where the Army of Light began and ended. There was talk of the High King and his ideals, but most was conjecture with little action. He was a cultural concept and his ideas a throwback to prior days. The members of the Round Tower sought to soften the harder lines of the past with blends of Keep cliché and insipid castle musings. They fancied themselves more sophisticated in managing the King's standards than their hard-line ancestors, the radicals, the agitators, or the always-zealous youth not yet tempered by the wisdom of years.

Once in a while, a firebrand ignited a few folks' old loyalties, but whereas Zophos' agents—under the tutelage of Ennui—had once reacted with ferocity, they had learned a measured response was more effective. Almost always the fire burned itself out for lack of fuel. The instigator was insulated from the others for disturbing their tranquility, and all returned to normal. While she and her agents kept an eye on a fiery zealot until satisfied he was extinguished, Ennui believed isolation for disturbing the peace was a stronger deterrent to other renegades than death in Gnarled Wood.

But lest the members of the Round Tower become suspicious of an obvious apathy, Ennui kept them busy with initiatives promoting noble-seeming labors. She initiated focus groups, and as planned, the members of the Keep cordoned themselves into exclusive groups. The distinctions of each group were irrelevant for the most part, but group pride and the security of belonging engendered devotion to group-think. At times, the group's devotion to their charter bordered on rabid. It was intense, but it was not an intensity that mattered to Ennui. All she cared about was that the Round Tower remain apathetic to the King and his wishes.

Ennui assigned agents to each group. In the more active and passionate groups, and those prone to zealotry, she deployed additional agents. Some of the more pallid organizations were managed together in a region, sometimes by a single agent. When the groups met—*en masse* or in smaller segments—the agents attended, participated as appropriate, and reported to Ennui.

It was a rare group that recognized an agent in their midst. Those who did dealt with them in short order. This wasn't a big deal to Ennui; she waited a few days—or weeks—and replaced the displaced agent with a new plant inside the group. More often than not, the new agent was welcomed and placed in a position of service since most presented themselves with a robust resume of noteworthy service in similar groups.

The groups managed themselves by committee. Some groups formed and became exclusive based upon their conviction about the proper size of the management committee. Some had as few in leadership as three while other groups believed every member was a guiding force. It didn't matter to Ennui. As she often said in secret, "A committee is a group of people doing the work of one." Some committees and groups were proactive, but the majority made decisions at such a languid pace that Ennui could anticipate their direction and have plenty of time to determine if preventive measures were necessary.

Every now and then a group formed around a single leader or married couple. These groups were insanely loyal and made quite an initial showing. Ennui learned that in spite of their bluster, the groups were fairly harmless and their longevity short lived. Often, the leader was corrupted by the unchecked power granted him by the group and a titular board. In addition, Ennui and her staff usually fueled the group's growth until the Tower was enamored by this "success" and emulated the style of the noteworthy group. But if the leader didn't die or fade away first, most stumbled drunkenly in the intoxication of their power and embezzled funds, afforded themselves excess compensation, broke the laws of private inurnment, committed adultery, or discredited themselves in some other fashion. In some respects, the failure of these Tower leaders was more remarkable and precipitous than their counterparts in the castle.

Ennui and her staff paid attention, but rarely had to take strong action. The best thinking of the group was usually sufficient to create a predictable death spiral.

The majority of the groups realized they needed a meeting management system, first to maintain order if opinions clashed—most common when discussing money—and second, to keep notes. Even in the smaller committees, the parliamentarian/moderator exercised great power as most were also responsible for preparing the agenda for the meeting. This too played into Ennui's hand.

Ennui's agent seated himself two-thirds of the way back, in the second auxiliary auditorium, on the fourth floor of the Round Tower, southeast corner. One of the more faithful groups was meeting to consider a new initiative. Moderator stepped to the lectern and rapped his knuckles on the wood three times. "Do I hear a motion to call our meeting into session?"

"So move," was barked from the side of the room.

"Do I hear a second?"

"Second," a woman said from the center.

"Thank you. We are in session," Moderator declared.

The early items on the agenda were perfunctory for the most part: the motion to accept the reading of the minutes from last meeting; the resolution authorizing Moderator and Secretary to liquidate non-cash gifts given to the group; the motion to accept the financial report as read. Apart from a discussion regarding the quarter-percent increase in funding for meal subsidies to home-bound widows, the agenda proceeded as planned and on time.

Fifteen minutes into their session, Moderator introduced the agenda item for which the meeting had been called: outreach to the castle.

It was part of group culture—this group in particular—to establish a presence in the castle in order to promote membership in the Round Tower. Members admired those who left the Keep and staffed these remote offices. Doing so meant changing their routine, culture, and not seeing family and friends for extended periods of time. Some duty was more demanding than others, but for the most part, the Round Tower's culture and standards were transferred to the field, so it wasn't as bad as it sounded. Nevertheless, members of the Round Tower lived vicariously through those who staffed the remote reaches of the castle and were anxious to associate themselves with them via their outreach reports as it helped them feel involved even if they never left the Tower themselves.

"Thank you for the financial report," Moderator said to Administrator. "Next on our agenda is our group's work in the eastern part of the castle. As you know, our staff there is under some duress given the political pressures you've read and heard about in the news. Our people are doing fine work—fine work—for a good cause, in an important part of the castle."

"How's our man's wife doing?" a woman asked. "Is she feeling better?"

Her outburst was a clear breach of order. Moderator was torn over what to do: Reprimand the woman, or have Director answer her question? *She shouldn't interrupt. It's not right,* he thought. *But it concerns the man's wife. Can't fault her for caring. After all, this is a Tower meeting, not a free for all, like those scurrilous folks in the castle have when they meet. Besides, she's a woman. Probably doesn't know any better.*

Moderator scanned the side of the auditorium until he located Director. He pointed for him to address the question from the floor; never mind that it was out of order.

Director stood half way, leaning on the bench in front of him, his massive belly protruding as if pregnant. "Last we heard—about six weeks ago, maybe five—she's still suffering from the infection in her jaw or tooth or somewhere. Believe it's an abscess...or somethin' like that. Correct me if I'm wrong." Director glanced around for assistance. Finding none—"You know the dental care in that part of the castle's not what it oughta be. She's had a fever going on what must be nearly three weeks." He paused to let that sink in and afford anyone with updated information to chime in. None was offered. "Well anyhow, as you already know, her mother died last month. Think it was the 23rd— or the 17th maybe. Many of you knew her. She sat real regular right over there," he said, pointing with his thumb. "A fine woman. Sure enough, she was. A fine woman. Member of our group for lots of years."

"Did we do anything for the family—after her mother's death?" The question came from his left.

Director looked to Secretary for assistance.

"No. It was discussed, but it's not in the budget. Besides, we have other people in the area capable of helping if needed," reported Secretary, still seated, taking notes, and not looking up.

With the question answered, Director continued, still half-standing: "Somebody told me the other day, think it was last week—don't remember who—that she's despondent too." Director lowered his voice at the shame he'd revealed. "That's understandable though, I suppose. This too will pass." He was more upbeat after pausing for reflection upon the despondency and shame. "Her husband is lookin' after the kids, I think. Don't know how he manages, but we ought to think of them more often. And you know, her mother had been sick for several weeks before she passed on."

"It's a blessing then that she's gone," Moderator concluded from the lectern. There were agreeing nods and umm's across the room. "Anything further, Director?" Moderator asked.

"When you think about it, you might mention them to the High King's staff when you see them." Director sat down.

"That's a good word. Thank you, Director," Moderator said, as he relocated his place on the agenda and resumed his remarks. "As I was saying, our man in the eastern office has expressed a need for materials to advance their work there. Seems there are people in that part of the castle who are interested in knowing more about the Kingdom. So, we'll entertain a discussion at this time regarding resources for our group's eastern office in the castle."

"How much will it cost?"

"Where will that money come from?"

"How will that reallocation of funds affect the stability of our group?"

After forty-five minutes of discussion about finances between the budgetary pragmatists and the bleeding hearts for outreach to the castle, Moderator asked, "Do I hear a motion to fund the creation of the requested resources for our office in the east?"

"So move," said a woman in the back, after an uncomfortable pause.

"I have a motion," declared Moderator. "Do I have a second?"

Silence.

"There's a motion on the floor. Do I hear a second?" Moderator asked again.

Silence.

"Motion fails for lack of a second," declared Moderator.

"Mr. Moderator."

"The chair recognizes the gentleman in the middle. Sorry I don't know your name, but you have permission to speak from the floor," Moderator managed.

"Thank you, Mr. Moderator. Has another group in the Round Tower developed any appropriate materials that we could use to assist our people in the field?"

"Good question." According to the rules, Moderator wasn't supposed to speak either against or in favor of questions, but he didn't often spare the group his opinion. "Director, can you speak to this question?"

Again Director half stood, resting his palms upon the back of the bench in front of him. "Competitor's created some excellent resources for their folks. I reviewed them five or six—or maybe four—months ago. They're done up real nice. Figure they must work all right or they wouldn't have created them." Director sat down.

"Who authored them?"

"How many pages is it?"

"Did they use a serif font?"

This question received twenty minutes of discussion, first to educate the audience regarding a serif, and once that was done, then to instruct on why the group—our group, as opposed to other groups—insists upon materials printed with serif fonts. In the end, Director didn't know if the materials in question utilized a serif or not. A motion was made—and passed without discussion—to form a committee to study the materials in question and find out if they did indeed use a serif, and if so, which serif since all serifs were not permissible. The matter now managed by a committee of the faithful until their follow up report at a subsequent meeting, the discussion continued regarding the pressing need for materials to be used in outreach to the eastern part of the castle.

"Does anyone know anything about the person who authored Competitor's materials?"

Director knew only the author's name, but nothing about him or his group in particular, other than what the biography on the back of the book stated. He had been educated at one of Competitor's schools. That did not bode well for the future of the materials, regardless of the serif.

As discussion volleyed back and forth, Mr. Stalwart stood to be recognized. It took several minutes before Moderator recognized him, but Mr. Stalwart didn't mind; he enjoyed the visibility. "The chair recognizes Mr. Stalwart to speak from the floor," Moderator said, in his best business tone.

"Mister Moderator, Director, Secretary, members of the group—friends all: Our people in the field—I've known them for many years—they are good people. They are our people. We've trained them, cared for them, raised them up right—the girl's mother sat here among us. We commissioned them. My wife and I visited them—three summers ago."

Mr. Stalwart digressed to tell a story about meeting an old friend while he and his wife were visiting the eastern part of the castle. It took seven minutes.

Circling back around to his original reason for taking the floor, he continued about the group's people in the east. "They are doing good work. They deserve nothing but our best. Competitor's work must be okay or Director wouldn't have complimented it." Mr. Stalwart nodded and smiled at Director who didn't acknowledge him.

"But we don't know enough," Mr. Stalwart continued, with added emphasis. "We don't have the confidence we need. These materials weren't developed by our group. The quality may not be up to our high standards, and they must be excellent. After all, these are our people. Good people. We shouldn't make a snap decision." Mr. Stalwart lowered his head, burdened by the thought of haste and waste.

"Let the committee we've formed do its work and bring us a report next quarter...or if need be, sometime in the spring," he counseled. "We should first answer the question of the serif. This is a serious decision that we must manage carefully—for the benefit of our people in the field. We owe it to ourselves. We owe it to them. After all, they are like family to my wife and me." Mr. Stalwart took a long time to sit down, his movement as ponderous as his speech.

"But wouldn't *some* materials be better than *no* materials?" The question came from a young person toward the back.

Mr. Stalwart began rising again. He stood for a time with his head bowed. He stroked his left hand backward over his balding head, then his right hand. He looked up, to the left, and then the right, then down again exaggerating his condescension. "Son, I admire the fire of passion in your question, but you are not old enough to understand. However, I do. I have weathered many storms. My wife and I know them, visited them last summer. I believe it was the summer."

Mr. Stalwart looked to his wife for confirmation. She frowned a discrete disagreement that he ignored.

"Yes. Well, our people in the field are going through a most challenging time right now. But they are called to their work. We must respect that. They need our group's resources, not materials from some-group-or-the other that's not part of us."

"But with all due respect, sir," the youth countered, interrupting. "They need resources *now*—any resources at all—and we have no resources of our own to send them."

"You do not understand this matter, son!" Mr. Stalwart shot back. "Perhaps in time, but not now. Our people in the field—and I remind you, I know them—are better off with no resources than they are with suspect materials from another group."

Again the youth spoke. "What difference does it make if the resources originate with another group or if the font has a serif?! They are in need!"

Moderator knocked his knuckles on the lectern! "Young man! You're out of order! Desist! If you do not, I will have you removed! Sit down! Mr. Stalwart has the floor." The audience turned around and cast glares at the red-faced youth.

Order returned, Mr. Stalwart continued: "Thank you, Mister Moderator. We mustn't go too hard on the boy. After all, we were all young and foolish once. But as I was saying…."

Mr. Stalwart paused for a long time before bending down to receive his wife's assistance in collecting his thoughts. He patted her shoulder.

"Yes, as I was saying, I make a motion that no materials be sent that are not our materials."

"I have a motion," said Moderator, while Mr. Stalwart continued to stand. "Do I have a second?"

"Second!"

"Very well. I have a motion and a second. All in favor of the motion indicate with a raised hand."

"All opposed indicate by like sign." The young man alone raised his hand, quick and slight.

"Motion carries with one in opposition and is duly noted by Secretary," Moderator said, pointing to Secretary, whose head was down.

"The chair will entertain a motion that we adjourn."

"So move," someone said.

"Second," was said before Moderator could ask for it.

"All in favor of the motion, say, 'Aye.'"

Instead of rapping again on the lectern, Moderator raised his hand after the chorus of "Aye's" and said, "Thank you for coming. Greet one another before you leave. Meeting adjourned."

The work of the Round Tower complete, the members of the group stood, shook hands, and congratulated themselves for their resolve in handling strategic issues. They greeted their friends. Couples made arrangements to meet for coffee. Parents went to retrieve their children from the nursery. Ennui's agent, who had been seated behind Mr. Stalwart, greeted him and his wife before leaving to meet Director for dessert.

In his embarrassment, the young man slipped out the side door closest to him, ran down the flights of stairs, and exited into a frigid rain. He pulled his hood over his head and hurried in no particular direction through the streets. An accomplice of Jester's was waiting to follow and interpret the experience for the youth's mind. *I will imprison my heart. Never again will it embarrass me like that! It's incapable of sound judgment or meaningful input.*

The young man agreed with Jester's accomplice and vowed to cap what was intended to be the wellspring of his life.

Jester's accomplice took note of the new territory gained for future reference.

CHAPTER 18

Camp at 10,550'

The wind shifted in the night, carrying the fire's smoke over Hank's bedroll. He awoke to the smell of smoke and coffee. Eight inches of new snow shrouded him, shielded from his body's heat by his cocoon of wool. He pulled his boots on, shook the snow from his bedding, and began his routine of stretches to free his muscles from pain's shackles.

"Where's Father?"

"Don't know," Hope said, "but those were here when I got up." Hank eyed the backcountry skis standing on their tails in the snow, poles like sentries by their sides.

"Maybe he went for a walk," Hank surmised.

"Maybe so."

Vassar entered camp with an arm full of wood just in time to hear the end of the conversation. "I spoke with him just before he left. Said we should head southwest, follow the ridgeline."

The group ate, broke camp, and put on skis equipped with climbing skins—the hairy hide of an elk or deer. The natural lay of the hair faced backward toward the tail of the ski. On the slide forward, the hair on the skin laid flat, but as the skier pushed against that ski in order to slide the opposite ski forward, the hair ruffed up to prevent the ski from sliding downhill. It was a simple solution mimicking the physics of stroking a dog's fur in the wrong direction.

Magician led them swishing through the backcountry to the southwest. The forest thinned and the terrain softened into undulations as they gained elevation. They skied single-file and covered a remarkable distance compared to the labor of the snowshoes they'd stashed and left behind.

It had been awhile since Hank had skied, but much to his delight, the habits etched into his brain years ago resurfaced. Apart from the irritant of Jester's petty nagging—an opportunistic constant that Hank was getting better at managing—Hank knew he was realizing more of his heart's desires. He could recall his days in the pit in an instant, but over time his default was to live in the light.

The demand of the weather and altitude would have been a trial for some, but not Hank. He relished the rigor of the mountains and was energized by the remorseless weather. While his pain remained implacable, the high places fed his soul.

They skied all day for four days. Apart from the thin air, their progress was unimpeded. They settled into their customary teamwork, taking turns in the lead so one man wouldn't get worn out breaking trail. On the climbs, the skins were invaluable. On the downhill runs, Hank resurrected his proficiency making telemark turns. He suspected there was a long, steep descent in his future.

At the edge of a broad, high-mountain meadow covered with blowing snow, Magician stopped in the lee of the trees to study their situation. The others skied up beside him. Across the meadow—perhaps a hundred yards—smoke curled against the cobalt sky. Was the builder of the fire friend or foe? Faith and Hope had both reported seeing signs of the enemy in the last two days, but the tracks were those of raiding parties—nothing new about that.

As he had learned to do, Hank adjusted his sense to the rhythm of the wilderness. Discord is discernable, provided you know what to listen and look for.

For all his cunning, Jester always created confusion no matter how hard he tried to do otherwise. That wasn't surprising, considering who had trained him. Zophos was the master of confusion, discord, and deception—his signature asset. He always created a disturbance; even his "peace" was tenuous.

So, Hank listened and observed. Were the bird's songs disrupted? Were they going about their daily chores in the usual manner? Were they chirping with their friends or were they complaining? Were they low in the shrubs or high in the trees? Did everything smell as it should? Wild odors didn't all smell pleasant, but they belonged. Hank knew an out-of-place scent was as sure a warning as the buzz of a Rattler's rattles back home in Texas.

They watched and waited for half an hour before concurring that all was as it should be. They decided Hank was best suited for the point. He didn't let on, but he knew it was an honor and sign of their trust that they selected him to lead over vulnerable ground to an exposed destination.

Swishing into the open, Hank focused on their destination and broke the trail. Strung out in a line with thirty or forty feet between them, they skied across the meadow toward the smoke. The men in the middle eyed their flanks. From his drag position, Vassar made certain there was no staging of the enemy behind them.

The closer Hank got to the smoke the more the vista beyond grew. He expected to find a campfire, but realized instead they were approaching a log and stone cabin surrounded by the meadow and facing a still-expanding view. The back of the roof was just above ground level, but from a distance—covered with snow—it appeared nothing more than a drift. Had it not been for the smoke, it would have been invisible. The meadow ducked off the edge of the mountain with a steep incline that plummeted several thousand feet into a valley laced with a river whose origin appeared to be the jutting peaks in the distance. Hank guessed the peaks to be over fourteen-thousand feet and perhaps thirty miles distant.

He slowed his pace as he approached the cabin. The wind raced up the slope from the valley and absorbed his breath and the ski's swishes as one more voice in its choir. While his approach was silent, his mind was a cacophony of advice.

He paused. With hand signals, Hank indicated he would secure the back, right corner. Next in line, Love, take the back left. Additional directions were unnecessary; they all knew to alternate sides until they were assembled and could move along both sides of the cabin toward the front.

He skied four slides toward the cabin and two giant dogs exploded over a snow drift, running and snarling toward him. Hank's heart jumped to his throat. His body rushed with an instant torrent of energy. Hank ripped off his right glove and whipped his dagger from its sheath.

A sharp whistle stopped the animals on-the-spot, their teeth still bared, roughs standing straight up. Hank crouched. With the dogs, he wanted to stand—intimidating—larger than life. But until he determined who whistled, he wanted to present a smaller target.

Hank watched the dogs. Someone must have come out of the cabin. They whined and glanced behind them. The standoff lasted an eternity—longer since Hank reverted to his bad habit of holding his breath when frightened—but it was more like five seconds.

Laughing as he came around the corner of the cabin, the King said, "Okay, dogs!" They bounded across the snow, as relieved as Hank, wagging and yelping and smelling and wiggling and licking and running in circles. The size of their pack had increased by six. A celebration was in order.

"Hank! I've been waiting for you. Come on! Come on! We need to sit on the porch."

The dogs liked Hank. By the time he worked his way through the dogs' greeting—again and again—the others had already kicked off their skis and stuck them tails first into the snow bank beside the cabin. They were shedding their packs and pointing at the view and talking all at once. The King stood waiting for his final guest. Accompanied by the massive dogs, Hank skied to a stop in front of the King.

"Hi, Father. I was hoping this was your place."

"This *is* my place, Hank. I can hardly wait to share it with you. It's the place I retreat to in my head and heart when I need to rejuvenate."

"That's interesting. I figured you hung out…" Hank searched for the right word to describe the illusive place he pictured the King dwelling.

"…On my throne, in some remote, inaccessible place far from reality, and even farther from you?" the King suggested.

"Well, yeah, I suppose. Something like that."

"Now you know," the King said. "Let me have your pack."

Hank followed the King across the porch and through the front door. The cabin's appointments reminded Hank of the room where he had his tryst with Significance, except that the ceiling was lower. Vassar had taken it upon himself to tend the fire, and while he was at it, to lift the lid on supper. Steam boiled out of the pot carrying with it the fragrant blends of a stew.

"While you're there, Vassar, give that a stir, will you please?" the King said.

"Oh my. That smells great," Hope said.

By the time they unpacked and settled in, it was time to eat. They small-talked over dinner, laughed more than usual in the safety of the King's cabin, sometimes carried on two or three conversations at once, and went back for second helpings until they couldn't eat any more. They asked the King more than once how he'd made the stew. He claimed a memory lapse for which he received no small amount of ribbing.

With supper done, the dishes cleared and cleaned, the dogs fed, the wood box replenished, and the fire stoked they reassembled around the King's fireplace along with the dogs.

"Guys, I'm glad you're here," the King began. "I'd like to review what we know about conditions in and around the Round Tower. My people are suffering. Their hearts are shriveling for lack of vision. They've substituted activities in the Tower for loyalty to the Kingdom and love for me."

Magician picked up, "Zophos has created an illusion of light."

"And he's done a good job," Hank chimed in. "He's made it appear as though his troops are part of the Army of Light."

"It's very deceptive," Magician concurred.

"So much so," continued Love, "that the Army of Light has relaxed their guard. Not only do they mingle with the enemy, but they've incorporated them into the culture and structure of the Keep as though they're family."

"They've substituted loyalty to you, sir, with a mixture of Kingdom-like principles and Zophos' mandates," said Faith.

"It's difficult—if not impossible—to discern who's with us and who's against us," reported Hope. "The majority look the same, dress the same, and talk the same."

"Zophos is a formidable foe," Vassar said. "But Father, I suspect you didn't bring us to this place just to be certain we had a hot meal. Do you have something on your mind?"

"I do," the King said. "I've guided our adventure to this precise moment. It's part of my master plan."

"I'm listening," Faith said.

Leaning forward, the High King said, "Zophos has made a tactical error. He believes territory and infrastructure are important to me, so he's seized as much as he can. Now he has to manage all of it and that dilutes his focus and disperses his resources. Plus, he's controlling the people in these territories with fear and threat. That requires a lot of energy. His tactics work initially, but in time they devalue the property and the people."

"So, he's always fighting a losing battle no matter how many victories he claims," Hope said.

"Right."

"And the more territory and people he grabs, the more frustrated and desperate he becomes," Hank said.

"Exactly. Here's the deal: Territory isn't important to me," the King explained. "While Zophos' current control appears expansive, it's an insignificant fraction of my Kingdom. So negligible as a matter of fact, that I don't worry about it. My real initiative is internal, not external. I'm interested in the hearts and souls of the men and women in the Round Tower and the castle. I'm interested in changing their lives. Zophos isn't interested in that, and even if he were, he can't affect lasting change inside a heart. He pretends he can, and positions himself as if he has the power, but it's a deception."

"Father's right," Vassar said. "He and I agreed in our covenant that our focus would be on the heart, not holdings. While Father's Kingdom is wealthy beyond calculation, the glimmer of its gold is a deception Zophos has clutched as the key to fulfillment and authority. But not so. The coalition Father seeks to build is a community of hearts bonded to his forever. Zophos is only out for Zophos."

"Great strategy!" Love said, and they all agreed.

"Okay. With this in mind, I've assembled us here to lay out my plan, first into the Round Tower, then to the castle, and ultimately into the surrounding area." They all leaned closer.

"Some years ago I sent Vassar to reclaim the hearts and minds of my people. As you know, he did a spectacular job in spite of tremendous opposition. This evening, I have gathered us here to commission Hank as my advocate to continue the work initiated by Vassar." All eyes turned to Hank—who was dumfounded—and then back to the King who continued detailing his plan. "Faith, Hope, Love—I'm assigning you to the Round Tower. More on that in a minute. Magician, I'd like for you and Vassar to…."

Finding his voice in the middle of the King's sentence, Hank interrupted, "…Wait a minute! Wait. Please." He stammered in his near-vain attempt to assemble his divergent thoughts and wild feelings. "Just hold on." Hank scratched his head with both hands.

"Father, with all due respect, your plan is flawed—fatally flawed."

"How so? I haven't even explained it yet."

"Well, to begin with, everyone in the room is better suited to be your advocate than I am. Have you forgotten?" Hank ducked his head and then raised his eyes to look at his Father.

"Forgotten what?" The room was stone quiet.

"Have you forgotten that I denied you? Disregarded your Kingdom? There's no way. How could you forget? I haven't. Don't you remember my arrogance in the pit? I stood before you naked and defied you, there in the darkness. I told you I didn't need you, told you I could take care of myself. I'd devoted my life to independence. Remember?" Hank stopped, but everyone knew he wasn't finished.

"Father, I slept with the enemy." There were tears in Hank's eyes as he looked into his past. This was the first time he'd looked into the pit long enough for his eyes to acclimate to the darkness.

"I cursed you. Accused you."

Hank was surprised at how fast his shame boiled over. It was too late to replace his emotional lid and cover his candor. "I'm disloyal, unfaithful, and irresponsible. I'm a cripple." Jester drove his declarations into Hank's gut like body blows into a boxer against the ropes. Hank absorbed his punches. "Every day's a desperate fight just to walk. I fail. I scream and curse and spit and complain—often at you. I cry and whimper in the night. I'm not courageous. I don't sleep. I drink too much. I'm a pretender, Father. I don't belong in the high places." Motioning to the others, "You all are warriors, knights. But not me. I'm a brawler—a knife fighter."

Turning again to the King: "I can't represent you. In spite of your love and faithfulness, and all my posturing in the pit, I still dream of sleeping with Significance." Hank shook his head. "No. For your own sake, choose someone else." Tears lapped over the spillway of Hank's eyes and coursed down his cheeks. "I'm just a stupid, incompetent…," his words drifted off into the clear implication: "You can do better than me."

Hank closed his eyes and reacquainted himself with his old name and old haunts in the pit. He didn't see his Father's tears or hear the crackle of the fire's inviting warmth. He focused instead on the shrieking wind in the storm outside. He listened to Jester and thought, *I should leave now. The storm will cover my tracks.*

He'd not felt such disappointment since the pit. *It's time I faced the truth,* Jester suggested, asserting that these last moments had jerked him to his proper sense of reality. *They'll be better off without me. I'll disappear into the mountains.*

He inventoried where his belongings were. All he needed to do was grab his coat, back out the door, and put on his skis. *Can't let the dogs out. I'll be gone in twenty seconds. My tracks will be covered as I make them.*

Jester knew he had Hank, knew Zophos would be proud of his work. He angled in for the kill. *Freezing's like going to sleep, they say. Then the catamounts and the wolves—ultimately the ants. Before long I'll be bits of feces.*

"Hank?"

The last time Hank had heard that tone in his Father's voice was in the pit. He'd fought against the heart behind that voice, but knew it was persistent.

"Hank?"

I've got to go now, he thought, in cahoots with Jester.

In the split second before Hank made his exit into the storm, Magician wiped the tears from Hank's face with his scarlet cravat. Just as he had done many times before, Magician whispered in his ear, "I will not in any way fail you. You asked me to accompany you. I will

307

not—I cannot—leave you. I will not, I will not, I will not in any degree leave you helpless, nor forsake nor let you down, nor relax my hold on you. Absolutely not! Take comfort and be encouraged. Confidently declare, 'Magician is my helper! I will not be seized by alarm. I will not fear or dread or be terrified. If he is with me, what force can stand against me?!'"

Magician's words were the leverage Hank needed to look at his Father. He saw his eyes, remembered the incident with the squirrel, and understood his heart.

He waited.

Jester cursed at Magician's counter attack.

"Hank, you're the one who doesn't remember," the King said. "You're forgiven. You can't disappoint me. I know you, and I believe in you. You're my son. I'm pleased with you. I love you beyond words."

"Look into your heart," the King continued. "What do you see?"

Magician touched Hank's elbow for reassurance. Hank looked inward. His eyes were still blinded from stepping back into the light. Magician saw him blinking and dabbed his eyes with his cravat. Hank looked inside. There was writing on the walls of his heart. Hank stepped out of the doorway and into his heart so the King's light could shine in and he could read. Written in his distinctive hand were his Father's hopes and desires—his dreams.

He'd taken the time to express himself in writing in this sacred place.

Do not be troubled. Believe me.

Hank turned and read more,

I have prepared a place for you and me. We will live there forever.

You know me.

I trust you.

You are in me, and I am in you.

Nothing can separate us, not even darkness.

You are my son.

Whatever you ask in your heart,
believing in me, I will do that for you.

I will give you a helper. He will never leave you.

Magician, Hank thought.

I will not leave you.

I live in and through you.

I love you. My dream is that you love me.

Hank's eyebrows raised as he read.

Our hearts are bonded.

I will talk to you. Listen.

Believe me.

I do. I do.

I will guide you.

I will teach you.

Wow. Have I ever learned a lot since crossing Malden Creek.

Do not worry.

Do not be afraid.

I've been afraid more since I got here than in my whole life. But, fear's not as bad as I feared. Hank smiled.

I am your source, like a vine, and you are like a branch. You are connected to me.

The King had drawn a picture of a grape vine. *He's good,* Hank thought, eyeing the drawing.

I am your life. Live in me. Walk in the light.

I live through you.

I love you just as much as I love Vassar.

You are my friend. I like you.

Hank stopped and stared at that statement.

Hank meandered through his heart. His Father had written on the walls, the ceiling, and the floor as well. There was so much more to read and consider. He determined to return when he had more time. As he turned to leave, etched above the door—in his Father's hand—was:

You are my dream, Hank

When Hank emerged from his heart and looked at his Father, the King knew the final words his son had read. "Hank, when you endorse Jester's accusation—that you're stupid, incompetent—not only do you reinforce his lie, you trample on my dream."

His Father's words cut quick and deep, exposing Jester and his tactic without mercy. Hank hadn't associated this ruthless condemnation of himself with Jester; hadn't recognized that his pet name—Stupid—dismissed the King's valuation of him and his worth. Sorrow rose up for his offense and patent abuse of his Father's dream.

There was no explanation necessary. "You're right, Father. I've trampled on your dream. I'm sorry. I didn't realize."

"I know you didn't. Listen Hank, I knew Jester would make a concerted effort to seize your life. I've been waiting until the right time. He played into my hand. You've had glimpses into your heart, but tonight was the right time for you to go inside and have a look around."

Vassar said, "Our hearts—Father's, yours, and mine—are bonded. Connected. They're interwoven—like fabric. We're family. We share the same nature."

"To see yourself as you really are. That's powerful medicine," Magician remarked for Hank's benefit.

"It sure is," Hank said, as he willfully adopted his Father's opinion of him.

The dogs roused and went to the door. The King got up and let them out. As he was coming back to sit down, Hank said, "Well Father, where were you with your plan before I sidetracked you?"

"Ah yes, my plan. Actually, it's an initiative."

"What's the difference?" Faith asked.

"None. Just seeing if you're paying attention," the King said.

Faith rolled his eyes.

"Alright. Here's what I'm thinking," the King began. "Faith, Hope, Love—you guys go to the Round Tower. I've selected a few trusted associates who will meet you there. They know you're coming. Together, you will assess the Keep and prepare the way for Hank. When he arrives, he'll lead you in the battle for the Round Tower. Okay so far?" They affirmed that they were.

"Good. Now Hank, I want you to serve as my representative and advocate inside the Round Tower."

The word "advocate" gave Hank pause, but he associated that with some shenanigan by Jester and nodded for the King to continue.

"I'm going to give you additional training before I send you to the Tower. That will give Faith, Hope, Love, and the others time to prepare for your arrival. More on the timing of that in a minute. You still alright?"

"Yes," Hank said.

"Great. Magician—I'm going to deploy you inside Hank's heart."

Hank's eyebrows rose with this news, but he saw the benefit. If Magician lived in his heart, there would never be an occasion when they were not with one another.

The King paused until Hank's eyebrows returned to their normal position. "Okay. From inside his heart, I want you to encourage, guide, and strengthen my son. Provide commentary for him about the writings I've inscribed on the walls. Tell him about our relationship. Talk with him about our plan. Help him realize his desires and express them."

Hank said. "Magician's been a great ally ever since the pit."

"Yes, you have, haven't you?" the King said to Magician.

"Through thick and thin," Magician confirmed.

"Vassar." The King stopped and admired his eldest. "I'd like for you to stay close to your brother. Don't let him out of your sight. Look out for him. And Hank, you do the same for Vassar."

Outside, the King's dogs joined a cacophony of wolves discussing the weather, the wind, and the wild. Everyone inside stopped to listen.

"Gentlemen, the Round Tower is compromised," the King said after the dogs got quiet. "The Army of Light and residents of the Keep have unwittingly made concessions with Zophos' agent, Ennui, and thereby with Zophos himself. As a result, their resolve is pithy. In their hearts, which most do not acknowledge, they sense insecurity but do not know how to remedy their uneasiness."

"And now they have a control game going," Faith anticipated.

"Have they ever! In lieu of living from their hearts, they've tried to codify desire and stuff it into cubbyholes of their own making. The spirit of what I meant has been lost. What I intended to be issues of the heart and wild desire, the officers of the Keep have reduced to principles, strategies, points-of-order, programs, objectives, and the like. There's no vision. Nothing beating in their chests. They've lost the fierce passion they're capable of in lieu of appearing to be nice folks. Their souls are weak and withering. Their thoughts, shallow and undisciplined. They believe themselves capable of managing the affairs of the Tower like they manage their businesses.

"Self-reliance! Their hearts vibrate to that iron string instead of resonating to the symphony of my love. The outcome is that I'm a noble ideal—part of their jargon—not the white-hot furnace that loves them furiously and fuels Kingdom dominance."

"This makes sense," added Vassar. "Zophos is no fool. He recognizes the innate power of the truth, and therefore, utilizes it ninety-nine percent of the time. At first, his one-percent compromise is indiscernible. But after time passes, what started out as a small error results in an undesirable outcome."

The King continued, "The correct course is formidable, and counterintuitive. Zophos is adept at convincing a lost wanderer that their desired course can be attained by proceeding with renewed determination, periodic correction, and heroic effort. But, this isn't true. People who are lost walk in circles."

"I can vouch for that," Hank contributed.

"So can I," said Hope. "See it happen all the time. And you know, unless a man pays attention, even when he circles back, he'll not recall that he's passed that way before."

"Well stated," confirmed the King. "When people find themselves on the wrong road, the first man to turn around and go back is the most progressive man."

"Ah," said Hank. "And therein is the counterintuitive part of correcting course."

"Right," the King said.

"In order to go forward, you first have to go backward," Hank said.

The King nodded at Hank and continued. "In failing to consult with me, and relying instead upon their own judgment, they opened themselves to Zophos' suggestions. He portrayed himself as part of the Army of Light, but it was a deception. And now the enemy mingles with the Army of Light throughout the Tower. Few can discern who's who."

"That's the conclusion we came to when we visited the castle," Hank said. "Remember talking to the waitress at Hoi Polloi?" he said, looking around at his traveling companions.

"Yes," Magician and Love said in unison.

The King exhaled. "It's sad. The residents of the Keep have come to regard their activity in the Round Tower as just another aspect of life in the castle. Zophos' goal is to deceive people into believing that residency in the Round Tower is optional—or irrelevant—as though it's a decision of preference."

"If there's no intervention, the Round Tower will be captured from within," Magician concluded.

"Exactly, Magician. It's time for us to refocus, reenergize, and reform the Army of Light within the Round Tower."

"And that's where we come in," Hope guessed. "What do you propose?"

"Letters and speeches, literature and programs—these won't do much good. They've been tried—and abused, with Ennui's deft supervision—until they're ignored. Not that this has changed anything. The Tower has more programs than the government, and like any bureaucracy, they're heavily invested in them. Doesn't matter if the programs work or not. They don't care. Ennui's seen to that. Programs are part of the routine. Gearing up for the next program is about all the change folks in the Keep are equipped to tolerate, so they live according to tradition."

"That's not much of a life," Hope said.

"No. But they defend it like a dog with a bone," the King said. "Others treasure their programs as though they're sacred. They're associated with their particular group. That's something else the Tower has plenty of—groups. It's not Kingdom mentality; it's club mentality." The King's increased intensity was palpable.

The King took a couple of deep breaths. "Hank, you're my advocate. I'm commissioning you as my representative to the Round Tower."

"He'll be a revolutionary," Love said.

"Yeah," Faith said, looking at Hope. "We've got our work cut out for us getting ready for Hank's arrival."

"You all do," the King confirmed. "This is a dangerous assignment, Hank. But you're the perfect person for it. You know me, know my ways, and understand my heart. I trust you to act and speak on my behalf."

"How will I get in? I mean, when we were at the castle, we heard stories of torture—even death—in the Tower, and I don't mean for enemy combatants. I'm talking about the folks they believe are revolutionaries."

"According to the plan, that would be you, little brother."

"Thanks, Vassar. Aren't you just a ray of sunshine? Don't forget. Father said you had to look out for me."

"Well guys, I hate to say it, but the stories are true. These days, there's no more dangerous place than the Round Tower."

"And I thought battling wild animals in the swamp was tough!" Hank exaggerated to laughs.

"That's the bad news. The good news is I've blessed you. I've made you. I've called you. I'll place you where I want you, and I'll build the right platforms for you to advocate on my behalf—I'll cause you to succeed, but remember, success will be on my terms."

"So that means you, and Vassar, and I need to consult on a regular basis," Hank said hopefully.

"Yes. We need to spend time together. As long as we do that, you're in good shape. Again, I wouldn't have chosen you if I didn't believe in you."

Nobody said anything and the King let them think for awhile.

"Alright. Any questions before I proceed?"

No one said anything, so the King continued. "If we all head down to the Tower together the guards will think they're being invaded and kill us all before we get through the gates."

"Not good," said Hank.

"So in the morning, Faith, Hope, Love—you guys leave together. Go back the way you came—northeast along the ridge and then east, down along the river. I'll keep in touch."

They talked about miscellaneous details, but not for long; they were seasoned warriors and understood what the King desired.

"Vassar—you, Hank, Magician, and I will delay here two days. Then, we'll ski into the valley on the morning of the third day. Good?"

"It's a good plan," Vassar said.

"I still don't understand," Hank confessed, "and I'd like to—but that's neither here nor there. Of course, Jester disagrees, but I've recommended a destination to him. So, I'm good to go, Father."

CHAPTER 19

The High King's Refuge, 11,250 feet

Hank dug his fingers into the dense fur of one of his Father's dogs as he watched Faith, Hope, and Love ski toward the line of trees. He believed he would see them again, but sensed in his heart that treacherous days lay ahead. Sensing his nostalgia, the great dog leaned against him. Hank stood up and watched until they were out of sight. Without the dog close to him, he chilled in the cold morning air. He rubbed the dog's head and went inside where Magician was refilling his coffee cup.

Hank sat down by the front window with a fresh cup of coffee and a book from the King's shelf. He pulled a blanket over his legs and stared out the window onto low clouds cloaking the valley floor with an early Spring snow storm. All four of them dozed and read and dozed and read until late morning. They repeated this sequence in the afternoon, but from the porch. The second day's schedule unfolded as the day prior.

Late morning, Hank stepped onto the front porch. It was a warm, glorious day. The sun had burned off the ground fog rendering a stunning view of the valley and its signature stream. Hank wondered if there were trout in the river and thought back to their camp in Montana, the llamas—no doubt dead and consumed by now—and his fly rods, tent, and other gear. He wondered if the park service had impounded his rental car and wondered how much late fee he'd amassed for keeping the car so long. He turned his thoughts away from the inevitability of the llamas' demise and the charges on his credit card and back to the stream in the valley. He decided that one day he'd craft a semblance of a fishing rod and explore the pockets of the river. He figured that his mission to the Round Tower would be stressful, and that while his view of life had changed considerably, he could still retreat to the river for replenishment.

He dragged a chair into the sunshine and sat down, wondered how Faith, Hope, and Love were progressing—if they were safe—and eyed the dogs curled up on the snow sunning.

The King stepped outside and pulled a chair up. "Mind if I join you?"

"Not at all. Quite a day."

"It is. It's a beautiful day. Love it up here."

"I can see why."

"No matter the weather, this place feeds my soul."

Hank and his Father chatted sporadically, but there was more silence than talk. The afternoon drifted along with a rotating combination of the four out front. Late in the afternoon, the cold began to reclaim its purchase in preparation for nightfall, and once again it was just Hank and his Father sitting above the darkening valley.

"How do you feel about tomorrow?" the King asked.

"I'm scared and excited and sad all mixed together."

"I understand," his Father said.

"I've been thinking though—about a couple of things," Hank said.

"Okay. I'm listening."

"First, I have no interest in charting my own course or determining my own destiny. Been there, done that. I feel like tomorrow is the beginning of a new journey, or as I've been thinking of it, a new adventure."

"I like that," said the King. "It is an adventure, isn't it?"

"I think it is," Hank said. "But what I mean is, in my heart I need to know I'm with you—not vice versa."

The King turned from the vista toward Hank, "You're with me, son. I'll never let go of you, never lose track of you, and I'll never fail you."

One of the dogs came up and rested his head in Hank's lap. Scratching the animal behind the ears, he continued, "Second, I need your reassurance that whatever you see along the way, and whatever you dream about, I need to know—or, I ask—that you share your view of our adventure with me. Please Father, point out what you see. Tell me what you're thinking. I want to see what you see and think like you think."

The King eyed his son. "Okay. Under one condition."

Hank cocked his head.

"Provided you'll respond to me, to the best of your ability, as my friend. Walk with me. Talk with me. Listen to me. Cause me to laugh with the sheer joy of your heart's presence."

Hank smiled at his Father. "You sounded like Vassar when you said that."

His Father just grinned at him.

Their deal was sealed.

Vassar stuck his head out the door to announce that dinner was almost ready.

"C'mon dogs," the King said, as they crossed the porch.

Magician placed another log on the fire and stoked it with the poker. A militia of shadows marched back and forth around the room as Hank, the King, and Magician took their seats. Vassar brought a bottle of red wine that had been decanting while he prepared the meal and handed it to Hank to pour and pass. When the bottle came back to him, Vassar poured a glass and raised it. "To a great group of men, chosen, and set apart for the Kingdom and the King, my Father."

They touched glasses, drank, and talked about the day.

Vassar brought a bowl of greens to the table, and as he had done with the wine, handed it to Hank to serve himself and pass. Once everyone was served, they took a bite of their salads. Hank's mouth puckered involuntarily and his eyes scrunched as the bitter dressing took effect.

"Hank, I prepared this salad to remind you of your bitter bondage in the pit. You believed in yourself, believed that if you could just overcome the disappointments you'd suffered before we left on our fishing trip, and believed that if you could just have Significance in that cozy room Jester arranged for you, that your life would come together and you'd be fulfilled. But like our enemy Zophos is prone to do, you overplayed your hand, following his counsel. You misjudged your step and fell into the darkness of your own proficiency and self-sufficiency. Your days in the darkness were a bitter disappointment."

Vassar got up and returned with a basket of flatbread he'd grilled and wrapped in a white cloth. He handed the basket to his Father. The King took the basket and stared at it a long time before asking Magician to hold it while he lifted the contents out and set them in front of him. He unfolded each corner of the cloth and laid it out smooth on the table. Hank could see that there was a piece of flatbread on top and underneath; in between was another piece of bread wrapped separately from the others in its own white cloth.

The King looked at Vassar.

Hank had seen this look once before. It was when Vassar and the King explained their blood covenant to him—after the incredible day on the mountain, where the three of them had hunkered behind the rock, and where Vassar had taken the despicable "D" onto his own chest and borne the bitterness of its disappointment as though it were his own.

They watched as the King went about his business. He removed the middle piece of flatbread, unwrapped it, revealing its dark scars from the grill, and broke it in half. He reverently wrapped one half again in the cloth and placed it inside his shirt against his heart. He took the remaining bread and passed it around the table.

When they each had a piece of bread, Vassar handed Hank a bowl of apples and nuts in a honey-wine sauce and recommended he rake some onto his salad. Hank did so and passed the bowl.

Once he'd served himself, Vassar held a piece of the flatbread and put some of his salad onto it. The others followed his lead. With the first bite, Hank remarked that his salad went from bitter to the best he could ever recall eating.

"This too is a reminder," Vassar said. "While your life in the pit was hopelessly bitter, Father came looking for you, found you, called your name out in that dark place, and blessed you with a great friend in Hope."

Hank picked up the explanation from his brother. "And on the mountain, because of the covenant between you and Father, you took the bitterness of my disappointments and wounds on yourself. You blessed me with the sweetness of your love and forgiveness. You helped me understand and believe that I'm significant."

Vassar nodded.

The King stood and refilled their glasses—almost to the rim. Retaking his seat, he said, "Just a sip now, in memory for Vassar's sacrifice of his reputation to prove Hank's significance." They sipped.

"In memory of his companionship to help Hank remember that he is loved." They sipped.

"In memory of his faithfulness to help Hank trust." They sipped.

"In memory of his plan to bring Hank behind the waterfall, to Erymos, and through the pit to help him overcome." They sipped.

"In memory of his steadfast endurance to help Hank overcome the distraction of pain." They sipped.

"In memory of his sorrow to help Hank celebrate the joy that is now his." They sipped.

"In memory of his promise to never leave Hank alone, and in so doing, help him live each day in the light." They sipped.

They each had one swallow left in their glasses. The King thought a minute and said, "In memory of the meal he's prepared so we won't starve to death." They clinked glasses, laughed, and drank.

Magician gathered the bowls off of the table and held them while Vassar ladled helpings of his lamb stew. Hank had learned to not question where things like lamb and bottles of wine and skis came from. He chalked it all up to his Father's provision.

After they finished their stew, Hank and Magician gathered the bowls from the table, stoked the fire, let the dogs out—and back in—and sat back down. The King reached into his shirt and pulled the broken flatbread wrapped in cloth from next to his heart. He unwrapped it, and holding it with both hands, handed it to Vassar.

Vassar took the bread, held it up face-high, and said as he broke it apart, "Hank, this is a symbol of my life, broken so you can live. It's a reminder of what transpired up on the mountain when I took your shame, disappointment, unfaithfulness, and insignificance—made them mine—and replaced them with my honor, hope, forgiveness, and value." Vassar passed a piece of bread to each of the others and they ate it, chewing slowly, thinking about what Vassar did and said.

After he'd swallowed, Vassar took the wine, refilled his glass, and passed the bottle. Once the glasses were refilled, he said, "Hank, this wine is symbolic of my life, given in the darkness, so you can live in the light." They drank and celebrated, and sipped and considered.

The King could tell Hank had something to say. He caught his eye and handed the bottle across the table to him. Hank filled his glass and passed it to Magician, who passed it to the King, who filled his glass and Vassar's.

After collecting his thoughts, Hank said, "I am struck this evening by this fact: By all rights, I deserve to be in the pit, wrecked on the rocks of my own self-endeavor. There's no explanation for my blessing apart from your lovingkindness." He looked at his Father and Vassar. "I don't possess any words grand enough to convey the gratitude flooding my heart. Thank you is all I can muster, but know that it comes from the core of my being."

Hank paused to think. "Vassar. Brother. What can I say? I thought we were going on a fishing trip, but you've escorted me to Father's heart—and you've done so at your own expense. You're the finest big brother anyone could ever dream of having. You have my eternal respect, honor, and loyalty." Hank lifted his glass and they drank.

Hank continued, "And Father. You dreamed all this up, before I ever booked the fishing trip to Montana, no doubt. You gambled—knowing all along the dice were loaded—that I would relinquish self-rule and see things from your perspective. You bet Vassar's life that I'd show no mercy to Jester, to my backward priorities, and to my life. What if you'd lost? You cut a deal—all or nothing—in hopes of winning us both back. You bet everything—your whole Kingdom—knowing full well you could lose us both. You're crazy! Why'd you do it? I'll never know I suppose, but I'd like to hear you try to explain it one of these days. Bet you can't, apart from love and the desire of your heart. I'll tell you this though: I'm glad you did it." Lifting his glass to each, Hank said, "Father. Vassar." They drank.

It was quiet at the table. The dogs were sleeping by the fire in need of tending. The candles had burned low and the light in the room flickered.

"Father, could I ask a favor?" Hank said.

"Ask anything, Hank."

In a flash of memory, Jester recounted all the reasons why Hank should not trust his Father. He felt his emotions react, but he dismissed both.

"Would it be alright if I called you, Papa?"

That night, the wind hurried through the trees and brushed alongside the cabin casting a foot of new snow in pristine preparation for their departure the next morning.

The four were up early. Magician laid out food for the trail—the usual things. Each man arranged his provisions in his pack and then tightened the laces on his boots before grabbing coat and hat and assembling on the porch.

The King was last out. He closed the door and checked it to be certain it had latched. The others were already in their skis, a task accomplished in spite of "help" from the dogs who knew something was up.

The King knelt down. Both dogs came to him nuzzling, licking, pushing against him, whining. He held each by the face and looked into their eyes. They grew quiet. The King stood up and patted them on the head. Simultaneously, they sat down, tilted their heads back, and howled.

In the books Hank had read, howling was described as mournful, and he'd accepted the description without much thought. But after being in the woods and listening to the wolves and coyotes—and listening now to Papa's dogs—he'd changed his mind. This morning the sound came from a deep place inside their chests, and as they howled, they took time in between to lick each other's face and muzzle.

The first wolf to appear peered around the edge of the cabin, exercising its natural wariness of humans. The King greeted the wolf and walked toward it with his palm open. He knelt a few feet from the animal—entirely black—and waited for him to overcome his hesitancy. He looked behind him a couple of times, then sniffed the King's hand, and moved in close to be petted. He was followed by several others. In seconds the porch was a wagging, whining, growling, mass of wolves oblivious to Hank and thrilled to see the King and his two dogs.

The pack moved off the edge of the porch except for the Alpha male and the King's dogs. Once again kneeling down, the King took each of his dogs by the face, looked into their eyes, and then held their face against his. He did the same with the Alpha male. After he'd looked into the Alpha's eyes and held his face against his, the wolf nuzzled in against the King and licked his chin. The King patted him and stood up.

"Alright dogs," the King said, waving his arms. Led by the Alpha, the King's great animals dashed off with the wolf pack toward the tall timber. He watched them run until they were out of sight, then turned back to get his skis.

"Aren't they fine animals? Wow. Love 'em. We go through the same ritual every time I leave. And when I get back, the Alpha and my dogs are always sitting on the porch waiting for me. No doubt been watching from the trees."

The King stepped into his skis and fastened the bindings. Unlike the others, he skied old-style—using his hiking staff instead of ski poles. He grasped his staff, wiped his nose with the back of his mitten, and took a deep breath. "Ready?"

He pushed away from the porch, kicked a few steps until he gained momentum, and pointed his skis into the valley.

The exhilaration of unbroken powder filled Hank's chest. He found his telemark rhythm and carved back and forth across the arcs left by Magician as if he skied powder every day. As the downhill narrowed, they closed the lateral distance between them—more waltzing now than skiing.

By the time the King stopped to rest, Hank's quads were burning, his eyes watering, and his lungs gasping for any measure of oxygen. But he was euphoric; they all were. They looked back up the mountain. Their trails looked like repeating infinity signs resolving in snow and sky.

The King didn't wait long before pushing off. For one, he was having too much fun, but he also wanted to keep moving. Their skiing became tight and technical. Instead of arcing turns, they pivoted around increasing numbers of rocks and trees.

It didn't take near as long to get down the mountain as it had to get up. Inside of two hours, they were kick-slide-kicking across decreasing accumulations of crusty snow. Hank could hear the stream he'd seen from the cabin, but because of the thickening timber he couldn't see it.

Hank noticed that his right boot felt loose. Sure enough, his lace was undone. He stopped, and since he was skiing drag, he scanned behind, and to his left and right, before kneeling down to tighten and tie his laces. It took a minute to break the ice and snow off of the stiff lacing, but soon he was on his way. He picked up his pace in order to close the gap that had grown between him and the others.

Hank noticed that the woods were unsettled—quieter than normal. He slowed. Stopped. Listened. Nothing. He swished forward, an easy step-at-a-time, assisting his balance with careful pole plants. Stopped again. Something was different. He couldn't place the "sense" in his intuition. It didn't feel wrong, just odd.

He skied forward a few kicks. Through the undergrowth he could see into a small clearing where the King, Vassar, and Magician were facing seven soldiers—horsemen, all of whom were dismounted. The men might not have heard him, but the horses sure did. Their ears pricked up in his direction.

There wasn't much he could do. Turning around on skis in tight surroundings was not an inconspicuous maneuver. Hunkering down to hide was pointless; he was already discovered.

Hank took off his gloves and secured them through his belt. With his hands ready, he swished ahead into a vacant spot between Magician and the King. Hank had a sense of *déjà vu* and wanted to look around, but he kept his eyes on the horsemen.

The ranking officer stepped forward still holding his horse's reins, bowed, and said, "Prince Henry. I am honored to be at your service."

Hank looked at his Father who said, "Thank you, Captain. Hope we haven't kept you waiting long."

"Not at all, sir."

"Is the area secure?" the King asked.

"Yes, sir. It is, except for Jester."

"Yes, Jester. Thank you Captain. Jester's nothing to worry about. All bark and no bite. Always plays right into Magician's hands. Right, Hank?"

The question caught Hank by surprise, but he understood his Father's point. "That's right, Papa. Provided Magician's on duty."

That got a rise out of Magician. "On duty? I'm always on duty."

"I know," Hank said. "Just kidding." Hank was relieved the soldiers were Army of Light troops.

"Alright, guys," the King said. "Hank, look around. Recognize this place?"

Hank studied his surroundings. They did look familiar. Then it all came together in a rush. This was the clearing where his adventure had begun. As his mind recollected, a soldier stepped into the clearing with a folded, oiled tarpaulin that he set down. Another trooper stepped up to assist him in unwrapping the tarp while two other soldiers spread blankets on the ground between patches of snow.

Hank's memory was still lagging a step behind the events his eyes were witnessing. Consequently, he was greeted with surprise after surprise as the soldiers laid out his waders, wading boots, socks, long underwear, shirt—all the paraphernalia of the modern world he'd dismissed from his mind. Vassar's things were there as well, none the worse for the wear.

The blankets and the tarp and the clothes were laid out like an invitation, but Hank thought they were a temptation—all of this in exchange for the adventure of going with his Father, wherever he was headed. What was odd was that he didn't hear an opinion coming from Jester.

"Papa, I don't want those things."

A soldier came forward with a pouch containing Hank's ring, watch, GPS, wallet, and cash. Hank pushed the soldier's hand away. "I don't want that. I don't want any of it."

The soldier was confused and looked back at the Captain.

"Papa, I want to go where you're going. You said I could go with you. You promised to take me with you, to talk to me about everything on your mind. You said you wouldn't ever leave me."

The King's heart was full, so full it overflowed from his eyes. He pulled Hank close. Holding him by the shoulders, he said loud enough for all to hear, "You are my son—my beloved son. I will not leave you. I cannot leave you. We are bonded together with an inseparable bond. It would kill us both if anyone or anything tried to separate our hearts. Nothing—not death, or life, or angels, or principalities, or things present, or things to come, or powers, or height, or depth—nothing will separate you, and Vassar, and me. I promise."

Hank was relieved. He took a deep breath and looked at Vassar. He looked around. "Where's Magician?"

"He's in you. Just like I asked, he's taken up residence in your heart to guide you, to explain my ways and wishes to you, to protect you, and comfort you when you need it."

"That's weird."

"You'll get used to it," the King said, as he guided Hank toward the blanket and his change of clothes.

"But Papa, what about the Round Tower? I can't wear that stuff there. They'll kill me—they'll kill us. Right, Vassar?"

Vassar was already agreeing.

"You're right. They would kill you."

The Sergeant holding Hank's belongings added his opinion. "Dang straight they'll kill you. Kill you, kill your brother, an' kill the horses you ride into town on."

"Thank you, Sergeant," the King said, unthreatened by the unsolicited input.

"Any time, sir."

"I can't ride in waders," Hank continued. "They'll chafe my legs and…"

…The King raised his hand for quiet. "You're not going to ride to town in waders. Let me explain."

"Won't be able to keep my feet in the stirrups with those boots either," Hank added for good measure.

His Father raised his hand again for quiet.

"Sorry, Papa."

"Don't worry about it. Now, here's the deal: Hank, you need some time, time to solidify and turn the remarkable revelation you have had since Erymos into resolute confidence. Magician will guide the process from inside your heart." The King pointed to a large tree. "That tree adds pulpy fiber—or new growth—for about two weeks over the course of a year's time. The other fifty weeks are spent solidifying the pulp into hardwood. That's what you need right now—time to solidify. Then it will be time to go to the Keep."

"How will I know when I'm solidified?"

"I'll let you know. It'll be part of the stuff we talk about."

"How long's this going to take?"

"A while. But don't worry about it. Neither you nor I will be a moment late getting to the Tower."

Hank looked at Vassar for reassurance. He felt Magician's warm confirmation in his heart and was confident in his Father's promise.

Hank and Vassar changed clothes. Hank noticed that while he had been warm in his wool clothing, he was a little chilled in his high-tech fabrics.

"Papa, you coming?"

"I am. I'm going before you, and behind you, and in you, Hank. I'll never leave you. Now remember what I said at the cabin. Vassar, Hank, you look out for one another. You are brothers don't forget, and you're my sons." The King hugged them both, kissed them on the forehead, and reiterated his love.

"Captain."

"Here, sir." The officer handed the first of two boxes to the King.

Giving the first box to Vassar and the second to Hank, the King said, "The daggers I gave you served their purpose here—and they'll be here when you return—but you need something different now. Something more appropriate, more practical—and a bit more understated."

Hank and Vassar opened their boxes to find custom-designed pocket knives. The knives were each unique but crafted upon the same theme. Their initials were monogrammed on the bolster below an intricate detail of the family's coat of arms.

"I'm proud of you guys. Couldn't ask for two better sons—or friends."

Hank reached inside his waders and stuffed the knife deep into his front pocket. He looked at the soldiers and at his Father, the High King. Hank took a deep breath, turned, and he and Vassar headed into the woods toward the waterfall.

As he got down on his knees to crawl through the vegetation alongside the creek, Hank looked back toward the clearing. It was empty and had begun snowing. *Papa thinks of everything,* he thought. *Our tracks will be covered in minutes.*

Hank crawled into the thicket after Vassar and lowered himself down the embankment, holding onto the vines and roots. He and Vassar inched along behind the cascading water, crabbed around the protruding rock, and eased down the slick face of moss-covered stone to the other side of Malden Creek. They both noted the large Brown trout holding to the side of the pool beneath the waterfall. *Tomorrow,* Vassar thought.

Vassar guessed they had an hour or so before nightfall. That seemed about right to Hank. They didn't say much on the downhill walk. Hank's mind was turning over various images of what their camp might look like after all this time. Then, he caught a whiff of smoke.

"Vassar," he hissed. "I smell a fire." Vassar stuck his nose in the air, sniffed, and agreed. They proceeded with the utmost caution. The undergrowth was damp along the river. That, combined with the noisy tumble of the water, made the brothers as stealthy alongside Malden Creek in Montana as they had been beyond the waterfall in the snows of Gnarled Wood.

They sneaked along until they were behind a clump of firs growing up around a lichen-covered boulder. Easing himself into position, Hank took off his cowboy hat and peeked around the edge of their hiding place into the camp. He studied the camp for a long moment before sitting back against the rock. He motioned for Vassar to have a look.

"What do you think?" Hank whispered.

"Looks like our camp."

"Yeah, I know."

Hank sneaked another peek. Three llamas were chewing their cuds, and they looked like their llamas. He leaned back again against the rock next to Vassar. Rubbed his eyes with the index finger of both fists.

"Brother, you needed something special," Vassar began. "You needed to meet with Father—on your terms—and eventually on his. You're a changed man because of the adventure we've been on, but nothing's changed here. Time stood still in Montana. Everything's just like we left it."

Hank was trying desperately to comprehend.

"Come on," Vassar said, getting up and walking into camp.

The llamas noted their entry, batting their long eyelashes, and twitching their pointed ears. Hank noted his fly rod was where he'd left it, and even that the fly was still damp. The tent looked fine and the fire appeared about right for cooking steak.

Hank turned in a circle eyeing his surroundings. He stopped. Something *was* different. The bottle of wine they had packed up the trail—that he'd so thoughtfully chilled in the creek—was right where he left it, but it was corked and sealed as though never opened. Next to it, a log was set on end with another bottle sitting on it, and opened to decant. A used camp cup sat beside it with a note underneath.

Hank—

I know you like Argentinean reds. Got this on a recent trip—had you in mind. It's rated 97. Will be great with your steaks. Tasted it to be sure it was good—couldn't resist. When you drink, remember!
You make me significant.

I love you,
Papa—

Hank read the note again and folded it once over his thumb. He stared into the laughing, tripping waters of Malden Creek as they rushed toward the Gulf of Mexico. He looked upstream and thought of the waterfall, his journey, the mystery of time, and of his Father. He closed his eyes, turned in his mind, and looked into the gray fog of the pit. He relished the indiscernible details, rejoiced that he was no longer captive to his mat, and embraced his freedom from the cloaked faces of expectation. Hank took a deep breath, his personal reminder to walk in the light, and deliberately turned his heart toward his Father.

Hank picked up the wine bottle and smelled. He smiled, and thought, *Papa, you're too much. Thank you. Thank you for liking me. Thank you for making me significant.*

Hank set the bottle down and walked over to where Vassar was struggling to tie a piece of 7X tippet to his fly line. Vassar looked up. Saw tears in Hank's eyes. "You alright?"

"Yeah. I'm fine."

Hank grabbed Vassar and hugged him—hugged him with the intensity Vassar had hugged him on the mountain. He let go and backed away.

Hank tried to think of some words, but there were none. Only sighs inside his heart.

ACKNOWLEDGEMENTS

It is not possible to adequately thank the people who have contributed to this book. Reny Madjarska—whose third language is English—made remarkably astute editorial comments, encouraged me unceasingly, and led the Prayer Tribe. You can find out more about Reny by searching on her name at PrestonGillham.com.

Thank you to the Prayer Tribe for praying. I dedicated this book to you because I know the vital part you played in its creation. You can read the Prayer Tribe entries at PrestonGillham.com

I was utterly astounded at the perseverance and thoughtful comments given by these friends who reviewed the manuscript before it was worth reading: Amy, Caryn, Colby, Dianne, Frank, Heather, Karla, Kevin, Lamar, Marshall, Randy, Reny, Tom, Victor, Wade, and Will. Thank you.

No Mercy is not my first book, but it is the first book I've written where I felt my editor was on my team. Steve Parolini did a great job of editing and a wonderful job of encouraging. Thank you, Steve.

Dianne, my wife, has never once—for even a moment—doubted, wavered, or flinched in her belief in me and this book. I have consistently run aground. She has been rock solid. She has encouraged, listened, and helped me prioritize my heart's desire: to write this book. There are insufficient words to capture or convey my gratitude. The best I have to offer is: Thank you, Dianne. I love you.

Finally, I recognize you, my reader. Thank you for reading, and in so doing, sharing my adventure. And if you have gotten this far, I presume you have told others about the book. Thank you.

ADDITIONAL RESOURCES

To contact the author about speaking engagements,
locate additional resources, or to find out more about
Preston's consulting practice, visit:
www.PrestonGillham.com

For bulk orders in quantities larger than those offered in the
online store at PrestonGillham.com,
write:
Bonefish Publication
2020 Wilshire Blvd.
Fort Worth, TX 76110
or email:
info@BonefishPublication.com

ABOUT THE AUTHOR

Preston Gillham has counseled, spoken, written, and consulted on leadership and spiritual formation for over thirty years. He fly fishes for fun, rides a bicycle to stay in shape, and loves his wife, Dianne. To discover additional resources by Preston, to read his blog, contact him about a speaking engagement, or to consider him as a consultant, please visit, www.PrestonGillham.com

ABOUT THE BOOK

No Mercy was edited by Steve Parolini. Leslie Carroll laid the book out and prepared it for print. The cover was designed and created by Stephen Cox of stellarvessel.com. The book was printed by Versa Press in East Peoria, IL. The font is Garamond, a typeface originally designed by Claude Garamond (1480-1561). The types are considered clear, open, and elegant.